Gothic Manners and the Classic English Novel

Gothic Manners and the Classic English Novel

Joseph Wiesenfarth

The University of Wisconsin Press

117263   ONLINE

The University of Wisconsin Press
114 North Murray Street
Madison, Wisconsin 53715

The University of Wisconsin Press, Ltd.
1 Gower Street
London WC1E 6HA, England

Printed in the United States of America

Library of Congress Cataloging-in-Publication Data
Wiesenfarth, Joseph, 1933–
    Gothic manners and the classic English novel.
    Bibliography: pp. 217–228.
    Includes index.
    1. English fiction—History and criticism.   2. Manners
and customs in literature.   3. Gothic revival (Literature)—
Great Britain.   I. Title.
PR830.S615W54   1988   823'.009'355   88-40195
ISBN 0-299-11900-9

For

Jay Clayton
Paul Goetsch
Badri Raina

shemblable freers

Contents

Preface

The argument of this book builds on premises set forth by Mikhail Bakhtin in *The Dialogic Imagination*. The first of these is that one basic task of the novel is to lay bare "any sort of conventionality" and to expose "what is vulgar and stereotyped in human relationships" (162). Thus a novelist like Jane Austen, says Joseph Sittler, lets "real cats out of phoney bags" (20). The second premise asserts that "ideological forms . . . become hypocritical and false" as "real life . . . becomes crude and bestial" (162). Thus Emily Brontë portrays Heathcliff manhandling Lockwood, who is a stodgy representative of stereotyped religious, social, and cultural attitudes. The third premise argues that "laughter alone remains unaffected by lies" (236) and manifests itself in the "parodic destruction of preceding novelistic worlds" (309) that are "false, hypocritical, greedy, limited, narrowly rationalistic, [and] inadequate to reality" (311–12). Thus we have not only novels of manners like *Pride and Prejudice* and new Gothic novels like *Wuthering Heights* but also novels of Gothic manners like *Middlemarch*, which scrutinize every aspect of life and fiction with caustic wit and skeptical humor.

Within the context of these premises, the argument of this book is that elements of two genres, that of the novel of manners and that of the new Gothic novel, come together and form a synthesis in the novel of Gothic manners. It is this synthesis which accounts, in good part, for the greatness of "classical" English fiction in the late nineteenth and early twentieth century. Moreover, the argument continues, in this synthesis the manners become the horror. If I say nothing new in presenting *Pride and*

Prejudice (1813) and *Barchester Towers* (1857) as novels of manners
and *Wuthering Heights* (1847) and *Great Expectations* (1861–62) as
new Gothic novels, I do say something new in redefining these
genres by sets of opposing categories: myth of concern/myth of
freedom, case/riddle, cardinal virtues/last things, complementary love/affined love. The first term of each pair is characteristic
of the novel of manners, the second term of the new Gothic
novel. These defining elements provide a way of looking at these
novels and their respective genres that leads to insights into the
nature of the genres and consequently into the novels themselves. They help, in H. R. Jauss's words, to alter our "horizon
of expectations": they help to change our notion of what we anticipate finding in what we read. This notion of a synthesis of the
novel of manners and the new Gothic novel helps us to see how
manners become horrors in such diverse novels as *Middlemarch*
(1871–72), *The Portrait of a Lady* (1881), *Jude the Obscure* (1895),
and *Parade's End* (1924–28). It also allows us to speak of these
works as novels of Gothic manners without denying them their
acknowledged place in the realistic tradition of English fiction.
Indeed, novels that incorporate Gothic manners help us better
to understand the social realism of the tradition itself.

The eight novels that illustrate my theoretical position mark
for me the clearest examples of my argument at the same time
that they reveal the inner dynamics of the genres themselves.
They are likewise exemplary in illustrating the movement from
one position to another in the evolution of Gothic manners.
Readers will of course think of other novels and other inner
dynamics on their own. Insofar as it proves flexible in accom-
modating these further instances, the theory that I set out here
will provide a standpoint from which to view the landscape
of English fiction. This book is therefore meant to be enabling
rather than definitive: a set of signposts, not a map of the whole
territory.

Acknowledgments

I am grateful to the friends, colleagues, and institutions that helped me while I was writing this book. My primary debt is to those to whom I have dedicated it: Jay Clayton (formerly my colleague at the University of Wisconsin–Madison) of Vanderbilt University, Paul Goetsch of the University of Freiburg in West Germany, and Badri Raina of Kirori Mal College, University of Delhi, in India. Jay gave me the benefit of his advice both at the beginning and toward the end of this enterprise; Paul helped me move it along apace by his generosity to me during my Fulbright lectureship in Freiburg; and Badri has been my guru ever since I was his teacher: I suspect the inspiration of this book came from him. I am delighted to salute them in Joyce's words as *shemblable freers*—as Shems to my Shaun, as brothers in a profession enriched by their intelligence and magnanimity.

I want also to thank other colleagues at the University of Wisconsin–Madison and elsewhere who, at different stages in the composition of this book, talked with me, read chapters of my work, and offered me their suggestions. In this regard I think especially of Emily Auerbach, John Halperin, Gordon Hutner, Hans Robert Jauss, Joseph A. Kestner, James R. Kincaid, Ira Bruce Nadel, and William Veeder. I owe a special word of appreciation to Mohamad Javadi of Houston, Texas, too; he helped me in various ways with my research while he was a graduate student. I am also grateful to the graduate and undergraduate students who worked with me in courses and seminars and contributed to my selection and understanding of the novels I have written about.

The Graduate School and the Vilas Foundation of the University of Wisconsin-Madison supported me substantially by providing me time for research and writing. To the administrators of both entities I wish to express my appreciation. I wish also to thank Allen N. Fitchen, Director of the University of Wisconsin Press, and Susan Tarcov, who served as my editor, for their encouragement and very practical help with this book. I owe a tip of the hat, too, to Thomas E. Nord, my companion over fairways and foul copy, who read proof with me and has looked to my punctuation as well as my putting for as long as I can remember. And I am grateful to the editors of *Studies in the Novel*, *Literaturwissenschaftliches Jahrbuch*, and *The Henry James Review* for permission to reprint the parts of chapters 1, 5, and 6 that appeared in their journals.

And finally I must thank my wife Louise for taking me back again after my protracted flirtations with Jane Austen, Emily Brontë, and George Eliot—to say nothing of my late-night gadding about with Trollope, Dickens, James, Hardy, and Ford; and I must thank my son Adam, too, for letting me win occasionally at Eight Ball when I was so distracted by Gothic manners that only his good manners at billiards could save the day.

Gothic Manners and the Classic English Novel

Introduction

Jane Austen sandbagged the old Gothic novel in *Northanger Abbey*. When Henry Tilney happens upon Catherine Morland searching haplessly for horrors, he examines the sand grain by grain:

> "Remember the country and the age in which we live. Remember that we are English, that we are Christians. Consult your own understanding, your own sense of the probable, your own observation of what is passing around you—Does our education prepare us for such atrocities? Do our laws connive at them? Could they be perpetrated without being known, in a country like this, where social and literary intercourse is on such a footing; where every man is surrounded by a neighbourhood of voluntary spies, and where roads and newspapers lay every thing open? Dearest Miss Morland, what ideas have you been admitting?" (199–200)

Bad as it may on occasion be, Henry Tilney is saying, a mannered social order precludes Gothic horrors, makes them obsolete. The world "may not follow virtue or beauty," but Henry "assures Catherine that it will not tolerate any major detour from law and

3

common sense" (Novak 56). England here and now is not like the
Continent once upon a Gothic time. Mary Shelley's *Frankenstein*,
published the same year as *Northanger Abbey* (1818), and Charles
Maturin's *Melmoth the Wanderer*, published two years later, were
among the most important of the novels which, for all their de-
partures from it,[1] originated in the old Gothic formula used by
Horace Walpole in 1764. It was precisely this romance formula
of *The Castle of Otranto* that Jane Austen, as the measured and
realistic voice of the educated middle class, knocked out of style.[2]

The Castle of Otranto follows the romance pattern that involves
a hero first in a conflict, then in a death struggle, and finally
in a discovery, all of which help him to defeat a villain and
win a bride (Frye, *Anatomy* 186–206). Theodore and Manfred
are hero and villain in *Otranto*. The one is described in the
imagery of spring, dawn, youth, fertility, and order; the other
in the imagery of winter, darkness, age, sterility, and confusion.
Theodore is consequently presented as life-giving; Manfred as
death-dealing. Theodore survives to redeem Otranto and marry
Isabella; Manfred kills Matilda, his daughter, loses Otranto, and
retires to a monastery to die. The romance pattern that brings
Theodore both princedom and princess reveals his identity as the
heir of the unjustly deposed Alfonso, former master of Otranto.
In this Manichaean world of black and white romance, good
triumphs over evil decisively in a way it seldom does in life.

But if the romance pattern of *Otranto* is clear, human motivation in the novel is not clear because "the Gothic does not simply create ambiguous or ironic romance," according to William
Patrick Day, "but subverts the mythology of the whole genre"
(7). Such a crucial debility substantiates Robert Kiely's contention that "Gothic fiction was not only *about* confusion, it was
written *from* confusion" (36). The reason for its confusion may
be that the Gothic novel is "one kind of treatment of the psychological problem of evil" (Hume 287). But it is demonstrably not a
satisfactory treatment of that problem. *Otranto* shows "no correspondence between human behavior and the demands of soul,
mind, heart, and body" (Kiely 40–41); moreover, Walpole shows
no awareness of this.[3] *The Castle of Otranto* is therefore filled with
"unnatural acts performed by improbable characters in unlikely

places" (Kiely 42).[4] Anthony Trollope found the same to be true of Mrs. Radcliffe's *The Mysteries of Udolpho*. "What may be done by impossible castles among impossible mountains, peopled by impossible heroes and heroines, and fraught with impossible horrors," he wrote, "*The Mysteries of Udolpho* have shown us" (*Thackeray* 190). In a similar vein of realistic commentary, Henry James asked, rhetorically, "What are the Apennines to us, or we to the Apennines?" (*Literary Criticism: Essays* 742). The answer is that they are nothing to us because, as George Haggerty observes, "Ann Radcliffe, the most polished of Gothic writers, allows the thrill of the immediate to undermine the overall impression of her works, even as she attempts to resolve her contorted plots with ruthless ingenuity" (381).

Like Walpole's before her, Mrs. Radcliffe's reach exceeds her grasp: she searches for sublimity but finds confusion. *Udolpho* duplicates the typical character types of Gothic romance found in *Otranto*: Manfred becomes Montoni, Theodore becomes Valancourt, Isabella and Matilda become one in Emily St. Aubert. But now the heroine is the center of the action rather than the hero, and her money is more a temptation to the villain than her virtue. Furthermore, her imagination dominates the action. Emily's life is "'like the dream of a distempered imagination,'" and the "achievement of *The Mysteries of Udolpho*" is "the projection of a nonrational mentality into a total environment" (Kiely 77). Emily St. Aubert, who half creates what she fears, shows that "the Gothic world . . . is a world of utter subjectivity" (Day 22). Insofar as her experience makes her, in Jane Austen's epithet, "a true quality heroine" of Gothic romance (*Northanger* 46), Emily enacts a prototypical pattern of events that Catherine Morland reenacts during her visit to Northanger Abbey. But the difference between Austen's Gothic vignette and Radcliffe's Gothic fantasy is that Austen knows precisely how to use confusion in such a way as to achieve order. As Cervantes did in *Don Quixote*,[5] Austen destroys once again what has become perverted in the "episteme or sign-system" (Jameson 27) of romance to emphasize, for better or worse, the contemporary manners of her society.

The Gloucestershire chapters of *Northanger Abbey* are cast in the mold of romance, and Catherine Morland plays the role of "true quality heroine" in chapters 20 through 24. But her mortification at the hands of a new kind of hero, Henry Tilney, and his villainous father returns her to the role Jane Austen wants her to have as "my heroine" (230), the heroine of a comic novel of manners. Catherine reassumes her proper role when the romance section of *Northanger Abbey* becomes a functional event in the comic structure of the novel. In *Northanger Abbey* Jane Austen leads the heroine by way of her romantic quest to the peripety and discovery of comedy. Catherine's exploration of the abbey is also an exploration of the self, and her mortification is a dying to Gothic illusion and an awakening to middle-class realities. "The visions of romance were over" (203), we are told by the narrator, and "the anxieties of common life began soon to succeed the alarms of romance" (203). Catherine's successful negotiation of the unpleasant trip from Gloucestershire to Fullerton, from abbey to parsonage, is a reversal of the romantic quest and shows "my heroine" retreating from the role of "true quality heroine" that she played on her way to and at Northanger Abbey. Catherine gets home safely by employing the resources of a steady head and a healthy constitution. The very events in the perilous quest that fails—the quest for the awful truth about Mrs. Tilney's untimely death—serve the heroine's advance toward the happy goal of marriage. The comedy of manners thereby uses the structure of Gothic romance to its own ends. Comedy assimilates romance to produce a catharsis of laughter and to precipitate a happy ending. In *Northanger Abbey* a novel of manners swallows a Gothic romance whole. The salutary effect is a healthy fit of laughter.

Joseph Conrad's *The Shadow-Line* is like *Northanger Abbey* in its ingestion of a Gothic romance. It is unlike Austen's novel in the way it proceeds and in the effects it produces. Each of Catherine Morland's suspicions is immediately tested and dismissed. When she is caught precipitately projecting fantasy onto life, she does not die; she lives to be mortified. Her suspicions are scolded into sense, and she becomes steadfast against a species of bourgeois villainy that constitutes a middle-class form of terror. Conrad's Gothic world is different from Austen's. Where she is dramatic, he is psychodramatic; where her characters are types, his are alter egos. Jane Austen's alternative to Gothic horror is the pain of dealing with the meanness of everyday life;

Conrad's alternative is psychic pain in the face of a meaning-less universe. Personal identity, which Austen took for granted as implicated in society, becomes for Conrad an insistent and inexorable question.

Conrad's narrator has no name. His experience is endowed with a universal meaning: he crosses that shadow-line from youth to maturity which defines a rite of passage. In that sense his is everybody's story, so that the narrator needs no name. He stands in for us, just as he stands in for an officer in the trenches on the Western Front who, in 1917, the year the novel was pub-lished, was going through his rite of passage in the war. Conrad pointedly dedicated the novel "TO BORYS AND ALL OTHERS who like himself have crossed in early youth the shadow-line of their generation WITH LOVE." Conrad's eighteen-year-old son, Borys, was an officer at the front when the novel was dedicated to him and his comrades. The Great War—itself deemed to be the war to end all wars—was likewise deemed civilization's rite of pas-sage, its transition, to an enduring maturity. The new captain, the narrator of the events of the novel, must cross the shadow-line by taking command of his ship. But the story shows that such a command is absurd. The sailing ship has no winds to move it; the captain has no crew to man it. The ship is becalmed with a sick crew. How can a captain be in command when there is no thing and no one to command? He can be in command only by commanding himself. He must not allow his fancy to overcome his sense of what is real.

The agent of fancy in *The Shadow-Line* is the chief mate, Mr. Burns, whose name describes his fevered mind. When disaster strikes, Burns tries to get the captain to believe that his ship is becalmed at latitude 8 degrees 20 minutes because the former captain of the ship is buried there. This old captain utterly failed to take command either of himself or of his ship. The new captain fears that he may be the old captain's double. Consequently, "the true terror" of this situation "lies in the possibility that the Gothic atmosphere will take over completely and that the conventional, stable division between self and Other will disappear forever" (Day 30). Burns tries to get the new captain to believe in ghosts. He tries to get him to open the nautical equivalents of old chests and cabinets and act like a fantasy-ridden Catherine Morland afloat. To the extent that the new captain loses command of his imagination, he is projected in Burns. To the extent that he does not, he is projected in Ransome, the ship's steward and best seaman, who has a weak heart. Though the captain's heart is also at times weak—Burns's fancies work on it—he is an excellent seaman too. He saves the ship. He finally refuses to believe Burns's Gothic tale of horror and accepts the reality of horror in a sick crew, windless weather, and his fear of his own failure. These bore into his mind and virtually overwhelm him until he takes command of himself in an absurd situation and sees the ship through. He crosses the shadow-line by confronting the *"grand miroir / De mon désespoir"*—the unmoved ocean holding his image in itself. The terror within and the terror without become one. And what is worse, both are real. What Conrad "makes us see" is the transformation of Gothic parody into psychodrama.

Like Jane Austen, Conrad encapsulates a Gothic tale— Burns's story of the devil-dodging old captain—inside a realistic novel. For both writers, to accept such a tale is to assess falsely the actual problems that life presents and to invite disaster: for her, social disaster; for him, existential disaster—madness or death. Catherine Morland deals with the characters in her drama as individuals external to herself; the new captain deals with the characters in his drama as extensions of himself. Jane Austen's heroine stands on one side of a line drawn by romanticism and Freudian psychology; Conrad's hero on the other side. This book, then, is about some of the changes the novel undergoes as it moves from Austen's world into Conrad's and beyond.

Since my argument is that elements of two traditional genres— that of the novel of manners and that of the new Gothic novel— came together in the latter part of the nineteenth century to yeild a new synthesis in fiction, I want to make clear what I mean by the novel of manners and the new Gothic novel. Lionel Trilling described manners as "the rules of personal intercourse in our culture" which create "culture's hum and buzz of implication." Manners are

> expressions of value . . . hinted at by small actions, sometimes by the arts of dress or decoration, sometimes by tone,

gesture, emphasis, or rhythm, sometimes by the words that are used with a special frequency or a special meaning. They are the things that for good or bad draw people of a culture together and that separate them from the people of another culture. They make the part of a culture which is not art, or religion, or morals, or politics, and yet it relates to all these highly formulated departments of culture. It is modified by them; it modifies them; it is generated by them; it generates them. In this part of culture assumption rules, which is often so much stronger than reason. (200–201)

A novel of manners, then, is one in which "assumption rules," implication is manifold, and cultural expectations have political, moral, and religious interaction. This description can be read as a subtle amplification of the *OED*'s definition of *manners* as "habitual behaviour or conduct" (4.a)—a definition that has a more literal amplification in the title of La Bruyère's famous work (to say nothing of the book itself) *Les caractères ou les moeurs de ce siècle*.[6] The *OED* continues: "In a more abstract subject of study, the moral code embodied in general custom or sentiment" (4.a,b)—a definition that Henry James amplifies when he declares that "everything hangs together, . . . and there's no isolated application of taste, no isolated damnation of delicacy. The interest of tone is the interest of manners, and the interest of manners is the interest of morals, and the interest of morals is the interest of civilization" (R. B. J. Wilson 276).

Whereas Trilling conveys to us a rather general *feeling* for manners, Martin Price, working out of Trilling, helps us to appreciate more precisely how manners exist in society:

Manners are concrete, complex orderings, both personal and institutional. They are a language of gestures, for words too become gestures when they are used to sustain rapport; most of our social ties are established in "speech acts" or "performance utterances." Such a language may become a self-sufficient system: polite questions that expect no answers, the small reciprocal duties of host and guest, of elder and younger; the protocol and management of deference. Such a code provides a way of formalizing conduct and of

distancing feeling; we do not feel the less for giving that
feeling an accepted form, which allows us to control its expression in shared rituals. . . . To the extent that manners
allow us to negotiate our claims with others, they become a
system of behavior that restrains force and turns aggression
into wit or some other gamelike form of combat. (265–67)

Price's description can be taken as an amplification of another
definition of *manners* in the *OED*: "External behaviour in social
intercourse, estimated as good or bad according to its degree of
politeness or conformity to the accepted standards of propriety"
(6). If one sees Price's specificity ("polite questions that expect
no answers" and the like) as modulating into Trilling's generalizations ("culture's hum and buzz of implication"), and Trilling's
generalizations modulating into Price's specific examples of conduct, then one gets a sense of the way I conceive of manners and
the novel of manners in this study.

Robert B. Heilman used the term "new Gothic" to describe
a revival of the Gothic tradition in novels that turn from older
forms of external terror to something more nearly psychological:
"the discovery and release of new patterns of feeling, the intensification of feeling" (99).[7] The new Gothic novel rehabilitates
the extrarational world not by emphasizing supernatural, preter-
natural, and "marvelous circumstance" but by moving "deeply
into the lesser known realities of human life" (101). Whereas
the novel of manners presents individual thought and feeling
indirectly through a code of usage established by social custom, the new Gothic novel presents individual thought and feeling at variance with social custom. The one emphasizes social
circumstance; the other, psychological states. In discussing the
development of Gothic fiction from the eighteenth to the nineteenth century, Haggerty fixes upon a dichotomy very much like
that just stated—a dichotomy between realism (social custom)
and romanticism (thought and feeling)—as the point where old
Gothic fiction deconstructs because it could not bring together
the metonymic writing characteristic of realism and the metaphoric language characteristic of romanticism. "Gothic fiction,"
he explains, "demanded . . . a means of resolving the metaphorical richness of the moment of Gothic intensity and the met-

onymic demands of time, space, character, and setting essential to the novel form" (382). Haggerty sees this dichotomy moving toward unity in *Melmoth the Wanderer*: "Moncada makes the private [metaphorical] dimensions of his experience more and more available to the reader by giving [metonymic] objective expression to his imaginings" (390). Maturin "makes the physical details so precise in order for the reader to understand more fully what is happening to Moncada psychologically" (389). When this kind of writing pervades a novel, rather than just passages of a novel, a new Gothic fiction takes form. When this formal integration of subjective and objective, metaphorical and metonymic is complete, the new Gothic novel avoids that "discontinuity with the real world" (Day 13) characteristic of old Gothic fiction, which "is one of unresolved chaos, of continuous transformation, of cruelty and fear, of the monstrous that is the shadow and mockery of the human" (Day 8). When, however, "the language of interiority becomes fully objectified" (Haggerty 390) so as to dramatize "the discovery and release of new patterns of feeling" and so as to penetrate "more deeply into the lesser known realities of human life," we hold in our hands what I call the new Gothic novel. My subsequent reflections on the new Gothic novel and the novel of manners presume these descriptions of each and move toward a further identification of these genres in a new way.

My contention is that the novel of manners can further be defined by its dramatization of a myth of social concern, its use of the structure of the "case," its literal depiction of the cardinal virtues, and its dramatization of a love of complementary partners. The new Gothic novel, for its part, can further be defined by its dramatization of a myth of freedom, its use of riddles, its metaphorical depiction of the last things, and its dramatization of a love of affined partners.

The myths of freedom and concern are at least as old as Plato, and they influenced Marx and Engels in the formulation of the dialectic of history. Their classical origin is complemented by their appearance in the Bible—in "Judaeo-Christian myth[ology] as set out in the Bible, and as taught in the form of doctrine by the Christian Church" (Frye, *Critical Path* 37). As myths they function as "possible models for human experience" (Frye, *Edu-*

cated Imagination 22). These myths, as elaborated by Northrop Frye, embody the conflict of the individual with society; they show themselves in such things as the tension "between the instincts of the individual" and society's "code of manners that does not at every point fit" those instincts (Paulson 267). They are based, on the one hand, on a correspondence of statement to fact which emphasizes evidence and logic (freedom); and on the other, on a coherence of doctrine and order which emphasizes belief and authority (concern). They present two sides of every man's existence: his belonging to a society that is concerned that he keep its laws and preserve its order, and, at the same time, his being an individual who rebels against law and order for the sake of establishing his freedom.[8] Consequently, "the myth of freedom is born from concern and can never replace concern or exist without it; nevertheless, it creates a tension against it" (Frye, *Critical Path* 131). Myths of freedom and concern are two complementary responses to human endeavor, but they often find themselves embodied in opposing ideologies of the right and left. "Satire shows us in *1984* the society that has destroyed its freedom, and [satire likewise shows us] in *Brave New World* the society that has forgotten its concern. They must both be there, and the genuine individual and the free society can exist only when they are" (Frye, *Critical Path* 55).

The case and the riddle are literary categories that were isolated for structuralist study by André Jolles in *Einfache Formen* (137–58). The case evolves as a literary form from law, courtly love, and theology; it emphasizes the mind's ability to propose solutions to difficult problems and solve them so as to allow life to continue within an orderly society. The appearance of the case in the novel of manners gives substance to Hayden White's contention that "narrative in general, from the folktale to the novel . . . has to do with topics of law, legality, legitimacy, or, more generally, *authority*" (17). Whereas the case admits of more than one approach and resolution,[9] the riddle does not. The riddle evolves from magic and religion, is seemingly insoluble, and punishes failure to produce the one right answer to it. The form of the riddle is like that of an examination in which only one answer is acceptable. The examiner asks a question that the one examined must answer or else fail the examination. The riddle therefore produces constraint. In the Sphinx's riddle (*Question:* What is that which walks on four legs, and two legs, and three legs? *Answer:* Man: a baby crawls, an adult walks upright, and an elderly person uses a cane) the constraint is clear: Oedipus must solve it or die. When he does solve it, the Sphinx dies. The riddle is the "unwelcome cipher" that Edward Said finds "at the beginning of the quest, the end of which is 'decipherment' " (144–45).

Plato was the first to define the cardinal virtues, and in the *Republic* he declared them necessary to the state and, since the state is the aggregate of its citizens, to each individual in it. Then in *The Laws* he examined them more particularly, having previously treated only justice at length. The cardinal (from Latin *cardo*) virtues are the hinge virtues because all others depend on them: every cardinal virtue "fulfils the conditions of being well judged, subserving the common good, being restrained within measure, and having firmness; and these four conditions also yield four distinct virtues" (Rickaby 343). In *De Finibus* Cicero writes, "Each man should so conduct himself that fortitude appears in labours and dangers: temperance in foregoing pleasures: prudence in the choice between good and evil: justice in giving every man his own" (Ricaby 343). He amplified this formula in *De Officiis*, a concerned father's letter to his dissipated son. The cardinal virtues might nowadays be better recognized by other names, such as wisdom, justice, courage, and discipline. Without such virtues society, presumably, cannot function effectively because these virtues oversee the establishment, individually and communally, of an orderly life: "the rules of good form," as Charlotte E. Morgan has shown, "were made dependent on the principle of right living" (90).

The notion of "last things" derives from theology. The last things are set out as death, judgment, heaven, and hell. The judgment of God follows upon death, and the reward of heaven or the punishment of hell follows upon judgment. These ideas of good and evil, reward and punishment point toward an unmasking, a revelation, an apocalypse. Eschatology and apocalypse go hand in hand because both depend on and point to the significance of death.

In traditional romantic literature death is frequently a *Liebes-*

tod, a "love-death" (Boone 38–39). Lovers who die for love are invariably affined lovers who have the same nature, disposition, and tastes. They are so much like one another that they define themselves as one heart and soul: "the real fierceness of desire, the real heat of passion long continued and withering up the soul of man, is the craving for identity with the woman that he loves. He desires to see with the same eyes, to touch with the same sense of touch, to hear with the same ears, to lose his identity, to be enveloped, to be supported" (Ford, *Good Soldier* 114–15). Such affined, romantic lovers differ from lovers in realistic fiction who usually bring distinct but complementary qualities of mind and heart to a marriage which welds their differences into a bond that does not sacrifice their individuality. Plato again supplies the primary text for the discussion of affined love in the *Symposium*, especially in Aristophanes' speech on the original androgynous condition of the man-woman. Zeus split the entity into two sexes because he feared that man-woman was strong enough to overthrow the gods themselves. Affined lovers in consequence seek in each other the primal unity of their original androgynous creation (189C–194E). "Thus," as Randall Craig writes, affined love "on earth can at best achieve an imperfect approximation of the original harmony and wholeness of self" (163). The psychoanalytic theory of Jacques Lacan is permeated with this sense of "lack," of imperfection: "I can't be you. But I can try." [10] Lacan's fractured human being is forever seeking something lost (*objet petit a[utre]*); "lack" originates in the loss of androgynous identity; this is the primary instance of the subject's being split and divided (thus *le corps morcelé*). Lacan even returns to Aristophanes' discourse in Plato's *Symposium* to give us a sense of the human subject's lost perfection as embodied in the myth of androgynous creation (*The Four* 196–97, 295). For Lacan the ideally unified human being figuratively projected in this myth does not and cannot exist. [11] His vision of man thus captures some of the romantic agony of new Gothic fiction in which affined lovers forever seek an impossible unity in each other.

The Judeo-Christian tradition supplies the primary text for complementary love in the Bible, where God, who is irrevocably different from man, loves man for what he is. This becomes the ultimate model for sacramental marriage when a man's love for his wife is seen as a symbol of Christ's love for the church. Shirley Robin Letwin summarizes the practical consequences of this theological tradition of complementary love in everyday life: "Christian love is a relationship between beings who recognize one another to be irrevocably different. They do not see themselves as members of the same class, instances of the same species or incarnations of the same universal principle. They do not use one another, desire to possess or fuse with the other. They remain wholly separate and unlike, and their appreciation of one another does not depend on any common element" (157). Complementary lovers provide strength where there is weakness, and together as a couple they are stronger than either can be alone. Mikhail Bakhtin's theory of utterance embodies a historical sense of the radical uniqueness of the individual subject: "Every word gives off the scent of a profession, a genre, a current, a party, a particular work, a particular man, a generation, an era, a day, and an hour. Every word smells of the context and contexts in which it has lived its intense social life; all words and all forms are inhabited by intentions" (Todorov 56–57). Simultaneously, Bakhtin's theory of utterance as dialogue shows that this radical uniqueness is formed and strengthened dialogically: "in Bakhtin, the more of the other, the more of the self" (Clark and Holquist 206). Bakhtin's theory of social relationships, consequently, suggests some of the possibilities for a renewal of life implicit in the novel of manners.[12]

The novel of manners assimilates the myth of concern, the case, the cardinal virtues, and complementary lovers into its structure as a matter of course. Manners require a stable society which the cardinal virtues promote. These virtues are in turn promoted by a myth of concern for their coherence in the present and their continuity in the future. Difficult cases are judged in the context of this myth. Such cases most frequently involve differences between a man and a woman who resolve them and eventually marry. The new Gothic novel assimilates the myth of freedom, the riddle, the last things, and affined lovers into its structure as a matter of course. Release and intensification of feeling is frequently frustrating and seldom fulfilling. Frustrated desire intensifies into emotional pain that becomes a kind of hell

on earth, just as emotional fulfillment brings a joy that is a kind
of heaven on earth. Only romantic lovers whose hearts and souls
are one another's can experience such intensity of feeling. But
affined lovers find that their relationship is very much a riddle
to them not only because of their unique two-in-oneness but
also because one lover is often legally bound in marriage to a
third party. This situation invariably leads the lovers to emphasize their freedom from the concern of society—the new Gothic
novel "trespasses on laws that are fundamentally social in character" (Clayton 81)—and makes a judgment of their actions, and
sometimes their death, inevitable.

The new Gothic novel, in addition, calls into question personal identity which is seldom, if ever, in question in the novel
of manners. Whereas in the old Gothic novel it is a question of
who your parents are, in the new Gothic novel it is a question
of who you are. The need for personal identity runs up against
social norms defined by words like *gentleman* and *lady*. But in
the new Gothic novel the norms that exist in the novel of manners to judge the awarding of such titles have disappeared. Too
frequently a *gentleman* is a monied man only, be his manners
what they may. Such a man's mind is alien to his heart. To be
a *gentleman* for the hero of a new Gothic novel becomes a riddle
of personal identity. That riddle as it is embedded in the word
gentleman further leads to an intense desire on the part of the new
Gothic hero or heroine to be freed both from old ties carrying
moral constraints and from new ties to money carrying a betrayal
of the heart. To be a gentleman in the way that Heathcliff and
Pip want to be gentlemen is to be devoid of an authentic self.
Darcy and Arabin, on the other hand, are defined as gentlemen
by birth and social custom; their struggle for identity is an educational process which helps them toward a better understanding
of their desires and their roles as gentlemen. They are, however,
never in doubt as to who as individuals they are.

The problem of identity is dramatized in both the novel of manners and the new Gothic novel by what has come to be called
the "bourgeois dream" (Houghton 189–90). John Ruskin set out
its constituent elements in "Traffic" in *The Crown of Wild Olive* as
the middle-class aspiration to use money acquired by hard work

to achieve the status of a gentleman—to buy a great house, settle down in it, and live a leisured existence. Addressing a Bradford audience that had asked his advice on the design of their Exchange, Ruskin, on 21 April 1864, excoriated their ambition:

> Your ideal of human life then is, I think, that it should be passed in a pleasant undulating world, with iron and coal everywhere underneath it. On each pleasant bank of this world is to be a beautiful mansion, with two wings; and stable, and coach-houses; a moderately-sized park; a large garden and hot-houses; and pleasant carriage drives through the shrubberies. In this mansion are to live the favoured votaries of the Goddess [of Getting-on]; the English gentleman, with his gracious wife, and his beautiful family; he always able to have the boudoir and the jewels for the wife, and the beautiful ball dresses for the daughters, and hunters for the sons, and a shooting in the Highlands for himself. (453)

This rejection of the Goddess of Getting-on is also a rejection of the Gospel of Getting-on as preached by Samuel Smiles in his runaway best-seller *Self-Help* (1859), in which the lowly workman with a spark of genius characteristically becomes the lordly millionaire. *The Life of George Stephenson, Railway Engineer* (1857), Smiles's popular curtain-raiser to *Self-Help*, is an up-close and personal look at one of the rich and famous; it created a demand for more of the same, which *Self-Help* satisfied.

Smiles is clearly the hagiographer of the industrial revolution that made England the workshop of the world and made the Great Exhibition "the peak of English confidence in the industrial economy and in the technology that made it possible":

> during the thirty years between 1851 and 1881 the national product rose from £523 million (£25 *per capita*) to £1,051 million (£75 *per capita*). And exports, on which Britain's international strength depended, rose, too, from £100 million in the decade 1850–59 to £160 million in the following decade and £218 million in the next. The tonnage of British shipping rose from 3,600,000 tons in 1850 to 6,600,000 in 1880 and the production of cast iron increased three-fold between

1850 and 1875. Industry itself was certainly not in decline. The greatest Victorian boom had ended by 1875, but while it lasted it was striking enough for Disraeli to describe it as a "convulsion of prosperity." (Briggs, *Social History* 195)

This convulsion of prosperity propelled in its turn two great leaps toward democracy in the two Reform Bills of 1832 and 1867 which enfranchised the middle class and the working class, respectively. The combination of prosperity and democracy made even more characteristic of the nineteenth century what Adam Smith had said of the eighteenth: "Merchants are commonly ambitious of becoming country gentlemen" (in Briggs, *Social History* 171). This is the common ambition that Ruskin condemns in his Bradford address. But whether he is aware of it or not, he is really rejecting Robinson Crusoe, who bought an estate in Bedfordshire after all those lonely years of toil on his desert island. And Crusoe is himself simply symptomatic of something deeply embedded in English folk tradition in "The History of Whittington," the story of the beggarly boy who becomes Lord Mayor of London.

For Ruskin, undoubtedly, past legend and present-day conditions of human existence are two different things. The bourgeois dream is nonetheless, in its roots, radically human because it encapsulates in its structure a basic difference between labor and leisure that divides our days into "working hours" and "after hours" and our weeks into "work days" and "weekends." The bourgeois dream seeks to dissolve days into afterhours and weeks into weekends. It seeks to recapture a world before the fall—before man was condemned to earn his bread by the sweat of his brow. The bourgeois dream as Ruskin articulated it, then, is a middle-class displacement of the biblical myth of Eden and comes into the novel having come out of the idyll.[13] In the complex evolution of religious and social and economic norms, Edenic leisure was deemed a gentleman's prerogative, and, conversely, a gentleman was someone who no longer needed to work. *Wuthering Heights* reenacts the fall of man when Heathcliff, having lost an Edenic preadolescent youth with Catherine Earnshaw, condemns one gentleman's son, Hareton Earnshaw, and another gentleman's daughter, Catherine Linton, to me-nial work, he himself having traveled the opposite route from labor to leisure. The gentlemen's children find their redemption when Hareton helps Catherine plant a garden, an event which initiates Heathcliff's rapid decline toward death. *Great Expectations* affords the best example of striving (but not succeeding) to overcome the labor/leisure, work-hours/after-hours, weekday/weekend dichotomies in John Wemmick, who gets "portable property" in Little Britain in order to live like a gentleman at Walworth. When in *The Last Post* Christopher Tietjens renounces the status and estate of a gentleman to cultivate a garden with his own hands, he accepts the fall of man, which the Great War all too vividly witnessed to, and brings the man of labor and the gentleman of leisure together in himself. The bourgeois dream is thereby given a sharp rebuke. The only bit of the garden world that a gentleman can recapture is peace, but that must come from cultivating his own garden. One invariable element common to novels of manners, new Gothic novels, and novels of Gothic manners is that they all make some response to this deeply rooted urge to rise in rank and fortune as it works itself out in contemporary society.

Sir William Lucas in *Pride and Prejudice* is an early example of a character in pursuit of the bourgeois dream; so too is Charles Bingley, whose father, after making a fortune, died before realizing the dream of buying an estate—a dream which his son fulfills. Heathcliff chases the bourgeois dream in *Wuthering Heights* in an attenuated way: he wants to use property as a stick with which to beat the old established property-owning class. And he succeeds because he enters the novel an orphan and leaves it the master of two estates. Trollope has Arabin and Slope jostle each other for the rich deanery of Barchester. Dickens' Pip tries to follow in the footsteps of Dick Whittington in *Great Expectations*. George Eliot rewrites Pip's story in those of Fred Vincy and Will Ladislaw in *Middlemarch*. In James's *The Portrait of a Lady* Isabel Archer undergoes a metamorphosis from middle-class girl to aristocratic lady by inheriting a fortune; that fortune also turns the reclusive aesthete, Gilbert Osmond, into a class-conscious European gentleman. Even Hardy's less worldly-minded Jude Fawley wishes to be a bishop and live on a fraction of a lordly income. Ford Madox Ford rejects the whole tradition of the bourgeois dream in *Parade's End* when Christopher Tietjens refuses his inheritance, rejects the title to his estate, and begins life anew as an antiques dealer and a home gardener.

The treatment of this central theme of the bourgeois dream in the novel from Jane Austen to Ford Madox Ford constitutes a reflection of and a reflection on the dynamics of the democratic process in English society from the end of the Napoleonic Wars to the end of World War I. The novel of Gothic manners, by synthesizing the opposing elements of earlier forms, enabled George Eliot to be a critic of an England thriving on respectability, Henry James to be a critic of a Europe entrenched in convention, and Thomas Hardy to be a critic of Western civilization and its medieval, indeed, its Gothic roots. Ford depicts the end of the old episteme in World War I: Tietjens' shell shock buries the eighteenth-century Tory gentleman and resurrects the modern man as *l'homme moyen sensuel* from the muddy trenches of the Western Front. It is not Tietjens' life alone that begins anew on 11 November 1918. On Armistice Day the whole world sees rebirth to the music of a French puppet show: *"Les petites marionettes, font! font! font!"* If Thackeray ended his merciless social history of the Battle of Waterloo by putting his puppets back into the showman's box at the end of *Vanity Fair*, Ford feels comfortable with letting his loose at the end of *A Man Could Stand Up* (the third novel of his tetralogy, *Parade's End*). Having worked out its implications in the horrors of Ford's war, Thackeray's "parade of mechanistic behavior, the money system, the mirror of art, the novel as fetish of escapism" (Polhemus, *Comic Faith* 150)—"the little world of dolls, puppets, artifacts, small histories, and private matters" (140)—gives way to a different and, Ford perhaps hopes, a better world. And thus the novel once again renews itself as a "developing genre . . . [that] reflects more deeply, more essentially, more sensitively and rapidly [than any other genre], reality itself in the process of its unfolding" (Bakhtin, *Dialogic* 7).

From *Pride and Prejudice* to *Barchester Towers* manners change from being a means of self-definition to being a means of social exclusion: Darcy and Elizabeth wed conduct to intelligence and affection and they wed each other; Bertie and Madeline Stanhope, however, leave the city of Barchester for more tolerant climes. In *Wuthering Heights* the conventions of Gothic fantasy are domesticated and in *Great Expectations* they are personalized: Heathcliff becomes master of two country houses; Pip's feelings are so skewed that he thinks himself akin to Dr. Frankenstein's monster. The novel of manners shows society gradually cultivating respectability as a virtue; the new Gothic novel shows the individual defining home and personality in terms of strong feeling. The novel of manners and the new Gothic novel become what Alan Liu called "pressure points where the entire generic field is beginning to rearrange around the massive intrusion of specifically historical reality" (527). Consequently, "the relationship between the individual text and the series of texts formative of a genre presents itself as a process of the continual founding and altering of horizons" (Jauss, *Toward* 88).

When the genres of manners and new Gothic fiction come together in *Middlemarch*, respectability replaces Gothic horror because it denies legitimacy to strong feeling. Indeed, respectability has the same effect on the human spirit that Mrs. Radcliffe posited for horror, which she said "contracts, freezes, and nearly annihilates" the faculties of the soul, closing them to the sublime (Hume 284–85). George Eliot shows the reversal of manners into this species of Gothic horror. When social formulations are unable or unwilling to admit new demands, the result is either the clerical conservatism of a Barsetshire or the emotional constraint of a Middlemarch society. In defiance of such constraint—such contraction, freezing, and near annihilation of the soul—Ladislaw asserts, essentially, the same freedom as Heathcliff, except that it takes a more aesthetic and political form. Opposition to valorized middle-class manners in both characters is nonetheless very much the same. When George Eliot shows manners as a species of Gothic horror in *Middlemarch*, the myths of concern and freedom are put in tension. The cardinal virtues are debased and come to exist more or less as simple manifestations of sanctioned social conduct. The last things are seldom named but dramatize themselves in states of feeling where they are revealed as dead metaphors interred in repression (death), guilt (judgment), joy (heaven), and sorrow (hell). Complementary love degenerates into the delusion of unsuitable partners who think that their differences will be their strength but whose marriages almost invariably turn out badly. Affined love becomes a romantic love that exists as an alternative to marriages already made. And the case becomes the riddle, the riddle the case: where intelligence may see a way out of a riddle-like case, society precludes a solution because the problem is frequently a miserable marriage. But miserable or not, marriage is the foundation of society's respectability: it is "the all-subsuming, all-organizing, all-containing contract." It is, as Tony Tanner remarks, "the structure that maintains the Structure" (*Adultery* 15). The realism of late Victorian novels of Gothic manners derives from the circumstances of the conflict between this structure within a Structure and the intense individual feelings that threaten it. In addition, "the taste for emotions of recognition" replaces, in Henry James's words, "the taste for emotions of surprise" (*Literary Criticism: Essays* 1354); consequently, suffering in fiction now seems to belong less to romance and more to a realistic rendering of contemporary life.

All of this is demonstrated at length in the chapters that follow, which, taken together, are projected as a study of the changes in English fiction that bring about the novel of Gothic manners. The book takes into consideration the demonstrable relations of one novelist to another as well as the palettes they use to paint the shifting picture of human life they variously depict. Its purpose is to present the classic English novel from the perspective of Gothic manners and to demonstrate how the art of the novel renewed itself as a criticism of life.

Part One

Manners

1

Pride and Prejudice
Manners as Self-Definition

Jane Austen makes a case in *Pride and Prejudice* for a prudent marriage and against a mercenary marriage. Her spokesman inside the novel for this point of view is Mrs. Gardiner. Her aunt cautions Elizabeth against encouraging Wickham's affections because marriage between them would be decidedly imprudent. She discusses this with her niece and puts forward considerations of family and fortune for particular attention. Elizabeth is not to encourage Wickham because it would be foolish for her to marry a man with even less money than she herself has. Such a marriage would require unreasonable sacrifices on the part of her family. This advice proves sound once Lydia marries Wickham: Darcy and Elizabeth must help the improvident couple in ways that the Bennets cannot afford. Nevertheless, when Mrs. Gardiner warns Elizabeth against getting into such a fix herself, her niece becomes petulant and sees no reason why she should be better than her neighbors (181–82). But Wickham's subse-

quent neglect of Elizabeth in favor of Miss King allows Mrs.
Gardiner to raise the subject a second time:

"But, my dear Elizabeth, . . . what sort of girl is Miss
King? I should be sorry indeed to think our friend mercenary."

"Pray, my dear aunt, what is the difference in matrimonial affairs between the mercenary and the prudent motive?
Where does discretion end, and avarice begin? Last Christ-
mas you were afraid of his marrying me, because it would be
imprudent; and now, because he is trying to get a girl with
only ten thousand pounds, you want to find out that he is
mercenary."

"If you will only tell me what sort of girl Miss King is, I
shall know what to think."

"She is a very good kind of girl, I believe. I know no
harm of her."

"But he paid her not the smallest attention, till her grandfather's death made her mistress of this fortune."

"No—why should he? If it was not allowable for him to
gain *my* affections, because I had no money, what occasion
could there be for making love to a girl whom he did not
care about, and who was equally poor?"

"But there seems indelicacy in directing his attentions
toward her, so soon after this event."

"A man in distressed circumstances has not time for all
those elegant decorums which other people may observe. If
she does not object to it, why should *we*?"

"*Her* not objecting does not justify *him*. It only shews her
being deficient in something herself—sense or feeling."

"Well," cried Elizabeth, "have it as you choose. *He* shall
be mercenary, and *she* shall be foolish."

"No, Lizzy, that is what I do *not* choose. I should be
sorry, you know, to think ill of a young man who has lived
so long in Derbyshire." (188–89)

In this conversation between aunt and niece, we see a logical,
intelligent opponent confronting an illogical, cynical one. The
difference between this chapter and the later one that depicts
the harsh confrontation between Elizabeth and Lady Catherine

is that Elizabeth is as dull with her own aunt as she is sharp with Darcy's aunt. Mrs. Gardiner forces Elizabeth to accept distinctions that she wants to ignore—distinctions that Elizabeth later uses to destroy Lady Catherine's illogical arguments against the suitability of a Darcy marrying a Bennet. In fact, the distinction between a prudent and a mercenary marriage that Mrs. Gardiner insists upon is crucial to the case that Jane Austen makes in *Pride and Prejudice*.

The *case* is a literary genre that was given theoretical prominence by André Jolles in his book *Einfache Formen* (1930). It is common to law and theology and to courtly love literature. In a case a set of real or hypothetical circumstances is offered to support a particular judgment of an action; arguments for other competing interpretative judgments are also made and set in opposition to the first judgment. Thus Charlotte Lucas and Elizabeth Bennet argue the case of Jane's response to Bingley's attentions to her, Charlotte arguing that Jane should make a public show of affection for Bingley and Elizabeth arguing that that affection is already evident enough. "In nine cases out of ten, a woman had better show *more* affection than she finds," says Charlotte. "But if a woman is partial to a man, and does not endeavour to conceal it," Elizabeth replies, "he must find it out" (68). Insofar as Bingley leaves Jane and goes to London with his sisters, Charlotte's judgment is vindicated; insofar as Bingley returns to Longbourne and marries Jane, Elizabeth's judgment is vindicated. According to Jolles—as this example shows—the case shows a disposition of mind that takes the world as an object which can be evaluated according to norms.[1]

It presents a process of deliberation but not necessarily the result of such deliberation. This is especially so in stories that embody cases argued in the Courts of Love. If a lady having two suitors accepts a new crown from one but gives her own crown to the other, which has she shown the greater favor? (Jolles 153). Does a husband who allows his wife to keep a promise that will result in her infidelity to him—a promise she made in fear of his life—show himself more generous than the lover who exacted the promise but who sends the lady back to her husband, refusing to allow her to keep it? Chaucer has the Franklin end his tale of these noble actions with a question: "Lordynges, this question, thanne, wol I aske now, Which was the mooste fre, as thynketh you?" (Robinson 144).

Austen more typically presents the results of deliberating a case. Nonetheless, a novel that is a case or contains a case or cases imposes an obligation on its readers to think along with the narrator and characters and also to think independently of them. Cases exist to be argued, to be settled, ideally, by the discourse of reason. *Pride and Prejudice* is by and large composed of a series of cases. "And so, you like this man's sisters too, do you? Their manners are not equal to his" (62). Thus it is that Elizabeth opens the case of Charles Bingley's sisters with Jane. The debate between the Bennet sisters continues as evidence is gathered and interpreted, but Jane finally has to give up her position and admit that Caroline Bingley and Mrs. Hurst are rather shabby friends at best: "My dearest Lizzy, will, I am sure, be incapable of triumphing in her better judgment, at my expence, when I confess myself to have been entirely deceived in Miss Bingley's regard for me" (184). Mr. Bennet later has to say just about the same thing to Elizabeth after Lydia elopes with Wickham. Elizabeth has earlier told her father that Lydia is too compacted of "wild volatility, the assurance and disdain of all restraint," to be allowed to go to Brighton. Mr. Bennet argued that "Colonel Forster is a sensible man, and will keep her out of any real mischief" (258). Both put their sides of the case well, but he is wrong and she is right, as Mr. Bennet himself later admits: "Lizzy, I bear you no ill-will for being justified in your advice to me last May, which, considering the event, shews some greatness of mind" (315). Once Lydia elopes, Jane and Elizabeth discuss her case: Jane argues the possibility of a marriage taking place; Elizabeth argues that it cannot take place because there is no money to tempt Wickham. When Darcy supplies the money, Wickham is tempted enough to marry Lydia. In these three instances the case functions as a heuristic device by which Mr. Bennet, Jane, and Elizabeth improve their knowledge of character and circumstance in their world.

The principal cases in the novel have a similar function and are precisely related to the major problems that develop between Darcy and Elizabeth. The question of how a woman should act to secure a husband—the question that Charlotte Lucas and Elizabeth debated—reappears when Darcy writes his celebrated letter to Elizabeth, following her refusal of his proposal of marriage. He substantiates the case Charlotte made: "I shall not scruple to assert, that the serenity of your sister's countenance and air was such, as might have given the most acute observer, a conviction that, however amiable her temper, her heart was not likely to be easily touched" (228).

The most difficult case is Darcy himself. "I hear such different accounts of you as puzzle me exceedingly," Elizabeth tells him as they dance at Netherfield (136). Remembering Darcy's finding her tolerable but not tempting at the Meryton ball, she willingly believes Wickham's lies about him and makes a case against Darcy by indicting his ill manners to her and his injustice to Jane and to Wickham. Elizabeth has been warned against taking this position by Charlotte and Jane and even by Caroline Bingley; but she refuses to respect their evidence and logic and prefers her own. Just how wrong she is she learns from Darcy's letter and from her visit to his estate. In chapter 18 she tells Darcy that she is working toward "the illustration of [his] character." He asks her "not to sketch [his] character at the present moment" (136). But Elizabeth feels that she cannot wait, and she draws for herself an ill-mannered, unjust Darcy. At Pemberley she finds a portrait of Darcy that sets to rights the caricature of his likeness that she took at the ball. She finds, in short, the picture she tried but failed to draw: "In the gallery there were many family portraits, but they could have little to fix the attention of a stranger. Elizabeth walked on in quest of the only face whose features would be known to her. At last it arrested her—and she beheld a striking resemblance of Mr. Darcy, with such a smile over the face, as she remembered to have sometimes seen, when he looked at her" (271).

Cases, then, abound in *Pride and Prejudice*. The novel itself is conceived as a case containing cases: we are asked to judge the circumstances of Darcy's two proposals to Elizabeth and find against the first and for the second as an offer of a prudent marriage. Jane, Mr. Bennet, and the Gardiners show us the way by taking the lead in doing just that. All the other cases contribute to our affirming this judgment beyond the shadow of a doubt. At Darcy's first proposal Elizabeth refuses to make a

mercenary marriage; at Darcy's second proposal she willingly
makes a prudent marriage. Between the two proposals Darcy
and Elizabeth are purged of their pride and prejudice and consequently redefine themselves for themselves. What Elizabeth
says to herself while center stage Darcy says to himself offstage:
"Till this moment, I never knew myself" (237). In light of what
they learn about themselves when measured against the norms
their society upholds—norms of justice, temperance, reason, fair
play, and good manners—in the light of these norms that are
made manifest in the first proposal scene, Darcy and Elizabeth
examine their conduct and find it wanting. Purging themselves
of what led each of them to be "blind, partial, prejudiced, absurd" (236), they then meet as reasonable and affectionate people when the novel begins again. Insofar as *Pride and Prejudice*
dramatizes what Walton Litz sees as "a harmony between characters and the base of reality" (69), Jane Austen is able to begin
her novel again in chapter 53 by having Bingley return and by
having Mrs. Bennet ask her husband to call on him. The novel
here demonstrates that it has a *da capo al fine* structure like that
of a piece of music. The same notes sounded at the beginning
are now played in a different key, the key of reason and affection. Jane Austen seems in effect to be saying that now that they
have at last come to a proper sense of themselves and their own
best good, Darcy and Elizabeth should, if they are given another
chance, get the ending of their story right a second time round.
And that is exactly what happens in the second proposal scene.
The moral and emotional revolutions that Darcy and Elizabeth
experience by facing hard, unpleasant truths about themselves
bring them to the realization that they can be equal and complementary partners in marriage. That realization shows that Jane
Austen has established a new norm to answer the old question
asked in the Courts of Love: Should a man love a woman who is
superior to himself in riches or rank, or one who is *inferior*? (Jolles
153). As long as the marriage is prudent, Austen replies, neither
superior nor inferior weighs in the balance. So *Pride and Prejudice*
can finally dramatize no greater wisdom than having Darcy and
Elizabeth marry. Such a union would obviously be a prudent
marriage, for, as Dr. Johnson tells us in his *Dictionary, prudence*

is "wisdom applied to practice." And *wisdom*, in its turn, is "the power of judging rightly."

If we conceive of the structure of the novel in terms of Darcy's two proposals to Elizabeth, we must see her rejecting the first offer because it would lead to a mercenary marriage and her accepting the second because it leads to a prudent marriage. When she refused Darcy's first proposal to her, she told him that he was not a gentleman: "You are mistaken, Mr. Darcy, if you suppose that the mode of your declaration affected me in any other way, than as it spared me the concern which I might have felt in refusing you, had you behaved in a more gentleman-like manner" (224). After Elizabeth accepts his second proposal of marriage, Darcy tells her that those very words led to his refor- mation: "Your reproof, so well applied, I shall never forget: 'had you behaved in a more gentleman-like manner.' Those were your words. You know not, you can scarcely conceive, how they have tortured me;—though it was some time, I confess, before I was reasonable enough to allow their justice" (376). The reference to justice, the chief of the cardinal virtues, is deliberately and precisely made here. Darcy has done Elizabeth justice: he has given Elizabeth's words their due and found himself wanting. The word justice thus reminds us of what C. S. Lewis affirmed when he said that Jane Austen used "the great abstract nouns of classical English moralists" uncompromisingly. "These are the concepts by which Jane Austen grasps her world. . . . All is hard, clear, definable" (60). Having done Elizabeth justice, Darcy can demand that she do him justice. Thus when he writes his long letter to her, he does not just ask her to read it attentively, he requires her to do so: "I demand it of your justice" (227). If Elizabeth learns prudence in her debate with Mrs. Gardiner, temperance in controlling her affection for Wickham, and forti- tude in standing up to Lady Catherine's merciless attack on her and her family, she also learns justice in dealing with Darcy's let- ter. She thereby completes the definition of the cardinal virtues in herself. After she reads the letter repeatedly, she submits her own conduct to judgment. Without "any wish of doing him jus- tice" (233), she comes to believe him: "the justice" of Darcy's words "struck her too forcibly for denial" (237). Drawing evidence from her conversations with others, Elizabeth correlates it with Darcy's explanation of his own conduct and finds herself at fault: "she had been blind, partial, prejudiced, absurd" (236). Elizabeth, judging herself accurately, does Darcy the justice that he demanded of her. The word *justice*, then, ties his first proposal to his second, just as the word *tempt* ties his refusal to dance with Elizabeth—"She is tolerable; but not handsome enough to tempt *me*" (59)—to her refusal of his first proposal: "Do you think that any consideration would tempt me to accept the man, who has been the means of ruining . . . the happiness of a most beloved sister?" (222). By the repetition of two words —*tempt* and *justice*—Jane Austen draws the introduction, climax, and conclusion of her novel together: the scene in which Darcy rejects Elizabeth at Meryton, the scene in which Elizabeth rejects Darcy at Hunsford, and the scene in which Darcy and Elizabeth accept each other at Longbourn.

The first time that Darcy proposes to Elizabeth, she has a chance to make a mercenary marriage and refuses to take it: "You could not have made me the offer of your hand in any possible way that would have tempted me to accept it," she tells him (224). The second time he proposes to her (375), Elizabeth has a chance to make a prudent marriage and takes it because "she began now to comprehend that he was exactly the man, who, in disposition and talents, would most suit her. His understanding and temper, *though unlike her own*, would have answered all her wishes. It was an union that must have been to the advantage of both; by her ease and liveliness, his mind might have been softened, his manners improved, and from his judgment, information, and knowledge of the world, she must have received benefit of greater importance" (325, italics added). This thorough understanding of their love as complementary and strengthening dictates the wisdom of their marrying. It has a firm hold on Elizabeth's mind when Lady Catherine comes to demand that she not marry Darcy. Elizabeth's fortitude is grounded on the certainty that her union with him would be very prudent indeed. What Lady Catherine wants, for her part, is a mercenary marriage between Darcy and her daughter: "Their fortune on both sides is splendid" (365). But she does not get it. Her visit backfires and precipitates Darcy's second proposal to Elizabeth.

Darcy's marriage to Elizabeth is prudent because they are complementary partners whose differences in temperament generate a stronger entity in marriage. Jane Austen's organization of the novel by way of building up, stating, and solving a set of problems is meant to demonstrate this beyond doubt. The center of this structure—and physically the center of the book too if one counts pages—is Darcy's proposal to Elizabeth, followed by her refusal, his letter, and her revaluation of their relationship.

Darcy's offer ends all confusion between him and Elizabeth by defining four problems that stand between them: she does not like him because he separated Bingley from Jane, because she believes he treated Wickham unjustly, and because he now acts and has previously acted in an ungentlemanlike way. Darcy tells Elizabeth that her family has shown itself wanting in common sense and civility. Up to this point Jane Austen has developed these problems dramatically, but she has never reduced them to a set of simple, unambiguous statements. Now, however, Darcy and Elizabeth come to understand each other perfectly. His letter to her treats the problems of Jane and Wickham so minutely that Elizabeth can no longer reasonably doubt that her indictment of Darcy was a mistake. She also admits that her family has always made a poor show of itself and calls the Netherfield dance to witness: there the Bennets seemed to have agreed "to expose themselves as much as they could" (243). Along with her family's bad behavior, Darcy's "proud and repulsive" manners remain a problem for Elizabeth (236). In short, Darcy's letter solves two problems (those of Bingley's separation from Jane and of Wickham's accusation against Darcy) and leaves two unsolved (those of the Bennet family's conduct and of Darcy's manners). The visit to Pemberley brings these last two problems to a resolution too. Darcy accepts Elizabeth's family in the person of the Gardiners and acts consistently like a gentleman. When Lydia's elopement calls both into question again, Darcy acts more like the gentleman than ever. He sees to it that Wickham marries Lydia, and then he asks Elizabeth to marry him. "Brother-in-law of Wick-

ham!" exclaims Elizabeth. "Every kind of pride must revolt from
the connection" (338). But not Darcy's. Having made the Bennet
family worse than it was before, he marries into it.

The reason for Darcy's change is evident at Pemberley, where
the Gardiners see that he loves Elizabeth but are not sure that
she loves him: "Of the lady's sensations they remained a little in
doubt" (281); but "it was evident that he was very much in love
with her" (283–84). This situation duplicates Bingley's earlier on,
just as Lydia's elopement with Wickham closely resembles Georgiana's near-elopement with him. In these dramatic sequences
Jane Austen resolves by empathy the problems detailed in the
first proposal scene. She makes Elizabeth feel Darcy's antipathy
to Wickham, and she makes Darcy feel Elizabeth's objection to
his interference between Jane and Bingley. The problems that
once made Darcy and Elizabeth see each other as irrevocably
divided give way to solutions founded on intelligence and empathy that show them to be complementary partners: "it was
an union that must" be "to the advantage of both." By the time
therefore that Bingley and Darcy re-enact the beginning of the
novel by settling at Netherfield a second time, Darcy and Elizabeth have come to know themselves and love each other by
virtue of "sense" and "affection." When Lady Catherine tries
to prevent the happy ending to this inevitable union, she not
only duplicates Darcy's earlier interference between Jane and
Bingley but also demonstrates that Darcy's aunt can easily be
as troublesome as Elizabeth's mother. If Darcy has complained
about Elizabeth's mother, she is equally entitled to complain
about his aunt. That she does not and that she finally convinces
him to make peace with Lady Catherine shows how the novel
moves relentlessly from a firm sense of self to a harmonizing of
familial and social orders. In *Pride and Prejudice*, in Leo Bersani's
words, the "ordered self contributes to a pervasive cultural ide-
ology of the self which serves the established social order" (56).
This is just about the last novel in the nineteenth century that
accomplishes this convincingly by a mastery of aesthetic means.
Jane and Mr. Bennet's acceptance of the union as a good marriage after first thinking it a bad one helps carry this conviction
to the reader. Jane tells Elizabeth that she must "do any thing
rather than marry without affection" (382); Mr. Bennet fears

that Elizabeth will be "unable to respect" her "partner in life" (385). But they quickly come to approve the marriage once they see that what they thought were irreconcilable differences in character and temperament are, when viewed in the light of Elizabeth's startling revelations about Darcy's good offices in the Wickham-Lydia debacle, really complementary traits of character that augur nothing but good for the couple.

Mr. Bennet and Jane initially voice their concern for Elizabeth's well-being. They worry that the chance freely to choose her husband may ruin her life. Lady Catherine voices a concern for society, stating that Elizabeth's free choice will tear, if not totally destroy, its fabric. "You refuse to obey the claims of duty, honour, and gratitude," she scolds. "You are determined to ruin him in the opinion of all his friends, and make him the contempt of the world." But Darcy and Elizabeth know that this is nonsense: "the world in general would have too much sense to join in the scorn," Elizabeth tells the dowager (367). Darcy's proposal simply confirms Elizabeth's conclusion. But Lady Catherine, like Mrs. Bennet, never does see the *prudence* of the match. As soon as her mother hears of it, Elizabeth becomes her favorite child— for all the wrong reasons:

> "Good gracious! Lord bless me! only think! dear me! Mr. Darcy! Who would have thought it! And is it really true? Oh! my sweetest Lizzy! how rich and how great you will be! What pin-money, what jewels, what carriages you will have! Jane's is nothing to it—nothing at all. I am so pleased —so happy. Such a charming man!—so handsome! so tall!— Oh, my dear Lizzy! pray apologise for my having disliked him so much before. I hope he will overlook it. Dear, dear Lizzy. A house in town! Every thing that is charming! Three daughters married! Ten thousand a year! Oh, Lord! What will become of me. I shall go distracted." (386)

Lady Catherine's reaction is given in the same mercenary key as Mrs. Bennet's, though it is sounded by a more powerful voice.

Taken together—with Mr. Collins' droning voice added to the hue and cry—Mrs. Bennet's and Lady Catherine's voices, when set against the narrator's voice, are instances of Jane Austen's dialogic imagination at work. Using the theories of Mikhail

Bakhtin to discover some of the subtler aspects of Austen's narrative technique, Jay Clayton has demonstrated that in *Mansfield Park* Austen's "text at many places appears 'double-voiced' [in] her awareness of [1] the 'stratification' of various styles of language and manners that occur within a presumably shared code, [2] her sensitivity to the danger that lies in privileged or 'ennobled' terms, [3] the risk that such terms may become instruments of social domination through their misuse by ignorance . . . or vice . . . , and above all, [4] her use of dialogue to express conflicting attitudes and irreconcilable perspectives" (122). The same can be said of *Pride and Prejudice.*

Mrs. Bennet's values are mindlessly bourgeois; they have about them what Nina Auerbach rightly called an "aura of awfulness" (50). Her mother registers Elizabeth's *success* in pin-money, jewels, carriages, and townhouses, going from the least expensive to the most costly items, and giving an inventory worthy of a Moll Flanders who has reached respectability after a successful life of crime. Lady Catherine, for her part, speaks with the voice of the Establishment, which seeks to limit such measurable *success* to its own kind by intermarriage within an aristocracy of birth and wealth. Her vituperative voice is worthy of the conventional preacher who mindlessly parades "gratitude," "honour, decorum, prudence, nay, interest" (365) before a congregation that knows better than he the true value inherent in such virtues. Mr. Collins' moral position is as incongruous as Lady Catherine's when he parades before Elizabeth three logical reasons (147) for "the violence of [his] affection" (148). His real reason for wanting to marry is to retain Lady Catherine's good will and patronage. So Mr. Collins as a young man in possession of a good fortune who is in want of a wife, Lady Catherine as a dowager who sends him off to find a wife, and Mrs. Bennet as a mother who is willing to supply him with a wife are three different voices that literally affirm the universally acknowledged truth that begins *Pride and Prejudice.* Their literal understanding of this truth is set in contrast to Jane Austen's ironic dramatization of it. But they are too self-interested and too humorless to share in her irony. With purely mercenary motives, then, Mrs. Bennet, Lady Catherine, and Mr. Collins support Jane Austen's case for prudent marriage in *Pride and Prejudice* by joining their distinct voices in a fugue of folly favoring mercenary marriage. Indeed, Lady Catherine finds it so hard to believe that Elizabeth will become a lady who has pin-money, jewels, carriages, and a town house that she does go distracted. She simply believes that "the upstart pretensions of a young woman without family, connections, or fortune" (365) must irrevocably separate her from a man with family, connections, and fortune. "You *are* a gentleman's daughter," Lady Catherine acknowledges to Elizabeth. "But who," she asks indignantly, "was your mother? Who are your uncles and aunts?" (366).

But it is clearly too late in this novel for Lady Catherine to object to raising oneself in society. Elizabeth is simply taking a step upward, just as Sir William Lucas, Mr. Bingley, and the Gardiners have already done. Having made "a tolerable fortune and risen to the honour of knighthood by an address to the King," Sir William quit his business in town, bought a country house, and settled down to "occupy himself solely in being civil to all the world" (65). Sir William is a prototype of the nineteenth century's "middle-class businessman [who] longed to escape from drudgery in hideous surroundings into a world of beauty and leisure, a life of dignity and peace, from which sordid anxieties were shut out" (Houghton 189–90). In short, he succeeds admirably in living to the hilt the "bourgeois dream." In doing so he surpasses Charles Bingley's father, "who intended to purchase an estate, but did not live to do it" (63). But with an inheritance of "nearly an hundred thousand pounds," the son does what the father wanted to do. Charles buys an estate just thirty miles from Pemberley "in a neighbouring county to Derbyshire" (393). And Mr. Gardiner is likely to follow the same path: "A sensible, gentlemanlike man" such as he would not be expected to live out his life "within view of his own warehouses" (177). By the end of the novel he is on "intimate terms" with Darcy and is frequently at Pemberley. In objecting to Elizabeth's marriage, then, Lady Catherine is actually objecting to the changing social pattern of English society itself—a pattern set in motion by the industrial revolution and spurred on by the Napoleonic wars during which *Pride and Prejudice* was first conceived and finally completed. In approving the marriage, Jane Austen endorses this pattern and shows herself, in Donald Greene's words, a "Tory democrat"

(165). In boasting of her pedigree and wealth, Lady Catherine demonstrates that she does not know that the basis of social progress has shifted, as Henry Sumner Maine argued in *Ancient Law*, "from Status to Contract" (Tanner, *Adultery* 5): "Not many of us are so unobservant as not to perceive that in innumerable cases where old law fixed a man's position irreversibly at his birth, modern law allows him to create it for himself by convention; and indeed several of the few exceptions which remain to this rule are constantly denounced with passionate indignation" (*Adultery* 3). Lady Catherine remains one of the few who is unobservant. For her a "gentleman" is born to family, fortune, and connections. For Jane Austen a "gentleman" is someone who, as Elizabeth brings Darcy to understand, agrees to act in a gentlemanlike manner. In the changing society that Jane Austen depicts and endorses, such a man deserves power and influence.

This endorsement is one instance of Jane Austen's showing how the virtue of the individual consolidates the strength of society. *Pride and Prejudice* thus enacts in the form of fiction something akin to Plato's social vision as presented in the *Republic* and the *Laws* where the strength of a society similarly arises from the virtue of its citizens. This inextricable connection between individual and social good is articulated by Mrs. Gardiner as a myth of concern when she insists that Elizabeth distinguish between a prudent and a mercenary marriage. The other side of this concern is voiced by Jane and Mr. Bennet when they urge Elizabeth not to marry without love and respect lest she lose her freedom along with her happiness. Among the three we see freedom and concern interacting and defining individual, familial, and social good. Neither Lady Catherine nor Mrs. Bennet has an appropriate sense of the issue when she speaks to Elizabeth about marriage. As the principal characters who address this issue with Elizabeth, Mrs. Gardiner and Lady Catherine define the polarities of meaning in the novel. They demonstrate that society's myth of concern is susceptible to intelligent and unintelligent interpretation. Mr. Bennet and Jane finally stand with Mrs. Gardiner; and Mrs. Bennet, unwittingly, stands with Lady Catherine. Mrs. Bennet and Lady Catherine are the novel's blocking characters because they stand in the way of the intelligent heart and the renewal it brings to life. They represent at the novel's conclusion the position that Darcy and Elizabeth represented at its beginning: ignorance of one's own, another's, and society's best good. The action of the novel is designed therefore to move Darcy and Elizabeth to moral intelligence through individual reformation and mutual love.

When Jane Austen dramatizes the growth of individuals to a freedom of action emanating from an intelligent heart, she suggests that their society has moved from feudal-aristocratic conventions that are static and portrayed in a Lady Catherine to bourgeois conventions that are dynamic and portrayed in a Mr. Gardiner, who, equally with Darcy, can be called a "gentleman." This society is both orderly and dynamic; it is strengthened spiritually by assimilating virtuous and independent people into it. Lady Catherine does not understand this. She makes a case against Elizabeth's marriage from the viewpoint of a prospective mother-in-law who loses the fortune and alliance she had counted on. As Elizabeth carefully steps around the obstacles that Lady Catherine drops in her path, it becomes clear that all that Darcy's aunt really wants is the fulfillment of a cradle engagement in which neither Darcy nor her daughter has had any say. She attempts to make the moral imperative of society's myth of concern shape itself to her own narrow desires; in short, she argues from "custom." To counter Lady Catherine, Elizabeth argues from "nature." Dr. Johnson distinguished between the two when he remarked, in an essay on tragedy, that we must "distinguish nature from custom, or that which is established because it is right, from that which is right only because it is established" (*Rambler* 5:70). The structure of *Pride and Prejudice* makes the case that the marriage of Darcy to Elizabeth is as natural as it is prudent: it is established because it is right. It is a *true* monogamous marriage even in Frederick Engels' classic sense of such a marriage as one based not on property and inheritance but on individual choice and compatibility. Engels argued that monogamy developed because *private* property had to be passed on, and this could not happen in a situation where offspring were common and families were tribes. *True* monogamy would be possible only after the end of the institution of private property because people would then marry for love, which recognizes the equality of men and women and is, consequently, the only right reason to marry (141–43). Clearly Jane Austen's fiction comes not at the end of such a millennium but in the middle of a society with constitutionally guaranteed rights to life, liberty, and property. Nevertheless, Elizabeth's repudiation of a mercenary marriage at Darcy's first proposal puts her squarely in a position to be prudent and make a *true* marriage at the end of the novel. Furthermore, the truth and rightness of this marriage are demonstrated because it cultivates perception, strengthens sense and affection, fosters the growth of the cardinal virtues, follows historical precedent, and promotes society's well-being by founding it on individual happiness.

Jane Austen classically articulates *Pride and Prejudice* as a novel of manners by casting it in the form of a case that dramatizes the development of the cardinal virtues in two individuals of complementary character whose freedom to love each other satisfies society's concern for its coherence and continuity. This marriage further demonstrates that the one satisfactory approach to a difficult case is through intelligence and affection. In a disillusioned world like our own, one value of a novel like this lies in its reminding us that its demonstration that intelligent and affectionate people can bring difficult problems to a happy resolution was once convincing. With *Pride and Prejudice* Jane Austen turns the face of her fiction toward life by presenting the intelligent heart as the key to happiness. "I am the happiest creature in the world," Elizabeth writes to Mrs. Gardiner. "Perhaps other people have said so before, but no one with such justice." The justice of such happiness is the case that *Pride and Prejudice* finally and wittily establishes: "I am happier even than Jane," Elizabeth tells her aunt, "she only smiles, I laugh" (390).

2

Barchester Towers

Manners as Social Exclusion

The bourgeois dream makes a completely casual appearance in *Pride and Prejudice* because it is a given of life, a *donnée*. Jane Austen is quite comfortable in treating it either literally or ironically as occasion requires. Charles Bingley has arrived where Mr. Gardiner is going; Darcy lives the life they both seek to emulate. Sir William Lucas is a parody of all three, and Lady Catherine is nervous about upward mobility because she is afraid that as others come up she must go down. By drawing sketches of the Lookalofts and their fellows at the Thornes' fête champêtre, Bertie Stanhope presents from the artist's point of view what Andrew Wright has called the "unlovely struggle" toward positions of power that goes on "not far beneath the surface of decorum" in Barsetshire (44–45). The ambition implied in the unlovely struggle is one of the subjects of *Barchester Towers*.

Austen's novel betrays less anxiety about individuals rising in society than Trollope's. Trollope seems finally not quite sure of what he really wants to see happen: the spokesman for society in him says one thing; the artist in him suggests another. Trollope seems to want only a very select few in positions of wealth and power. Whereas Austen's view is inclusive—even Lady Catherine visits Pemberley before *Pride and Prejudice* ends —Trollope's is exclusive: Mr. Slope is removed from the diocese, Mr. Harding is denied the hospital and deanery, and Bertie and Madeline Stanhope are sent off to Italy. They are simply not the right kind of people. Trollope's society requires sterner stuff than they are made of.

Jane Austen was worried not about the fate of her society but only about the fate of individuals in it. Trollope, however, seems preoccupied with preserving the old order against both revolution and invasion. Archdeacon Grantly is as hard on Eleanor Bold (to say nothing of the late John Bold) as he is on Mr. Slope and Mrs. Proudie. And the archdeacon and the lady bishop are more memorable than Arabin and Eleanor, the romantic couple in the novel, because Dr. Grantly and Mrs. Proudie have a single-minded determination to preserve what they believe in: their precisely opposed notions of church, power, and prerogative. Archdeacon Grantly and Mrs. Proudie are the shakers and the movers of their respective camps, the generals of opposing armies fighting for the spoils of Barsetshire. That the church as the spiritual property of the state should be so perilously up for grabs makes Trollope nervous and conservative and full of concern. Love is therefore second in importance to power in *Barchester Towers*; indeed, when love is portrayed, it is presented as power extending itself into the affective realm.

If Jane Austen makes a case for prudent marriage as against mercenary marriage, Trollope makes a case for Arabin's ambition as against Slope's. Consequently, the cardinal virtues take a peculiar turn in the hero of this novel: prudence shows itself in Arabin's interest in clerical advancement, justice as the cause of his party, fortitude as his bravery in fighting Obidiah Slope, and temperance as his abandoning chastity as a stoical ideal and adopting instead marriage as a comfortable way of life for a gentleman. This focus on and characterization of Arabin shows

Trollope developing and protecting a more fragile (and therefore a more boldly held) myth of concern in *Barchester Towers* than we saw projected in *Pride and Prejudice*. And the relative lack of growth in character in the complementary lovers, Arabin and Eleanor, further demonstrates that the world Trollope creates in this novel is more nearly middle-aged and much less youthful than the one Austen created before him. *Barchester Towers* also shows more discrete social units than *Pride and Prejudice*, where social integration is greater. These distinctions do not of course mean that Trollope's is less a novel than Austen's. They mean that from one writer to the other the genre of manners has undergone a subtle shift in emphasis—reflecting, undoubtedly, the rapid upward mobility of the Crystal Palace decade during which British society was ever more deeply plunged into commerce and industry.[1] In Trollope's novel the myth of concern more nervously holds the foreground than in Austen's.

Trollope's use of proverbs, maxims, songs, and poetry reveals an uncertainty in his society, which must seek its justification in the accepted mores of days gone by. Mr. Harding hesitates to take the wardenship on Slope's terms because "It's bad teaching an old dog tricks" (107). Bishop Proudie casts his lot with Mr. Slope against Mrs. Proudie, convinced that *"Ce n'est que le premier pas qui coûte"* (293); nevertheless, he is fairly warned not to: "Better the d[evil] you know than the d[evil] you don't know" (231). Mr. Slope is content to make progress with Eleanor slowly because he knows that "Rome was not built in a day" (138). But having drunk deeply at the fête champêtre, Mr. Slope resolves to go ahead with a proposal of marriage, saying to himself, "That which has made them drunk, has made me bold" (380). This literature of one-line worldly wisdom shapes the matrix of Slope's most humiliating defeat. And appropriately so, for, as Northrop Frye says, "the proverb is typically the expression of popular wisdom: it is generally addressed to those who are without exceptional advantages of birth or wealth, and it is much preoccupied with prudence and caution, with avoiding extremes, with knowing one's place, with being respectful to superiors and courteous to inferiors" (*Critical Path* 41). Obadiah Slope needs such good advice because he is without the advantages of birth or wealth;

nevertheless, he seeks to rise rapidly in Barchester society. Un-
fortunately, he has no respect for authority, and he treats those
below him ignobly. Therefore, throwing caution to the wind, he
takes no heed of popular wisdom, acts imprudently, and finds
himself severely judged. He is sentenced to death and turned
over to Madeline Neroni for execution: "He was the finest fly
that Barchester had hitherto afforded to her web" (242). Indeed,
she "sat there . . . looking at him with her great eyes, just as
a great spider would look at a great fly that was quite securely
caught" (249). Mr. Slope fails "to be off with the auld luve" before
he is "on wi' the new" (241), mingles "love and business," falls
"between two stools" (244), and finds himself fatally entangled
in the spider's web. Slope meets this awful fate because he has
ignored the accumulated wisdom of the ages, which expresses
society's myth of concern. This is one reason why his ambition makes him such a threat to Barchester society and moves
Trollope to pull out all the stops to dramatize society's myth of
concern as it relates to Eleanor and the deanery. Should Slope
succeed in his ecclesiatical designs, the church would suffer from
his lust for power; should he succeed as a suitor, marriage would
be reduced to an economic adventure. Slope is consequently a
threat to the family, society's smallest unit, and to the church,
society's greatest bulwark of right conduct. Eleanor's situation
is a personal reflection of the church's public position; one is an
image of the other. Both are misunderstood by clergymen who
are called "men of the world"; both are worth £1,200 in yearly
income; both are pursued by Arabin and Slope; both are adhered
to unswervingly by Mr. Harding; and both, finally, get the same
dean. The case that Trollope is making in the novel is that Slope,
whom he describes as a devil—and as befits a devil, a liar—is
undeserving of the good things that should belong to gentlemen
only: a powerful position, a handsome income, a beautiful wife,
and a comfortable house.

Barchester Towers sets out four prizes representing money, position, and power for two ambitious men to seek: the bishopric
of Barchester, the wardenship of Hiram's Hospital, the cathedral
deanery, and the hand of Eleanor Bold. Slope contends for all

four prizes; Arabin for two. Slope's pursuit of them without regard to prudence, justice, or temperance is set out in volume 1
(chaps. 1–19) of *Barchester Towers*. Arabin's more virtuous pursuit of them is presented in volume 2.[2] And the results of their
ambitious efforts are made known in volume 3.

Volume 1 sets Slope in action. He vies with Mrs. Proudie for
the bishopric while trying to retain the goodwill of the bishop;
he uses the vacant wardenship callously to maneuver Mr. Harding and Mr. Quiverful; and he plays suitor to Eleanor Bold at
the same time that he is Madeline Stanhope's professed lover.
The weakness of Slope's position is exquisitely revealed in chapter 19 when he visits the Stanhopes and is uneasy that everyone expects Mr. Harding to be named warden and embarrassed
that Madeline greets him as an intimate while Eleanor looks on.
Slope's dilemma is that he wants too much and cannot decide
who is likely to give him even a little. His is an intemperance that
tramples on justice to satisfy ambition. Trollope therefore makes
Slope's case for a lot more money and a much better position
hopeless.

Volume 2 sets Arabin in action and develops his success in
opposition to Slope's maneuvering. "A Morning Visit" (chap. 5),
for example, shows Slope abusing the archdeacon by express-
ing his discontent with the physical amenities of the palace; "St.
Ewold's Parsonage" (vol. 2, chap. 2) shows Arabin restraining
the archdeacon from repairing the parsonage, which suits him
well enough as it is. "War" (chap. 6) finds Mr. Slope preaching
his "doctrine, and not St. Paul's" for thirty minutes in the cathedral and leaving "all Barchester . . . in a tumult" (48); "Mr Arabin
Reads Himself in at St Ewold's" (vol. 2, chap. 4) finds Arabin
preaching "the great Christian doctrine of works and faith combined" for twenty minutes and sending his congregation home
"to their baked mutton and pudding well pleased with their new
minister" (206). This set of contrasting events presents Arabin as
a preeminently prudent man and Slope as his opposite.

Volume 3 disposes of the ambitions of Arabin and Slope.
Trollope judges their cases and metes out justice according to his
lights. In Act 2 of Ullathorne Sports Mr. Slope loses Eleanor and
allows Arabin to win her hand. Slope's grab at Eleanor's waist

earns him an immediate slap in the face that ends his untimely pursuit forever. Slope also fails to dispose of the wardenship as he would like to. Quiverful gets the nod from Mrs. Proudie, who has appropriated the bishopric, another goal that Slope has fruitlessly pursued. Finally Mr. Harding and then Mr. Arabin are offered the deanery, and the bishop's chaplain is offered nothing. Arabin, the prudent man of moderate ambition, gets the better of Slope, the intemperate man of unbridled ambition. And Madeline, who helps Arabin with Eleanor, exposes Slope to the laughter of his political and clerical rivals, Thorne and Arabin, by revealing his double-dealing in preferment and love. Slope is made to swallow the bolus of poetic justice whole as he is expelled from the bishop's palace, slapped in the face, and laughed to scorn.

Arabin is nonetheless linked to Slope by way of a proverb: "Truly he had fallen between two stools" (178). But Arabin fell because he underwent a series of changes connected with a growing understanding of himself and his place in life, not because he was intemperate or imprudent. He is shown as a man who was once a Tractarian, once a lonely bachelor, and once a poorly paid professor of poetry. He is now no longer content with these things because "the daydream of his youth was over" (176). That daydream was founded on a stoicism that Trollope exposes as a pernicious doctrine which "can find no believing pupils and no true teachers" (177). Indeed, the idea of renouncing "wealth and worldly comfort and happiness on earth" is pronounced "an outrage on human nature" (177). When Arabin belatedly comes fully to understand his own human nature, he regrets not having the good things in life: "no wife, no bairns, no soft sward of lawn duly mown for him to lie on, no herd of attendant curates, no bowings from banker's clerks, no rich rectory" (178). Arabin's ambition, in short, complements his maturity.

By way of these radical changes that Arabin undergoes before he enters into the action of the novel with his arrival in Barchester, Trollope maintains that to interfere with the comforts of an English gentleman—established religion, family, money, and position—is unnatural. Arabin at age forty is a convert to the doctrine that Trollope as narrator preaches at age forty-two.[3] And, one should carefully note, Slope is a true believer too.

Slope wants only a little more than Arabin as far as the good life is concerned. Although Arabin never wants to be bishop, both he and Slope want to be Eleanor's husband and Barchester's dean. But Slope is an English gentleman neither by birth nor by conduct; he is a scion of Sterne's Slop family—he adds the *e* to his name for gentility's sake—who tries to subvert High Church practice, who makes love to a married woman, and who lies repeatedly in seeking a wife and deanery. Slope's ends tally with natural ambition, but Slope's means make him an overreacher. Trollope makes him a red man—hair of "pale reddish hue," face "a little redder," and nose like "red-coloured cork" (25)—a liar and "the d[evil] you don't know" (231). The low-bred, mean-minded, callously manipulative Slope is a comic form of devil. Arabin, on the other hand, has so forthright a character that he is seen as "a little child" (371). Therefore, whereas Slope is struggled against, Arabin is helped. Dr. Grantly gives him St. Ewold's, Madeline delivers Eleanor into his hands, Mr. Harding renounces the deanery in his favor, and a Whig government improbably appoints him to clerical office. Arabin represents for every faction in the novel the best of what one reviewer of *Barchester Towers* called, in a happy phrase, "the second-class of good people": Trollope "has the merit of avoiding the excess of exaggeration. He possesses an especial talent for drawing what may be called the second-class of good people—characters not noble, superior or perfect, after the standard of human perfection, but still good and honest, yet with a considerable proneness to temptation, and a strong consciousness that they live and like to live, in a struggling, party-giving, comfort-seeking world" (*Saturday Review* [30 May 1857] quoted in Smalley 510). With Arabin the second class of good people finds its hero and *Barchester Towers* touches ground and stands four-square. Francis Arabin's reasonable ambitions are completely satisfied within the limits of the cardinal virtues, and the novel's conventional wisdom is thereby thoroughly justified.

Arabin's success is a perfect realization of the political and social myth that Trollope promulgated in his *Autobiography*—a myth of concern that appeals to God, authority, doctrine, and belief to preserve the coherence and continuity of Victorian society as Trollope sees it:

Make all men equal to-day, and God has so created them
that they shall be all unequal to-morrow. The so-called Conservative, . . . being surely convinced that such inequalities
are of divine origin, tells himself that it is his duty to preserve
them. . . .

The divine inequality is apparent to him, but not the
equally divine diminution of that inequality. That such diminution is taking place on all sides is apparent enough;—but
is apparent to him as an evil, the consummation of which it
is his duty to retard. He cannot prevent it; and therefore the
society to which he belongs is, in his eyes, retrograding. He
will even, at times, assist it; and will do so conscientiously,
feeling that, under the gentle pressure supplied by him, and
with the drags and holdfasts which he may add, the movement will be slower than it would become if subjected to his
proclaimed and absolute opponents. . . .

. . . The equally conscientious Liberal is opposed to the
Conservative. He is equally aware that these distances are
of divine origin, . . . but he is alive to the fact that these
distances are day by day becoming less. . . . What is really
in his mind is,—I will not say equality, for the word is offen-
sive, and presents to the imaginations of men ideas of communism, of ruin, and insane democracy,—but a tendency
towards equality. In following that, however, he knows that
he must be hemmed in by safeguards, lest he be tempted to
travel too quickly; and therefore he is glad to be accompanied on his way by the repressive action of a Conservative
opponent. Holding such views, I think I am guilty of no absurdity in calling myself an advanced conservative liberal.
A man who entertains in his mind any doctrine, except as
a means of improving the condition of his fellows, I regard
as a political intriguer, a charlatan, and a conjurer,—as one
who thinks that, by a certain amount of wary wire-pulling,
he may raise himself in the estimation of the world. (252–53)

In *Barchester Towers* the conservatives are represented by Archdeacon Grantly and the liberals by Bishop and Mrs. Proudie.
Mr. and Miss Thorne stand somewhat to the right of the archdeacon, and Mr. Slope somewhat to the left of the bishop. Slope

is the hated wire-puller seeking a place of undue importance in Barchester society. Arabin is the man in the middle, the advanced conservative liberal, and Eleanor Bold, as her name indicates, occupies a position a little more advanced and a little more liberal in the middle ground. The final matrimonial and ecclesiastical triumph of Dean and Mrs. Arabin is as complete a triumph of Trollope's public position and society's myth of concern as is possible. From his spiritual office in a state-affiliated church Arabin has the best opportunity to hold society on a course of gradualism and prudent change. The case that Trollope makes for the successful issue of Arabin's ambition is therefore airtight.

The difference between *Pride and Prejudice* and *Barchester Towers* is that Austen's charcters are more imaginative, intelligent, and dynamic, and their society more fitted to infuse these qualities into its changing structure; Arabin is no Darcy and Eleanor no Elizabeth. Arabin and Eleanor, for instance, undertake no personal revaluations of their conduct as a result of their encounters; their love does not reveal each to the other. The movement toward personal realization attendant on Darcy's proposal to Elizabeth in *Pride and Prejudice* is absent from *Barchester Towers*. The movement toward social realization that comprises the last half of Austen's novel is the whole of Trollope's novel. Eleanor and Arabin's marriage is everything. The social fabric has worn thinner in Trollope, so that traumas caused by critical thinking, such as Arabin's flirtation with Roman Catholicism and his later renunciation of stoicism, are antecedent to the action of the novel. Trollope's comedy is also more physical than intellectual, more farcical than ironic. His society finds it harder to deal with troublemakers too: a persistently egregious character like Lady Catherine de Bourgh is drawn back to Pemberley at the end of *Pride and Prejudice*, but the awful Mrs. Proudie is never integrated into the mainstream of society in *Barchester Towers*. Trollope's social manner is more anxious and exclusive than Austen's because his "vision [is] more troubled and more complex" (Kincaid, *"Barchester"* 596). Although both write comedies of manners, the ground rules for living have changed in the forty-odd years separating their novels. For Austen the cardinal virtues allow for growth of character and change in society; for Trollope they set limits and draw boundaries that are not to be crossed. When Madeline Neroni and Bertie Stanhope and Septimus Harding are finally accorded secondary importance in Barchester—especially when the sister and the brother, who pose a threat to Arabin and Eleanor, are sent out of the city —*Barchester Towers* invokes the shade of Plato's *Republic*.

Plato insisted that society's guardians be protected from imaginative people, especially if they make them laugh (338E).[4] Madeline and Bertie do even worse: they make inferiors laugh at their superiors. And the greatest imaginative aberration in the republic is the artist who imitates and thereby leads the guardians astray: "imitation is a wretched thing begetting wretched things on a wretched stock" (602C; Gilbert 50). Imitation destroys the ability of a man to be "a good administrator of important affairs" (394D; Gilbert 38). Artists must therefore be sent out of the city: "If we do admit the muse who is so sweet with her lyrics and epics, pleasure and pain will rule in our city instead of law and what is generally accepted as right reason" (606E; Gilbert 54). Madeline as an actress who plays a part and Bertie as a sculptor who cuts forms from marble must go back to Italy where no one expects much right reason. In England Rabelais is kept locked in a drawer; in Italy people do what Rabelais shows people doing.

But here we meet with a paradox: logically, Plato and Trollope should be put outside the gates of the city too. Plato has Socrates discuss imitation in a dialogue, a purely imitative form. So much so that Schlegel held that "novels are the Socratic dialogues of our day"; Bakhtin, following suit, called the Socratic dialogues the "novels of Antiquity" (Todorov 87). In them Plato has a lot of very stupid people, whom no one would ever want to imitate, feed straight lines to Socrates. Yet Plato, the founder of the Academy, allows himself to imitate those very impercipient people by making them characters in a dialogue. His reason for doing this is made clear by Bakhtin, who argued that Plato "understood thought as a conversation that a man carries on with himself" (*Dialogic* 134). In a Hellenic society in which there were "no mute or invisible spheres of existence" (134), thought was externalized in characters talking. Just as thought varies from dull to acute, so do characters in the Platonic dialogues. Shades of character vary with shades of thought; therefore, Plato's depiction of a variety of characters in dialogue is deliberate and

. . . You try to despise these good things, but you only try;
you don't succeed." . . .

"Come, Mr. Arabin, confess; do you succeed? Is money
so contemptible? Is worldly power so worthless? Is feminine
beauty a trifle to be so slightly regarded by a wise man?"
(366)

Madeline draws out of Arabin that rejection of stoicism that Trollope earlier endorsed. She is an intensification of the narrative
voice that refuses to live with lies. She ranges from low to high,
from Mr. Slope to Mr. Thorne, revealing what should be revealed
about each. But since her weapon is sex, the Victorians objected
to her and called her "desperately wicked."[6] Trollope even crip-
pled her to keep her from circulating too much; nevertheless,
he refused to give her up when Longman's reader called her "a
great blot on the work" (Sadleir 170). After all, she was a part
of himself; she was his truth within the action of the novel; she
was Arabin's "inner spirit" (366); she even delivered Arabin into
Eleanor's hands. In Madeline's case, actions speak louder than
words. And this is a principle to be kept in mind when judging
Bertie Stanhope and Septimus Harding, who are the heroes of
Trollope's imagination in *Barchester Towers* just as Madeline is his
heroine.

Some pretty harsh things are said about Bertie in the course
of the novel, the harshest being that "he had no principle, no
regard for others, no self-respect, no desire to be other than a
drone in the hive, if only he could, as a drone, get what honey
was sufficient for him" (72). Yet he refuses to propose marriage
to Eleanor in any way that could tempt her to accept him. The
idea of a prudent marriage and domestic tranquility that attracts
Arabin and Slope gives Stanhope's stomach a turn: "the most
desirable lady becomes nauseous when she has to be taken as
a pill" (401). Far from being a man without self-respect, principle, and a concern for others, Bertie is a free spirit, a bohemian
oddity,[7] who does not share the financial or marital goals of ambitious men. What has Bertie to look forward to as Eleanor's husband? "Having satisfied his creditors with half of the widow's
fortune, he would be allowed to sit down quietly at Barchester,
keeping economical house with the remainder. His duty would
be to rock the cradle of the late Mr Bold's child, and his highest

excitement a demure party at Plumstead Rectory" (401). Bertie cannot bear the idea of living by the code of "the second-class of good people." Is he, therefore, to be condemned? If the narrator says *yes* in his harsh words, the novel says *no* in its most brilliant episodes. The artistic truth about Bertie is that he has the very best scenes in the novel—those that call in question the sacred cows of Barchester's bourgeois existence: church, university, family, and work.

At Mrs. Proudie's reception he deflates the obsessive preoccupation of High and Low Church clergymen with their intense partisan versions of ritual and doctrine by announcing himself as having been, first, an Anglican who aspired to a bishopric; next, a Roman Catholic who was an acolyte of the Jesuits; then, a Jew who admired Disraeli's Sidonia; and now, obviously, a genially persistent gadfly to Barchester clergymen. Bertie also deflates the timely preoccupation of these contentious churchmen with the English university system—timely because a royal commission had investigated the state of academic dilapidation at Oxford in the early 1850s[8]—by suggesting in no uncertain terms that German universities are far superior. And in a justly famous unveiling scene, Bertie defrocks the pretentious, usurping lady bishop: "As Juno may have looked at Paris on Mount Ida, so did Mrs. Proudie look on Ethelbert Stanhope when he pushed the leg of the sofa into her lace train" (85). Bertie deflates everything overblown in Barchester's clerical politics and serves the office of novelist-surrogate even more delightfully than his alluring sister. Bertie is Trollope speaking with the voice of a bohemian and wearing Victorian drag, "dressed in light blue from head to foot. He had on the loosest possible blue coat, cut square like a shooting coat, and very short. It was lined with silk of azure blue. He had on a blue satin waistcoat, a blue neckhandkerchief which was fastened beneath his throat with a coral ring, and very loose blue trousers which almost concealed his feet" (82). From tip to toe Bertie incarnates and celebrates a myth of freedom.

Bertie's other great scene is a domestic triumph. He is equally adept at destroying pretension at home as he is abroad. Dr. Stanhope turns his illogical, sanctimonious parental wrath against Bertie after he learns that Eleanor is not going to marry his son.

As Bertie draws caricatures from his recollection of the Thornes' fête champêtre, his father rages against him while his sister tries to mediate between the wrath of the one and the calm of the other:

> "Give over drawing," said Charlotte, going up to him and taking the paper from under his hand. The caricatures, however, she preserved, and showed them afterwards to the friends of the Thornes, the Proudies, and De Courcys. Bertie, deprived of his occupation, threw himself back in his chair and waited further orders.
>
> "I think it will certainly be for the best that Bertie should leave this at once; perhaps tomorrow," said Charlotte; "but pray, Papa, let us arrange some scheme together."
>
> "If he will leave this to-morrow, I will give him £10, and he shall be paid £5 a month by the banker at Carrara as long as he stays permanently in that place."
>
> "Well, sir! it won't be long," said Bertie, "for I shall be starved to death in about three months."
>
> "He must have marble to work with," said Charlotte.
>
> "I have plenty there in the studio to last me three months," said Bertie. "It will be no use attempting anything large in so limited a time; unless I do my own tombstone." (436–37)

Bertie manages this confrontation by the simple device of taking his father's pretensions to a concern for him to their logical conclusion, and he finds the task so easy that he can simultaneously leave a record of the social climbing he witnessed at Ullathorne. Bertie's victory is in its own way an updating of Elizabeth Bennet's logical destruction of Lady Catherine de Bourgh's ridiculous argument against her marrying Darcy. Bertie allows his father to push him to the brink, and then he steps aside as the last shove leaves Dr. Stanhope spread-eagled in the empty air. There is more farce than wit here, but it is as subtle—with the drawings and the third-party meditating—as farce gets to be. Consequently Bertie shares the honors of comic success with the heroine of *Pride and Prejudice*, a book that Trollope once thought "the best novel in the English language."[9]

"Mr Harding was by no means a perfect character," says the

narrator. "In his indecision, his weakness, his proneness to be
led by others, his want of self-confidence, he was very far from
being perfect" (151). He is dismissed as not in the least suited
to the warfare that gives the conflict its metaphorical texture in
the novel. Mr. Harding subscribes to peace and not to Arabin's
doctrine that "peace on earth and good-will among men, are,
like heaven, promises for the future" (186). He believes in "that
beautiful love which can be true to a false friend" (257). He is
by temperament and principle unsuited to Barchester's peculiarly fractious interpretation of the Church Militant; he is "a man
devoid of all the combative qualifications" (255) of a soldier in
Archdeacon Grantly's army. He would rather direct the cathedral choir and play the violoncello than fight tooth and nail. He
seems to be neither prudent nor courageous. Yet in spite of all
these things Mr. Harding is given the last word in the novel:
"The Author now leaves him in the hands of his readers: not as a
hero, not as a man to be admired and talked of, not as a man who
should be toasted at public dinners and spoken of with conventional absurdity as a perfect divine, but as a good man, without
guile, believing humbly in the religion which he has striven to
teach, and guided by the precepts he has striven to learn" (499).
What this sentence says, in effect, is that Mr. Harding cannot be
judged by the conventions of Barchester society. It affirms the
very things that make him seem weak: "Ah, thou weak man;
most charitable, most Christian, but weakest of men!" (256). No
word of condemnation could be sweeter to a clergyman's ear.

Mr. Arabin is the novel's successful priest and Mr. Harding its failure, we are told. But it is well to remember that what
Arabin gets, Harding gives—his daughter and his deanery. Also,
what Arabin represents is actually less satisfactory to Trollope's
mind than what Harding represents. In his *Clergymen and the
Church of England* Trollope praises the parson of a parish above
the dean of a chapter. "A dean," he writes, "has little to do and a
good deal to get" (42). Indeed, if one adopts a hard line toward
Arabin, one could say that he is made dean because he is not
suited to be a parson. Trollope objects to a man who "is ordained
in order that he may hold his fellowship," accepting in middle
age the functions of a parish parson (*Clergymen* 84): "Can anyone, we say, believe that such a one at the age of forty can be

fit to go into a parish and undertake the cure of the parochial souls?" (*Clergymen* 86). Yet Arabin at age forty does precisely that. But the former professor of poetry is rapidly promoted to the deanery to which he is more nearly suited: "It is required that a clergyman shall have shown a taste for literature in some one of its branches before he can be regarded among the candidates proper for a deanery" (*Clergymen* 36). Mr. Harding, however, does not get to be warden and refuses to be dean. He remains vicar of St. Cuthbert's: he remains the parson of a parish. His essential charity, which makes him fail as a combatant, allows him to succeed as a parson; and by the word *parson* "the parish clergyman is designated as the palpable and visible personage of the church of his parish, making that by his presence an intelligible reality which, without him, would be an invisible idea" (*Clergymen* 54). Mr. Harding finds at St. Cuthbert's the truth of his calling: "The parson in his parish must know that he has got himself into a place for which he has been expressly fitted by the orders he has taken" (*Clergymen* 57).

Mr. Harding's quietly but tenaciously held sense of his vocation suggests the shortcomings of Barchester society. Whereas it is good to be Arabin and get Eleanor and the deanery, it is better to be Bertie Stanhope and Mr. Harding and refuse Eleanor and the deanery. They are essentially unambitious men who stand outside the main action of the novel. Their imagination indicts ambition and shows us precisely why Trollope is nervous about a society whose makeup and manners he feels called upon publicly to defend. That society cannot stand up to a penetrating imaginative critique. By the time Trollope wrote *Barchester Towers* both Dickens and Emily Brontë had proven this statement true. They, like Trollope with the Stanhope siblings and Mr. Harding, dismantled the pretensions of society's typical "second-class of good people." Francis Arabin is such a typical "second-class" citizen and thereby satisfies a conventional demand; Bertie and Mr. Harding are unconventional and satisfy an imaginative demand. Arabin's path leads to domestic contentment; theirs do not. But Bertie scales the height of Trollope's comic genius and Mr. Harding sounds the depth of his moral sensibility. Insofar as Trollope's England is an updated version of Plato's republic in its concern for its future guardians—"girls" and "lads"

need to be taught "truth," "honor," and "simplicity" (*Thackeray*
202–3) [10] and so become like Arabin and Eleanor—flashy Bertie
Stanhope and immodest Madeline Vesey Neroni must be sent
back to Italy and weak Septimus Harding must return to his
modest lodging in Barchester High Street. But insofar as these
three have the best scenes in *Barchester Towers*—a novel must
after all teach by *amusing* (*Thackeray* 207) [11]—Trollope clearly casts
his lot with them. His political conservatism cannot subdue his
artistic inspiration. [12] What he consciously condemns by word he
unconsciously affirms by deed. In giving the best scenes of his
novel to a sculptor, an actress, and a musician, the novelist casts
his lot with his fellow artists. And by doing so he not only calls
into question the adequacy of the values they refuse to acknowledge but also looks toward the kind of novel in which outcasts
are more significant than the society that casts them out.

In Trollope the cardinal virtues that characterize the novel of
manners are tarnished by what R. H. Hutton called in 1882 "the
aggressiveness of the outer world": "Everybody in Mr Trollope
is more or less under pressure, swayed hither and thither by
opposite attractions, assailed on this side and on that by the strat-
egy of rivals; everywhere someone's room is more wanted than
his company; everywhere time is short" (Smalley 510). Keenly
aware of this, Noel Annan remarked that "prudence is undoubtedly a cardinal virtue; but one can't help thinking that a world
governed by her and her sisters, temperance, fortitude, and justice, would be dispiriting" (11). Quite so. The comic world of
Barchester Towers is a dispirited world—a world dispirited by a
myth of concern centered on middle-class comfort and privilege
and troubled not only by the aggressivity of Mr. Slope but also
by the conscience of Mr. Harding, a man whose place, above
all, not whose company, is wanted. And Mr. Arabin, who takes
his father-in-law's place in the deanery, is not quite colorful
enough—certainly even less colorful than his complementary
lover, Eleanor Bold—to get it on his own merits. Though Trollope makes out a convincing enough case for Arabin's succeeding
where Slope has failed, he prepares us by his penetrating survey
of social manners for the more aberrant world of new Gothic
fiction where society's shortcomings are seen as decidedly in-

imical to individual freedom. So decidedly inimical, in fact, that Emily Brontë must be as much a mistress of abnormal psychology as Trollope is a master of normal psychology. For the greater the deprivation of individual freedom that is encoded in a myth of social concern, the greater will be the deviation of individuality from normality. We enter the darker world of new Gothic fiction then with Heathcliff, whose critique of a code of manners is as explicit as Mr. Harding's was implicit. "This darker world . . . make[s] the niceties of moral conduct and warm generosity grossly irrelevant" (Kincaid, "*Barchester*" 612). *Wuthering Heights*, which preceded *Barchester Towers* by ten years, repudiated everything that we have just seen Barchester value: the cardinal virtues, reasonably argued cases, a myth of concern, and complementary love. Consequently, Heathcliff's is a world of death and hell, of riddles, individual freedom, and affined love. It is the world of the new Gothic novel.

Part Two

The New Gothic

3

Wuthering Heights
The Gothic Tradition
Domesticated

Walter Scott was the most significant influence on the revival of chivalry in the nineteenth century. Marc Girouard argues that Scott turned the medieval knight-errant into the modern gentleman. He created "a type of character" that was "to be imitated in innumerable later novels" as well as in "real life" (37). Scott gave the medieval world its first hard shove into modern life. He stands behind its domestication in such episodes as the Ullathorne Sports that Trollope presents in *Barchester Towers*: Harry Greenacre boldly attacks the quintain while Miss Thorne plays "queen of beauty" (*BT* 345), and Lady de Courcy mistakenly enters the social lists in a staring contest with "the mother of the last of the Neros" (*BT* 351). Trollope has the Thornes imitate in fiction an actual contemporary rage for medievalism that Scott inspired. Lord Eglinton's famous tournament of August 1839 was the real-life standard (at least in conception; rain ruined the reality) against which the Victorians measured themselves (Girouard 85–110). But the holding of tournaments was not of the highest priority; first came the renovation of country houses in the Gothic style, and second the further domestication of medievalism in the "muscular Christian," that peculiarly Victorian version of the knight-errant. In an age when faith came to be doubted and English social history found class pitted against class (as the Chartist Movement and the Hungry Forties made painfully evident), the muscular man split off from the Christian. For Tom Hughes this non-Christian strongman became the "muscleman" who had "no belief whatsoever as to the purpose for which his body was given him, except some hazy idea that it [was] to go up and down the world with him, belabouring men and captivating women for his benefit or pleasure" (Girouard 142). With the impetus of social exclusion as practiced by the elder Lintons and Edgar and by Hindley Earnshaw—and even for a time by Cathy Earnshaw—Heathcliff becomes the most famous "muscleman" in English fiction: he belabors men and captivates women for his financial benefit and his pleasure in revenge.

With Heathcliff, Emily Brontë advances Scott's domestication of the medieval world by taking horrors out of castles and cloisters and putting them into country houses. "It was the essence of Gothic characters to be exotic," writes Winifred Gérin; "Emily Brontë brought them home" (224). She brings the horrors of Gothic fiction home to one country house kitchen and to another country house drawing room and directly into the bedrooms of both houses where Cathy Earnshaw slept as one gentleman's daughter and where she sleeps as another gentleman's wife. Like Scott in *The Black Dwarf*, as Florence Swinton Dry has shown (34–48), Emily Brontë dramatizes the force of love in its destructiveness.[1] She gives us a "muscleman" with motivation: she gives us horrors that make sense to us. Brontë "shows Heathcliff not only as hateful, cruel, and destructive; she shows us also how he became so" (David Wilson 111). Heathcliff is a homely presence because—like the workingmen of the West Riding in the Chartist days during which Emily Brontë matured as a writer—"after enduring suffering and degradation at the hands of his 'betters' . . . [he] turned to defiance and destruction" (110). When, then, violence and fraud—the *forza* and *froda* of Dante's Inferno—directly oppose the cardinal virtues of fortitude and prudence in *Wuthering Heights*, we know why.

Violence and fraud were given heroic stature by Achilles, the wrathful hero of the *Iliad*, and by Ulysses, the cunning hero of the *Odyssey* (Frye, *Secular* 65–66). They are practiced villainously to a heroic degree by Heathcliff in *Wuthering Heights*. He thinks nothing of poking Nelly Dean, beating Catherine Linton, throwing a knife at his wife, Isabella, terrorizing his son, Linton, battering Hindley Earnshaw, and brutalizing Hareton Earnshaw;[2] he seduces Isabella Linton, subborns Lawyer Green, bribes the church sexton, and defrauds Catherine Linton and Hareton Earnshaw of their property and money. Heathcliff gives epic vice a romantic turn in a bourgeois setting. He domesticates Gothic villainy at the hearths of Wuthering Heights and Thrushcross Grange, the houses he would destroy. Heathcliff becomes violent and treacherous to revenge himself on the Earnshaws and Lintons. He relieves himself of pain by inflicting pain on those who conspired to spoil Cathy's love for him. He makes himself diabolical and sadistic and he makes everyone else as miserable as hell itself.[3] Suffering and darkness and death, consequently, are the ordinary condition of *Wuthering Heights*. Only by becoming orphans like Heathcliff and by suffering a personal degradation akin to his own can Catherine and Hareton walk out of the shadow of this valley of death. They have to live Heathcliff's death to find their own life.

Casting *Wuthering Heights* in the form of a romance, Emily Brontë filled it with two generations of light and dark heroes, with orphans and sadomasochists, with prophecy and insanity, with sex, cruelty, kidnapping, and death. Events exist in an apocalyptic framework where death, judgment, heaven, and hell are familiar words. Indeed, *Wuthering Heights* celebrates the "last things," beginning with death: "Time wore on at the Grange in its former pleasant way, till Miss Cathy reached sixteen. On the anniversary of her birth we never manifested any signs of rejoicing, because it was, also, the anniversary of my late mistress's death. Her father invariably spent that day alone in the library;

and walked, at dusk, as far as Gimmerton kirkyard, where he would frequently prolong his stay beyond midnight" (246). It may be an overstatement to say that Edgar Linton has a "romantic tendency to necrophilia" (Goodridge 168); nevertheless, he cannot forget that his wife died the day his daughter was born, and he chooses to commemorate the death, not celebrate the birth. Heathcliff, in a rare moment of patience, explains Edgar's disposition to Edgar's unhappy child: "Catherine, his happiest days were over when your days began. He cursed you, I dare say, for coming into the world (I did, at least). And it would just do if he cursed you as *he* went out of it. I'd join him. I don't love you! How should I? Weep away" (306). When Edgar dies with his daughter at his bedside, he thinks of her joining him, not surviving him: "I am going to her, and you, darling child, shall come to us" (315). Here, then, is a man who seeks fulfillment in death, not in life.

When the much-put-upon Catherine Linton Heathcliff finally wins the love of Hareton Earnshaw, a last judgment takes place. The biblical-minded Joseph calls on heaven to adjudge this marriage wicked and unnatural: " 'It's a blazing shaime, ut Aw cannut oppen t' Blessed Book, bud yah set up them glories tuh sattan, un' all t' flaysome wickednesses ut iver wer born intuh t'warld! Oh! yah're a raight nowt; un' shoo's another; un' that poor lad 'ull be lost atween ye. Poor lad!' he added, with a groan; 'he's witched, Aw'm sartin on 't! *O, Lord, judge 'em, fur they's norther law nur justice amang wer rullers!* " (339; italics added). Here a happy course of events that promises marriage for two relatively sane, normal young people is set down to witchery.

Catherine is called a witch by Heathcliff too. He condemns her as a "damnable witch!" and an "accursed witch!" (350) to emphasize the infernal misery she causes him. Heathcliff blames the daughter of Edgar for taking her mother's life when she was born. That is part of her witchery for him. Furthermore, Catherine looks enough like her mother to call her to mind: "Their eyes are precisely similar," and she has "a breadth of forehead . . . and a certain arch of the nostril that makes her appear haughty, whether she will, or not" (352). In the daughter he hates, Heathcliff sees the mother he loves. "He was tired of seeing Catherine," says Nelly Dean (340–41); therefore, he tells her not to "come into my sight again!" (350). Heathcliff is bewitched by Catherine Linton because to be reminded of Cathy Earnshaw is hell for him: "Two words," he tells Nelly, "would comprehend my future—*death* and *hell*—existence, after losing her, would be hell" (186). "Oh God! it is unutterable!" "I *cannot* live without my soul!" (204). Heathcliff's life without Cathy is explicitly depicted as death and hell—a hell that is made worse by the bewitching daughter of the beloved mother who exacerbates Heathcliff's torments until all that is left for him is to die another death. Not only do we have a novel littered with eleven corpses over two generations, but we also have a novel in which heaven and hell are states of consciousness; and devils and witches, like Heathcliff and Catherine Linton, are everyday antagonists. Because this is so, the metonymic and realistic elements of Brontë's novel constantly provide a grounding for its metaphoric and poetic elements, which readers have always tended to emphasize.

The poetic quality of Brontë's novel is embedded in the effect its language has on the reader. Imagery domesticates Gothic monstrosity to express the extremity of anguish; death and damnation become table talk. The unusually horrible becomes the horribly normal. In *Pride and Prejudice* no one dies and the only intrusion of the supernatural into the affairs of men is Darcy's closing his letter to Elizabeth with the words "God bless you." Reasonable people are left to solve their problems themselves. In *Wuthering Heights* the only supposedly reasonable people are Lockwood and Nelly Dean, two middle-aged celibates immersed in self-satisfaction, voyeurism, and vicarious emotional living.[4] They "never fully separate themselves from the hero and heroine they are meditating upon," says Walter L. Reed (110). Lockwood and Nelly are too deeply involved in their own emotional difficulties to be anything but nominally rational. Nelly is "sister" to Hindley before Cathy is born and "mother" to Hareton after Frances' death and to Catherine Linton after Cathy Earnshaw's death. Cathy is Nelly's rival for the love of old Mr. Earnshaw and Hindley, and Nelly thinks herself a better mother than Cathy could have been. Lockwood is Hareton's rival for Catherine Linton's affections. Both Nelly and Lockwood are always narrowly observing their rivals and delighting in their ills and scorning their successes. Neither is as handsome nor as emotionally liberated as their rivals and, like it or not, their only approach to love and hate is to watch others loving and hating.

No matter what its disguise, then, irrationality has to dominate Emily Brontë's novel because nothing else is available for her to use. Her imagination must try to push beyond the bounds of normal realistic fiction. One way she does succeed is by allowing herself to say and us to hear what to Heathcliff is "unutterable." In this vein Jay Clayton has remarked that "the very words that bind the figures [of Heathcliff and Cathy] together—'like' and 'resemble' and 'as'—reveal the pressure on the terms to spring apart. In place of the perfect silence of *is,* we receive the compensatory beauty of *as*" (83). In this way the imagery of heaven and hell says what is meant by love and hate.[5] In addition, the virtues that underlie civility, society, and manners are repudiated: "I have no pity! I have no pity! The more the worms writhe, the more I yearn to crush out their entrails!" says Heathcliff (189). When Nelly Dean tells Heathcliff that Edgar is attending the weakened and deranged Cathy and that he sustains his affection for her by "common humanity" and a "sense of duty" (185), Heathcliff scorns Edgar's virtues: " 'That is quite possible,' remarked Heathcliff, forcing himself to seem calm, 'quite possible that your master should have nothing but common humanity and a sense of duty to fall back upon. But do you imagine that I shall leave Catherine to his *duty* and *humanity*? and can you compare my feelings respecting Catherine, to his?' " (185). Shortly after, Heathcliff takes up the same theme again: "You talk of her mind being unsettled—How the devil could it be otherwise, in her frightful isolation? And that insipid, paltry creature attending her from *duty* and *humanity*! From *pity* and *charity*! He might as well plant an oak in a flower pot, and expect it to thrive, as imagine he can restore her to vigour in the soil of his shallow cares!" (190). Cathy suggests the same thing when she says: "Whatever our souls are made of, . . . [Heathcliff's] and mine are the same, and Linton's is as different as a moonbeam from lightning, or frost from fire" (121). Pity, charity, duty, and humanity, virtues that sustain a myth of concern, also sustain souls compounded of frost and moonbeams, but not souls welded by lightning and fire. Only passionate, irrational love makes such souls—souls living out their myth of freedom—one. So not only are prudence and fortitude submerged beneath the violence and fraud that pervade the plot but anything that seems an adjunct to the cardinal virtues—pity and charity, duty and humanity—is explicitly rejected because it inhibits the freedom of the two supremely affined lovers, Heathcliff and Catherine Earnshaw. But the price of the rejection is the pervasiveness of death, judgment, and hell. Nevertheless the mysterious oneness of soul that exists between Heathcliff and Cathy remains the burden of what is real as well as what is poetic in the novel.

Cathy says of Heathcliff that "he's more myself than I am" (121) and "I *am* Heathcliff" (122). Heathcliff calls Cathy "my life" (194) and tells her "that I could as soon forget you, as my existence!" (196). He reproaches her for her infidelity to him, saying, "I have not broken your heart—*you* have broken it—and in breaking it, you have broken mine" (197). She is not only his heart but his soul too: "Oh God! would *you* like to live with your soul in the grave?" (204). These exclamations posit an existential identity between Heathcliff and Cathy. They are each other's being, life, existence, heart, and soul. The notion of "adjusting private feeling to public order" is consequently foreign to them (Kinkead-Weekes 95). Emily Brontë frets the language to find the words to express what seems to be inexpressible—that Heathcliff and Cathy are a single seamless human entity. "The self is not contained in an 'I'; has no sustaining 'existence' or 'being' in itself." Cathy "can only fully exist, be herself, in existing and being beyond herself in Heathcliff; as he can only fully exist, be, live in her" (Kinkead-Weekes 88). Once they are separated from one another, their "body" becomes what Lacan calls *le corps morcelé*, a body in bits and pieces, that can never regain in this life the unity it had when they roamed the heath together, as one, savage and hearty and free. Also, once they are separated, their ordinary time becomes apocalyptic, not chronological.

Bakhtin pointed out that the Gothic novel inscribes "castle time," measured by architecture, inscriptions, heirlooms, armaments, portraits, and the like ("Forms of Time" 245–46). Aside from the portal markings at Wuthering Heights, this is not the way that time is measured in any significant way in this novel. In *Wuthering Heights* we have diary entries (1801, 1802), visits,

meals, prayers, births, deaths, weddings, wakes, and burials
as well as the changing of seasons and years and generations.
Wuthering Heights in consequence becomes what Bakhtin calls
"the family novel and the novel of generations" ("Forms of Time"
231). The inscription of ordinary time in the novel is another
instance of Emily Brontë's domesticating the Gothic by substitut-
ing domestic time for castle time. But what we as readers note
in particular is that domestic time kills Catherine Earnshaw and
has no claim on Heathcliff's attention aside from Cathy's death
itself. The focus of Heathcliff's attention is her death and his
own death. The one separates him from her, the other unites
him with her. Those are the only realities for him. Everything
in between is a waste of time, given over to his punishing the
Earnshaws and the Lintons until he realizes that his sadism is a
useless exercise in frustration. No matter how much his enemies
suffer, he suffers more.

  Because Cathy momentarily denies her identification with
Heathcliff by marrying Edgar, she goes insane. This is precisely
what chapters 9 and 12 tell us by dramatizing a "cleavage between the person and the ideological environment that provides
its nourishment"—a cleavage that "ultimately lead[s] to the complete disintegration of consciousness, to disorder or insanity"
(Todorov 70). The sudden abandonment by Cathy of her and
Heathcliff's myth of freedom (embodied in their oneness of heart
and soul) for society's myth of concern (embodied in Cathy's
social sense that marrying Heathcliff would be a degradation)
has immediate and deadly consequences. Once Heathcliff leaves
Wuthering Heights—after hearing Cathy say that to marry him
would be to degrade herself—a ravaging storm breaks, Cathy
is taken desperately ill, and Mr. and Mrs. Linton contract her
sickness and die. The storm leaves behind it a symbolically riven
tree: "There was a violent wind, as well as thunder, and either
one or the other split a tree off at the corner of the building; a
huge bough fell across the roof, and knocked down a portion
of the east chimney-stack, sending a clatter of stones and soot
into the kitchen fire" (125). With the splitting apart of Cathy
and Heathcliff, life at Wuthering Heights is irreparably damaged.
Cathy had threatened anyone who separated her from Heathcliff

with the "fate of Milo" (121, 370), who was trapped in the cleft of a tree which he had split apart and was eaten by wolves. Milo's fate becomes that of the Lintons and Earnshaws. They split apart Cathy and Heathcliff, and he, in the imagery of the novel, becomes the wolf that destroys them.[6] Brontë uses the imagery associated with the riven tree to explicate the inexplicable. She dramatizes the tragic split of the androgyne in primordial time by reenacting it in domestic time by the separation of Heathcliff from Cathy at Wuthering Heights.

If we think of this set of events in Lacan's terms, we can see that Brontë is here writing psychodrama. The external events act out the trauma of unfulfilled desire that Lacan posits as human fate: thwarted "desire is affirmed as the absolute condition" of human life (Silverman 176). At one time one in the womb, Heathcliff-Cathy can now only be Heathcliff *and* Cathy until they are one in the tomb. The womb in the imagery of the novel, Joseph A. Boone has conclusively demonstrated, is "the enclosed oak-paneled bed that the two share at the Heights until Heathcliff is fourteen and Catherine twelve" (153). Their separation is a pubescent reenactment of the primal scene of mitosis in the womb. Even better than their pinafores which Catherine pins together to shelter them from their oppressors or the single cloak that makes them one on the moorland, the oak-paneled bed defines Heathcliff and Cathy's personal sexual identity. Split apart by Hindley at puberty, Cathy and Heathcliff each take a socially sanctioned husband and wife. But Edgar and Isabella Linton have nothing to do with the constantly thwarted desire of Cathy and Heathcliff to be one again as they once were in the womblike oak-paneled bed. It is the constant thwarting of desire wherein their identity and therefore their freedom lies that produces the madness in Cathy and the sadism in Heathcliff and that requires death, judgment, and hell to reign in the novel. Heaven in life can only be what was: Heathcliff and Cathy in the womb. But heaven can also be what will be in death—a return to the womb in the tomb. That takes place when the wooden bed gives way to the wooden coffin. With the sides knocked out of Heathcliff's and Cathy's coffins, their dust mingles and their integral androgynous condition is restored to them. Heathcliff therefore longs to die to find his heaven of eternal oneness with Cathy in the grave.

Cathy's illness, a fever accompanied by a delirium willfully brought on, is the natural effect of her losing a part of herself in losing Heathcliff. And the death of the Lintons is a retribution exacted of those who first separated Cathy from Heathcliff and introduced her to a way of life that led her to prize gentility above passionate love. In the "interior dialogue" within Catherine Earnshaw's being, the Lintons speak with what Bakhtin calls the voice of "a typical representative of the social group" to which one belongs; nevertheless, what the Lintons stand for "does not occupy a stable position [in Cathy's makeup] but consists in an incoherent series of reactions exclusively determined by the circumstances of the moment" (Todorov 70). To separate Cathy from Heathcliff, her heart and soul, for the sake of a momentary incoherent series of attachments to the gentility the Lintons represent and Edgar embodies is clearly to invite disaster. And if the law in the person of Mr. Linton (a magistrate who wants to hang Heathcliff as soon as he sees him [91],[7] if common sense in the person of Nelly Dean (she calls Cathy's identification of herself with Heathcliff "folly" [122]), and if religion in the person of Joseph (he thanks "Hivin for all" when he thinks Heathcliff has drowned [125]) do not understand this basic truth, the cosmos does. There will be nothing but storms of one kind or another until Cathy and Heathcliff are together in the grave. Insofar as duty, humanity, pity, and charity are the virtues of a public order that does not comprehend the meaning of Heathcliff and Cathy's being one, they have no part in the moral vitality of *Wuthering Heights*. In a central paradox of the romantic agony as it is enacted here, *Liebestod* animates the novel.

Chapter 12 supports this conclusion. It follows upon Edgar's enforcing a separation between Heathcliff and Cathy after he tries to run Heathcliff off his property with armed men. Separation again makes Cathy desperately ill: "Our fiery Catherine was no better than a wailing child!" (162). The "threatening danger" is "permanent alienation of intellect" (169). In other words, Cathy without Heathcliff is on the verge of irrevocable insanity. The advice that Kenneth gives is that she not be vexed or crossed. The chapter makes clear why. In her illness Cathy harks back to what she once was: "a girl again, half savage and hardy, and free . . . and laughing at injuries, not maddening under them!" (163). She throws off the facade of civilized willfulness (her fragile mirror image of herself as Mrs. Edgar Linton) and returns to her savage girlhood when Heathcliff, who shared her bed till she was twelve years old—"I was laid alone for the first time" (163)— was "my all in all" (163). It makes good sense psychologically not to cross Cathy. Uncrossed, she can play the role of Mrs. Linton; crossed, her repressed passionate and savage life, the Heathcliff in her, overwhelms her. Not only is Heathcliff the "fierce, pitiless, wolfish man" (141) who terrorizes the lamb Edgar (154), an "evil beast . . . waiting his time to spring and destroy" (146), he is also the savage, passionate soul of Catherine Earnshaw that she tries to repress at the ultimate cost of her sanity and her life.[8] From his perspective, if not from hers, he speaks nothing but the truth when he berates Cathy on the very eve of her death:

> "*Why* did you betray your own heart, Cathy? I have not one word of comfort—you deserve this. You have killed yourself. Yes, you may kiss me, and cry; and wring out my kisses and tears. They'll blight you—they'll damn you. You loved me —then what *right* had you to leave me? What right—answer me—for the poor fancy you felt for Linton? Because misery, and degradation, and death, and nothing that God or Satan could inflict would have parted us, *you*, of your own will, did it. I have not broken your heart—*you* have broken it— and in breaking it, you have broken mine." (197)

Heathcliff's accusation, in a word, is that Cathy has not done him justice. The cost of that injustice is her literal death and his metaphorical death—his having to live when his soul is in the grave. At this point the *Liebestod* is incomplete; Heathcliff's literal death completes it. The cost prior to her death is her actual insanity; the cost after her death and prior to his death is his seeming insanity—his acting in such a way that he seems a devil.

Catherine Earnshaw suffers psychotic episodes and eventually dies because she chose to be Catherine Linton and not Catherine Heathcliff. Accordingly, the writing that Lockwood sees in chapter 3 proves to be the riddle at the heart of the novel[9]: "The ledge, where I placed my candle, had a few mildewed books piled up in one corner; and it was covered with writing scratched on the paint. This writing, however, was nothing but a name repeated in all kinds of characters, large and small—*Catherine Earnshaw;* here and there varied to *Catherine Heathcliff,* and then again to *Catherine Linton*" (61). What Catherine Earnshaw tries to do is become Catherine Linton although she can only truly be Catherine Heathcliff: "Nelly, I *am* Heathcliff" (122). Cathy is seduced by the trappings of gentility that present themselves to her in the image of a bourgeois heaven: "We should have thought ourselves in heaven!" says Cathy when recalling her and Heathcliff's first glimpse of the world of Thrushcross Grange: "—ah! it was beautiful—a splendid place carpeted with crimson, and crimson-covered chairs and tables, and a pure white ceiling bordered by gold, a shower of glass-drops hanging in silver chains from the centre, and shimmering with little soft tapers" (89). But going to a bourgeois heaven by marriage to Edgar is a dream that her soul rejects: "heaven did not seem to be my home; and I broke my heart with weeping to come back to earth; and the angels were so angry that they flung me out, into the middle of the heath on the top of Wuthering Heights, where I woke sobbing for joy" (120–21). In the very moment that she asks Nelly Dean's advice on marrying Edgar, Cathy knows that she should not marry him: "In whichever place the soul lives—in my soul, and in my heart, I'm convinced I'm wrong" (119). Following the logic of the language of the novel, we can say with H. D. P. Lee that "you have only to be sufficiently determined to realize heaven on earth to be sure of raising hell" (46). And that is exactly what happens.

Catherine Earnshaw betrays her heart and soul and consequently betrays her instinctual life—the Catherine Heathcliff within her. Cathy's madness and death proceed then from this existential betrayal. She tries to have what she *has* by being what she *is* not. In her bedazzlement and confusion she tries to solve the riddle of her life by being Catherine Earnshaw, Catherine Heathcliff, and Catherine Linton simultaneously. This she cannot do. The result is that she shatters her identity, goes crazy, and dies. Her death ends the first half of *Wuthering Heights.* The second half deals with her daughter, who runs the sequence of names backward through her life by being first Catherine Linton, then Catherine Heathcliff, and finally Catherine Earnshaw. The daughter ends where the mother began. But she preserves the balance of her mind and the vigor of her youth by never betraying her soul and by growing into these identities sequentially and not trying to live them simultaneously. Her reward is to have in her early maturity what her mother had lost at her puberty. What the oak-paneled bed and the moors were to Cathy and Heathcliff when they were savage and hardy and (more or less) free, Hareton's little garden is for Catherine Linton Heathcliff. She rejects the simultaneity of apocalyptic time and accepts the slow working of domestic time. She thereby solves the riddle and lives.[10]

This riddle in *Wuthering Heights* mediates between its old Gothic forebears and its new Gothic character because the riddle is inextricably bound up with terror. It is "The word carved on a sill / Under antique dread of the headsman's axe" (Graves 11). The simplest forms of riddles have a questioner and a respondent; one ciphers (makes the riddle) and the other deciphers (solves the riddle). If Oedipus does not solve the Sphinx's riddle, he dies; when he does solve it, the Sphinx dies. Riddles are terrific; they terrify. When riddles appear later in literary forms they tend to take on characteristics determined by another genre. (Detective stories are an obvious example.) In *Wuthering Heights* the romantic quest for identity through love is short-circuited by the bourgeois dream (heaven on earth) that leads lovers to ask questions of themselves that they cannot answer. Catherine Earnshaw scratches names in paint. Frantic to know which name should be hers, she asks Nelly Dean who, not knowing the answer herself, then puts her through a catechism. But Nelly's simplification of the riddle elicits no answer from Cathy that can translate conviction into action. Cathy ciphers but she cannot decipher; therefore, she must die. Fittingly, her death, like Heathcliff's later on, is largely self-induced. Once Lockwood enters onto the scene and takes Edgar's place, the terror of the riddle reasserts itself. Will Catherine Linton be able to answer the question her mother asked? Will she too die? No, she will not. Solving the riddle of who she is serves as an initiation into a new life, just as the solution of riddles originally did. That new life is first pictured in the garden Hareton prepares for her and is formally announced in their wedding (a rite of passage) scheduled for the New Year (a time of renewal).

This sequence of events is innovative in that it breaks a repetitive pattern of action in the novel. Catherine's movement from being Edgar's daughter to Linton Heathcliff's wife to Hareton's bride saves her from repeating her mother's mistakes. Like Cathy, who repudiated Heathcliff, Catherine first repudiates Hareton because she finds him degraded and socially her inferior. But having lived as the wife of Linton Heathcliff prevents Catherine from persisting in her dislike of Earnshaw. The one alternative to Hareton that the novel presents is Lockwood. Chapter 32 of *Wuthering Heights* rewinds the novel and allows it to begin again. Chapter 1 opens with the date 1801; chapter 32 with the date 1802. These are dates in Lockwood's diary where all the events of the novel are recorded for us to read (Homans 10).[11] In chapter 1 Lockwood comes to Wuthering Heights the first time and takes a fancy to Catherine. In chapter 32 he comes a second time, and the threat implied in the pattern is that his fancy for Catherine might become a reality. But having been married to Linton Heathcliff, Catherine knows what it means to be the wife of a "gentleman." A marriage to Lockwood could be only a repetition of the disaster and an image of her mother's rejection of Heathcliff who, like the plowboy Hareton, was degraded. Life would then be a hopeless circular series of similar mistakes. As it is, Lockwood returns to be disappointed in love. An intricate pattern of repetition is broken, and the novel ends, looking for once toward life, not death.[12] Just as death has been associated with the first generation of lovers who established their identity within each other, life is now associated with a second generation of lovers who establish their identities outside each other. Death gives way to life as affinity gives way to complementarity. Hareton and Catherine's wedding therefore becomes possible when Heathcliff joins Cathy in the grave. Love is literally consummated in death as the sides of Cathy's and Heathcliff's coffins are broken open and their dust mingles in the grave.

Heathcliff dies as he has lived—as little a Christian as possible. No minister is wanted; no prayers are said. What need when, as he says, "I have nearly attained *my* heaven" (363). If life without Cathy is hell, death with Cathy is heaven. Heathcliff has always had his sacred time and sacred place. The time, when he and Cathy roamed the heath together. The place, her old room where they slept together as children and where Lockwood so witlessly raised her ghost, real or imagined. Ever since then Heathcliff has been poignantly haunted by his desire to rejoin Cathy. Edgar Linton's death is a spur to his own, for he does not want to lose in death what he lost in life.[13] The pattern of his life, then, remains the same. Unceasing rivalry with Edgar Linton for Cathy's love leads to the grave. The devilish, fiendish, infernal avenger is, in the end, the man whose love is as strong as death.

These words of biblical wisdom are proven true by every unholy means in *Wuthering Heights*. Once Heathcliff survives Cathy's death he proves that his love for her is strong enough to perpetrate outrage after outrage on those who kept them apart. He gladly watches Hindley die by inches; he weakens Edgar's already feeble grip on life by kidnapping Catherine; he allows his son Linton to die unnoticed. He swears on his salvation (266) to ruin his enemies to the second generation. "By heaven, I hate them," he says, as well as, "By hell, I hate them" (302). That he can support his hate by swearing on heaven, hell, and his salvation suggests the tremendous disordering effects that un-requited passionate love can have on life. Everyone associated with him calls him a devil and a fiend and labels his machina-tions hellish or infernal. When Heathcliff is called a devil, it is not only because he carries on the functions of the devil in old Gothic fiction. He is also an updated Zofloya (*Zofloya*), Matilda (*Monk*), and Zatain (*Abbot*) who makes a deal and gets the better of his partner. His marriage to Isabella, for example, is totally to his advantage: it gives him power over her, over their son, and over their niece, Catherine Linton; it gives him Thrushcross Grange too. In seeing Heathcliff achieving these and his other goals, we see the labyrinthian architecture of Gothic fiction (the dark passages, subterranean tunnels, and secret doors of castles and monasteries) give way to the labyrinthian machinations of one whose own domestic arrangements are actually very simple. Heathcliff shows us, as Jennifer Gibson argues, that "Gothic vil-lainy" need not be "chaotic or individualistic at all," but can take "the form of organized schemes motivated by the structure of social relationships" (66 n. 18). Because Heathcliff is a superior Machiavel those who suffer at his hands label him a devil.

This inspired name-calling is a happy meeting of metaphor and metonym. Emily Brontë makes what is diabolical and hellish a very down-to-earth matter in order to suggest the power of love. Heathcliff is *so* bad that there must be something good about him. Paradoxically, as everyone's fiend, Heathcliff gives witness to the salvation that lies in love. He is not one of the saved because he is not one of the loved: he is a devil because Catherine Earnshaw abandoned him for Edgar Linton and the bourgeois heaven of Thrushcross Grange. His only way to gain his own version of heaven is to die and mingle his dust with hers. What is good about this man whom all think bad is the testimony that he gives to love as *the* one basic, ineluctable human value. Heathcliff is at last therefore what Mr. Earnshaw called him at first as a child: "a gift of God": "See here, wife . . . you must e'en take it as a gift of God; though it's as dark almost as if it came from the devil" (77). Most who know him see Heathcliff as coming from the devil, and he himself takes that reputation with him to the grave: "Th' divil's harried off his soul," says Joseph, "and he muh hev his carcass intuh t' bargain, for ow't Aw care!" (365). But Heathcliff from the very beginning forces a discrimination of values on those associated with him. Mr. Earnshaw values him above Cathy's whip and Hindley's fiddle and bids his family do the same. The Earnshaws cannot bring themselves to do so, nor can the Lintons after them. Mr. Earnshaw's "gift of God" becomes their "imp of Satan" (80). Heathcliff is set up by Brontë as a sign to be contradicted because he witnesses to values of the spirit that are rejected by a materialistic civilization. Nelly suggests Heathcliff's importance in the simplest of sentences: "He said precious little, and generally the truth" (79).

Arnold Kettle attempted to demonstrate that Heathcliff spoke at least one kind of truth when he argued that Heathcliff manipulates marriage and private property to expose them as social evils and through them to attack the foundation of middle-class society. By way of Heathcliff, therefore, Emily Brontë turns *Pride and Prejudice* upside down and *Barchester Towers* inside out. Whereas

Austen supports civility's virtues with the rewards of marriage and property, Brontë does not. And whereas Eleanor Bold amplifies our sense of Arabin's and Slope's ambition for wealth by becoming the goal of their striving (she *is* marriage and property personified), Cathy's marrying Edgar and her moving to Thrushcross Grange are portrayed as mistaken acts carrying dire consequences. Marriage and property enable *Pride and Prejudice* and *Barchester Towers* to look toward life, but they force *Wuthering Heights* to look toward death. Repulsion dominates Emily Brontë's novel and manifests itself in one dead body after another until Heathcliff starves himself to death and becomes the novel's last corpse. The ultimate object of man's repulsion, death, is the ultimately attractive thing to Heathcliff. In *Wuthering Heights* love has become so contaminated by property and marriage that they remain only as props in a revenge drama that must be consummated in Heathcliff's death.

If Heathcliff is only one of many who die in the novel, so too is he only one of many who are repugnantly brutal. He is an especial witness to the close connection between frustration and savagery in human nature, but he is not singular in his actions. "No other novel so completely defines its characters in terms of the violence of their wills" (Miller, *Disappearance* 167). Indeed, *Wuthering Heights* "cauterizes sentimental feeling" by turning it into psychological truth (Goodridge 169). Not surprisingly, then, the more hurt Heathcliff gets, the more hurt he gives. He thereby becomes the starkest instance of a psychological truth revealed in Hindley, Hareton, Lockwood, and Catherine Linton (see Hagan, "Control" 73–75), who are "modified versions" of Heathcliff (Bersani 199). Once Frances dies, Hindley's brutality increases with his loneliness. Hareton—in some of his actions, if not substantively—becomes, under Heathcliff's subjugation, what Heathcliff became under Hindley's: their crude treatment of Catherine Linton and their hanging of dogs are obvious parallels. Outraged by his reception at Wuthering Heights, Lockwood cruelly cuts the wrists of the spectral Cathy who seeks, just as he did, entrance to the house. Zillah says of Catherine Linton, "She has no lover, or liker among us. . . . She'll snap at the master himself, and as good as dares him to thrash her; and the more hurt she gets, the more venomous she grows" (328). Heathcliff is not a villain lifted whole from the page of old Gothic fiction, an Ambrosio with amnesia. He is the stark embodiment of a psychological truth common in the novel. He needs to say "precious little" because he acts out "the truth." That is why Heathcliff is terrifying.

Heathcliff is devil and fiend in *Wuthering Heights* not because he is the father of lies but because he tells and supports with hideous hardheartedness the paradoxical truth that a man cannot live rationally without irrational love. Catherine comes closest to describing the diabolical in Heathcliff when she says to him:

> "Mr Heathcliff, *you* have *nobody* to love you; and, however miserable you make us, we shall still have the revenge of thinking that your cruelty arises from your greater misery! You *are* miserable, are you not? Lonely, like the devil, and envious like him? *Nobody* loves you—*nobody* will cry for you, when you die! I wouldn't be you!" (319)

At the end of the novel Heathcliff loses his infernal character once he sees Cathy in the grave at the time of Edgar's funeral. The character of passionate lover comes to supersede that of lonely avenger. He rapidly loses his hardness as he and Cathy meet everywhere. Hareton is no longer the hated Hindley's son; he is the personification of Heathcliff: "Hareton's aspect was the ghost of my immortal love, of my wild endeavours to hold my right, my degradation, my pride, my happiness, and my anguish" (354). Hareton is also the personification of Cathy: "his startling likeness to Catherine connected him fearfully with her" (353). Heathcliff's love for himself and for Cathy meet in Hareton. Heathcliff can no longer enjoy destroying Hareton: it would be too much like murder and suicide. Hareton is a "hybrid" (Bersani 200). He brings together the two who have been apart for twenty years (see Tristram 187–88). Hareton in reincarnating Heathcliff and Cathy is a trace of the original androgynous human being that Aristophanes spoke of in Plato's *Symposium* (189C–191D). He is a stark visual realization of Cathy's irrational assertion that "I *am* Heathcliff."

In Plato's myth the human person was originally both man and woman. But rivalry with the gods caused man-woman to be split apart, and ever since the sexes have sought to rejoin each other and become one again. *Wuthering Heights* restores the androgynous entity when at its conclusion Cathy and Heathcliff become momentarily one in Hareton, and then they become eternally one in the grave. The personality of Heathcliff as avenger disintegrates as he becomes lover once again. For him Cathy is everywhere:

"I cannot look down to this floor, but her features are shaped on the flags! In every cloud, in every tree—filling the air at night, and caught by glimpses in every object, by day I am surrounded with her image! The most ordinary faces of men, and women—my own features mock me with a resemblance. The entire world is a dreadful collection of memoranda that she did exist, and that I have lost her!" (353)

Hareton is the memorandum that kills Heathcliff. He can bear no more. He starves himself to death, his spirit hungry for eternity.

Robert B. Heilman argued that the "new Gothic" fiction of the Victorians appropriated standard Gothic conventions to move "deeply into the lesser known realities of human life" and to discover, release, and intensify "new patterns of feeling" (99, 101). *Wuthering Heights* does precisely this because it is a primary example of what Northrop Frye calls "secular scripture": a "work of literature [that] is expanding into insights and experiences beyond itself": "a shell that contains the sound of the sea" (*Secular* 59).

The life we know is defined in *Wuthering Heights* by a preexistence and a death we do not know. The sufferings of Heathcliff's life are connected to the mysteries of Plato's *Symposium* and the Apocalypse of St. John; that is, to the mysteries of what is before life and what is after it—to androgynous creation and sexual division and to the last things of eschatology. "The failure of reason ever finally to decide the questions raised by such a text makes it properly apocalyptic" (Clayton 86). By defining Heathcliff and Cathy as one human entity, by splitting them apart, by casting their joy and sorrow in the language of heaven and hell, and by fulfilling their love in death, Emily Brontë dramatizes the riddle of life by making what is humanly imaginative touch what is spiritually real:

> whether we be young or old,
> Our destiny, our being's heart and home
> Is with infinitude, and only there.[14]

But if the heart's home is infinite, it is also Wuthering Heights —indeed, it is a room within a house, Cathy's bedroom at the Heights, the holy place of Heathcliff's heart. Brontë's new Gothic novel in this way domesticates apocalypse. *Wuthering Heights* is apocalypse here, now.

4

Great Expectations

The Gothic Tradition
Personalized

Wuthering Heights is new Gothic fiction in the form of the family novel; *Great Expectations* is new Gothic fiction in the form of the *Bildungsroman*. *Great Expectations* presents Pip's personal perspective on the human condition. This is immediately evident in the opening scene, which is as horrific as any old Gothic romancer could initiate; except, of course, that Pip has lived to tell and laugh at his tale of terror, as Paul Goetch indicates: "Dry, amused, cynical, with irony and an eye for the grotesque, yet sidestepping rhetorical exaggeration, Pip exposes his previous follies and errors."[1] This narrative perspective makes what was horrific for the boy grotesque for the man. The opening scene shows Dickens sounding just the right personal note to establish a gripping but carefully modulated tone for his entire novel.

The novel immediately focuses on death and judgment. It opens in a graveyard from which a gibbet can be seen. Pip is forced to face his orphaned condition as he looks at the graves of "Philip Pirrip, late of this parish, and also Georgiana wife of the above" and of his brothers Alexander, Bartholomew, Abraham, Tobias, and Roger, who "were also dead and buried" (35). A convict appears, sets him on a tombstone, and threatens his life. This is Pip's introduction to death and judgment. Mrs. Joe is subsequently murdered, Compeyson and Drummle die violent deaths, Magwitch is sentenced to death but dies before he can be hanged. Miss Havisham dies like Magwitch of injuries, Bill Barley drinks himself to death, and Orlick almost murders Pip after accusing him of killing Mrs. Joe. In addition, Pip visits Newgate and sees criminals who will soon be executed. Mrs. Joe's funeral is a grotesque celebration of death, "a kind of black Bazaar" (298). And, finally, in the last chapter the frightening events of the first chapter are recalled as the narrator takes the new young Pip to the same old place on the marshes: "And I took him down to the churchyard, and set him on a certain tombstone there, and he showed me from that elevation which stone was sacred to the memory of Philip Pirrip, late of this Parish, and Also Georgiana, Wife of the Above" (490).

Not only does *Great Expectations* constantly remind one in these ways of death and judgment but it also presents characters whose very lives embody death and judgment. Dickens' remarkable achievement with Miss Havisham and Jaggers is not only that they deploy metaphors for death and judgment—from the decaying wedding shroud of Satis House to the scented lemon soap of Little Britain—but also that they serve as metonyms for Death and Judgment, living out their lives as particular instances of these haunting abstractions so pervasive in the novel. Such a fusion, as George E. Haggerty indicated, escaped the old Gothic novelists whose formulas Dickens reinvents for his new Gothic novel.

Miss Havisham parades Death just as Jaggers parades Judgment. She is one of the living dead. She has a broken heart and looks like a corpse: "waxwork and skeleton seemed to have dark eyes that moved and looked at me," says Pip (87). Satis House is her tomb: it has shut out the sun and stopped the clock; it is damp, cold, and moldy; it is overrun by mice, beetles, and spiders. Miss Havisham has embraced death in place of life because to live is to risk loving again. That is a chance she cannot take; so she sits in front of a mirror loving herself to death. As a reincarnated Narcissus, she is a figure out of a scenario by Jacques Lacan, deriving a sense of her own uniqueness from the image of a brokenhearted lover that she sends back to herself from her looking glass, yet never content with what she has become or can be: "The *mirror stage* is a drama whose internal thrust is precipitated from insufficiency to anticipation . . . and, lastly, to the assumption of the armour of an alienating identity, which will mark with its rigid structure the subject's entire mental development" (*Ecrits* 4). Thus fixed and alienated, Miss Havisham has only one ambition—to murder Love; but Love she insists, in her image of herself as dead bride, has murdered her. With Estella as her tool, Miss Havisham makes Pip her victim: "You can break his heart," she tells Estella (89). Miss Havisham's desire for revenge literally makes the place of the "bridal feast" a "funeral room" (260) and anticipates the Widow Edlin's declaration in *Jude the Obscure* that weddings have become funerals. Dickens has telescoped the charnel house and the castle of old Gothic fiction into a bourgeois manor house run to ruin by a greed that left love unrequited and made revenge insatiable. Miss Havisham is the wronged innocent heroine who has become the ghost in the haunted house. Satis House *is* Miss Havisham, just as Walworth *is* Wemmick: we cannot think of one without the other. A man's house may be his castle, but his castle is also an expression of himself. In Satis House and in Walworth Dickens transforms the old Gothic convention by personalizing it with an indispensable genius loci.

Jaggers lives as though the world were one vast courtroom in which everything is related to an all-encompassing and ongoing judicial process (see Winner; Tick). As long as one lives, therefore, one is subject to arrest, indictment, trial, judgment, and punishment. Jaggers thinks the worst of everyone because he has lived his professional life in "an atmosphere of evil" (424). "The man who fills the post of trust never is the right sort of man" (265), Jaggers remarks not only of Orlick but of every man. "Of course you'll go wrong somehow, but that's no fault of mine" (194), he tells Pip, suggesting that lemon soap bathes his conscience as well as his hands. He makes Pip feel that it is hardly worth coming of age in such a "guarded and suspicious world" (311). Jaggers makes Herbert think that "he must have committed a felony and forgotten the details of it" (311). Jaggers sees Bentley Drummle as "a promising fellow" because he is likely to mistreat Estella, and he calls him the "Spider" (402). Only Estella has ever made Jaggers deviate from his hard, cynical professional ways: she became for him "one pretty little child out of the heap, who could be saved" (425). Everything else with Jaggers is lawyerlike in the extreme: "Have you paid Wemmick?" (191); "I execute my instructions, and I am paid for doing so" (307); "If you say a word to me, I'll throw up the case" (191); "That's a question I must not be asked" (308); "I think for you; that's enough for you" (191); "I'll put a case to you. Mind! I admit nothing" (424); "Get out of this office. I'll have no feelings here. Get out" (427).

To Jaggers the world is a dangerous place that is safe only if one makes oneself a "mantrap" by being a lawyer all the time. Life must be treated as a series of cases. Death masks of convicted felons must be preserved to remind one of what happens if one's case is lost. Home must simply be an extension of the office lest one forget that life is a trial. Gerrard Street like Little Britain must harbor an acquitted criminal and be filled with law books and legal briefs. A vigorous washing with lemon soap is the only rite of passage allowed between the office and the home. If a lawyer is any less vigilant than this, a Jaggers might easily become a Magwitch. Indeed Magwitch is the case that proves Jaggers' point. Magwitch lives in fear of the law and twice loses his case: once to transportation and once to the sentence of death. Magwitch is always, when he appears in the novel, a "hunted dunghill dog" (337).

The essence of Dickens' new Gothic fiction is to personalize the horror of old Gothic fiction. As a frightening story, *Great Expectations* is actually Pip's own tale, constantly revealing something about him as he grows up.[2] Death and Judgment are not faceless abstractions either; their horror is personalized. Miss Havisham lives her death; Jaggers lives his judgment. Just as Satis House bears her stamp, Gerrard Street bears his. And just as Satis House decays, Gerrard Street thrives, suggesting that in nineteenth-century Gothic fiction "the landed estate . . . has been touched by the hand of death" while "new city types . . . with hardened heart and jaded virtues" are invigorated (Lehan 103). If places in the old Gothic fiction exist to terrify as they exemplify disputes over inheritance and succession to power, places is new Gothic fiction, as Dickens writes it, exist to exemplify dislocated psyches that are the product of an economy based on commerce rather than real property. Consequently Satis House represents a dying order, Walworth represents an attempt to preserve a fraction of that order with city money, and Gerrard Street represents the city's cynical attitude toward that order, regarding it as nothing but a source of income for a professional class. And yet while reflecting these cultural and economic shifts, Dickens personalizes them in Miss Havisham, Wemmick, and Jaggers.

Characterization is as personalized as setting in *Great Expectations*. Magwitch is always "*my* convict" to Pip (italics added). Magwitch, moreover, combines death *and* judgment in himself: directly, by being adjudged a felon who is sentenced on pain of death to transportation; indirectly, by Pip's mistakenly investing Miss Havisham with the power Magwitch actually exercises and by Pip's experiencing that exercise of power through the agency of Jaggers. By dramatizing death and judgment in this way, Dickens allows Pip to demonstrate that his life is shaped by deadly, not quickening, forces. Furthermore, Pip gives us an insight into the personal and social dynamics of these forces.

Money is used by Magwitch and Miss Havisham to shape Pip and Estella into a gentleman and a lady. Jaggers as the agent of monied clients becomes richer himself; Wemmick gets more personal property. Both the lawyer and his clerk also make money in the citadels of judgment and death, the Old Bailey and Newgate. This conflation of money with death and judgment has about it the same instinctive wisdom and implications of perversity as Silas Wegg's sexual arousal (the symbolic erection of his wooden leg) when reading about money buried in a dungheap (*Our Mutual Friend*, chap. 39). The conflation dramatically illustrates one meaning embedded in the name *Havisham:* to-have-is-sham. If Dickens requires Pip to solve the riddle of *gentleman,* he requires the reader to solve the riddle of *Havisham.* This is precisely what George Eliot, one of Dickens' most astute readers, did. When, in *Middlemarch,* Dorothea tells Ladislaw, "I hate my wealth" (chap. 83), she throws off the incubus of Casaubon, who seeks to control her affective life by controlling the terms of her inheritance. Miss Brooke refuses to be an updated version of Miss Havisham: she refuses to give herself over to hugging his money to her death and making his dark house her half-acre tomb.

Pip's personal life then is shaped by the forces of death and judgment because money governs social intercourse. His growing up a gentleman is therefore a particulary poignant growing up under the judgment of death. All humankind grow up this way, of course, but Pip's life intensifies our sense of our mortality. And Dickens quickens that sense with the sham-of-having that Pip's adventure exposes. From his first moment in Satis House as a boy, Pip sees himself as someone who does not have enough. This is as much his mirror image as the mirror on the bridal table is Miss Havisham's. His ideal is to have enough; her ideal is to be miserable enough. But his mirror image satisfies him no more than hers satisfies her. Once Pip has got enough, he fritters away his humanity. Having got what he wanted, he is more than ever out of touch with himself. So when Magwitch dies, Pip nearly dies too. With the source of his money and his life gone, there is virtually nothing left of Pip. The mirror is shattered. Pip's imaginary self is annihilated. Only someone who knows Pip's real self can save Pip's life. That person is Joe Gargery.

Like Miss Havisham and Magwitch, Joe Gargery is truly unique. But in making Joe and Miss Havisham and Magwitch singularly strange (and in making Jaggers and Wemmick strange too) Dickens makes death, judgment, and life itself singularly strange as well and thereby forces us to see things that are seemingly familiar in a new way—a *defamiliarized* way—which Victor Shklovsky argued was characteristic of great fiction (13–14). Furthermore, insofar as judgment and death and rebirth are phases of every individual life, Dickens' art makes Pip a unique version of Everyman—especially, a nineteenth-century Everyman: "the emblem of an age" (Lindsay 371).

In seeking money, gentility, and love Pip strays from Joe and the forge where he already has identity, approbation, friendship, security, and love. To find happiness he leaves the ground of his being behind him. He gives up the edenic life he does not know he has in order to find the Edenic life he supposes he can have. But what he finds is the fallen world. In this way, as Badri Raina remarks, Dickens' Pip reminds us of Emily Brontë's Catherine: "the quality of experience that defines Cathy Earnshaw's betrayal of herself also illuminates the nature of Pip's self-betrayal" (114): "The *Gestalt* of Pip's first visit to Satis House recalls that of Cathy Earnshaw's visit to Thrushcross Grange. In Edgar Linton, Cathy encounters her first gentleman, superior to the dirty-nailed Heathcliff. In Estella, Pip senses the power of poise that similarly derives from grooming and from the solid security of property" (113). The major difference between Cathy and Pip is that his expectations lead him into a drama of redemption while hers do not. Pip falls into sin on his first visit to Satis House; he is punished with the return of Magwitch; he undergoes a symbolic death in his illness; and he returns to life after Joe nurses him through his fever.[3] The same events are subject to another familiar pattern of interpretation. Pip's expectations lead him into a drama of integration: he repudiates his superego in Joe, with whom he is also in oedipal conflict over Biddy; his id asserts itself in his irrational and erotic love for Estella; and his ego is integrated with both when he learns to love and nurse Magwitch in the same way that Joe loves him and soon will nurse him—when, in short, Pip integrates his experience of the world with his experience of the forge.[4]

Both the theological and the psychological pattern of events applies not only to Pip but to Everyman. His adventure represents what Hegel found to be the "biography of the 'general spirit,'"

representing the consciousness of each man and Everyman, the course of whose life is a painfully progressive self-education, rendered in the plot-form of a circuitous journey from an initial self-division and departure, through diverse rec-

onciliations and ever-renewing estrangements, conflicts, re-
versals, and crises of spiritual death and rebirth. This plot
turns out to be the unwitting quest of the spirit to redeem
itself by repossessing its own lost and sundered self, in an
ultimate recognition of its own identity whereby . . . it can
be "at home with itself in its otherness." (Abrams 229–30)

Part of the appeal of *Great Expectations* to readers during six-score
years is their sense that Pip's story, for all its manifestations of
callousness and moral stupidity, is their own; it is Everyman's
story cast in a special mode.[5] Moreover, *Great Expectations* is a
rewriting of a popular wish-fulfillment dream set forth in the
well-known tale (Captain Cuttle's favorite story in *Dombey and
Son*) of Dick Whittington, the orphan boy who is violently mis-
treated by Cecily, the cook, but who, through the efforts of his
cat (not through his own efforts) gains a fortune, marries his rich
master's daughter, and becomes Lord Mayor of London. Whittington's good fortune is the incarnation of the bourgeois dream
and the pattern of Pip's expectations.

These expectations make Pip a visionary in a dangerous and
death-ridden world. He holds unswervingly to a vision of affined
love for Estella. His experience of Estella haunts him in the way
that Cathy haunts Heathcliff in *Wuthering Heights*: "The entire
world," Heathcliff lamented, "is a dreadful collection of memoranda that she did exist, and that I have lost her!" (353). Pip's
experience of Estella—he speaks to her in the following passage
—is exactly the same as that of Heathcliff, who spoke of Cathy
as his heart, soul, and existence:

"Out of my thoughts! You are part of my existence, part of
myself. You have been in every line I ever read, since I first
came here, the rough common boy whose poor heart you
wounded even then. You have been in every prospect I have
ever seen since—on the river, on the sails of the ships, on
the marshes, in the clouds, in the light, in the darkness, in
the wind, in the woods, in the sea, in the streets. You have
been the embodiment of every graceful fancy that my mind
has ever become acquainted with. The stones of which the
strongest London buildings are made, are not more real, or

more impossible to be displaced by your hands, than your
presence and influence have been to me, there and everywhere, and will be. Estella, to the last hour of my life, you
cannot choose but remain part of my character, part of the
little good in me, part of the evil." (378)

Part of the little good in Pip manifests itself in his desire for
freedom. Like Magwitch, he wants to knock off his manacles.
The manacles are manifest in the obsessive concern for order
and obedience that Mrs. Joe and Pumblechook express. In their
world there is no place for boys like Pip. There is however a
place for girls like Estella. Pip is made to understand this during his first visit to Satis House. His total absorption in Estella
—evident in her being in every line and every prospect in his
purview—is an expression of Pip's desire for freedom. Acceptance of any difference between them is for Pip acceptance of
his inevitable bondage and her alienating freedom. Money, position, and influence confer freedom. Estella has them; Pip feels
he must have them too. If she is a lady, he must be a gentleman.
Pip says of Estella that "I loved her against reason, against promise, against peace, against hope, against happiness, against all
discouragement that could be" (253–54). He thereby expresses
the irresistible driving force of his desire to be free. Estella is,
as he tells her, "the embodiment of every graceful fancy that
my mind has ever become acquainted with." The only kind of
lover that Pip's intense desire allows him to be, therefore, is an
affined romantic lover. If she is the "Princess," he must be "the
young Knight of romance" who marries her (253). His freedom
demands that he and Estella be one: she must be, as he says,
"part of my character, part of the little good in me, part of the
evil."

The evil part of Pip manifests itself after his first meeting with
and rejection by Estella when he has a vision of Miss Havisham
hanging in the brewery. One thing that Estella's hardness trig-
gers in Pip is a death wish for hard women like Mrs. Joe and
Miss Havisham. And Dickens renders his relationship to these
hard women in a psychodrama. Both women indeed do die, and
Pip is involved in their deaths. Orlick accuses him of murdering
Mrs. Joe: " 'Wolf!' said he, folding his arms again, 'Old Orlick's

a going to tell you somethink. It was you as did for your shrew
sister'" (437). Orlick's bizarre statement makes Pip one with
Orlick, the actual murderer.[6] When Pip returns to Satis House in
chapter 49, he fancies he sees "Miss Havisham hanging to the
beam" again. Shortly after, when she is afire and Pip smothers
the flames, they struggle "like desperate enemies" (414). Pip's
unconscious desire to punish punishing women manifests itself
in his language—they are "enemies"—and in his visions that
function like Rorschach tests in which he projects a hanging
woman onto a configuration of objects in the setting of the brewery (see also Moynahan 163–66). Just as Orlick gets at Pip by
murdering Mrs. Joe, Pip gets at Estella by hanging Miss Havisham in his imagination. Eventually Estella experiences a fate
that links her to Mrs. Joe too. Drummle batters the girl just as Orlick battered the woman. "I have been bent and broken," Estella
tells Pip, "but—I hope—into a better shape" (493). The imagery
is that of metal worked by a blacksmith, just as the fire that burns
Miss Havisham and the manacle that batters Mrs. Joe are also
related to the forge (and, of course, to life itself, as Joe suggests
when he says that life is "made of ever so many partings welded
together, as I may say" [246]). By being burned, battered, and
bent, the hard women in the novel take on a new shape. Each
eventually asks Pip's forgiveness (301, 415, 493). Thus reshaping
through adversity leads, finally, to salvation, as Dickens suggests
here and as John Donne suggested in Holy Sonnet 14:

> Batter my heart, three person'd God; for you
> As yet but knocke, breathe, shine, and seeke to mend;
> That I may rise, and stand, o'erthrow mee, and bend
> Your force, to breake, blowe, burn and make me new.

Pip's intensely personal visions are thus joined psychodramati-
cally by a pattern of imagery to major themes of death and judgment as they touch suffering and salvation.

Joe Gargery dramatizes values opposite to those held by Miss
Havisham and Jaggers; where they value money he values love.
Pip is bound over as apprentice and passes from Miss Havi-
sham's into Joe's hands. In chapter 13 Joe does not speak to

Miss Havisham.[7] The twenty-five pounds she gives to him are immediately given to Mrs. Joe in confirmation of one exchange at Satis House:

> "You expected," said Miss Havisham, as she looked them [the articles of apprenticeship] over, "no premium with the boy?"
>
> "Joe!" I remonstrated; for he made no reply at all. "Why don't you answer—"
>
> "Pip," returned Joe, cutting me short as if he were hurt, "which I meantersay that were not a question requiring a answer betwixt yourself and me, and which you know the answer to be full well No. You know it to be No, Pip, and wherefore should I say it?" (129)

As far as Joe is concerned, money cannot set a value on his love for Pip: " 'This is wery liberal on your part, Pip,' said Joe, 'and it is as such received and grateful welcome, though never looked for, far nor near nor nowheres' " (129). The ceremony by which Pip further passes from Joe's loving care to Jagger's legal guardianship is more elaborate than his being bound over as an apprentice blacksmith, but it too nicely separates the claims of love from those of money. When Pip passes out of Joe's hands and into Jaggers' in chapter 18, the lawyer is so insistent on setting a price on Pip that Joe threatens to serve Jaggers as he did Orlick by knocking him down.

> "But if you think as Money can make compensation to me for the loss of the little child—what come to the forge—and ever the best of friends!—". . .
>
> "Now, Joseph Gargery, I warn you this is your last chance. No half measures with me. If you mean to take a present that I have it in charge to make you, speak out, and you shall have it. If on the contrary you mean to say —" Here, to his great amazement, he was stopped by Joe's suddenly working round him with every demonstration of a fell pugilistic purpose.
>
> "Which I meantersay," cried Joe, "that if you come into my place bull-baiting and badgering me, come out! Which

I meantersay as sech if you're a man, come on! Which I
meantersay that what I say, I meantersay and stand or fall
by! (168–69)

To Miss Havisham and Jaggers Pip is worth a specified amount of
money. It is crucial to Dickens' indictment of his society that the
agents of death and judgment in the novel both set a price on Pip.
But the agent of life and love does not. To Joe Pip is "ever the best
of friends" and valuable beyond price. Pip eventually realizes the
same thing about Joe: because "I am soon going abroad, and . . .
shall never rest until I have worked for the money with which
you have kept me out of prison, and have sent it to you, don't
think, dear Joe and Biddy, that if I could repay it a thousand
times over, I suppose I could cancel a farthing of the debt I owe
you, or that I would do so if I could!" (488). If, as Herbert Pocket
insists, in agreement with his father, Matthew, a man must be a
gentleman at heart before he can be a gentleman in manner, then
the blacksmith is the novel's true gentleman from beginning to
end because his love has no price tag attached to it. And this too
Pip finally comes to realize: "O God bless this *gentle* Christian
man!" (472; italics added).

Insofar as *Great Expectations* is a *Bildungsroman* that contains a
mystery story within it, this crucial word *gentleman* is the riddle
at the heart of the mystery. The mystery is the identity of the
benefactor who, with one magnanimous gesture, makes Pip a
gentleman. The riddle resides in the question of what it means to
be a gentleman. Because Pip comes so close to failing to realize
the meaning of *gentleman*, he comes close to dying—the ancient
conjunction between failing to solve a riddle and paying for the
failure with one's life is here rendered in a modern fashion. Because he finally learns the meaning of *gentleman*, Pip lives. The
rite of passage that takes him into a world that has the trappings
of gentility is presided over by Jaggers in chapter 18. That rite
takes place in the state parlor, involves a change of guardians,
of clothes, and of names; and it insists on the persistence of
mystery: no inquiry concerning the identity of Pip's benefactor
is allowed him. This rite of passage immediately estranges Pip
from the forge: he spends the most miserable night of his life
there because the true meaning of *gentleman* is a riddle to him.

Writing at one period (the 1860s) about another (beginning "between about 1810 and 1830" [Calder in *GE* 14]), Dickens draws on a wide variety of ideas of what a gentleman is. The gentleman of birth appears in the Pip who is reborn at age eighteen and changes his name, dissociates himself from Joe, and later tries to repudiate Magwitch. The gentleman of wealth appears in Pip at age twenty-one who comes into £500 a year. The gentleman of honor appears in the Pip who defends Stella's name and wants to restore Satis House. The gentleman of breeding appears in the Pip who learns manners from Herbert. And the gentleman of education appears in the Pip who studies with Matthew Pocket.[8] But the true gentleman does not appear in *Great Expectations* until Pip provides for Herbert's expectations, accepts Magwitch's love, and seeks Joe's forgiveness. These different models of a gentleman show that Pip cannot be what he does not understand. It takes him a while to realize that he who is a gentleman is he who does the gentle deed.

For the longest time Pip understands nothing of *gentleman* beyond the cash, clothes, and city life implied in birth, wealth, honor, breeding, and education. Pip cannot distinguish an interior from an exterior mode of existence. For £500 a year he exchanges his identity to live with a riddle encased in a mystery. The rite of passage that takes him back to his identity is his sickness subsequent to Magwitch's death and his own loss of fortune. This rite in chapter 51 is presided over by Joe, whose unselfish love gives Pip the clue to the riddle of *gentleman:* the word *Christian* signifying that love and forgiveness must stand between *gentle* and *man:* "O God bless this gentle Christian man!" (Gilmour 143; Castronovo 50–51). With Pip's invocation of this blessing on Joe, he deciphers what he ciphered early in the novel: " 'Why, here's a J' said Joe, 'and a O equal to anythink! Here's a J and a O, Pip, and a J-O, Joe' " (75). In those early days, Joe found his name; now Pip finds the meaning of that name: "a J and a O" means *gentleman*. Not until Pip figures this out for himself does the internal action of his self-realization come to a conclusion. If Pip's acceptance of Magwitch, as Peter Brooks argues, is the denouement of the mystery plot in *Great Expectations* (136), Pip's recognition of Joe is the denouement of the growing-up plot in the novel.[9]

Joe is Dickens' version of the muscular Christian who has none of the vulgarly violent characteristics of Charles Kingsley's version of the type. Joe has the bodily strength of Kingsley's gentleman but the spiritual strength of Newman's gentleman: "he is too clear-headed to be unjust; he is as simple as he is forcible" (Haight 467). His heart is animated by the virtue that ideally distinguishes followers of Jesus: their love for one another. Love then lies at the heart of true gentility: if Pip must decipher the meaning of the word *gentleman*, he must also decipher the meaning of the word *love*. If *gentleman* is the riddle within the mystery, *love* is the enigma within the riddle. Dickens therefore presents the complexities of love in every phase of the novel.

If love at the forge issues in a blessing, love at Satis House issues in a curse:

> "Hear me, Pip! [says Miss Havisham of Estella] I adopted her to be loved. I bred her and educated her, to be loved. I developed her into what she is, that she might be loved. Love her!"
>
> She said the word often enough, and there could be no doubt that she meant to say it; but if the often repeated word had been hate instead of love—despair—revenge—dire death—it could not have sounded from her lips more like a curse. (261)

Pip can find no better way to be accursed than by loving Estella: "I never had one hour's happiness in her society, and yet my mind all round the four-and-twenty hours was harping on the happiness of having her with me unto death" (319). A boy who carries with him both a common origin and criminal associations can hardly find a better way of punishing himself for those things than by loving a girl who will not love him. A boy who hates his "mother" (in Pip's case Mrs. Joe) cannot vex himself more completely than by trying to marry someone equally unloving either to prove that he is lovable or to make her over, on the model of Pygmalion, into an ideal wife (see Kubie 24–25; Freeman and Greenwald 85–87). Pip expresses these unconscious desires in his vision of a renovated Satis House, a renewed Miss Havisham, and a new Estella: Miss Havisham "had adopted Estella, she had as good as adopted me, and it could not fail to be her intention to bring us together. She reserved it for me to restore the desolate house, admit the sunshine into the dark rooms, set the clocks a going and the cold hearths a blazing, tear down the cobwebs, destroy the vermin—in short, do all the shining deeds of the young Knight of romance, and marry the Princess" (253). This is simply another version of the bourgeois dream that we saw in "The History of Whittington." Here the poor boy grown rich establishes himself in a gentle way of life happily ever after. Pip wants love to be a blessing for Satis House as it is for the forge, but it turns out to be a curse. The fire that blazes to white heat at the blacksmith's forge, Dickens suggests, is kindled by Joe's love. Fire touches the dark dankness of Satis House only after Miss Havisham declares her love for Pip by asking his forgiveness. Once she does that, Satis House is no longer a personal expression of her life so Dickens immediately burns it down. But the forge endures to the end as an expression of Joe Gargery's love.

In a novel that presents many ways of loving, Joe's way is characterized by fidelity and stability. He goes to the length of maintaining that Mrs. Joe is "a-fine-figure-of-a-woman" (78). He marries her as much for Pip's sake as for her own: " 'And bring the poor little child. God bless the poor little child,' I said to your sister, 'There's room for *him* at the forge!' " (78). From that moment on, for Joe, he and Pip are "ever the best of friends." And even though Mrs. Joe dies and Pip leaves, Joe stays at the forge where he takes another wife and begets a son. Joe's love, in both marriages, is in part inspired by compensation: " 'It were but lonesome then' [after his mother died], said Joe, 'living here alone, and I got acquainted with your sister' " (77–78). Pip's sister takes the place of Joe's mother, and his toleration of her ("your sister comes the Mo-gul over us" [79]) makes up for his father's violence ("he took us home and hammered us" [77]) to his mother and himself. Joe brings to life as a husband and a father the words he intended for his own father's gravestone: "Remember reader he were that good in his hart" (77). In his second marriage, Mrs. Joe's place is taken by Biddy, and Pip's place by the second Pip.

There, smoking his pipe in the old place by the kitchen fire-
light, as hale and as strong as ever though a little grey, sat
Joe; and there, fenced into the corner with Joe's leg, and sit-
ting on my own little stool looking at the fire, was—I again!
  "We giv' him the name of Pip for your sake, dear old
chap," said Joe, delighted when I took another stool by the
child's side (but I did *not* rumple his hair), "and we hoped
he might grow a little bit like you, and we think he do." (490)

Joe's love, then, as simple as it may seem and as heartwarming
as it may be, is psychologically a complex matter. Although Joe
can say to Pip, "What larks," his life with his parents and with
Mrs. Joe and with Pip is anything but a lark. Biddy and their son
make up for a great deal that Joe has suffered and lost.

Wemmick presents another approach to love. He is both like
and unlike Joe. When Pip abandons the forge, he visits Walworth, where the generous and positive love that characterizes
the forge has another incarnation. It has turned the threatening
castle of Gothic fiction into a fun house. There Joe's ingenuity
resides in Wemmick and Joe's endearing qualities in the Aged
P, who hears just about as well as Joe writes and whose an-
tics with buttered toast are as happy as Joe's with bread and
cheese. But Joe's professional and personal life are one at the
forge; Wemmick's are divided between Little Britain and Walworth. In paraphrase of Sir Edward Coke, Joe's saying that "a
Englishman's ouse is his Castle" (475) is literally true for Wemmick, whose office is far to the other side of the moat.[10] As a
crypto-businessman-commuter, Wemmick has a life-style which
asserts that half one's life must be lived without love.[11] However delightful a Dickensian creation, Wemmick in his approach
to love shows at best a bizarre accommodation that admits of
a Miss Skiffins only late in middle age. The younger Wemmick
has spent much of his life in the Old Bailey and Newgate getting
hold of portable property. Wemmick embodies in himself—as
Pip does in his own relation to Estella—the precarious relation
between the myths of freedom and concern, the one associated
with love at Walworth and the other with the law at Little Britain. But, as Mr. Bumble said, "The law is a ass" (*Oliver Twist*
461).[12] The law is "a ass" because it is inextricably bound up with

hardheartedness, prevarication, trial, guilt, imprisonment, and execution. The values that Dickens affirms in *Great Expectations* show little if any sympathy for any of these things.

Herbert Pocket is most indelibly etched on the reader's mind as the pale young gentleman who is repeatedly knocked down by Pip and who repeatedly gets up to face his adversary once again. He is most like Pip in that he has expectations that are satisfied. He is most like Joe in that he is a constant and faithful friend of Pip's. He is most like Wemmick in that he is a successful businessman. His expectations, constancy, and success enable him to marry Clara Barley. The good-heartedness that character- izes Herbert in every phase of his life and career suggests that unlike Wemmick he does not have two selves, one personal and the other professional. By the good fortune of friendship with Pip, who fulfills his expectations, Herbert seems to be the one character in the novel who finds romantic love least enigmatic. Perhaps this is so because Dickens allows him so little dramatic engagement with love itself. Herbert stands in the novel more as a hope that a solution to the enigma of love can be found than as someone who shows us how to find it. In a novel that is in- tensely personal, Herbert's relation to love is noticeably abstract. And although his life seems more integrated than Wemmick's, Wemmick's precarious balancing of work and love seems closer to actuality. Herbert's great expectations come true; Wemmick never had any expectations and made his life what it is.

On the subject of love *Wuthering Heights* is very much a dia- logue of one: Heathcliff. *Great Expectations*, to use Bakhtin's term, is very much a heteroglossia on love. Many voices speak of love from different backgrounds and perspectives. The novel is a symposium in which Dickens' characters are no wiser than Socrates' friends at their banquet at Agathon's house in Athens. Like Plato, Dickens urbanizes irrational love. The country house, Satis House, is destroyed, and the forge harbors Biddy and Joe; as locales of unsuccessful and successful romantic love they of- fer neither place nor possibility to Pip. In the canceled ending of the novel Pip meets Estella for the last time in the city. In the published ending of the novel he walks "out of the ruined place"

(493) with her. London, one presumes, is their destination. In both endings as in the body of the novel itself Dickens brings not only Pip but passion to the city. He makes Pip test romance in a hard but ineluctable world. Two city men, Herbert and Wemmick, suggest alternative ways for Pip to accommodate work to home, hand to heart, money to love. Each ending suggests a different model for Pip to follow. The canceled ending shows Pip as an early middle-aged professional man whose bachelor ways indicate that marriage, if it comes at all, will come in later middle age. That is the Wemmick model. The published ending suggests that Pip has achieved some of his expectations: having become a gentleman and done well in business, he now gets Estella too. He follows, in short, in the footsteps of Herbert. Neither ending is alien to patterns in the novel. But how in fact Pip finally deals with love in *Great Expectations* remains—as the endings and the endless debate over the endings indicate—an open question.[13] If the riddle of *gentleman* and the mystery of Pip's benefactor are finally solved, the enigma of *love* properly remains unsolved.

Great Expectations, then, is a new Gothic novel that in working out Pip's growing-up explores love in its various manifestations. One of these is the protagonist's affined love that in its erotic drive expresses his search to be free from society's stagnant myth of concern. In Pip's telling his own story, in the personalization of death and judgment in a set of characters that surround the protagonist, in Pip's need to work out his salvation among them, and in his initial failure and subsequent success in solving the riddle of *gentleman* and consequent experience of death and rebirth, *Great Expectations* is an intense personalization of the new Gothic novel. As such it moves the genre of new Gothic fiction a giant step toward a yet more realistically rendered psychological approach to characterization that appears when elements of the novel of manners combine with elements of the new Gothic novel to produce the Gothic manners of *Middlemarch*.

Part Three

Gothic Manners

5

Middlemarch

Gothic Manners in England

Between *Pride and Prejudice* and *Barchester Towers* manners cease to be a means of self-definition and become a means of social exclusion: Darcy and Elizabeth wed conduct to intelligence and affection and then they wed each other; Bertie and Madeline Stanhope, however, leave the city of Barchester for more tolerant climes. In *Wuthering Heights* Gothic conventions are domesticated, and in *Great Expectations* they are personalized: Heathcliff becomes master of two country houses; Pip's feelings are so skewed that he thinks himself akin to Dr. Frankenstein's monster. The novel of manners shows society gradually cultivating respectability as a virtue; the new Gothic novel shows the individual defining home and personality in terms of feeling. When these genres come together in *Middlemarch*, respectability replaces Gothic terror because it denies legitimacy to strong feeling. "Respect" becomes, as Georges Bataille suggests, "really nothing but a devious route taken by violence" (Tanner, *Adul-*

tery 11). In *Bleak House* Dickens' presentation of the voracious Mr. Vholes, a lawyer who preys upon his clients for the sake of "his three daughters [at home] and his father in the Vale of Taunton" (483–84), is a merciless indictment of respectability as a devious route to violence:

> Mr. Vholes is a very respectable man. He has not a large business, but he is a very respectable man. He is allowed by the greater attorneys who have made good fortunes, or are making them, to be a most respectable man. He never misses a chance in his practice; which is a mark of respectability. He is reserved and serious, which is another mark of respectability. His digestion is impaired, which is highly respectable. And he is making hay of the grass which is flesh, for his three daughters. And his father is dependent on him in the Vale of Taunton. (482)[1]

Dickens has Mr. Vholes lurking behind a black door, buttoned up in black clothes, working at a desk that is "as hollow as a coffin" (485); when he raps the desk it makes "a sound as if ashes were falling on ashes, and dust on dust" (486). All of which indicates that respectability and death are law partners. Mr. Vholes's respectably bad digestion makes him "but a poor knife and fork man at any time" (542), but that is not to say he has no appetite and does not eat. Mr. Vholes is a cannibal "always looking at the client, as if he were making a lingering meal of him with his eyes as well as with his professional appetite" (485). Mr. Vholes is really "the official cat who is patiently watching a mouse's hole" (485). But this legal cat is a respectable cannibal. He dresses and undresses with respectability: "Mr. Vholes, quiet and unmoved, as a man of so much respectability ought to be, takes off his black gloves as if he were skinning his hands, lifts off his hat as if he were scalping himself, and sits down at his desk" (484). That this "Mr. Vholes is considered, in the profession, a *most* respectable man" is confirmed by the minutes of a parliamentary inquiry (483). Why? Because Mr. Vholes has a code: "I never give hopes, sir. . . . I never give hopes"; "I never disparage, sir, I never disparage"; "I never impute motives. . . . I never impute motives" (486–87). Above all, Mr. Vholes never violates the one great principle of English law: "The one great principle of English law is, to make business for itself" (482). For Dickens, the bottom line of the business ledger equals "undoubted respectability" (483). But even such undoubted respectability gives the cannibal only the appearance of civility: "Make man-eating unlawful, and you starve the Vholeses!" (483). George Eliot takes over Dickens' carnivalization[2] of respectability in *Middlemarch*—like Dickens she emphasizes man-eating[3]—where "the devious route taken by violence" is anatomized in a ladylike basil plant, a cannibal clergyman, and a devilish banker who devours the competition.

Middlemarch is a novel about the horrors of respectability. Impeccable manners ravish the peccant heart. George Eliot demonstrates that there is no longer a need for Gothic villainy; a bourgeois code of conduct is horror enough. She lets fall "Damocles' sword of *Respectability*" which Thomas Carlyle saw hanging "for ever . . . over poor English life" (157). Along with Dickens and Carlyle, Eliot reminds us that "it was not only that 'self-help,' 'character' and 'respectability,' essential elements of Victorianism, began to be questioned, or that manifestations of these Victorian qualities in action . . . were under attack, but that the tone in which the qualities were discussed was very different from before" (Briggs, *Social History* 231). Thus it is that George Eliot has Rosamond Vincy make her entrance into *Middlemarch* telling her mother not to speak in a "vulgar" manner and further insisting that she herself is never "unladylike" (73). Rosamond persists in this course of conduct and marries a gentleman to detach herself forever from a grandfather who was an innkeeper. Throughout her marriage to Tertius Lydgate she insists on the decorum of her conduct and the indecorousness of his. The very profession that makes him splendid she maintains is not "nice" (335). At the end of the novel this pattern card of Mrs. Lemon's school is presented in a horrible image. Lydgate calls her "his basil plant; and when she asked for an explanation, [he] said that basil was a plant which had flourished wonderfully on a murdered man's brains" (610). No wonder then that Henry James saw in the "gracefully vicious" Rosamond the perfect representative of the "fatality of British decorum" (*Literary Criticism: Essays* 963).[4]

Edward Casaubon decides to marry in conformity with soci-

ety's "sanctions" and thereby leave it "a copy of himself." He
thinks only about what he requires of a wife and nothing about
what a wife requires of him: "Society never made the prepos-
terous demand that a man should think as much about his own
qualifications for making a charming girl happy as he thinks of
hers for making himself happy." He finds that his wife falls short
of expectations; nevertheless, he determines to act like "a man of
honour according to the code" and to be "unimpeachable by any
recognised opinion." He is determined to act "with propriety"
and fulfill "unimpeachably all [outward] requirements" (207).
When most annoyed with his wife, he calls her "my love," his
"irritation reined in by propriety" (149). He sees Dorothea as a
woman of "affectionate ardor" and "Quixotic enthusiasm" and
determines to recall her to decorum and prevent her from being
anything but a gentlewoman. This he does by adding a codicil
to his will to control her actions from the grave: "the prevision
of his own unending bliss could not nullify the bitter savours
of irritated jealousy and vindictiveness" (308). Thus he forbids
Dorothea to marry Will Ladislaw on pain of losing her inheritance. Casaubon's constant attention to the requirements of a
social code ironically costs him his position in society. "Ladislaw is a gentleman," says Mr. Brooke. "I am sure Casaubon was
not," says Sir James (356). What was he then? The narrator suggests that he was an ancient dead pagan awaiting Charon on
the banks of the river Styx while masquerading as a clergyman:
"To Mr Casaubon now, it was as if he suddenly found himself
on the dark river-bank and heard the plash of the oncoming oar,
not discerning the forms, but expecting the summons" (311).[5] As
far as Sir James is concerned, Dorothea is given as "a horrible
sacrifice" to Casaubon (210). To Ladislaw, Dorothea's marriage
with Casaubon is "the most horrible of virgin-sacrifices" and
Casaubon is a monster growing "grey crunching bones in a cavern" (264). The man who would fulfill perfectly all the external
requirements of a gentleman becomes, in one mythic analogy
in *Middlemarch*, the Minotaur, half man and half beast, feeding
on virgin sacrifices. His path to this horrible transformation has
been perfect propriety.

The scion of middle-class respectability, Rosamond Vincy
who would be a lady, ends her quest feeding on a murdered

man's brain. The irreproachable gentleman-clergyman, Edward Casaubon, ends his quest for respectability feeding on a virgin sacrifice. Both have become horrible by seeking justification of their conduct in standards maintained by "good society."

Nicholas Bulstrode seeks justification by a yet higher standard: the will of God as made known through a Calvinist doctrine of predestination. As one of the elect who will go to heaven willy-nilly, he does his worst and finds that it is what God demands of his "instrument." But God's cause is conveniently connected to man's society. Wealth and power are the signs of God's election. These Bulstrode allocates to himself:

> Who would use money and position better than he meant to use them? Who could surpass him in self-abhorrence and exaltation of God's cause? And to Mr. Bulstrode God's cause was something distinct from his own rectitude of conduct: it enforced a discrimination of God's enemies, who were to be used merely as instruments, and whom it would be as well if possible to keep out of money and consequent influence. Also, profitable investments in trades where the powers of the prince of this world showed its most active devices, became sanctified by a right application of the profits in the hands of God's servant. (453)

What Bulstrode has achieved is a "respectability [that] had lasted undisturbed for nearly thirty years" (452–53). It is disturbed, however, at precisely the moment that it has achieved its goal. Raffles shows up when Bulstrode has secured the goal of the bourgeois dream—at precisely the moment that the hardworking middle-class businessman claims the goal of his work in a large estate and looks forward to retirement and living like a gentleman: "he had bought the excellent farm and fine homestead simply as a retreat which he might gradually enlarge as to the land and beautify as to the dwelling, until it should be conducive to the divine glory that he should enter on it as a residence, partially withdrawing from his present exertions in the administration of business, and throwing more conspicuously on the side of Gospel truth the weight of local landed proprietorship, which Providence might increase by unforeseen occasions of purchase" (381).

With all the external trappings of a gentleman in hand, however, Bulstrode ends his days at best as a rascal and at worst as a devil, as Mrs. Dollop indicates to Mr. Limp: "If one raskill said . . . ['if the hairs of his head knowed the thoughts of his heart, he'd tear 'em up by the roots'], it's more reason why another should. But hypo*crite* as he's been, and holding things with that high hand, as there was no parson i' the country good enough for him, he was forced to take Old Harry into his counsel, and Old Harry's been too many for him" (529). The devil shows up as Raffles, a "loud red figure," who is Bulstrode's incarnate past and who forces the banker to see in him an image of himself: "a handsome family likeness to old Nick" (386).[6] With a genius for psychodrama George Eliot produces Raffles as the devil within Bulstrode. Once he exorcises that devil Bulstrode is only a shell of himself and is driven from Middlemarch in disgrace. The end of the bourgeois dream is not gentlemanly leisure but weeping and gnashing of teeth. Respectability has produced a basil plant, a Minotaur, and a devil in *Middlemarch*; horror is the natural product of decorum. In *Middlemarch* George Eliot has made the Gothic novel and the novel of manners one and the same thing. The riddle that one usually finds in Gothic fiction now entails understanding what words like *lady* and *gentleman* truly mean; and the legal case characteristic of the novel of manners now dissociates justice from justification, money and power from nobility of character.

What George Eliot advances to its logical conclusion, then, is Dickens' earlier perception in *Great Expectations*—a perception buried in the pun on Miss Havisham's name—that to have is a sham. She quite consciously makes her novel into an *expectations* story in which characters improve humanly in proportion to the amount of money they lose, refuse, or give up.

The story of Fred Vincy, Mary Garth, and Peter Featherstone offers the most obvious parallel to Pip, Estella, and Miss Havisham's adventures. Satis House becomes Stone Court, the grasping Pockets become the grasping Waules, and legacies are arranged in wills that disappoint almost everyone. Fred is deferential to Peter Featherstone because he expects him to make his fortune. He dreams of taking over Stone Court and hunting his way into gentility. He visits Mary Garth there under the pretext of visiting Featherstone; when he does see Featherstone, Fred marches the enfeebled old man around the room as Pip once did Miss Havisham. The Waules are called "vultures" and "assiduous beetles" and take over Stone Court as the Pockets once did Satis House. Their expectations are as seriously disappointed as Fred's are by Joshua Rigg, who is left Stone Court and money on the condition that he take the name Rigg Featherstone—just as Philip Pirrip had once agreed to be known legally as Pip. Like Pip's, Fred's disappointment is followed by a serious illness that brings him to the brink of death. Like Pip he finds his best friend in a lowly acquaintance. Caleb Garth becomes the Joe Gargery of *Middlemarch*, and not only does he pay Fred's debts but he makes his expectations come true. By dint of hard work Fred eventually buys Stone Court long after he marries Mary Garth, who thinks of herself as Fred's last expectation: " 'Fred has lost all his other expectations; he must keep this,' Mary said to herself, with a smile curling her lips" (423). And should the reader have missed all these explicit parallels, George Eliot allows Mary to remind the reader that Fred's story draws on Pip's: "I have heard a story of a young gentleman," she says to Fred, "who once encouraged flattering expectations, and they did him harm" (606). "O possibilities!" cries the narrator, "O expectations founded on the favour of 'close' old gentlemen! O endless vocatives that would still leave expression slipping helpless from the measurement of mortal folly!" (246).

What George Eliot does in *Middlemarch* is rewrite the expectations story of mortal folly within the context of a society more ample and various than the one created by Dickens, whose *Bildungsroman* becomes one element seeking redefinition in Eliot's middle-class epic. The grotesque elements of Pip's story reemerge in the circumstantial realism of Fred's as the new Gothic novel is assimilated to the novel of manners. Fred, Mary, Featherstone, and Caleb Garth are less extraordinary than Pip, Estella, Magwitch, Miss Havisham, and Joe because they arise out of a society rather than out of a dark and misty landscape. And Peter Featherstone lying dead among his coins, cash box, and papers is more immediately probable than Miss Havisham planning her wake on a vermin-ridden banquet table. *Great Ex-*

pectations functions then as a prototype for *Middlemarch*. The later
novel deconstructs the grotesquerie and the poetic presentation
of the earlier, making a sharper social point by reducing the
mythic and the Gothic elements to everyday reality. George Eliot
thereby provides room not only for the point but for the counterpoint as well. The counterpoint of Fred Vincy's adventures is
Will Ladislaw's expectations.

Ladislaw seeks out Dorothea in a dark house, as Pip does
Estella; Miss Havisham gives way to Casaubon, Satis House
to Lowick, and the banquet room to the library as the most
death-ridden room in the house. As Will's supposed benefactor,
Casaubon turns out to be his worst enemy; anyone but Ladislaw can have Casaubon's widow and his money. The codicil becomes as disenfranchizing a legal document as any ever written.
Furthermore, Will refuses Bulstrode's offer of £500 a year (precisely the sum that Magwitch allowed Pip) and tells the banker
—contrary to Bulstrode's belief in his instrumentality—that "It
ought to lie with a man's self that he is a gentleman" (457).

The precise difference between Will's story and that of Fred
and Pip is that Ladislaw is a gentleman by birth and they are
not; and whereas Ladislaw renounces money, they seek it. Social
status and money are never the objects of Ladislaw's expectations. He awaits the call of the universe to activate his genius. If
that never quite happens in any way he could foresee, he uses
what is genial in him to promote political reform and to liberate
a woman. Ladislaw tells Dorothea that his religion is "to love
what is good and beautiful when I see it" (287). He does precisely that as a politician and a lover. In the case of Ladislaw
the expectations story unfolds not within the material nexus of
gentility and money but within the spiritual nexus of justice and
love. Consequently those who love money and status before all
else—those who like Casaubon and Rosamond and Bulstrode
are interested in their own justification—treat him as an outcast: Mr. Hackbutt calls Ladislaw a "loose fish from London"
(262); Mr. Hawley calls him a spy, an "emissary" (278); Lydgate
finds him "a sort of gypsy" (319); Sir James denounces him as
an "Agitator" (356); and Mr. Toller thinks him an "adventurer"
(441). Will is labeled a "Byronic hero" (278) and "Mr Orlando
Ladislaw" by Mrs. Cadwallader (460) and "a sort of Daphnis" by

Lydgate (364). And he is denounced as a "Polish emissary" (339), "an Italian with white mice" (359), and the "grandson of a thieving Jew pawnbroker" (566). Mr. Hawley sums up Middlemarch's dislike of Ladislaw when he denounces "any cursed alien blood, Jew, Corsican, or Gypsy" (527). The point could not be more precisely made: Ladislaw is cursed alien blood. Will is treated unjustly because he is an alien in Middlemarch society. This may be the most telling difference in the expectations story as used by Dickens and Eliot. In *Great Expectations* Pip's alienation is an evil; in *Middlemarch* Will's alienation is a good. Eliot's alien is like Arnold's: he is the thinking man who provides the only hope for the future of England.

The alien pursues the inbred goods of neither the Barbarian nor the Philistine nor the Populace: he pursues neither honors nor consideration, neither fanaticism nor moneymaking, neither brawling nor smashing. Aliens, according to Arnold, are "persons who are mainly led, not by their class spirit, but by the general *humane* spirit, by the love of human perfection" (538). That perfection is attained by the happy union of an ability "to see things as they really are" with "conduct and obedience"—that is, by the happy union of Hellenism with Hebraism (559–60). When Ladislaw tells Dorothea that his religion is "to love what is good and beautiful when I see it" (287), he is telling her that he is an alien seeking human perfection and he emphasizes the Hellenism of his nature. When Dorothea says to Will, "You care that justice should be done to every one" (395), she emphasizes the Hebraism of her nature. Each enriches his nature through the best characteristics of the other. Will teaches Dorothea the "language of art,"[7] and Dorothea helps Will find his vocation in Reform politics. Will and Dorothea seek human perfection—the sweetness and light of their best selves, in Arnold's words—in each other. They are two individuals formed dialogically, on the Bakhtin model: each finds the self through the other; their subjectivity is intersubjectively formed. Understandably, then, Dorothea like Will is an alien in Middlemarch society too:

> Sir James never ceased to regard Dorothea's second marriage as a mistake; and indeed this remained the tradition concerning it in Middlemarch, where she was spoken of to

a younger generation as a fine girl who married a sickly clergyman, old enough to be her father, and in little more than a year after his death gave up her estate to marry his cousin—young enough to have been his son, with no property, and not well-born. Those who had not seen anything of Dorothea usually observed that she could not have been "a nice woman," else she would not have married either the one or the other. (612)

Dorothea's marriage to Will—which proves to society that she is not "a nice woman"—represents a process of growth into her best self. To grow into one's best self, consequently, is to grow into alienation from society. This deflection of the law within a person from the laws outside him divides emotional reality from social expectation and demands a new way of rendering the modes of Gothic fiction and the novel of manners. George Eliot finds that new way in a remarkable psychodrama that frees Dorothea to be herself—to be the alien wife of an alien Will.

In chapter 1 of *Middlemarch*, Dorothea, called upon to divide her mother's jewelry with Celia, finds her thought and feeling at odds with each other—her moral sensibility and her emotions working against each other. When Celia induces Dorothea to divide their mother's jewelry, she takes Dorothea away from working on plans for the rebuilding of cottages on tenant farms. Architecture is important to Dorothea because she expects it to have practical results in better buildings on the Freshitt and Tipton estates. The things that are important to her are those that affect the quality of other people's lives. Indeed, Dorothea is like Caleb Garth, who praises her plans and implements them, in part, on Mr. Brooke's and Sir James Chettam's estates. Both manage to take part in the historical movement for reform while staying out of politics proper. Each has an organic sense—Dorothea's perhaps more limited than Caleb's—of the relations of one thing to another in life. So that when she sees a set of emeralds that she instinctively likes but thinks she ought not to like because "miserable men find such things, and work at them, and sell them!" she is troubled. Her intense concern for others interferes with her freedom to feel comfortable in liking the emeralds for herself.

She salves her Puritan conscience by saying that "gems are used as spiritual emblems in the Revelation of St. John"; she keeps the emeralds for herself, Scripture supplying an excuse for feeling. Nevertheless, Dorothea senses that it is wrong to keep them and shows her feeling when she answers Celia's enquiry—"Shall you wear them in company?"—sharply: "I cannot tell to what level I may sink" (10–11). Dorothea vents her anger with herself on her sister. This vignette at the beginning of the novel reveals the astringent Hebraism in Dorothea's makeup. Her sense of duty makes her natural delight in beautiful things, her latent Hellenism, an evil: her delight in brightness and color is wrong. At the novel's very beginning, then, George Eliot presents her heroine at odds with herself as the myths of freedom and concern make contradictory claims upon her. *Middlemarch* explores the implications of these myths by presenting them in the psychodrama of Dorothea's dissociated sensibility, which takes the form of the agon of her marriage to Casaubon.

In chapter 29 the split in Dorothea's sensibility is externalized in her argument with her husband, who is intensely engaged in a process of self-justification, preparing to publish "a new Parergon, a small monograph of some lately-traced indications concerning the Egyptian mysteries whereby certain assertions of Warburton's could be corrected" (207). Two letters from Will Ladislaw—whom Casaubon has made quite clear to Dorothea he dislikes—come across his desk; he passes one on nastily to Dorothea, saying that he has no intention of seeing Will "whose desultory vivacity" fatigues him and distracts him from his work. A few moments before, in chapter 28, Dorothea was revealed in her boudoir as revolted by Casaubon's unfeeling attitude toward Ladislaw and as sympathizing with Will to such an extent that the miniature of his grandmother is transformed by her imagination into a picture of Ladislaw himself: "Nay, the colours deepened, the lips and chin seemed to get larger, the hair and eyes seemed to be sending out light, the face was masculine and beamed on her with that full gaze which tells her on whom it falls that she is too interesting for the slightest movement of her eyelid to pass unnoticed and uninterpreted" (203). Dorothea has forced her way into the library to be of assistance to her husband: "but for her pleading insistence" she would not be there.

The boudoir world of sexual feeling and the library world of wifely duty are quietly sleeping together within Dorothea until Casaubon awakens them by his harsh comment to her. Dorothea resents the implication that she would want what Casaubon does not want, and she bluntly tells her husband what she thinks: "The fire was not dissipated yet, and she thought it was ignoble in her husband not to apologise to her" (208). Not long afterward Casaubon has a heart attack. Revolted by the effects of her strong feelings on Casaubon, Dorothea ends the chapter in repentance, "kneeling and sobbing by his side" (209–10). Here is the id doing battle with the superego, and losing as the ego collapses into feelings of guilt. Casaubon has aligned himself with the Puritan conscience of chapter 1, Ladislaw with the shining emeralds, and the ego of Dorothea is caught guiltily between them.

By chapter 37 Dorothea, alarmed by Casaubon's collapse, cannot respond to another of his attacks on Ladislaw. Her life of wifely duty has by now become a horror for her: "Hearing him breathe quickly after he had spoken, she sat listening, frightened, wretched—with a dumb inward cry for help to bear this nightmare of a life in which every energy was arrested by dread" (275). And the nightmare leaves her completely shaken: "her ardour, continually repulsed, served, with her intense memory, to heighten her dread, as thwarted energy subsides into a shudder" (311). Two chapters later Dorothea tells Ladislaw, "I am always at Lowick" and "I have no longings." In short, no longer free to feel, Dorothea is determined not to feel at all. Ladislaw senses this and says to her, "That is a dreadful imprisonment" (287). Lowick as the physical extension of Casaubon's dark mind is a prison. Casaubon as the extension of Dorothea's own superego has shut her up in her own prison. Insofar as he is twice her age, Casaubon, in the *Name-of-the-Father*, to use Lacan's phrase, "has identified his person with the figure of the law" (Bowie 134–35) and imprisoned Dorothea's affective self. Casaubon's own feelings, such as they are, have become Dorothea's law. Her concern is to obey the law, but she cannot. For a moment, in chapter 42, Dorothea rebels. Going to her boudoir as Casaubon retreats to his library, Dorothea says bitterly: "'It is his fault, not mine.' In the jar of her whole being, Pity

was overthrown. Was it her fault that she had believed in him—
had believed in his worthiness?—And what, exactly, was he?—
She was able enough to estimate him—she who waited on his
glances with trembling, and shut her best soul in prison, paying
it only hidden visits, that she might be petty enough to please
him" (312–13).

In chapter 48 Casaubon asks her to intensify her pettiness by
finishing his "Key to All Mythologies" should he die. He asks
her, in effect, to take on his judgment and sensibility; having
failed to produce a copy of himself from her body, he asks her
to produce a copy of himself from her mind.

> "You refuse?" said Casaubon, with more edge in his
> tone.
> "No, I do not yet refuse," said Dorothea, in a clear voice,
> the need of freedom asserting itself within her. . . .
> "But you would use your own judgment: I ask you to
> obey mine, you refuse."
> "No, dear, no!" said Dorothea, beseechingly, crushed by
> opposing fears. (350)

Casaubon demands that Dorothea give up not only her freedom
but also her personality wholly and completely: she is to be what
he wants her to be and not to be herself. This is the final and logical conclusion of the posture she has taken as a dutiful wife: "She
was always trying to be what her husband wished, and never
able to repose on his delight in what she was" (348). This extinction of self is the ultimate psychological horror Dorothea faces,
and for pity's sake she is willing to submit to it. Wifely duty has
led her Puritan conscience to what Ladislaw calls in chapter 22 a
"fanaticism of sympathy": shut up in her prison away from Will,
Dorothea is will-less. The one man who has praised her feelings,
called her a "poem," and told her that "the best piety is to enjoy
—when you can" (163) is kept from her. In the absence of any
joy in herself, Dorothea lets pity overwhelm her in her concern
to be a good wife. Fortunately for her, Casaubon dies, and she
gradually returns to a sense of her self and her freedom. In chapter 54 she repudiates his mind and his will by repudiating his
"Key": *"Do you not see now that I could not submit my soul to yours,
by working hopelessly at what I have no belief in?"* (393). Dorothea

literally takes her soul back into her own keeping. Symbolically, if one thinks of the phallic implications of "Key," she takes her body out of bondage too. Again, quite literally, the last vestige of Casaubon's will that Dorothea has to deal with is the codicil forbidding her to marry Ladislaw. One will is meant effectively to keep another Will out of her life.[8]

With his codicil Casaubon forfeits his right to be called a gentleman, but he also martials social opinion against Ladislaw. Social opinion and Casaubon's will have a hold on Dorothea's life until she grows comfortable enough with her freedom to accept her feelings and to choose according to her liking. After Casaubon's death Dorothea and Will meet and part a number of times, each parting becoming more difficult than the last because Dorothea sees ever more clearly that she and Will love each other. With a keenness for mythological analogy, George Eliot equates their first such parting with that of Cupid and Psyche: "She did not know then that it was Love who had come to her briefly, as in a dream before awaking, with the hues of morning on his wings—that it was Love to whom she was sobbing her farewell as his image was banished by the blameless rigour of irresistible day" (399). In *Middlemarch*, as in *The Golden Ass* where Eros and Psyche's story is told, pettiness and jealousy keep Ladislaw and Dorothea apart for a time, but Love and the Soul cannot live without each other. When Will returns again in chapter 62, Dorothea, like Psyche with her lamp, sees and recognizes her lover for the first time; and Ladislaw, like Love, is gone in an instant: "it was all one flash to Dorothea—his last words— his distant bow to her as he reached the door—the sense that he was no longer there" (464).

Dorothea's task now consists in overcoming obstacles that keep her and Ladislaw apart. The first and most important obstacle that Dorothea has to deal with is the codicil of Casaubon's will. The second is her jealousy of Rosamond, itself the product of Rosamond's romantic vision of Ladislaw as her own jealous lover. In chapter 81 Dorothea faces her hardest task: she goes a second time to visit Rosamond after her first visit was aborted when she found Ladislaw at the Lydgates' holding Rosamond's hand. Only the greatest moral effort brings Dorothea back again. She seeks Rosamond's good in spite of believing that she has lost her own good. The epigraph from *Faust* suggests in part just how momentous Dorothea's effort is: *Zum höchsten Dasein immerfort zu streben*. Dorothea strives with all her powers to transcend her jealousy and attain the highest form of life. Her reward is to learn that Ladislaw loves her, not Rosamond. In chapter 83, then, she is able to act on that knowledge and overcome the crippling effects of Casaubon's will. Ladislaw says "good-bye" to her, but she absolutely refuses to let him go one more time. A flash of lightning moves them to join hands and in a moment they kiss. The Soul having grasped and tasted Love will not let go of Love again:

> "Oh, I cannot bear it—my heart will break," said Dorothea, starting from her seat, the flood of her young passion bearing down all the obstructions which had kept her silent —the great tears rising and falling in an instant: "I don't mind about poverty—I hate my wealth."
>
> In an instant Will was close to her and had his arms round her. (594)

Consequently the chapter ends with Dorothea in Ladislaw's arms and engaged to the man she loves. The allegory of Love seeking the Soul (and the Soul, Love) and overcoming every obstacle in the way is made complete in Will and Dorothea's lives.

This allegory also helps to work out the tension between the myths of freedom and concern dialectically: in her concern for Rosamond's marriage, Dorothea finds the freedom to love Will Ladislaw. In addition, the money that confers social respectability and becomes the object of material expectations—money that makes a dutiful and respectable widow of a disenchanted and rejected wife—is renounced with a scorn of the shackles it clamps on Dorothea. The money and respectability it brings, which society loves, Dorothea hates. This strong emotion of hate, hatred of Casaubon's money, ties Dorothea to Ladislaw, who hated Casaubon himself: "The poet must know how to hate, says Goethe; and Will was at least ready with that accomplishment" (166).[9] Dorothea finally gives voice to love and hate and finds her will in Will Ladislaw. And now she has no need for any justification outside her feelings themselves. Chapter 83 ends the psychodrama begun in chapter 1: the emeralds give place to

Ladislaw, the gleam of sunshine that irradiated them to the flash of lightning that welds Dorothea to Will, and the "current of feeling" that the gems started in her becomes "a flood of passion." The desire for the gems once justified by Scripture gives way to a desire for Will which now needs no justification whatsoever. Love has taken hold of the soul, as Eros did of Psyche, and the soul knows that each keeps the other alive. Anything else, as Dorothea's marriage to Casaubon proved, is death.

When elements of the genres of manners and new Gothic fiction come together in *Middlemarch*, respectability is transmuted into the equivalent of Gothic horror by denying validity to strong feeling: "to be a happy wife to a dead man is to be buried alive" (Gilbert and Gubar 503). In forbidding emotional explosions, respectability invites emotional implosions. The myths of concern and freedom are thereby constantly put in tension. The moral virtues come to exist more or less as simple manifestations of sanctioned social conduct; the last things are seldom named but dramatize themselves in states of feeling where they are revealed as dead metaphors: repression (death), guilt (judgment), joy (heaven), and sorrow (hell). Complementary love degenerates to the delusion of unsuitable partners who think that their differences will be their strength in marriages that almost invariably turn out badly. Affined love becomes a romantic love that exists as an alternative to marriages already made. And the case becomes the riddle, the riddle the case: where intelligence may see a way out of a riddle-like case, society precludes acting on feelings that allow a solution because the problem is invariably a miserable marriage and the solution is either separation, divorce, or adultery.

Miserable or not, marriage is the foundation of society's respectability: it is "the all-subsuming, all-organizing, all-containing contract. It is the structure that maintains the Structure" (Tanner, *Adultery* 15). The realism of the late-Victorian novel of Gothic manners derives from the circumstances of the conflict between this structure within a Structure and the intense individual feelings that threaten it. In addition, "the taste for emotions of recognition" replaces "the taste for emotions of surprise"; consequently, suffering in fiction seems to belong less to romance and more to life itself (James, *Literary Criticism: Essays* 1354). Simply by virtue of its scope and homely detail *Middlemarch* makes the everyday world of character and event more completely recognizable than it was in *Wuthering Heights* and *Great Expectations*. In *Middlemarch* the intense feeling liberated in these new Gothic novels is planted in the common ground of manners cultivated in *Pride and Prejudice* and *Barchester Towers*. The separation between Heathcliff and Cathy is denoted in *Wuthering Heights* by lightning that splits apart a tree; in *Middlemarch*, however, lightning inaugurates a new union between Dorothea and Ladislaw and functions as a metaphor of welding. It is an illuminating flash that not only has *Middlemarch* look back to the new Gothic tradition but also has it anticipate a further relation to the Gothic manners of *The Portrait of a Lady* where Caspar Goodwood sends a kiss through Isabel Archer like "white lightning, a flash that spread, and spread again, and stayed" (591).

6

The Portrait of a Lady
Gothic Manners in Europe

Henry James went to Harvard to read law, but he read Balzac instead, left Cambridge, and became a novelist. The precise details of this episode in James's education escaped Ford Madox Ford, who somehow thought that James had studied law at Geneva, a university which lacked the academic distinction of "Oxford, Bonn, Heidelberg, Jena or even Paris" (Hueffer, *Henry James* 101), but which conferred the social distinction of *respectability*. Consequently, Geneva was not James's tender mother; Geneva was James's respectable mother: "I allow myself to discover in Mr. James . . . a trace of—I won't say of affection, for the word would be ill-applied to this University that is *Mater*, not *Alma*, but *Respectiblissima*—a trace of remembrance of the respectability of this haunt of his contemplative youth" (106). This cachet of respectability is important to Ford's James whose "conscious or unconscious mission . . . was to civilise his people—whom he always loved" (140–41). But Europe failed to provide James the respectability he sought: "He had tried to find his Great Good Place—his earthly Utopia—in Italy, in France, in English literary life. He had failed" (146). James found himself therefore "in the same boat with Flaubert, with Zola, with Turgenieff, with Maupassant, and even with Baudelaire" (138).

> From Italy, France and England the dayspring was to have come; but half a century of pilgrimages . . . left [James] with no further message than that—that the soul's immortal, but that most people have not got souls—are in the end just the stuff with which to fill graveyards; that *cela vous donne une fière idée de l'homme; homo homini lupus*, or any other old message of all the old messages of this old and wise world. Bric-à-brac, pallazzi [*sic*], châteaux, haunts of ancient peace—these the pilgrim found in matchless abundance, in scores, in hundreds. Poynton, Matcham, Lackley, Hampton. . . . "The gondola stopped; the old palace was there. How charming! it's grey and pink. . . ." From the first visit to Madonnas of the Louvre, in *The American*, to the last days of the eponymous vessel of *The Golden Bowl*, there is no end to the *articles de vertu*. . . . But as for the duchesses with souls— well, most duchesses haven't got them! (141–42)

It is the James whose duchesses have no souls who wrote *The Portrait of a Lady*. If in *The American* a marquis and a marquise have no souls, in *The Portrait* "the cleverest woman" (176) and "the first gentleman" (430) in Europe have no souls; nor does the Countess Gemini: "The Countess seemed to . . . have no soul; she was like a bright rare shell, with a polished surface and a remarkably pink lip, in which something would rattle when you shook it" (449). James's subjects in *The Portrait* are Americans who go to Europe in search of civilization and find their own savagery. If Conrad uncovered the heart of darkness in the Congo, James uncovered it in cities. The unholy alliance of the Bellegardes, mother and son, in Paris, gives way to the unholy alliance of estranged lovers, Madame Merle and Gilbert Osmond, in Florence and Rome. This is what makes James an ally of Baudelaire. For if Henry James found the "fatality of British decorum" in *Middlemarch*, we today find the fatality of European decorum in *The Portrait of a Lady*.[1] If Ford made a mistake about James's studying law at Geneva, he made no mistake when he showed James depicting the decay of contemporary manners in the cultural centers of Europe.

When James saw "the fatality of British decorum" inscribed in George Eliot's characterization of Rosamond Vincy, he signaled his awareness of what could be done by driving a wedge of middle-class respectability between manners and morals. Whereas Casaubon is a gentleman in Middlemarch, Osmond is "the first gentleman in Europe." This ominous fact eventually makes the jaded Madame Merle say that "Society is all bad" (239). And certainly there is something of Henry James in that remark because he knew from reading Sainte-Beuve that "as soon as you penetrate a little under the veil of society, as in nature, you see nothing but wars, struggles, destructions, and recompositions" (*Literary Criticism: French* 688). The truth of that observation came home dramatically to Henry James in 1914 at the outbreak of World War I: he virtually ceased writing about society and took to reading to wounded soldiers and distributing tobacco in the hospital wards. *The Portrait of a Lady* penetrates Sainte-Beuve's veil of society by showing what it means for an American girl to become a *lady* in European society. This focus requires James to emphasize Isabel Archer's consciousness and sensibility more exclusively than Eliot did Dorothea Brooke's. Such a choice—primarily dictated by his study of Turgenev but also by what James called "the lesson of Balzac"—makes Henry James's novel a telling permutation within the fiction of Gothic manners that George Eliot practiced in *Middlemarch*.

Although Isabel Archer is far from being a New Woman of the kind that Henrik Ibsen and Bernard Shaw were to make the focus of attention, she shares with the New Woman a desire for a fullness of life beyond that allowed to women of a more conventional stamp.[2] Isabel wants to achieve "the union of great knowledge with great liberty: the knowledge would give one a sense of duty and the liberty a sense of enjoyment" (431). Because such knowledge and liberty are her goals, she turns down proposals of marriage from Lord Warburton and Caspar Goodwood. And she does so quite rightly because both men are modern displacements of medieval figures. Their ideas of woman as wife are feudal compared with Isabel's ideal of woman as knowing and free. In portraying them, James invoked the Victorian addiction to chivalry (which I noted in discussing *Wuthering Heights*), giving us a knight-errant in Goodwood and a feudal lord in Warburton. James presents an American businessman who is as "selfish as iron" (332), as a knight-errant. Goodwood is shown as "naturally plated and steeled, armed essentially for aggression" (155). His eyes "shine through the vizard of the helmet" (154). When he fights with Isabel, she penetrates his armor with her sharpness (156–57). When he asks her for a "pledge" (157), she gives him none at all. So he strides about "lean and hungry," keeps "his ground," and dresses his "wounds," determined to watch over her whether she likes it or not (158–59). Isabel is the Queen of Beauty to whom Goodwood vows loyalty and service and from whom he takes as reward a single kiss. But he differs from knights-errant of old in that he mostly battles his lady rather than battles for her. And when he at last proposes adultery to her, she finds him "mad" (588). Isabel can be neither his wife nor his mistress. If his passion frightens her—and it unmistakably does do that—his interdiction of her "love of liberty" (162) frightens her even more. Only after Goodwood leaves her is Isabel free: "She had not known where to turn; but she knew now. There was a straight path" (591).

Lord Warburton also offers Isabel an outdated model of what it means to be a woman. He addresses her as a feudal lord would and invites her to be his chatelaine. His sisters, Miss Molyneux and Mildred, illustrate the type of woman Isabel chooses not to be:

> "I suppose [Isabel said] you revere your brother and are rather afraid of him."
>
> "Of course one looks up to one's brother," said Miss Molyneux simply." . . .
>
> "His ability is known," Mildred added; "everyone thinks it's immense."
>
> "Oh, I can see that" said Isabel. "But if I were he I should wish to fight to the death: I mean for the heritage of the past. I should hold it tight."

"I think one ought to be liberal," Mildred argued gently.
"We've always been so, even from the earliest times."

"Ah well," said Isabel, "you've made a great success of
it; I don't wonder you like it. I see that you're very fond of
crewels." (77–78)

In the absence of a critical faculty, being a lady amounts only
to a taste in embroidery. Being a gentleman like Warburton is
largely a matter of property and power. "He owns fifty thousand acres of the soil of this little island," Mr. Touchett tells
Isabel, "and ever so many things besides. He has half a dozen
houses to live in. He has a seat in Parliament as I have one at
my own dinner table" (74). This hardly seems to qualify him as
"liberal," save perhaps in Mildred's terms. Warburton, according to Ralph, "regards himself as an imposition—as an abuse"
(71). But Warburton is not liberal enough to do away with that
abuse by disestablishing himself in any way. Ralph finds that
Warburton is "the victim of a critical age; he has ceased to believe in himself and he doesn't know what to believe in" (71).
A rich, privileged, landed feudal lord, Warburton is not suited
to be Isabel's husband. He doesn't even understand her: " 'He
thinks I'm a barbarian,' she said, 'and that I've never seen forks
and spoons' " (70). Warburton's failure of imagination is even
cruder in his pursuit of Pansy Osmond and in his eventual marriage to a woman whom he does not love. If Goodwood restricts
Isabel's freedom, so too does Warburton: she could really never
be herself with him and hope to be understood.

To marry, therefore, either the knight-errant or the feudal
lord, either Goodwood or Warburton, would be for Isabel to take
a step backward into the past rather than forward into the future.
Both men invite Isabel to choose deliberately to live intellectually and emotionally in the past. If she eventually finds herself
in a more horrifying version of a Gothic world with Osmond, it
is because she once saw herself finding "great knowledge" and
"great liberty" with Osmond. That she was frightfully mistaken
in her choice of Osmond does not at all argue that she was mistaken in her dismissal of both Goodwood and Warburton. That
she should not have married a Gothic villain does not logically
argue that she should have married either a knight-errant or a

feudal lord. As a young woman affronting her destiny, Isabel Archer cannot do herself justice by accepting either Goodwood or Warburton. Yet what she desires above all, once her quest for great knowledge and great freedom begins, is justice.

It is because Isabel is convinced that she is doing herself and Osmond justice that she agrees to marry him. When she passes her life in review in chapter 42, she asks herself a rhetorical question about Osmond: "Hadn't he all the appearance of a man living in the open air of the world, indifferent to small considerations, caring only for truth and knowledge and believing that two intelligent people ought to look for them together and, whether they found them or not, find at least some happiness in the search?" (429). To the Gilbert Osmond of this vision Isabel is determined to do the justice she feels is denied him by Ralph Touchett. "I can't enter into your idea of Mr Osmond," she tells Ralph. "I can't do it justice, because I see him in quite another way" (346). When she does come to see Osmond as Ralph sees him—as a "sterile dilettante" (345)—Isabel realizes that her husband's limitations are even greater than Goodwood's or Warburton's. The "aristocratic life" that to Isabel meant "the union of great knowledge with great liberty" is to Osmond "a thing of forms, a conscious, calculated attitude" (431). "There were certain things they must do, a certain posture they must take, certain people they must know and not know. When she saw this rigid system close about her, draped though it was in pictured tapestries," a "sense of darkness and suffocation . . . took possession of her; she had seemed shut up with an odour of mould and decay" (431). With this image of the tomb, so characteristic of Gothic fiction,[3] James gives us a pointed expression of the horror of respectability—of the fatality of European decorum, of the deadly propriety of Gothic manners. It is totally appropriate that the name Osmond should come out of a play by Monk Lewis entitled *Castle Spectre*. The Palazzo Roccanera is hardly more healthy a place: it is "the house of darkness, the house of dumbness, the house of suffocation" (429). In it, Isabel is buried alive.[4] She is no better off there than Claire de Cintré is in *The American*, a Carmelite nun in the Rue de l'Enfer—in a street named after hell itself.

Isabel had not of course expected anything like this in marrying Osmond. She had seen vistas opening to her as Osmond's wife that were not in the prospect of a Lady Warburton or a Mrs. Goodwood. But her first public appearance after her marriage presents her as bound in on all sides. The irony of Isabel's appearing as "framed" in a golden doorway is inescapable. Having been collected by Madame Merle, Isabel is framed by Gilbert Osmond. Isabel herself has supplied the gilding on the frame by bringing Osmond her fortune in marriage. The woman who above all wanted to be free—the woman whose fortune, by Ralph's reckoning, was to guarantee her freedom—has been "captured" by Gilbert Osmond's "beautiful mind" (428). The woman who wanted to combine great knowledge with great liberty sees that her "real offence . . . was her having a mind of her own at all" (432). Osmond's "egoism lay hidden like a serpent in a bank of flowers" (430). Isabel, as the image suggests, is the victim of the devil himself. She is now neither to think nor to act outside the boundaries he has set her: "he had expected his wife to feel with him and for him, to enter into his opinions, his ambitions, his preferences" (432). "Osmond's beautiful mind" gave her "neither light nor air; Osmond's beautiful mind indeed seemed to peep down from a small high window and mock at her" (429). Her function is now what Ralph once warned her it would be: "to keep guard over the sensibilities of a sterile dilettante" (345).

What James reveals in the drawing rooms of a man of taste is a degraded principle of life: Osmond pointed out to Isabel

so much of the baseness and shabbiness of life, opened her eyes so wide to the stupidity, the depravity, the ignorance of mankind, that she had been properly impressed with the infinite vulgarity of things and of the virtue of keeping one's self unspotted by it. But this base, ignoble world, it appeared, was after all what one was to live for; one was to keep it forever in one's eye, in order not to enlighten or convert or redeem it, but to extract from it some recognition of one's own superiority. On the one hand it was despicable, but on the other it afforded a standard. (430)

On this scale of values, the cardinal virtues are redefined and degraded. Prudence is degraded to a concern for worldly regard; justice is degraded to a husband's right to his wife's obedience; fortitude is degraded to her endurance of their miserable marriage; temperance is degraded to her suppression of all firm ideas and strong feelings of her own. The cardinal virtues are no longer the moral foundation of the good life as promoted by civilized manners; they are as corrupted as the manners themselves. Those manners, which should be integral to the civilized intercourse of life, are now only the empty civilities of a horrible life: Isabel sees that she and Osmond "were strangely married, at all events, and it was a horrible life" (433). Manners as dictated by respectability—extracting from the world "recognition of one's own superiority"—variously put Isabel in a dungeon that becomes a tomb and makes her the companion of an egotistical devil. Gilbert Osmond reveals to Isabel Archer what Henry James's novels suggested to Ford Madox Ford: "most people have not got souls—are in the end just the stuff with which to fill graveyards." Here where life turns deadly as manners become horrors, *The Portrait of a Lady* defines itself as a novel of Gothic manners.

One person with a soul who is nevertheless about to fill a grave is Ralph Touchett. Oddly enough—but then again not so oddly in a novel of Gothic manners—the dying Ralph is the most satisfying lover for the vital soul that is buried in Isabel Archer. The most extraordinary love scene in the novel takes place between them at his deathbed. In her intensely passionate last moments with Ralph, Isabel does justice to him and in so doing does justice to herself as well. This scene enacts the climax of the quest for justice involved in the question that *The Portrait of a Lady* asks: How can a woman give up being a girl to become a lady without giving up being her *self*? How can Isabel Archer give up being a naive American girl to become a sophisticated European lady without giving up what is vitally essential to being herself? Isabel, as a girl, flatters herself that she is "a very just woman" (59). She promises to do Warburton "justice" (109). She shows a "passionate desire to be just" and tells Ralph "I am very just"

(342) when they discuss Osmond. In the midst of her unhappy marriage she prays, "Whatever happens to me let me not be unjust" (404). And as her quest approaches its climax, Isabel finds her "old passion for justice" reasserting itself (537). Seeking justice, then, Isabel makes her life a case; but, at the same time, seeking an understanding of her *self*, she makes it a riddle. The case demands a judgment on whether she has acted justly; the riddle asks how she can be woman and lady, friend and fiancée, sister and wife, and still be herself. Isabel's gradual understanding of the full implications of justice and of selfhood informs her relationship with every man in the novel. It also reforms her relationships with Mrs. Touchett, Madame Merle, and Pansy. And, finally, it places Osmond, once her complementary lover, increasingly in tension with Ralph, who becomes ever more completely her affined lover. This telescoping of case (seeking justice) with riddle (seeking selfhood) is the focal point for James as he paints his portrait of Isabel Archer. The niceness of the case and the baffling quality of the riddle are immediately evident when Gilbert Osmond requires Isabel as his wife to bring her lover, Warburton, to propose marriage to his daughter, Pansy. How in this complex of demanding relationships is Isabel Archer herself to survive? How can she do justice to all the parties involved and to herself as well?

As Osmond's spouse, Isabel manifests a concern for their marriage by limiting her freedom of action and trying to do as her husband wishes: "It seemed to Isabel that if she could make it her duty to bring" Warburton to propose to Pansy "she should play the part of a good wife" (415). But whereas "play[ing] the part" satisfies Osmond's desire that she appear "a good wife," it threatens her personal integrity. Isabel has instinctively been opposed to a match between Warburton and Pansy—"at first it had not presented itself in a manner to excite her enthusiasm" (414)—but "the idea of assisting her husband to be pleased" allows her to rationalize the suitability of the proposed match (417). When she decides to help Osmond, she, for a moment, feels good about being a useful spouse. But James's subtle psychological dramatization of Isabel's emotional makeup shows her instinctive life rebelling against her rationalized sense of wifely duty: "After all she couldn't rise to it; something held her and made this impossible" (417). Without fully understanding the reasons for her actions, Isabel begins to play what Osmond later calls "a very deep game" (481). Before she instructs Pansy to obey her father and accept Warburton if he proposes, Isabel prevents Warburton from proposing. Her visit to Pansy becomes therefore simply a calculated act of self-justification. Isabel now lives in a world where such acts of casuistry have become a wearisome necessity. When Madame Merle tells Isabel that she, Madame Merle, is going to ask Pansy what Isabel had to say about Warburton, we know that Pansy will report that Isabel told her to accept Warburton if he proposes marriage. But we also know that Warburton will not ask Pansy to marry him. Isabel has had it both ways. She has done Osmond a legalistic kind of justice by literally following his advice in telling Warburton to send his letter of proposal and in instructing Pansy to obey her father; at the same time Isabel has done Warburton, Pansy, and herself justice too by seeing to it that Warburton does not send the letter and consequently that Pansy will not need to obey her father. James puts Isabel through this extraordinary performance to demonstrate what a tight spot she finds herself in; indeed, to demonstrate what it means for a once carefree girl now to have become a careful lady. The myth of concern that is generated in Isabel by her marriage is at this moment directly at war with the myth of freedom that is the spring of her vitality. James's realistic characterization of Isabel shows her adapting painfully to her surroundings. When James, as Theodora Bosanquet reported, "walked out of the refuge of his study into the world and looked about him, he saw a place of torment, where creatures of prey perpetually thrust their claws into the quivering flesh of the doomed, defenseless children of light" (33). Accommodation is necessary to survival. In Rome, Isabel does as the Romans do: she becomes supersubtle. Such are the measures the children of light must take to survive in the "darkened . . . world" (425). *Il faut hurler avec les loups*. That is what it means to be a *lady*.

But Isabel is not quite the Roman wolf that Madame Merle is. She avoids the trap that would make her so. In the chapters treating Pansy's courtship, Isabel has the chance to do for her husband what Madame Merle has already done for him: she has a chance to secure a spouse for an Osmond. Although Madame

Merle tries to revivify her life of feeling through Isabel—she has Isabel marry her lover and mother her child—Isabel refuses to give Serena Merle the last satisfaction she craves. Isabel refuses to become the damned creature that Osmond has made of his former mistress. Madame Merle—who tells Osmond, "You've dried up my soul" (522)—tells Isabel that "if we can't have youth within us we can have it outside, and I really think we see it and feel it better that way" (195). When we think about it for a minute, the differences between a Madame Merle and a Miss Havisham are superficial at best, as are the differences between a Compeyson and an Osmond. Both women are caught in the same Lacanian plot of trying to define themselves through others who are fated to act on their own as both Estella and Isabel (and in a small way Pansy too) do. Both Miss Havisham and Madame Merle seek to live the life they lost in younger versions of themselves who disappoint them. Serena Merle—who, according to Ralph, "got herself into perfect training, but had won none of the prizes" (252)—wants to win Warburton with Isabel's help so that she can live vicariously through Pansy. "She has failed so dreadfully," says the Countess Gemini of Madame Merle, "that she's determined her daughter shall make up for it" (547). But Isabel disappoints "the cleverest woman" in Europe turned emotional vampire. Isabel refuses, in the imagery of the novel, to serve the devil and lose her soul.[5] In playing the Roman lady by doing what the Romans do, Isabel finds and holds onto some shreds of her identity and begins to present herself as a woman to be reckoned with—an identity that she arguably possesses even more fully and formidably at the end of the novel when she leaves for Rome following Ralph's funeral.

Isabel's decision to return to Rome is the culmination of a pattern of knowing and choosing that first manifests itself dramatically in her decision to go to the dying Ralph against her husband's wishes. After talking with the Countess Gemini, who reveals to Isabel the past life of Osmond and Madame Merle, Isabel's head is "humming with new knowledge" (548), and she decides to go to Ralph at Gardencourt. This decision is the beginning of what becomes an abbreviated life of greater knowledge and greater liberty which, until that moment, eluded Isabel during her mar-

riage to Osmond. The structural logic of chapters 50 through 55 is
to provide Isabel with more and more knowledge so that she can
make a thoroughly enlightened choice at the end of the novel.
In chapter 50 Isabel learns from Ned Rosier that he has sold his
bibelots for fifty thousand dollars to make himself more acceptable in Osmond's eyes as a suitor to Pansy. In chapter 51 Isabel
learns from the Countess that Madame Merle was Osmond's
mistress and is the mother of Pansy. In chapter 52 Isabel learns
from Madame Merle that Ralph is the architect of her fortune.
In chapter 53 Isabel learns from Henrietta that Mr. Bantling and
Henrietta will marry and settle in England. In chapter 54 Isabel
learns from Mrs. Touchett that Lord Warburton is soon to marry.
And in chapter 55 Isabel learns from Goodwood the meaning
of passionate love. This new knowledge crowds in upon Isabel
and leads her to make a series of judgments: Madame Merle
is wicked, Osmond vulgar, Mrs. Touchett dry, Henrietta un-
original, Warburton dead, and Goodwood mad. Isabel finds all
her friends wanting, and, with Ralph in the grave, Isabel consequently finds herself very much alone, "humming with new
knowledge" and prepared to make a final choice.

This intensified pattern of knowing and choosing is a late
and realistic achievement of Isabel's earlier romantic desire for
great knowledge and great liberty. This pattern also rapidly
rounds out a compositional structure that has been leisurely built
on interior events like gaining knowledge, formulating judgments, and making choices. And this pattern is likewise James's
contribution to the form of the novel that he appropriated from
Turgenev, who said of his own work that it lacked architecture
(*PL* vii). So that finally this pattern allows James to provide a
frame for a view of life that he attributed to Turgenev but that
was also very much his own:

Life *is*, in fact, a battle. On this point optimists and pessi-
mists agree. Evil is insolent and strong; beauty enchanting
but rare; goodness very apt to be weak; folly very apt to be
defiant; wickedness to carry the day; imbeciles to be in great
places, people of sense in small, and mankind generally, unhappy. But the world as it stands is no illusion, no phantasm,
no evil dream of a night; we wake up to it again and for ever

and ever; we can neither forget it nor deny it nor dispense
with it. We can welcome experience as it comes, and give it
what it demands, in exchange for something which it is idle
to pause to call much or little so long as it contributes to swell
the volume of consciousness. In this there is mingled pain
and delight, but over the mysterious mixture there hovers a
visible rule, that bids us learn to will and seek to understand.
(*Literary Criticism: French* 998)

The Portrait of a Lady dramatizes Isabel Archer's life as a battle,
and it shows her experience of mingled pain and delight swelling
the volume of her consciousness and teaching her to learn to will
and to seek to understand.

Taking his cue from Turgenev, James attempted to reshape
the English novel as it was bequeathed to him by George Eliot:
Middlemarch "sets a limit" for James "to the development of
the old fashioned English novel" (*Literary Criticism: Essays* 965).
James thought of *Middlemarch* as both the "strongest" and the
"weakest" of English novels, and he identified the weakness
with what he saw as its "diffuseness": its unwillingness to center
on Dorothea Brooke and its giving nearly equal importance to
the stories of Lydgate, Bulstrode, and Mary Garth. For James,
then, *Middlemarch* appeared to be "a mere chain of episodes."
What he demanded in a novel was "an organized, molded, bal-
anced composition, gratifying the reader with a sense of design
and construction" (*Literary Criticism: Essays* 958). To achieve that
ideal James centers his novel on one character and, with that
choice, transforms Dorothea Brooke's struggles with duty and
respectability into Isabel Archer's passion for justice in a darkened world.

Along with the overall design of *Middlemarch*, James also
set out to reform its ending. The flash of lightning in *Middlemarch*, which leads to a kiss that unites Dorothea and Ladislaw
for life, becomes a metaphor in *The Portrait* for a kiss that separates Goodwood from Isabel. James transforms a sign of sentiment into a signal for separation; therefore, what he considered
a realistic ending for his novel leaves everything to the reader's
imagination.

But when darkness returned [Isabel] was free. She never looked about her; she only darted from the spot. There were lights in the windows of the house; they shone far across the lawn. In an extraordinarily short time—for the distance was considerable—she had moved through the darkness (for she saw nothing) and reached the door. Here only she paused. She looked all about her; she listened a little; then she put her hand on the latch. She had not known where to turn; but she knew now. There was a very straight path. (591)

This is the second time that Isabel pauses in this doorway. She leaves the novel as she entered it, through "the ample doorway" of Gardencourt (15). In chapter 2 she stepped into the light of "a splendid summer afternoon," a "tall girl in a black dress" (5), and declared, "I am very fond of my liberty" (21). Between the framed picture of the girl who is fond of her liberty and the framed picture of the woman who is free comes the portrait of a lady, framed in a doorway of the Palazzo Roccanera: "The years had touched her only to enrich her; the flower of her youth had not faded, it only hung more quietly on its stem. She had lost something of that quick eagerness to which her husband had privately taken exception—she had more the air of being able to wait. Now, at all events, framed in the gilded doorway, she . . . [was] the picture of a gracious lady" (367). The three presentations of Isabel as framed in doorways are three portraits of her at different stages of her existence. The first, Isabel framed in the Gardencourt doorway, shows her as an American girl in love with her freedom. The second, Isabel in the gilded doorway of the Palazzo Roccanera, shows her as the European lady hemmed in by a concern to present herself as Osmond's wife and handmaiden. The third, Isabel barely visible in the dark but once again framed in the Gardencourt doorway, shows her as the woman who has regained some modicum of her freedom. The three portraits represent Isabel in the three phases of her existence. The first shows her as a representative of the myth of freedom; in it the great round world lies before her as brightly and as broadly as the Gardencourt lawns in the summer sunshine. The second shows Isabel as a representative of the myth of concern, Osmond now having reduced her great round world to a tiny circle defined by his own exquisite "taste": "a thing of forms, a conscious, calculated attitude." The third shows Isabel as a representative of an integrated life of freedom and concern, Goodwood's proposal having given the last stroke to her characterization when she rejects his final plea: "We can do absolutely as we please; to whom under the sun do we owe anything? What is it that holds us, what is it that has the smallest right to interfere in such a question as this? . . . The world's all before us—and the world's very big. I know something about that" (590). Goodwood's argument articulates precisely what was once Isabel's sense of the world.

When she stepped out of the ample doorway onto the Gardencourt lawn for the first time, "she had a fixed determination to regard the world as a place of brightness, of free expansion, of irresistible action" (51). Isabel's rebuttal of Goodwood sums up the changes that four years have worked in her: "The world's very small" (590). Isabel's sense of herself is now such that it is only in that smaller world where she has planted the roots of her concern that she can allow her freedom to grow. She needs coherence and continuity in her life to face the facts that finally confront her: Ralph, generously, made her fortune, and Madame Merle, selfishly, made her marriage; Osmond, who once loved her but now hates her, vulgarly married her for her money; Ralph adored her, but Osmond wanted her to adore him; Ralph's life was beautiful, but others' lives are not; Pansy needs her, and Isabel has promised to help her; Osmond without Madame Merle, who is to leave Rome and even Europe perhaps, is at half strength at best; and, finally, "the day when she should have to take back something she had solemnly bestown" now rapidly approaches (462). What dominates *The Portrait of a Lady*, as James's analysis of Turgenev's novels suggests, is his heroine's need first to understand her situation and then to choose to do something about it. But as Elsa Nettels argues, the resolution of the novel cannot appropriately be effected by a change in Isabel's "external circumstances, for the rewards of Isabel's experience lie in the inward change, in her deeper knowledge of herself and the other characters" (13). No other character understands as much as she does by the time the novel ends. Isabel knows at last that she cannot be free without having the truths she has discovered become the basis of the last choice she makes.

The advantage that Isabel has over Osmond is that he fears these same truths because they threaten to expose his pose as "first gentleman in Europe." Because Ralph is dying and dying men tell the truth, Osmond objects to Isabel's visiting her cousin: "It's dishonorable; it's indelicate; it's indecent," says Osmond, for Isabel to "travel across Europe alone . . . to sit at the bedside of other men" (536). But Isabel does not finally care how things look; she finally does not care for her own or for Osmond's respectability. Isabel, the narrator says, "lost all shame, all wish to hide things" (575). Her last moments with Ralph, not her final minute with Goodwood,[6] consequently constitute the great love scene in the novel. Isabel, kneeling at Ralph's bedside, holding the dying man in her arms, is "supremely together" with him (575): " 'And remember this . . . that if you've been hated, you've also been loved. Ah but, Isabel, *adored*!' he just audibly and lingeringly breathed. 'Oh my brother!' she cried with a movement of still deeper prostration" (578). This follows on what the narrator calls Isabel's "passionate need to cry out and accuse herself, to let her sorrow possess her" (576). This is unmistakably a love scene of considerable power even though it contains no explicitly erotic event. It takes place in a man's bedroom, the woman has lost all shame, the man is dying in the woman's arms, the lovers are supremely together, and they experience a great moment of ecstasy, followed by exhaustion. James rewrote this passage to emphasize the ecstasy and the exhaustion. What Ralph said to Isabel in the 1881 edition of *The Portrait* was "that if you've been hated, you have also been loved." Nothing more. Isabel's response was, "Ah, my brother!" According to F. O. Matthiessen, the James of the 1908 *Portrait*, "felt impelled to a more high-keyed emotional register" (172). This passage shows that clearly. If John Donne once used a vocabulary of knowing and dying to express the power of sexual love,[7] James now uses a vocabulary of sexual love to express the power of knowing and dying. "In the world of Isabel Archer," Stephen Donadio writes, " 'the bribes and lures, the beguilements and prizes,' may be many, but the prize is still 'within' " (81). So Henry James's great love scene is a moment of truth in which Isabel Archer's soul is ravished by the adoration of Ralph Touchett.

Ralph is Isabel's lover in the romantic tradition of affined souls. Isabel's every encounter with Goodwood is a battle: they clash like knights in the lists with the clatter of arms overwhelming words of love. They are anything but lovers who are alike. Ralph, however, begins the novel as Isabel's "cousin," becomes her "best friend" (462), and ends it her "brother." Brothers and sisters are frequently lovers in Gothic novels; and, as Elizabeth MacAndrew reminds us, they exist as "uncorrupted figures in a harsh and wicked world" (67). Ralph is Isabel's affined lover because he is, in Tony Tanner's words, "her true image of what her self wants to be" ("Fearful" 157). Isabel, who wanted to make her life a work of art, now pronounces Ralph's to have been "beautiful" (570). Appropriately, Ralph never allows anyone to use the room that Isabel once used at Gardencourt; Ralph keeps Isabel's room inviolate in the same way that Heathcliff kept Cathy's at Wuthering Heights: "something told Isabel that it had not been slept in since she occupied it" (570). Ralph's serious decline in health begins with Isabel's engagement to Osmond: "He felt cold about the heart; he had never liked anything less" (339). So just as the last years of his life were centered on Isabel —"It was for you that I wanted . . . to live," he tells her (504)— so is his death. In the great tradition of romantic love, Ralph's death is a *Liebestod*.[8] James dramatizes in this love scene between Isabel and Ralph the truth that Hans Castorp nicely articulates to Claudia Cauchat in *The Magic Mountain*: that love (*l'amour*) and death (*la mort*) are so entangled in the body as to be scarcely distinguishable: *"Oui, ils sont charnels tous deux, l'amour et la mort, et voilà leur terreur et leur grande magie!"* (Mann 342). James makes it difficult for his readers to distinguish between *l'amour* and *la mort* when, by telling each other the truth, Isabel finds love and Ralph death.

Part of the truth they speak anticipates the ending of the novel:

> Then he murmured simply: "You must stay here."
> "I should like to stay—as long as seems right."

"As seems right—as seems right?" He repeated her words. "Yes, you think a great deal about that."
"Of course one must." (577)

After Isabel has thought a great deal about what "seems right" —about where justice lies—she starts back to Rome.[9] She goes back as a woman who has seen her lover's ghost. Ralph, "the only true living spirit she has ever known" (Banta 172), once told Isabel that to see such a ghost at Gardencourt was a "privilege" given only to those who "have suffered greatly, have gained some miserable knowledge" (48). "She apparently had fulfilled the necessary condition; for the next morning, in the cold, faint dawn, she knew that a spirit was standing by her bed. . . . She stared a moment; she saw his white face—his kind eyes, then she saw there was nothing. She was not afraid; she was only sure" (578–79). These eight words are Ralph's only legacy to Isabel; he leaves her no other. Having faced the past with Ralph, Isabel now faces the future without him. He has bequeathed her strength and certainty.

Writing of the fate of Louis Trevelyan in Trollope's *He Knew He Was Right*, James—finding Trevelyan "living in a desolate villa on a hilltop near Siena"—sees a conclusion so determinedly real that he judges it worthy of Balzac in its pitilessness: "Here and in several other places Trollope has dared to be thoroughly logical; he has not sacrificed to conventional optimism; he has not been afraid of a misery which should be too much like life" (*Literary Criticism: Essays* 1351). This should be taken as a comment as much on James's own endings as on Trollope's, in the same way that James's analysis of Turgenev's sense of life as a battle is really a comment on James's own sense of life. The ending of *The Portrait of a Lady* avoids easy solutions and the kind of closure that James constantly criticized in George Eliot's novels, not excluding *Middlemarch*.[10] The open ending of *The Portrait* is meant to stimulate the reader's moral imagination: reading the novel is meant to provide the reader with "great knowledge" which, in itself, ensures the reader "great liberty" in supplying a meaning for the conclusion of Isabel's story.[11] The novel is written to allow the reader to emulate life insofar as life bids us all to "learn to

will and seek to understand." Now among the many ways of
understanding the ending, two seem to represent opposite poles
of the range of choice: one reading follows Jacques Lacan and
pushes *The Portrait* more deeply into a world of Gothic manners;
the other follows Mikhail Bakhtin and suggests a gradual emergence from the world of Gothic manners; both readings require
a theory of the *Other*.

When Henrietta tells Goodwood that Isabel has left for Rome,
she is saying that Isabel—somehow, some way—is going to confront Osmond. Gilbert Osmond constitutes the principal Other
for Isabel. For Lacan the Other is definitive of the self. The
Other is the inescapable mirror image through which the subject acquires a self that is always inadequate because "to know
oneself through an external image is to be defined through self-
alienation" (Silverman 158). Osmond is perhaps the best example
of a person whose own identity has been and continues to be
defined by lack. Neither Osmond's first wife nor Madame Merle
nor Isabel has brought him fulfillment; in the delusive hope that
Pansy may, he has imprisoned her in a convent until she agrees
not to marry Ned Rosier and comes round to marrying a man he
selects for her. As a collector not only of women but also of art
objects and public adulation, Osmond is a classic Lacanian example of someone after an object (Lacan calls it *objet petit a[utre]*)
"that derives its value from its identification with some missing component of the subject's self, whether the loss is seen as
primordial, as the result of a bodily organization, or as the consequence of some other division" (Silverman 156). In the world
of hopeless cases, Gilbert Osmond is the most hopeless: "He has
a genius for upholstery" (385). For Isabel to return to Osmond
further allows him to attempt to define himself through her as
Other. Since he cannot do that by love, he must do it by mastery:
as her "appointed and inscribed master" (462). Osmond's first
wife died mysteriously; his estranged mistress accused him of
drying up her soul; his present wife knows he hates her. Even
if Isabel returns to Osmond under the impulse of being true to
"the most serious act—the single sacred act—of her life" (463),
the best she can hope for is the worst because such idealism
would be an indication only of some lack in her; it would de-

rive its value, just as in Osmond's case, from an identification with something missing in herself. Indeed, it would be Isabel's acquiescence to the cultural values which have been defined for women by men, "values which define male subjectivity within patriarchal society" (Silverman 183). These values, having established an outpost in her mind by her treating them as ideals, would overthrow her in her weakness which, delusively and ironically, presents itself to her as her strength, her virtue. In this Lacanian reading of the meaning of the ending of *The Portrait*, respectability would be preserved—Isabel would appear "as solemn . . . as a Cimabue Madonna" (210)[12]—and, in the soil of that respectability, the manners that sustain its horrors would flourish.

Bakhtin's reading of the process of self-realization is the opposite of Lacan's. If for Lacan there is an inevitable dismemberment of a total self, for Bakhtin there is a continual movement toward a self that is never total but always capable of further realization: "The Bakhtinian self is never whole, since it can exist only dialogically" (Clark and Holquist 65). Lacan looks back to what it is impossible to recover; Bakhtin looks forward to what it is possible to become. For Bakhtin there is no self without the Other: there is no subjectivity without intersubjectivity. "Bakhtin conceives of otherness as the ground of all existence and of dialogue as the primal structure of any particular existence, representing a constant exchange between what is already and what is not yet" (Clark and Holquist 65). For Isabel Osmond's ineluctable presence makes him the Other against whom she must define herself. Isabel has yet to do herself and Pansy complete justice. She has further to understand her obligations to the single sacred act of her life—"marriage meant that a woman should cleave to the man with whom, uttering tremendous vows, she had stood at the altar" (540)—by a revaluation of her marriage now that she knows about Osmond's past and has experienced Goodwood's passion and accepted Ralph's love. Isabel, having faced and routed Madame Merle, has demonstrated that she is capable of dealing with Osmond, whom Madame Merle represents: "that Madame Merle had lost her pluck and saw before her the phantom of exposure—this in itself was a revenge, this in itself was almost the promise of a brighter day" (552). The heterological nature of discourse that Bakhtin exposes and espouses has led Isabel to victory in this confrontation. She has learned from the world of gossip and infidelity that characterizes the Countess Gemini. She confronts the discourse of brilliant "deviltry" and "vile[ness]" that characterizes Madame Merle (522), "a woman who had long been mistress of the art of conversation" (551). In Pansy's convent, "a well-appointed prison" (549) that Osmond calls "a school for good manners" (532), Isabel intuits the discourse of her husband's heartless cruelty: "Osmond wished it to be known that he shrank from nothing" (553). She is deeply touched by the discourse of young love and tells Pansy, "I won't desert you" (557); "I'll come back" (558). In these scenes with Madame Merle and Pansy, Isabel grows in a strength and tenderness that carry over to her dismissal of Goodwood's passion and her acceptance of Ralph's love. In short, the closing chapters of *The Portrait of a Lady* may be read as showing Isabel Archer immersed in a world of heterological discourse and becoming more aware and assured of herself in the process: "She was not afraid; she was only sure."

Reading the end of the novel from the perspective of Bakhtin does not guarantee Isabel's triumph over Osmond or Pansy's marriage to Ned Rosier, nor does it shut down the moral imagination that James sought to stimulate in his readers. It suggests, simply, that Isabel is better prepared to enter into dialogue with the Other and that Osmond's world of Gothic manners now has less purchase on her because she better understands his "blasphemous sophistry" (537) as well as the complexities and commitments of justice and love. In other words, a Bakhtinian perspective makes sense of what Irene Santos identifies as "the central irony" of *The Portrait of a Lady*: "that in the cold and selfish Osmond Isabel finds the person who of all the characters can best bring to maturity her potential strength and nobility" (577).

7

Jude the Obscure

Gothic Manners in Western Civilization

Henry James and Thomas Hardy seem not to have had much in common.[1] James's review of *Far from the Madding Crowd* as an inferior *Silas Marner*—"the only things we believe in are the sheep and the dogs" (*Nation* 424)—is an indication of sensibilities that have little to do with each other. And Violet Hunt recorded in her diary for 3 January 1896 that "Henry James expressed his disapprobation, laboriously, of 'Jude'" (Secor 5). Indeed, the differences between James and Hardy achieved an epiphanic moment in A. C. Benson's unhappy attempt to entertain the two great men together: Benson "noted how deafness prevented either from hearing what the other was saying" (Gittings, *Thomas Hardy's Later Years* 107). A novel like *Jude the Obscure* seems, at first at least, much more in the tradition of Dickens, as Philip Collins suggests, and of Eliot too, than of James. Hardy uses a

thoroughly English tradition to give form to the raw material of
his life when he transmutes it into fiction in *Jude*.

Jude the Obscure is "a personal statement" (Millgate 329). Jude
Fawley is "the embodiment of, almost a scapegoat for, a long
accumulation of personal and family distress" (Millgate 350).
Hardy first named him Jack Head because his "suffering through
poverty" and the family curse that lies upon him were originally
associated with Hardy's grandmother, Mary Head of Fawley.
Her father died the year she was born and her mother when
Mary was only six years old. She was taken in by her uncle's
family, but his wife and sons died when Mary was eleven (Gittings, *Young Thomas Hardy* 329). Jack Head was a "parish boy relation" of hers, and, like Jude, was a "bird-scarer." The character
of Jude is further indebted to Hardy's uncle, John ("Jack") Antell,
and to his teacher and friend, Horatio ("Horace") Mosley Moule.
Antell was a self-taught man with a "fatal weakness for drink"
(*Young Thomas Hardy* 217, 218) A cobbler by trade, he taught
himself Latin and opened his own Latin school. "He dreamt of
going to college, but poverty, hard work, and drink banished the
dream." His death at age sixty-two was "hastened by exposure
through having spent the night in a ditch after a drunken bout"
(*Young Thomas Hardy* 15).[2] Jude dies after spreading his blanket
and lying down outdoors "in the teeth of a north-east wind and
rain" (*JO* 470). Moule also had a weakness for drink because, like
Jude, he at times became "melancholy mad" (*JO* 176) and drank
to forget his misery. He was a classical scholar who left Trinity
College, Oxford, in 1854 without a degree. Moule fathered an
illegitimate child by a Dorchester county girl and committed suicide in 1873. His bastard son grew up in Australia where he
died by hanging. The death of the brilliant, generous, and beloved Moule, who took "virtual control of Hardy's life in 1857,"
left the novelist a changed man (*Young Thomas Hardy* 38). After
it, "Hardy never portrayed a man who was not, in some way,
maimed by fate" (*Young Thomas Hardy* 186). In Horace Moule's
failure at Oxford and his problems with drink, sex, and suici-
dal depression, Hardy found essential aspects of Jude Fawley's
character; in Moule's hanged Australian bastard, he found the
figure of Little Father Time.

Both Antell and Moule gave Hardy a vivid illustration of Schopenhauer's pessimistic philosophy in which Idea falls victim to Will. He saw in their fate that the conception of the world as rational and ordered is an idealization which mistakenly insists that life can be understood and is worth living. Antell destroyed by drink and Moule destroyed by sex as well as drink showed man's mind as enslaved to a "blind, self-perpetuating force operating through man and nature alike." What Nietzsche said, Hardy believed and dramatized: "Apollo is, in effect, only the disguise worn by Dionysos for purposes of self-deception" (Rajan 35, 36). These early experiences of Hardy, along with an unhappy London love affair with "a schoolmistress" of "advanced or freethinking opinions," settled him "in the belief that any supreme power must be ignorant or indifferent to any form of human life" (Gittings, *Young Thomas Hardy* 93, 213). Hardy's loss of faith in 1865 translates into Jude's in the novel. Fawley's love for his cousin Sue also mirrors Hardy's for his cousins, the Sparks sisters, especially Tryphena, who studied at a training college, as Sue did, and worked for a bachelor schoolmaster not unlike Phillotson (*Young Thomas Hardy* 218). The rigid dogmatism that claims Sue's mind in the last part of the novel had its analogue in "the narrowest form of sectarian Protestant prejudice" that Hardy observed in his own wife, Emma, as well as in the "high Church leanings" of Mrs. Florence Henniker (*Young Thomas Hardy* 213, 219), whose first name became Sue's second and with whom Hardy was hopelessly in love in the 1890s. The marriage question that absorbs so much creative energy in the novel is directly related to Hardy's own unhappy marriage and his abortive romance. With Sue resembling one woman from whom he had grown estranged and another who would not accept his love, Hardy finally has Jude say to her, "Sue, Sue, you are not worth a man's love!" (469). That the name is repeated— Sue is both Emma and Florence—is telling.

Hardy shapes this raw material of his life in the tradition of *Great Expectations* and *Middlemarch* and shows both how alike and how different Jude's world is from those projected by Dickens and Eliot.[3] *Middlemarch* is echoed in the marriage of Sue and Phillotson. The May-January union reappears, the girl as wife-secretary to the middle-aged scholar repeats itself, and the "Key to all Mythologies" gives way to the "Roman Antiquities of Wessex." But in Hardy's novel the inconvenient husband does not die; the young lover does. *Jude* suggests what might have been had Casaubon lived and Ladislaw died. It announces the end of the possibilities that were so alive in *Middlemarch*. Ladislaw the alien becomes the leader that Arnold called for in *Culture and Anarchy*. Jude the obscure becomes nothing but a corpse. His sad life proclaims that there can be no more great expectations. Indeed, Jude begins his novel like Pip does his, but he ends it differently. Just as Pip's life is turned upside down by Magwitch at the beginning of *Great Expectations*, Jude's is set in a dizzying whirl by Farmer Troutham. From that moment his life changes. Gentle respectability becomes his goal too. Pip gets £500 a year to live on, precisely the sum Jude proposed to hold back for himself from the £5,000 a year he would get when he became a bishop. The difference between Pip and Jude is that Pip gets what he expects and learns a lesson; Jude gets nothing and curses the day he was born. Hardy explodes such romantic expectations. Heredity and environment, nature and society, the psyche and love are too much for one man to cope with. Pip succeeds because he is never alone; someone is always there and fellow feeling is alive. Jude fails because he is too much alone and fellow feeling is dead. Pip survives his brain fever because Joe is there. Jude dies of fever because no one is there: "Water—some water—Sue—Arabella!" (485), he cries, but no one answers. The death wish that Mrs. Joe had for Pip is thwarted; the death wish that Drusilla Fawley had for Jude is fulfilled. Dickens' novel may sometimes be grotesque, but Hardy's is frequently horrible.

These traces of Dickens and Eliot in Hardy's fiction lead us back to Hardy and James to suggest, if less insistently, what the similarities are between *The Portrait of a Lady* and *Jude the Obscure*. Given the differences between their authors' sensibilities, these novels show extraordinary affinities which demonstrate how Hardy pushes beyond James to a new philosophical position that pillories the manners of European society as historically anachronistic, intellectually arrested, and morally destructive. If James gives the lie to the surface of European culture, Hardy gives the lie to its roots in the feudal mores of Western civilization. James's symbol is the dark house, Hardy's is the dark city—the dark city that is supposed to be the city of light. If Isabel returns to Palazzo Roccanera and an ambivalent life at the end of her novel, Jude returns to Christminster and certain death at the end of his. *The Portrait* presents us with a *Liebestod* in the death of Ralph; *Jude* presents us with one in the death of Fawley. Isabel returns to Osmond; Sue to Phillotson. The death of Isabel's child marks, in the structure of her novel, the death of her love for Osmond: only after the child dies do Isabel and Osmond make their first appearance as husband and wife; by then, they are antagonists. The death of Sue's children marks her decisive break with Jude. Goodwood's kiss, metaphorically rendered as Isabel's drowning, shows passion and death as one, just as they are telescoped in the death of her child, the offspring of her and Osmond's first passion. The death of Sue's children indicates to her the evil of the passion that begot them. Nature's law of "mutual butchery" (378) is God's sign to Jude and Sue that their love is cursed. If Goodwood's kiss is an overwhelming force that influences Isabel's choice to go back, that choice is decidedly personal. For Sue the choice of Phillotson over Jude is cosmic: she is overwhelmed by God's acting through nature. She has to obey. Whereas Isabel's morality has an aesthetic dimension related to making her life beautiful, Sue's choice has a cosmological determination. We today might readily find that both Isabel and Sue invoke the aesthetics and cosmology of moral choice specifically as defenses against their own passional life. But that should not prevent our also seeing Isabel's choice as inwardly directed toward a harmony in her life and Sue's as outwardly directed toward a harmony with a natural order and its cultural embodiment in the social ethics of Christminster, the theological and philosophical interpreter of the cosmos.

Hardy's genius in *Jude* is to show how Christminster applies the final force that destroys individuals already weakened by nature (heredity and laws governing the survival of the fittest) and nurture (familial rejection and feudal concepts of right and wrong that form an imperious superego). Hardy presents in his novel characters who are pathetically weak, a nature that is tragically savage, and a society that is incorrigibly self-righteous. *Jude the Obscure*, consequently, dramatizes Christminster as a society that breaks characters like Sue and Jude who are already weakened in the fight for survival—"Cruelty is the law pervading all nature and society" (389)—by the simple fact of being human beings who were born, reared, and socialized. Whereas nature has no choice in what it does, society does have a choice. Thus while lamenting natural conditions,[4] Hardy fixes blame on social conditions. Sue and Jude are not so much to blame as the society that blames them. The enemy in the novel is the medieval mind and heart of Christminster, a modern city that refuses to come of age. If a certain lack of clarity pervades Hardy's novel because of the way his own life is implicated in those of Jude and Sue, he does nevertheless make a clear case against society by concentrating his attention on the marriage question. In that question—and consequently in the question of divorce too—Hardy finds God, man, and nature present to the degree that theological doctrine, moral and civil law, and sexual passion complicate marriage and divorce. Hardy shows that for individuals as physically, intellectually, and emotionally weak as Jude and Sue are, Christminster is a hindrance to life and living. He presents in Jude and Sue a species of modern man and woman; he presents in Christminster a species of medieval civilization: feudal in social law and Scholastic in moral law. Hardy shows, in short, modern feeling confronting outmoded forms for structuring that feeling. Insofar as a medieval consciousness is incorporated in every aspect of Christminster from stones to Scholastic theology, that city is a Gothic city. With this city at the center of his universe in *Jude the Obscure*, Hardy moves the novel of Gothic manners to a new permutation. He makes the Gothic city into the Gothic horror.

Hardy presents the central problem of *Jude the Obscure* as a case that turns into a riddle. The case centers on the meaning of marriage; and, when that cannot be determined, the word *marriage* becomes a riddle. Jude and Sue cannot solve the riddle; therefore, one dies and the other is doomed to find no happiness until she dies. Meanwhile each lives in torment: the word *torture* in one form or another haunts their marriages to Arabella and Phillotson and describes their inability to marry each other. Jude's life is summed up as "hell": "It *was* hell—'the hell of conscious failure,' both in ambition and in love" (176). Sue is also

in "hell" in her marriage to Phillotson (317): "I have been thinking," she says, ". . . that the social moulds civilization fits us into
have no more relation to our actual shapes than the conventional
shapes of the constellations have to the real star-patterns. I am
called Mrs. Richard Phillotson, living a calm wedded life with
my counterpart of that name. But I am not really Mrs. Richard
Phillotson, but a woman tossed about, all alone, with aberrant
passions, and unaccountable antipathies" (266). To be Phillotson's wife is for Sue to be "tortured . . . to death" by him (305).

Although Jude and Sue differ in their thinking on many
subjects, and so give the impression of being discordant, if not
complementary, lovers, they are really affined lovers—theirs, as
Shelley writes in "Epipsychidion," is "difference without dis-
cord" (line 144)—because they have the same soul: they are epi-
psyches, one of the other.[5] They are "counterparts" (197), "one
person split in two" (293), "two parts of a single whole" (361):

> One hope within two wills, one will beneath
> Two overshadowing minds, one life, one death,
> One Heaven, one Hell, one immortality,
> And one annihilation.
>
> ("Epipsychidion," lines 584–87)

In a passage in Hardy's manuscript that was deleted from the
printed text, Jude sees Sue as "the rough material called himself
done into another sex" (Millgate 352). This intense sense of identification of one with another is dramatically realized when Sue
changes into Jude's clothes and sits in his chair in his room. In
the best tradition of romantic love, then, Sue is Jude's "affined
soul" (170): "I am not thine: I am part of *thee*" ("Epipsychidion,"
line 52). Together they recall the androgynous entity that Aristophanes described in the *Symposium* as threatening the gods.

But neither the God of Christminster nor their spouses will
tolerate Jude and Sue as an entity. Their marriages to Arabella
and Phillotson are the marriages sanctioned by civil and canon
law. These loveless marriages to supposedly complementary
partners make Jude and Sue into romantic lovers who eventually experience *Liebestod* as a physical and emotional reality.
That is so because their socially approved marriages are expres-
sions of a myth of concern that has the blessing of canon law

and the sanction of civil law, whereas their extramarital love for each other expresses a myth of freedom struggling against that myth of concern to find some justice for the individual. Christ-minster's myth of concern has medieval roots and a middle-class respectability; consequently, it is not interested in the problem Sue describes when she talks about "social moulds" that are ill adapted to "actual shapes" of feeling. The myth of concern is interested only in the established, clear-cut solution to the case that Jude and Sue present it: they should return to their spouses. But that solution is their riddle. How can such unions be called *marriage*? If Jude's tortured relationship to Arabella and Sue's to Phillotson are called *marriages*, why would any society want to think of marriage as either sacramental or legally binding? Insofar as such marriages take no account of the individuals in-volved in them, insofar as the myth of concern provides only a brutally clear-cut solution to the case of Sue and Jude, insofar as that solution involves continued torture and inevitable death, the manners of the bourgeois Gothic society of Christminster violate justice, the most fundamental of the cardinal virtues. The horror story in *Jude the Obscure* is that such medieval concepts are the groundwork of modern middle-class respectability.[6] What makes the story even more horrible is that a supposed center of intel-lectual and ecclesiastical life like Christminster—"It is what you may call a castle, manned by scholarship and religion" (66)—supports outmoded ways of thinking and feeling. And perhaps what makes the story most horrible is that Jude as a stonemason is put to the task of having to repair church and college walls as well as the letters of the Ten Commandments. The tragic irony of the novel is that its aspiring spiritual and intellectual leader must, as a humble workman, make stronger the walls that ex-clude him and make more precise the letter of the law that makes him a sinner and social outcast.

Insofar as Gothic fiction depicts horror, this novel is Gothic because Jude (and Sue too) is caught in a circular pattern of unending mental riddles and emotional tortures. That circular pattern is generated by a myth of concern—embodied in the Ten Commandments as interpreted by church and university in Christminster—that produces the automatic solution to the case of unhappy marriages by insisting on them and thereby ensuring the continuance of fortitude and temperance, if not of real justice and true prudence. At the same time, the case so simply and unjustly dealt with produces a riddle for lovers with affined souls, tortures them inordinately, and leads them to an emotional hell, to condemnatory judgments, and to death itself. *Jude the Obscure* is therefore a novel in which manners become Gothic: it sets in tension the case with the riddle, the myth of concern with that of freedom, affined with complementary lovers, and the moral virtues with the last things.

In carrying on the tradition of *Middlemarch* with its May–January marriage, Hardy also carries forward the psychological analysis of character that we have seen in the use of alter egos in novels like *Great Expectations* and *The Portrait of a Lady*. Pip is forced to see in Orlick the possibilities of his worst self, so that Orlick's accusation that Pip murdered Mrs. Joe is cause for profound reflection; and Orlick's attempted murder of Pip is an outward manifestation of Pip's inward murder of his own best instincts when he abandoned the values of the forge for those of Satis House and when he left Joe for Jaggers in pursuit of the bourgeois dream. Isabel pursues the elusive image of *lady* in Madame Merle; and Isabel, in becoming Pansy's mother and Osmond's wife, achieves her desire to be such a lady only to find it intolerable. Hardy builds on incidental psychodrama of the kind found in Dickens and James and makes it encompass his whole novel. He splits Jude's character into Sue, Arabella, Phillotson, and Father Time. Then he allows Jude to experience these extraordinary elements of his character by seeing them act against each other. A. Alvarez first suggested the doubling of Jude's personality in Sue, Arabella, and Phillotson: "both women are presented less as characters complete in themselves than as projections of Jude, sides of his character, existing only in relation to him." And Phillotson is "a kind of Jude Senior: older, milder, with less talent and urgency, and so without the potentiality for tragedy" (413). We might say in more contemporary terms that in presenting the character of Jude in this way Hardy is giving us a dramatization of what Lacan calls "the anguish of the *corps morcelé*, the 'body in bits and pieces'" (Gallop 79). Jude as a character is dismembered, and he must suffer the pain of constantly aspiring to a better social and economic position while seeing himself so fractured that his expectations become impossibilities given the astringent realities of Christminster.

Enough has been said about Sue already to show that she and Jude are spiritual counterparts. One need add only that Sue has Jude's "own voice" (1325) and that they are alike "at heart" (262). Also as children both were "crazy for books" (52) and had the "same trick of seeming to see things in the air" (162). With Arabella, however, Jude is much closer to the ground: she smears his books with pig fat. As "a woman of rank passions" (457), the pig is her emblem, and she is consistently associated with it. Her father is a "pig-breeder" (83), and she attracts Jude's attention by hitting him with a "pig's pizzle" (*Collected Letters* 2:93). She and Jude chase "three unfattened pigs" (95) on their first date, and she seduces him with a cochin's egg wrapped in "a piece of pig's bladder" tucked between her breasts (99). Once married, they keep a pig. When Jude fears that Sue's leaving him will make his "another case of the pig that was washed turning back to his wallowing in the mire" (429), he immediately falls again into Arabella's hands. She takes him home to her father, now a "master pork-butcher" (456); Jude then dies slowly, the way a well-bled pig should. "The great Phillotson" (149), as Jude calls him, is "a man who had had no advantages beyond those of his own making" (216). He is Jude's model. Everything that Phillotson does, Jude is sure to do. They both go to Christminster, fail to get degrees, think of becoming licentiates, take Sue as a wife and lose her. Jude studies with Phillotson's books, plays his piano, precedes him to the altar with his fiancée, succeeds him as his wife's lover. The one obvious way that Phillotson differs from Jude is that Sue goes back to him. But even in this matter master and pupil may be subtly the same, for Sue will not be happy till she joins Jude in the grave.

Sue is clearly an extension of Jude's mind and heart, Arabella of Jude's animal instinct, and Phillotson of his ambition. Insofar as they do not get along with each other, they enact Jude's being torn apart by internal oppositions. If nature's law of "mutual butchery" (378)—the law that permeates *Jude the Obscure*—translates itself most painfully in Father Time's murder of Sue's children and his own suicide "because we are too menny" (410), it also operates in Sue, Arabella, and Phillotson, and in their destructive relationships with each other and with Jude. At Marygreen, Arabella's animal instinct demands Jude: "I shall go mad if I can't give myself to him altogether" (93). A "complete and substantial female animal" (81), Arabella, the "tigress," devours Jude (241). At Christminster again, Arabella needs Jude to survive. She gets him and survives; he dies. What is good for her is bad for him. His marriages to Arabella cost him Christminster, Sue, and his own life. Sue satisfies the emotional hunger of the lonely, solitary, and unloved Phillotson. Their second marriage sets Phillotson "right in the eyes of the clergy and orthodox laity" and helps him "get back" into his "old track" (442). But Phillotson's good becomes Sue's evil. Arabella and Sue fight for Jude; Phillotson and Jude fight for Sue in the arena of marriage. What is good for one is bad for the other. Arabella and Phillotson prove fittest to survive, she by an adherence to animal instinct and he by repudiating his "instinctive . . . sense of justice" to adhere to the social code of "an old civilization" (435). Phillotson's social survival complements Arabella's animal survival. Through Phillotson Hardy translates Darwinism into a social doctrine.

Phillotson is also inimical to Jude and Sue in another way. For both of them he takes the place of a father. With his father dead, the boy Jude, eleven years old, attaches himself to Phillotson. When as a young man Jude goes to Christminster, he hopes to find his surrogate father there, but Phillotson tells him when they meet, "I don't remember you in the least" (150). Rejected by the institution he would have be his "Alma Mater" (80), Jude finds himself unknown to his father too. And shortly after meeting Phillotson, Jude drives Sue into the schoolmaster's arms by revealing his own marriage to Arabella. Jude thereby becomes convinced of his individual worthlessness: he sees himself as "damn bad" (457). Sue has recently been repudiated by her father because she roomed with an undergraduate. Marrying Phillotson, old enough to be her parent—he is eighteen years her senior—she seeks to regain a father's love but puts herself instead into a psychologically incestuous situation. She has good reason to jump out of the window when Phillotson enters her bedroom: she is escaping incest. Phillotson at first seems to fill her need for both a father and a lover, but her unconscious knows him, horribly, as both in one; sexually, he can only be an incestuous lover. Sue therefore *feels* that her denial of conjugal rights to Phillotson is psychologically right but morally wrong. Consequently she feels, further, intensely guilty; after granting Phillotson his conjugal rights, she feels even worse. Sue's marriage is an insoluble riddle to her. Whatever she does is wrong. Running away from her husband makes her guilty, but so too does going back to her husband. Like Jude, Sue finds herself "worthless and contemptible" (429), a "vile creature" (425). The only way that Sue and Jude can find to increase their self-esteem is to do something that a father would approve.

In the Name-of-the-Father, as Lacan suggests, they seek the Other to validate their own sense of self. But also, as Lacan suggests, they cannot validate themselves because they cannot validate their sexual desire for each other. In Lacanian terms, therefore, Jude and Sue repudiate the penis for the phallus. In less puzzling terms that means that they repudiate the one thing that may help to make them more nearly themselves, sexual desire (the penis), for an approved male-dominated cultural code (the phallus) that will confer on them social approval at the same time that it imposes on them self-alienation. That cultural code resides in the Other. And the Other for both Sue and Jude is the church. He decides to become a "humble curate" and find "a touch of goodness and greatness" in the process. That is "a purgatorial course worthy of being followed by a remorseful man" (181). But his feelings do not allow him to become "a law-abiding religious teacher" (279). Jude must live with his guilt as "an ordinary sinner" (280). Sue repents her being "bad" (325), a "wretch" (425), saying, "I'll *hate* myself forever for my sin" (470) of leaving Phillotson for Jude. She repents by prostrating herself in the aisle of a church that is distinguished by the ironwork her father did there. She punishes herself in "a fanatic prostitution" (437) by giving herself sexually to Phillotson once again. The ultimate degradation, psychologically, becomes the only acceptable punishment. By another church wedding she allies herself with an accepted good hoping thereby to find her own goodness. Like Jude, she cannot find it. Guilt increases; it does not abate. The more Sue is Phillotson's wife the guiltier she feels. The Widow Edlin puts it graphically: "She can't stomach 'un" (490). Conse-

quently, as Arabella says at Jude's impromptu wake, Sue will not
be happy until she is dead: "She's never found peace since she
left his arms, and never will again till she's as he is now" (491).
The respectability conferred on Sue and Jude in the Name-of-
the-Father does nothing to restore that sense of the self when
each was the other's lover. Society's approval and individual
self-approval have nothing to do with each other. The alliance of
Phillotson with the father and the father with the church and the
church with goodness (whatever that may mean in the novel)
simply tears Jude and Sue to pieces. They are the hostages to a
chain of signifiers moving in a labyrinth wherein nothing emotionally satisfying is ever signified for lovers like them.

The self-destruction implied in the dramatization of Sue,
Arabella, and Phillotson as mutually destructive elements of
Jude's character comes to an epiphany in Little Father Time, who
dramatizes the death wish that haunts Jude. Once the child appears, they feel "a tragic doom" overhanging them (350). Time,
like Jude, is an unwanted child who feels he "ought not to [have]
be[en] born" (404). The words Jude quotes when he dies are the
ones he quotes when Little Father Time arrives on the scene: "Let
the day perish wherein I was born" (341). Jude sees his son as an
extension of himself at Christminster: "What I couldn't accom-
plish in my own person perhaps I can carry out through him?"
(345). This is ironically true: Jude failed to commit suicide, but
Time succeeds. Put in the same position as Jude when he was a
child without a mother, Time, finding Sue absent (and judging
himself and the other children a burden on their parents), feels
deserted and kills his siblings and himself. Later, Jude, deserted
by Sue, also kills himself, if more slowly than his son. *Tel père,
tel fils!* What the Fawleys do best is kill themselves. Little Father
Time dramatizes Jude's death wish. He is, gruesomely, a chip off
the old block.

Hardy's total projection of Jude's personality in the characters of Arabella, Sue, Phillotson, and Time makes his novel a
species of romantic psychodrama (see Kestner, *Spatiality* 130).
Over each of them hovers the specter of Christminster's respectability that constantly moves them away from Jude in the
process that pulls him apart. Jude is consequently "a tragic Don
Quixote" (265) who takes his view of life from books and makes

Christminster his ideal. Hardy transcends his own personal sorrow, out of which the novel grew, by creating a suffering surrogate in Jude. Hardy creates a world out of his own sorrows
by projecting them onto Fawley. Hardy's lost faith, miserable
marriage, unrequited love as well as Moule's failure and suicide
become the forces that destroy Jude. Hardy creates a world out of
them and requires Jude to move into it to experience the horror
of the self at war with itself. With Jude Fawley as his surrogate,
Thomas Hardy puts an end to the celebration of the romantic
individualism of the egotistical sublime.

If one thinks of romantic literature as projecting character onto
circumstance so as to mold circumstance to character,[7] then in
Jude the Obscure Hardy gives the lie and calls an end to romantic
aspiration. The novel is a "Song of Myself" scored as a dirge.
Nothing is perhaps more illustrative of this than Little Father
Time and the city of Christminster. Little Father Time comes to
Jude and Sue immediately after their first act of sexual intercourse. There is no fertilization, no gestation, no labor, no par-
turition. There is simply climax and a child—the saddest child
imaginable. Just as James plays in *The Portrait of a Lady* with a pun
on *dying* as both orgasm and physical death in Ralph's deathbed
love scene, so Hardy plays with it in Jude and Sue's first sexual
encounter. Arabella sends Little Father Time, the novel's premier symbol of death, into Jude and Sue's marriage immediately
following their sexual union. His name is Jude, but he is called
"Little Time." In short, Arabella gives just a little time to Jude
and Sue as sexual partners. With a preponderance of references
to Greek tragedy and with emphasis on "mutual butchery" and
"cruelty," Hardy suggests that Jude and Sue have little time before their tragedy is acted out to its horrifying end. Fittingly,
Jude is now a "Monumental Mason." The only thing that Jude
does not carve as a monumental mason is his own tombstone.
But there is no need for him to do so because he has already
carved its equivalent in putting "Thither J. F." on the milestone
outside Marygreen (120). "Thither," of course, is Christminster,
the city of ghosts. Little Father Time confirms this characterization of it when he kills his siblings and himself within sight of
Sarcophagus College, which throws "four centuries of gloom,

bigotry, and decay" into the Fawleys' rooms in Christminster (406).

The city is supposed to be a city of light, the citadel of faith and reason. The boy Jude sees it as such from the Brown House. Jude sees Christminster as the "centre of the universe" (391), the "new Jerusalem" (62), the "paradise of the learned" (163). It is a projection of everything that his own miserable life is not. He endows the city with ideal qualities, making it saintly, happy, noble-minded, harmonious, and beautiful. Christminster is the stuff that "magnificent . . . dream[s]" (84) are made of. It is an "ecclesiastical romance in stone" (76). Jude regards Christminster as "the intellectual and spiritual granary" of England (162–63). But, according to Sue, it is "a nest of commonplace schoolmasters whose characteristic is timid obsequiousness to tradition" (383). It is "new wine in old bottles" (204). Christminster makes Sue say, "I hate Gothic" (189). In actuality Christminster is a ghost town. When Jude enters it for the first time, he sees only the phantoms of its greatness: "thin shapes" and "mournful souls" in the "gloom" (126); when he enters it for the last time, these specters laugh at him (473).

Sue sees Christminster as a place of "fetichists and ghost-seers" (205). Its colleges look like "family vaults above ground" (130). They are "rotten," "crumbling," "decrepit," and "superseded" (130, 125). Christminster harbors a "deadly animosity" for "contemporary logic and vision" (131). It is "as dead as a fern-leaf in a lump of coal" (131). What, consequently, Christminster finally stands for are all those things that prove useless to Jude in his life: trust in "a ruling Power" (184), a "purgatorial course" of existence (181), scriptural reading, private prayer, church hymns, and religious sentiment (184). What Christminster initiates is Sue's repudiation of "Nature's own marriage" to Jude and her acceptance of "Heaven's" marriage to Phillotson (426). Affined love gives way there to complementary couples in whose marriage love disappears altogether. The good manners society demands of its married partners are satisfied, but the partners themselves are not. The substitution of the complementarity of manners for the affinity of romance proves to be Sue's emotional suicide. Giving up Jude for Phillotson is Sue's real-life way of changing Apollo and Venus into Saint Peter and Mary

Magdalen, a trick she does for Miss Fontover with chalk statues
of the pagan deities (142). Both substitutions lead to destruction: "Can this be the girl who brought the Pagan deities into
this most Christian city?—who mimicked Miss Fontover when
she crushed them under her heel?" "Where," wonders Jude in
dismay, "Where are dear Apollo, and dear Venus now!" (427).
What, in other words, has happened to Sue's mind and affections? Christminster has taken their place. "She's affected by
Christminster sentiment and teaching," says Phillotson; "I can
see her views on the indissolubility of marriage well enough,
and I know where she got them" (434). What Christminster represents here is a formalism that opposes and triumphs over life.
The consequences of its victory are remarriage and death. As
the Widow Edlin says, "Weddings be funerals 'a b'lieve nowadays" (479). When "respectability" triumphs over "human development in its richest diversity" (287)—when Jude and Sue
remarry Arabella and Phillotson instead of remaining together—
the novel becomes truly horrible. Weddings do become funerals.
And Christminster, Jude's city of light, becomes a world of darkness. The Gothic city replaces the Gothic castle as the Gothic
horror.

In *Jude the Obscure* Hardy demands that his readers revaluate the
nature of Gothic. The novel is set in the 1860s (Gittings, *Young
Thomas Hardy* 93–95), a decade after the publication of *The Stones
of Venice* in 1851 and 1853. In an England, as Marc Girouard has
shown, that had already gone mad for medievalism, Hardy requires his readers not only to stop and think about their fads
but also to stop and think about Ruskin's deadly serious chapter "The Nature of Gothic" in *The Stones of Venice* (vol. 2, chap.
6), which William Morris characterized as "one of the very few
necessary and inevitable utterances of the century" (Rosenberg
101). If Ruskin's advocacy of Gothic architecture depends on the
biblical event of the Fortunate Fall, as John D. Rosenberg has
persuasively argued; if it depends on a frank acknowledgment of
man's imperfection so as to leave something to the grace of God
to perfect, then it follows that an art that shows the imperfection
of its origins truly praises God. Ruskin can therefore say in ital-

ics: *"the demand for perfection is always a sign of a misunderstanding of the ends of art"* (*Genius* 183).

Christminster, however, is a Gothic city that has lost the sense of imperfection as a human characteristic. It is a city that has taken on a middle-class respectability and has the vice of its self-importance. Christminster tolerates neither crude workmanship nor crude morality. It certainly does not have any place for working men in its institutions, as T. Tetuphenay makes clear to Jude when he tells him, "I venture to think that you will have a much better chance of success in life by remaining in your own sphere and sticking to your trade than by adopting any other course" (167). Christminster does not tolerate any deviations from its code of conduct, as Phillotson finds out once he lets his wife return to her lover and as the Fawleys find out when they try to find decent housing for themselves in the city. The nature of Gothic has changed under the impulse of middle-class morality. Because the spirit of Gothic that incarnated the imperfection of man in the imperfection of stone is dead in Christminster, the city is socially and spiritually a ghost town. The pride that Ruskin saw in the Grotesque Renaissance's pursuit of perfection—perfection allocates all to man, leaving nothing to God—lives on now in bourgeois Christminster. The recognition of the "value of the individual soul and the fruits of its labor" (Rosenberg 96) is now a matter of class: "now it is a veritable difference in level of standing, a precipice between upper and lower grounds in the field of humanity" (*Genius* 179). Jude in wanting to be a bishop at £5,000 a year—"I'll be a D.D. before I have done!" (79)—is partially but not wholly caught up in this ethic, which the narrator indicates by calling him "a species of Dick Whittington whose spirit was touched to finer issues than a mere material gain" (124).

Harsh reality, however, makes Jude a stonemason, a descendant of the kind of men that built the Gothic cathedrals that Ruskin so much admired across Europe from the "irregular lake" of the Mediterranean to the "wild and wayward" northern seas (*Genius* 173–74). Jude is of that breed of artisans that Ruskin celebrated in *The Stones of Venice*. But he is different from the medieval stonemason in one important way: he does what he does merely as "a prop to lean on while he prepare[s] those greater engines" of scholarship which are his first love. So Jude is not happy in his work as stonemason. Yet the one question that Ruskin demands his readers ask themselves when judging a product of labor is this: "Was it done with enjoyment?" (Rosenberg 100). Jude's work of repairing college walls, carving the Ten Commandments, and cutting tombstones is not done "with enjoyment." The would-be scholar is happy with books not stones. Jude is a laborer alienated from his work because he must stick to his "own sphere." Ruskin argued that "the architecture of the Renaissance, incapable of stooping or conceding, 'was full of insult to the poor in its every line'" (Rosenberg 95). That is precisely the argument that Hardy is making about Gothic in middle-class Christminster. Ruskin, following Wordsworth who preferred "the language of the Cumberland peasant to the poetic diction of the Augustans," was thoroughly romantic in exalting "the 'crude' carving of the medieval stonemason over the polished perfections of the Renaissance architect" (Rosenberg 94). Hardy tests that romanticism and finds it wanting.

Hardy knows too much about Darwin, *The Origin of Species*, and *The Descent of Man* to believe in the nature the romantics glorified; he knows too much about middle-class respectability to think either crude work or crude workmen can be valued by it. Ruskin looked to reform the present out of the past; he tried to get Victorian society to value the last even with the first, to renounce progress for the sake of people: "we manufacture everything . . . except men; we blanch cotton, and strengthen steel, and refine sugar, and shape pottery; but to brighten, to strengthen, to refine, or to form a single living spirit, never enters into our estimate of advantages" (*Genius* 180). Hardy knew the soul of man—indeed, his own soul told him nearly enough—so well that he knew Ruskin's efforts were doomed to failure and that Ruskin's exaltation of a Gothic age was romantic nonsense in a Victorian society. Hardy set down Ruskin's description of St. Mark's in Venice as "humbug" (F. E. Hardy 253). Hardy insists in *Jude the Obscure* that everything Gothic is grievous in the modern age. In Raymond Chapman's words, "False medievalism and regression from reality are shown by addiction to the Gothic" (282). Not only the events of his novel but even the novel's six-part structure makes this painfully evident. Joseph A. Kestner demonstrated that each part of the novel is a manifestation of one of the characteristics that Ruskin assigned to Gothic style. Rudeness is seen at Marygreen, changefulness at Christminster, naturalness at Melchester, grotesqueness at Shaston, obstinacy at Aldbrickham, and redundancy at Christminster again (*Spatiality* 130). If Hardy is contemporary in his psychodramatic presentation of character, he is traditional in giving an architectural form to *Jude the Obscure*. The form is as rigid as the Gothicized bourgeois world of Christminster itself, which is "an image of outmoded but still constricting beliefs" (Chapman 286). Just as Ruskin argues that "Gothic architecture has external forms and internal elements" (*Genius* 171), so too does Hardy's novel have such forms and elements. Indeed, the extreme formalism of the novel mirrors the extreme formalism of society. Gothic is not only the substance of Jude's tragedy but the form of his tragedy too.

The six parts of the novel with their Gothic qualities worked out in detail embody a myth of concern founded on the medieval belief that earth exists between heaven and hell and that man moves toward one or the other depending on his adherence to or on his deviation from the Ten Commandments as interpreted by the laws of the church; man himself—made in the image and likeness of God—is held to be a creature of reason guided by Divine Providence and redeemed from original sin by the sufferings and death of Jesus Christ. This myth of concern as interpreted by Christminster, "the most religious and educational city in the world" (400), overwhelms Jude's attempt to establish a myth of freedom founded on his experience of modern life, which makes a claim for the here and now and not for an afterlife. For Hardy's modern man, heaven and hell are states of feeling; human life is one precarious step up from animal existence; and man is a creature of feeling redeemed by human love alone. These myths of freedom and concern collide with tragic consequences in this novel, as the narrator indicates in a single sentence: "To indulge one's instinctive and uncontrolled sense of justice and right, was not, [Jude] found, permitted with impunity in an old civilization like ours" (435). When Christminster "sentiment" shuts out "contemporary logic and vision" (131), it shuts out justice. If the personal, social, biological, and psycho-

logical conditions of human existence are excluded from the formulation of religious doctrine, there can be no true morality.
Hardy said as much at the outbreak of World War I when he
stated that "all the Churches in Europe should frankly admit the
utter failure of theology, & put their heads together to form a
new religion which should have at least some faint connection
with morality" (*Collected Letters* 5:43). For Hardy the churchly
society of Gothic Christminster is nothing more than an "ecclesiastical romance in stone" (76), not a living reality. Christminster's
medieval doctrine in Hardy's modern world sets itself against
the most fundamental of the cardinal virtues. There is no justice
in Christminster; there is only judgment, death, and hell. More
than any other novel of its time, *Jude the Obscure* repudiates the
romance of such a civilization and turns a human face toward
the awful realities of modern existence.

8

Parade's End

Gothic Manners in the Great War

Parade's End is in a "markedly 'English' fictional tradition." " 'The rescue into love' of Christopher Tietjens is the theme of Ford's tetralogy as it is of *Middlemarch*" (Green 129). And Ford takes up where Hardy left off.[1] There is a curse on the Tietjens family in *Parade's End* just as there is on the Fawleys in *Jude the Obscure*. If the Fawleys should not marry, the Protestant Tietjenses should not own Groby. But the real curse on Christopher is that he cannot be other than he is: "You are as conceited as a hog; you are as obstinate as a bullock," Campion tells him (481). Both Jude and Christopher are entrapped into bad marriages by women fearing or pretending pregnancy. As upholders of rules of conduct, each takes the woman for wife as the honorable thing to do. When children are born to Arabella and Sylvia neither husband is sure that he is the father of his son. So both Tietjens and

161

Fawley believe in a Providence that afflicts them with adversity
as a punishment for their sexual sins. Their wives' delight in
torturing them and tormenting the women they love intensifies
their punishment. Arabella's and Sylvia's patent sadism is joined
to a will to social survival that their husbands lack.

Such similarities are striking in light of the differences between *Jude the Obscure* and *Parade's End*, the one a novel about
the lower classes and a working man who aspires to gentility,
the other about the upper classes and a gentleman who aspires
to the common condition of humanity: Tietjens withdraws "from
a world of power and intrigue . . . to the company of men without class or country" (Wiley 247). But the workman and the
gentleman are so similar because they are caught by a feudal
order in its mortifying code. Both are also described as Christ-
like, which emphasizes that they are set apart to suffer because
they attempt to do what their contemporaries see as imprac-
ticable.[2] Jude's compassion moves him to principles fifty years
ahead of his time, Christopher's to practices one hundred and
fifty years behind his time: he is "an eighteenth-century figure
of the Dr. Johnson type" (151). Both become conspicuous when
the principles governing their sexual lives collide with society's
code of manners. Jude never comes completely to understand
his sexuality, though he does affirm it; Christopher comes to
understand his sexuality gradually as the tetralogy advances
from novel to novel. And when his own personal life is not
immediately involved, Christopher shows a clear-sightedness
about sexual entanglements that allows Ford to explore the place
of passion in the conduct of social and civil affairs. Indeed the
title of Ford's combined novels indicates that public conduct is
a parade[3]—an exhibition of "all those social rituals by which
a governing class has reassured itself of its hegemony" (Green
154)—a parade that, because of society's refusal to give man's
passionate life a legitimate accommodation, must violently come
to an end. The Great War is testimony to this. It is the inevitable
outbreak of suppressed passion that destroys the manners of the
supposedly rational and stable society that has made war the
ultimate horror.

Beginning with *Some Do Not* Ford makes "individual constraint
of passion a key to the rift in Victorian character between surface
amenity and the concealed violence of primal instincts which
can explode, on the one hand, in the mania of Duchemin or the
sexual tirades of his wife, or on the other, in the final conflagra-
tion of the war" (Wiley 226). The novel consequently makes a
case against sustaining the life of such a society.

Some Do Not portrays three significant journeys, each of
which stands for more than itself: a train ride from London to
Ashford, a dogcart ride on midsummer's night through the English countryside, and a taxi ride through London. The most
striking of these is the second. Tietjens, having driven the fugi-
tive suffragette Gertie Wilson to a safe haven, is returning with
Valentine Wannop to her mother's house. He and she are falling
in love. A low-lying fog has set in so as to obscure the ground,
the signposts, and everything below Tietjens' neck. Christopher
and Valentine are so hopelessly lost that she is on the road seeking a direction and he is in the cart holding the horse motion-
less. This extraordinarily managed scene derives its effect from
loss of direction, loss of sight, and the sound of voices. The
magical atmosphere of midsummer's night adds to it too. On
the shortest of acquaintances, Valentine calls Christopher "My
dear," and Christopher—in an unusual show of emotion for a
Yorkshire man—asks Valentine if she is "all right" (139, 129).
Tietjens has "an all but irresistible impulse" to kiss Valentine
(137), and she in fact does put "her arm over his shoulder" (143).
What Ford projects here is a night journey into a world of un-
settling emotions. While what is atop the body is visible, what is
low-lying is shrouded. A sensible gentleman and gentlewoman
are falling victims to love; passional life is beginning to break
through manners: "By God! Why not take a holiday? Why not
break all conventions?" (129). The journey ends at dawn when
General Campion crashes his motorcar into the horse, and his
sister, Claudine Sandbach, sets Christopher and Valentine down
as lovers. The night journey ends in disaster at break of day. The
scene is a *Parade's End* in small. The world is journeying in the
night of irrational impulses toward a fatal collision—the collision
of the Allied and Central Powers in World War I. Daylight reveals
that the last sentence of the chapter caps not only the events of a

night's journey but the events of the world's passage into chaos:
"The knacker's cart lumbered round the corner." Ford "makes it
quite clear," W. H. Auden said, "that World War I was a retribution visited upon Western Europe for the sins and omissions
of its ruling class, for which not only they, but also the innocent
conscripted millions on both sides must suffer" (Green 141).

The daylight world does not of course see itself as headed
for a disastrous collision. Like the well-appointed train that takes
Macmaster and Tietjens down to Sussex for a round of golf, the
course of the world seems well tracked and smooth-riding. It
leads to a station where Christopher meets his godfather, General Campion, and introduces Macmaster to him. The end of
the train ride becomes the beginning of Macmaster's rise just
as the end of the dogcart ride is the beginning of Tietjens' fall.
Macmaster's rise is abetted by his writing critical works on English authors. The first of these is a monograph on Dante Gabriel
Rossetti, whom Tietjens loathes: "Damn it," he says to Macmaster. "What's the sense of all these attempts to justify fornication? England's mad about it. . . . I tell you it revolts me
to think of that obese, oily man, who never took a bath, in a
grease-spotted dressing-gown and the underclothes he's slept
in, standing beside a five-shilling model with crimped hair, or
some Mrs. W. Three Stars, gazing into a mirror that reflects their
fetid selves and gilt sunfish and drop chandeliers and plates sick-
ening with cold bacon fat and gurgling about passion" (17). The
train ride then, inasmuch as Christopher Tietjens and Vincent
Macmaster are far from seeing eye to eye, is not all that smooth.
Rossetti's world also invokes the nighttime realm of passion.
And we are reminded that Sylvia seduced Tietjens on a train and
that Christopher is accused of being Edith Ethel's lover because
she, after fleeing Vincent's bed, is seen with Tietjens on a train.

The next day the Germans invade Belgium and the war begins. The conduct of that war involves the rapid movement of
troops by train, each side vying with the other for efficient loco-
motion.[4] "Transport," prays Mark Tietjens, "be thou my God"
(832). He is in charge of transport for all of England, and Christopher, in *No More Parades*, is in charge of transport from the
base camp in Rouen. The orderly, well-tracked, smooth-running
world that opens *Some Do Not* becomes the novel's primary illu-

sion. Disaster lurks just down the line. And as Tietjens tells
Macmaster, England has become too dishonest to avert disaster:
" 'War, my good fellow,' Tietjens said—the train was slowing
down preparatorily to running into Ashford—'is inevitable, and
with this country plumb centre in the middle of it. Simply because you fellows are such damn hypocrites. There's not a country in the world that trusts us. We're always, as it were, commit-
ting adultery—like your fellow!—with the name of Heaven on
our lips.' He was jibing again at the subject of Macmaster's monograph" (20). "Transport!" thinks Valentine. "There was another
meaning to the word" (275). And she is correct. The ecstacy of
sexual love and the logistics of bloody war are telescoped in its
two syllables.

The third journey in *Some Do Not* takes place after Tietjens
has already been damaged by the fighting, having suffered a
loss of memory from the concussion of an exploding shell. Four
months of convalescence at an end, he is to go back to France
in the morning. Having promised each other to be lovers the
night before he leaves, Christopher and Valentine find themselves taking her drunken sailor brother home in a taxi and settling him on the couch that was to be theirs for the night. Were
he not there, the situation would not be different, for Tietjens
has decided that "a decent fellow didn't get his girl into trouble
before going to be killed" (273). The scene is notable for the fragmentation of its prose—so different from the easy coherence of
the prose describing the opening train ride—and its allusiveness
too. The fragmentation suggests the world's condition; and the
allusions, especially one to "Dover Beach" (281), identifies the
world as one in which the sea of faith has receded and the lovers
have only one another as they face the drear and naked shingles
of the world. But in spite of that—perhaps even because of it
—they decide not to become clandestine lovers. Some do not.
They are of that group. In confusion those who can see clearly
must exercise some restraint. Christopher and Valentine can be
just and temperate in the midst of their passion because they
have at least tried to face it squarely. They can therefore make
a case both for their love and for their not becoming lovers. "I
stand for monogamy and chastity," Tietjens told Macmaster on
their train ride (18); circumstances now require him to prove it.

Changed circumstances will later require a change in principle:
"Tory rectitude" will find "no place in an environment perpetually full of 'unusual stresses' " (Green 157). Tietjens sees that in
face of "death, love, and public dishonour" a British sense of
good manners is not very useful (179).

Tietjens also told Macmaster that he, Vincent, stood for
"lachrymose polygamy" and the "polysyllabic Justification by
Love" (18)—that is, for fashionable morality of the Rossetti kind.
Macmaster's is a morality of expediency that Edith Ethel Duchemin joins him in professing. They become an updated version
of affined lovers in the romantic tradition. They see themselves
as so much alike that each calls the other "Guggums."[5] Their
romantic situation even recalls the new Gothic tradition of a
novel like *Jane Eyre*; but instead of a madwoman in the attic, there
is a mad parson in the rectory, Mrs. Duchemin's husband. And
this intensely romantic situation produces a calculatedly hypocritical morality. Macmaster and Mrs. Duchemin become sexual
partners because they can make society believe that they are
chaste lovers whose communion of mind is perfection itself.
Society demands that men and women maintain a show of propriety because it has refused to recognize the place of passion
in social life. Lawrence's bitch goddess Success was with good
reason sexless in the extreme.

The socially successful Macmaster and Mrs. Duchemin pro-
ject an extreme of sexlessness while becoming lovers the night
of the very day they meet. That was the day that Tietjens and
Macmaster discovered that "Breakfast" Duchemin, disciple of
Ruskin and Rossetti, was, although a clergyman, a scatological
maniac. In one of the supreme scenes of English comedy—the
tradition of manners meeting the tradition of horrors head on—
the Reverend Duchemin raves on about chastity and coitus while
everyone at the breakfast table pretends to hear nothing at all
and keeps up a parade of good manners and trivial conversation
until the clergyman, shouting *"Post coitum tristis,"* is dropped
to his chair with a kidney punch. "To Tietjens that seemed the
highest achievement and justification of English manners" (100).
At this "wildly bizarre breakfast worthy of the Marx Brothers at
their most surreal" (Gordon 89), the nighttime world of bed and
sex is simply not allowed to interfere with the daytime world

of breakfast and chatter. No more are Vincent and Edith Ethel allowed to disport their passion before society. But their pretense of restraint—their "parade of circumspection and rightness" (241)—cannot always keep its face. Edith Ethel is as mad as her husband on occasion: "For Mrs. Duchemin had revealed the fact that her circumspect, continent, and suavely aesthetic personality was doubled by another at least as coarse as, and infinitely more incisive in expression than, that of the drunken cook" (265). Macmaster's outlet is a madness of another kind. He betrays Christopher's friendship by stealing factitious statistics that Tietjens has devised for his own amusement; Vincent uses these to prove that a single command is not wanted for the conduct of the war. Insofar as this is precisely what the government wants to prove, Macmaster wins a knighthood.

Macmaster's rise from "son of a very poor shipping clerk" (13)—when she thinks she is pregnant, Edith Ethel calls Vincent a "dirty little Port of Leith fish-handler" (230)—to a KGB is a classic instance of the achievement of the bourgeois dream. Lady Macmaster explains to Valentine that Vincent cannot repay Tietjens the two thousand guineas he owes him because he has to keep up his establishment as a country gentleman:

> She was to be allowed, under her husband's [Duchemin's] will, enough capital to buy a pleasant little place in Surrey, with rather a nice lot of land—enough to let Macmaster know some of the leisures of a country gentleman's lot. They were going in for shorthorns, and there was enough land to give them a small golf-course and, in the autumn, a little —oh, mostly rough—shooting for Macmaster to bring his friends down to. It would just run to that. Oh, no ostentation. Merely a nice little place. As an amusing detail the villagers there already called Macmaster "squire" and the women curtsied to him. (243)

Edith Ethel also excuses Vincent from his indebtedness to Christopher by accusing Tietjens of all the sins that she and Macmaster actually committed. Having become successful by cleverly disguising her passions, she, from her position of success as Lady Macmaster, accuses Tietjens of the very sins she succeeded in hiding. In short, to be found out is really the only sin that counts.

Edith Ethel pretends to have found out Tietjens and is properly and publicly shocked to know such a "brute beast" (260)—such a lower form of life along the evolutionary scale. Because Tietjens knows the truth about the Macmasters and because they owe him a small fortune, he must be discredited. After he saves them, they destroy him. He becomes their scapegoat: "He saved others: himself he could not save!" (272).

As scapegoat, Tietjens goes to war; Macmaster stays home. At the front Christopher's hallmarks are wisdom and courage. The old Republic represented by the Macmasters and the government has none of the old virtues left: neither wisdom nor justice nor courage nor discipline: "Sham people pursuing their ways across the sham grass. Or no! In a vacuum! No! 'Pasteurised' was the word! Like dead milk. Robbed of their vitamines . . ." (273). Ford's England in *Some Do Not* is sham, vacuumed, and pasteurized.[6] London has become the Unreal City. The nation no longer deserves to flourish. Ford sees what Henry James saw when in *What Maisie Knew*—that "passionless masterpiece" about "the English habit of trying to shift responsibility" (Hueffer, *Henry James* 28, 147)—he asked the overwhelming question that Ford asks again in *Parade's End*: "Are the prizes of life, is the leisured life which our author [James] has depicted for us, worth striving for? If, in short, this life is not worth having—this life of the West End, of the country-house, of the drawing room, possibly of the studio, and of the garden party—if this life, which is the best that our civilisation has to show, is not worth the living; if it is not pleasant, cultivated, civilised, cleanly [,] and instinct with reasonably high ideals, then, indeed, western civilisation is not worth going on with, and we had better scrap the whole of it so as to begin again" (Hueffer, *Henry James* 62–63).

In a set of books that Ford modeled as an ironic comedy on *What Maisie Knew*, and in a set of books that uses the classical Jamesian point of view[7] and hourglass structure[8]—Macmaster rises and goes politically to the right as Tietjens falls and goes politically to the left—Ford asks pitilessly James's question: If this is the best we can do, should we do it at all? His answer is No. "I am not, you understand, a pessimist: I don't want our civilisation to pull through," Ford wrote in *Provence*. "I want a civilisation of small men each labouring two small plots—his own ground and his own soul. Nothing else will serve my turn" (*Your Mirror* 388). That is the case that *Some Do Not* makes for the new civilization that Ford gives us in *The Last Post*.[9] *No More Parades* and *A Man Could Stand Up* are signposts to a civilization of ground and soul.

When Valentine thinks about the contradictions in Lady Macmaster's character, she also thinks about the same contradictions in nations: "But, also, as Valentine Wannop saw it, humanity has these doublings of strong natures; just as the urbane and grave Spanish nation must find its outlet in the shrieking lusts of the bull-ring or the circumspect, laborious and admirable city typist must find her derivative in the cruder lusts of certain novelists, so Edith Ethel must break down into physical sexualities—and into shrieked coarseness of fishwives. How else, indeed, do we have saints? Surely, alone, by the ultimate victory of the one tendency over the other!" (268). Urbane and grave manners are an instance of a dialectical contradiction, for they require the shrieking lusts of the bullring. War also has its contradictory sides: battle and parade are military counterparts. Bloodletting requires discipline, and discipline promotes bloodletting. Not insignificantly, parts 1 and 2 of *No More Parades* are set in the night; they deal with troop movements and shelling as well as with seduction and near rape. Part 3 is set in the morning light; it deals with interrogation and inspection: General Campion puts Captain Tietjens' cook houses on parade. In an epiphanic moment, Tietjens elicits the contradiction from the parade. Campion is presented as a godhead who has descended into a cathedral formed of the cook houses where Sergeant-Cook Case is high priest. Tietjens sees the pomp and circumstance of this parade as his very own "funeral" (500).

Sylvia brings about this epiphanic moment. In the mode of Edith Ethel, the Spanish nation, and the war itself, she is a woman compounded of light and dark sides—a *lady* of sadistic passion—a human being filled with seemingly endless contradictions. She is a woman who has everything she wants but her husband's love, which, if she had it, she would not want. She cannot have Christopher's love because she enjoys making him suffer. She is caught in an endless round of torture and seduction and consequently announces herself "Bored":

> "I'm bored," she said. "Bored! Bored!"
>   Tietjens had moved slightly as she had thrown. The cutlets and most of the salad leaves had gone over his shoulder. But one, couched, very green leaf was on his shoulder-strap, and the oil and vinegar from the plate . . . had splashed from the revers of his tunic to his green staff-badges. She was glad that she had hit him as much as that: it meant that her marksmanship had not been quite rotten. She was glad, too, that she had missed him. She was also supremely indifferent."
> (156)

Baudelaire's *"monstre délicat—C'est l'Ennui"* (*Fleurs* 20)—has Sylvia acting in an elaborately outrageous manner in order to dispel her boredom; actually, however, her nonsense increases her boredom. She tries to be as bad as she can to get some little kick out of life. She dabbles in diabolism and black masses; she flirts with social disgrace by running off with an "oaf" named Perowne; she tempts Father Consett to exorcise her by threatening to corrupt her son. But even a lot of sadism goes only a little way for someone about to "swallow the world in a yawn" (*Fleurs* 21).

> "When I saw Christopher . . . Last night? . . . Yes, it *was* last night. . . . Turning back to go up that hill. . . . And I had been talking about him to a lot of grinning private soldiers. . . . To *madden* him. . . . You *mustn't* make scenes before the servants. . . . A heavy man, tired . . . come down the hill and lumbering up again. . . . There was a searchlight turned on him just as he turned. . . . I remembered the white bulldog I thrashed on the night before it died. . . . A tired, silent beast . . . With a fat white behind. . . . Tired out . . . You couldn't see its tail because it was turned down, the stump. . . . A great, silent beast. . . . The vet said it had been poisoned with red lead by burglars. . . . It's beastly to die of red lead. . . . It eats up the liver. . . . And you think you're getting better for a fortnight. And you're always cold . . . freezing in the blood-vessels. . . . And the poor beast had left its kennel

to try and be let into the fire. . . . And I found it at the door when I came in from a dance without Christopher. . . . And got the rhinoceros whip and lashed into it. There's a pleasure in lashing into a naked white beast. . . . Obese and silent, like Christopher. . . . I thought Christopher might . . . That night . . . It went through my head . . . It hung down its head. . . . A great head, room for a whole British encyclopaedia of misinformation, as Christopher used to put it. It said: "What a hope!" . . . As I hope to be saved, though I never shall be, the dog said: "What a hope!" . . . Snow-white in quite black bushes. . . . And it went under a bush. They found it dead there in the morning. You can't imagine what it looked like, with its head over its shoulder, as it looked back and said: "What a hope!" to me. . . . Under a dark bush. An eu . . . eu . . . euonymus, isn't it? . . . In thirty degrees of frost with all the blood-vessels exposed on the naked surface of the skin. . . . It's the seventh circle of hell, isn't it? The frozen one . . . the last stud-white hope of the Groby Tory breed. . . . Modelling himself on our Lord. . . . But our Lord was never married. He never touched on topics of sex. Good for Him. . . ." (416–17)

Sylvia obviously enjoys what Christopher calls "pulling the string of a shower-bath" (488) when he is unprepared for a dousing. Her most ambitious tug at the string comes when she visits him at base camp in Rouen for the purpose of getting him to sign a legal document (which requires no signature!) that gives her the right to live at Groby and makes their son Michael his successor to the estate. Sylvia's arrival at the western front presents Christopher with a riddle. He is particularly apt at solving all sorts of military problems and successfully advises both his superiors and subordinates in matters of the heart. Even Campion praises Tietjens for his extraordinary abilities: "He's got a positive genius for getting all sorts of things out of the most beastly muddles. . . . Why he's even been useful to me . . ." (409). But Sylvia's presence presents Christopher with a riddle wrapped in the word *Paddington* that he cannot solve. Ford had at one time intended *Paddington* to be the last word of *Some Do Not* but changed his mind (Griffith 148). It was the last word that Christo-

pher heard Sylvia utter before he left for the front a second time.
She ordered a taxi driver to take her to the railway station at four
in the morning shortly before her husband's own departure. She
was supposed to take a train to Birkenhead where she was to
go into more or less permanent retreat in a convent. *Paddington*
therefore meant to Christopher freedom—freedom to make a life
with Valentine Wannop once the war was over for him (401–2).
But in a characteristic reversal of that understanding Sylvia no
longer means to give Christopher his freedom. She means to
intensify his concern for her as his legal wife. She has come to
Rouen to "make his wooden face wince" (381)—to play "some
vampire . . . La belle Dame sans Merci" (386) yet once more.

What then does *Paddington* now mean? That is the question
Christopher asks himself. The word haunts him throughout *No
More Parades* as much as the death of O Nine Morgan, which
begins the novel, does. *Paddington* encodes the great riddle that
Tietjens for all his ability with puzzles and predicaments has not
been able to decode: "My problem will remain the same whether
I'm here or not," Tietjens tells Campion. "For it's insoluble. It's
the whole problem of the relations of the sexes" (491). "On the
basis of past experience," Carol Ohmann argues, Christopher
"can conclude that, provided she is sane, Sylvia has come to
Rouen for a purpose. But then he must ask: what purpose? And
he cannot answer. His chain of inference begins and ends with a
question" (143). The question of the sexes wrapped in the riddle
of *Paddington* becomes Christopher's death warrant. He is fated
to die like O Nine Morgan, who also had an unfaithful wife, if
he does not first go mad like McKechnie, whose wife has left
him for another man and who, like Tietjens, refuses to initiate a
divorce action against her. Christopher's one prayer at the front
is that he not lose his mind before he loses his life; so throughout
this novel and *A Man Could Stand Up* madness and death dog his
steps.

The contradictions of public and private life come together
on the western front when Sylvia comes to France with the fixed
purpose of making her husband wince: "To seduce Tietjens in
Rouen is her most ardent wish but one: to fail to seduce him"
(Ohmann 127). Ford combines the bloodlust of war with the
manner of parade when Tietjens has to fight both his private

war with Sylvia and England's war with Germany at one and
the same time. With O Nine Morgan dead because of his wife
and the war, with McKechnie mad because of his wife and the
war, and with Colonel Levin betrothed in spite of the war, Ford
makes it clear that the passional life complicates geometrically
the problem of fighting a war. A soldier has, so to speak, one
enemy before him and one behind him: " 'he has to go through
the public affairs of distracted Europe' with a 'private cannon-
ball' " (Stang 107).

Sylvia dramatizes this truth by lying to General Campion
about her husband, Captain Tietjens:

> "Hasn't it ever occurred to you that Christopher was a
> Socialist?"
>
> For the first time in her life Sylvia saw her husband's
> godfather look grotesque. . . . His jaw dropped down, his
> white hair became disarrayed and he dropped his pretty
> cap with all the gold oakleaves and the scarlet. When he
> rose from picking it up his thin old face was purple and
> distorted. . . .
>
> . . . He stopped, snorted and exclaimed: "By God, I *will* have
> him drummed out of the service. . . . By God, I will. I can
> do that much. . . ." (410)

Besides lying about Christopher, Sylvia as much as invites two
officers to her bedroom when she knows that Tietjens will be
there with her. The arrival of Major Perowne and General O'Hara
leads Christopher to throw both men out of the door at three in
the morning and brings about his arrest for striking his superior
officers. This makes it impossible for Tietjens to remain at the
Rouen headquarters. Campion refuses to take him onto his own
staff because that would smack of nepotism. Tietjens cannot be
sent to the post his brother Mark secured for him because he
has quarreled with both Lord Beichan and Hotchkiss, Beichan's
hand-picked commanding officer at that post, about the proper
treatment of horses. And Tietjens finally cannot be sent as a
liaison officer to the French because Sylvia's first lover, Colonel
Drake, has as much as accused Christopher of being a French
spy. So having solved every imaginable problem that the army
has presented him, Tietjens cannot solve his own problem: the

Paddington riddle—the riddle of the relation between the sexes
—does him in. A successful military career is undermined by an
unsuccessful marriage. Therefore in the grim comedy of *No More
Parades* Campion sends Tietjens to the trenches. Christopher
finds himself, as Campion says, "promoted," but "promoted,"
as Tietjens realizes, to "certain death" (476).

Christopher does not die. He skips that step and goes directly to hell.

> *Es ist nicht zu ertragen; es ist das dasz uns verloren hat* . . .
> words in German, of utter despair, meaning: It is unbear-
> able: it is that that has ruined us. . . . The mud! . . . He
> had heard those words, standing amidst volcano craters of
> mud, among ravines, monstrosities of slime, cliffs and dis-
> tances, all of slime [. . . .] and the slime had moved [. . . .]
> The moving slime was German deserters. . . . You could not
> see them: the leader of them—an officer!—had his glasses
> so thick with mud that you could not see the colour of his
> eyes, and his half-dozen decorations were like the begin-
> nings of swallows' nests, his beard like stalactites. . . . Of
> the other men you could only see the eyes—extraordinarily
> vivid: mostly blue like the sky! [. . . .] Those moving saurians
> compacted of slime kept on passing him afterwards, all the
> afternoon. . . . And he could not help picturing their immedi-
> ate antecedents for two months [. . . .] In advanced pockets
> of mud, in dreadful solitude amongst those ravines . . . sus-
> pended in eternity, at the last day of the world. And it had
> horribly shocked him to hear again the German language a
> rather soft voice, a little suety, like an obscene whisper. . . .
> The voice obviously of the damned; hell could hold nothing
> curious for those poor beasts. . . . His French guide had said
> sardonically: *On dirait l'Inferno de Dante!* (486–87)

This infernal vision of what Tietjens is to go to contrasts radically
with the supernal vision of what he has come from.

> Tietjens had walked in the sunlight down the lines, past the
> hut with the evergreen climbing rose, in the sunlight, think-
> ing in an interval, good-humouredly about his official reli-

gion: about the Almighty as, on a colossal scale, a great English Landowner, benevolently awful, a colossal duke who never left his study and was thus invisible, but knowing all about the estate down to the last hind at the home farm and the last oak; Christ, an almost too benevolent Land-Steward, son of the Owner, knowing all about the estate down to the last child at the porter's lodge, apt to be got round by the more detrimental tenants; the Third Person of the Trinity, the spirit of the estate, the Game as it were, as distinct from the players of the game; the atmosphere of the estate, that of the interior of Winchester Cathedral just after a Handel anthem has been finished, a perpetual Sunday, with, probably, a little cricket for the young men. Like Yorkshire of a Saturday afternoon; if you looked down on the whole broad county you would not see a single village green without its white flannels. That was why Yorkshire always leads the averages. . . . Probably by the time you got to heaven you would be so worn out by work on this planet that you would accept the English Sunday, for ever, with extreme relief! (365–66)

Heaven and hell: the country estate and the battlefield: the cricket pitch and the trenches. Heaven is gone and hell is here. The contradiction inherent in the heaven of the one—especially since country estates have fallen into the hands of the Macmasters and the Lord Beichans and will fall into the hands of the Mrs. de Bray Papes in *The Last Post*—has bred the hell of the other. Thus there can be no more such parades for Tietjens. There can only be the final parade of the inspection of the cook houses when the godhead—"Major-General Lord Edward Campion, V.C., K.C.M.G., tantivy tum, tum, etcetera" (444,662)—descends to officiate at Tietjens' funeral:

> The general tapped with the heel of his crop on the locker-panel labelled PEPPER: the top, right-hand locker-panel. He said to the tubular, global-eyed white figure beside it: "Open that, will you, my man? . . ."
> To Tietjens this was like the sudden bursting out of the regimental quick-step, as after a funeral with military hon-

ours the band and drums march away, back to barracks. (500)

After his funeral Tietjens is transported to the trenches for burial.

Part 2 of *A Man Could Stand Up* finds Tietjens commanding a frontline trench at "the most crucial point of the line of the Army, of the Expeditionary Forces, the Allied Forces, the Empire, the Universe, the Solar System" (598). Dawn is about to break, and Christopher and his men are awaiting a German attack to begin in forty-five minutes. The six chapters of part 2 cover these three-quarters of an hour and come to a climax when the shelling starts and Tietjens is buried in mud. At this time on this day as the darkness of night gives way to the light of day—"wet half-light, just flickering" (543)—Christopher Tietjens crosses the shadow line from youth to maturity. In a tribute to Conrad, Ford has Tietjens cross this shadow line by taking command of his troops. The nameless captain in Conrad's *The Shadow-Line*—a novel dedicated to his soldier son and his fellow officers on the Western Front—who takes command of a sailing ship and thereby finds his own personal maturity becomes in *A Man Could Stand Up* Captain Tietjens, promoted to major, who takes command of the 9th Glamorganshires.[10] As night turns to day Christopher finds that he has integrated his passional with his rational life and that he is ready to stand up to the world with Valentine as his lover: " 'You will be prepared immediately on cessation of active hostilities to put yourself at my disposal; please. Signed, Xtopher Tietjens, Acting O.C. 9th Glams.' A proper military communication" (630).

Christopher takes command of himself, his life, and his men by his decision to be responsible and reprehensible at the same time. He decides to give up his title to Groby, to give up his London club, and to live with Valentine:

He was going to write to Valentine Wannop: "Hold yourself at my disposal. Please. Signed . . ." Reprehensible! Worse than reprehensible! You do not seduce the child of your father's oldest friend. (632)

He drank his last cup of warm, sweetened coffee, laced

with rum. . . . He drew a deep breath. Fancy drawing a deep breath of satisfaction after a deep draft of warm coffee, sweetened with condensed milk and laced with rum! . . . Reprehensible! Gastronomically reprehensible! . . . What would they say at the Club? . . . Well, he was never going to be at the Club! The Club claret was to be regretted! Admirable claret. And the cold side-board! (633)

Reprehensible! . . . He snorted! If you don't obey the rules of your club you get hoofed out, and that's that! If you retire from the post of Second-in-Command of Groby, you don't have to . . . oh, attend battalion parades! (634)

Reprehensible! He said. For God's sake *let* us be reprehensible! And have done with it! (636)

This mature decision to take command of himself and of his battalion occurs because fighting the war has radically changed Christopher:

The war had made a man of him! It had coarsened him and hardened him. There was no other way to look at it. It had made him reach a point at which he would no longer stand unbearable things. At any rate from his equals! He counted Campion as his equal; few other people, of course. And what he wanted he was prepared to take. . . . What he had been before, God alone knew. But to-day the world changed. Feudalism was finished; its last vestiges were gone. It held no place for him. He was going—he was damn well going!—to make a place in it for . . . A man could now stand up on a hill, so he and she could surely get into some hole together! (668)

Ford dramatizes this change in Tietjens by putting him through a literal burial and resurrection and then making him face the godhead in judgment too. As he drinks his reprehensible cup of sweetened coffee laced with rum, a German shell explodes and buries him up to the neck and completely buries Lance-Corporal Duckett whose features remind Tietjens continuously of Valentine. Once he himself is extricated, Christopher digs out Duckett. This action intensifies a psychological process that has been going on throughout the war chapters of the novel which show Tietjens digging Valentine out of his sub-conscious.[11] Her name first breaks through to his consciousness in fragments ("Valen . . . Valen . . ." [563]) and then completely ("Valentine Wannop. . . . What! Is *that* still there?" [593]), and finally she appears in the person of Duckett ("it came suddenly into his head that he liked that boy because he suggested Valen-tine Wannop!" [602]). This moment is especially reminiscent of Christopher's midsummer-night ride with Valentine: she buried in the fog, he with only his head above it. Digging out Duckett and restoring him to life, Tietjens restores his own psychological equilibrium along with Duckett's breath. Having chosen to be re-sponsible by being reprehensible, Tietjens, now in command of himself as well as of his battalion, meets General Campion and is dismissed from his command for being covered from head to toe in mud. Reborn from the earth, Tietjens is sacked for being unwashed. It is as though the godhead had rejected Adam be-cause he was formed from mud! Campion still loves a parade: the world governed by the myth of concern is the world of parade. But for Christopher there are no more parades. The life governed by the myth of freedom chooses to be reprehensible rather than respectable. Tietjens has put up with Campion's preference for Macmaster since their meeting at Ashford, he has survived Cam-pion's crashing into Mrs. Wannop's dogcart at Mountby, he has accepted Campion's promoting him to "certain death" at Rouen; but he has had enough. Tietjens will simply have no more of Campion's high-handedness. "By God! I'll take the thing before the Commander-in-chief. I'll take the thing before the King in Council if necessary. By God I will!" (644). The man who relieves his drunken colonel of command and who drinks sweetened coffee laced with rum, the man who will live with the woman he loves and who will save the lives of his men—this man has crossed the shadow line from darkness to dawn and will stand up and be a man. And if he finds out that Campion has become his wife's lover in his absence—sex is a problem for the general too—he will call him out and shoot him.

If part 2 of *A Man Could Stand Up* shows Christopher Tietjens changing, parts 1 and 3 confirm that the old order has changed too. They are set on Armistice Day, 11 November 1918—Eleven Eleven Eighteen—the "crack across the table of History," the "parting of the ways of the universe" (513). Ford does for this day what James Joyce did for 16 June 1904. Just as the day of Joyce's first date with Nora Barnacle became immortal as Bloomsday, the day of Tietjens' reunion with Valentine Wannop becomes immortal as Armistice Day. Not only is it the world's rite of passage but it is theirs too. Just as there is an inquest and a funeral for Christopher in part 3, chapter 2, of *No More Parades* when Campion interrogates Tietjens and inspects his cook houses, so there is an inquest and a funeral for Valentine when Miss Wanostrocht questions her in part 1, chapter 3, of *A Man Could Stand Up*. "Still, it's I that's the corpse. You're conducting the inquest," Valentine tells the Head. "It *is*, you know, rather more my funeral than yours" (539). Such a motif of death followed by rebirth is integral to rites of passage. Consequently we find Christopher stabbing "furiously at the latchhole with his little key" to open the door of his flat for Valentine, and "she closed the door as delicately as if she were kissing him on the lips" once she enters his rooms. "It was a symbol," Valentine says (646–47). The new order has begun for them.

A Man Could Stand Up is very much about a new order for the world too. With the old world gone, what will the new world bring? What shape will the new Republic take? The novel hints at an answer. First the old rules will no longer apply: "No more respect . . . For the Equator! For the Metric system! For Sir Walter Scott! Or George Washington! Or Abraham Lincoln! Or the Seventh Commandment!" (511). Second, reason will have to give passion its due: "something human, someone had once said, is dearer than a wilderness of decalogues!" (510). Third, moral standards will have to change because they have failed so badly: "Middle Class Morality? A pretty gory carnival that has been for the last four years!" (534). Fourth, authority will have to give way to conscience because men have learned how to stand up for themselves: "no more feudal atmosphere" (633) because the "Feudal Spirit was broken" (597). And, fifth, the upper class must give way to the lower because "they're the only people in this country who are sound in wind and limb. They'll save the country if the country's to be saved" (18). *A Man Could Stand Up* dramatizes these conditions that are to bring about the new Republic.

Part 1 is set at a "Great Public Girls' School" where Valentine Wannop is an instructor in physical education. The school functions as a metonym for "the World" since its worries are those of society too. Miss Wanostrocht and the school mistresses worry about how to retain their authority once the armistice is declared at eleven o'clock and "the World" (510) in consequence becomes "The World Turned Upside Down" (511): "You had to keep them—the Girls, the Populace, everybody—in hand now, for once you let go there was no knowing where They, like waters parted from the seas, mightn't carry You. Goodness knew! You might arrive anywhere—at county families taking to trade; gentlefolk selling for profit! All the unthinkable sorts of things!" (511). In fear of just such unthinkable things the mistresses want Valentine, who does not share their views, to get six hundred girls to shout "Hurrah!" three times when the armistice is announced and then return to their classrooms for schooling: "to turn six hundred girls stark mad with excitement into the streets already filled with populations that would no doubt be also stark mad with excitement" would not be "expedient" (512). The mistresses' mentality is just one more instance of a restrictive fear of strong emotions and makes impossible a sensible assessment of what human life is about. Intense joy is too orgiastic for the Head —the name given to Miss Wanostrocht—to admit as acceptable. Such intensity skewers the rules and chucks out Authority. It proclaims the ascendancy of a myth of freedom over a myth of concern, which is what *A Man Could Stand Up* is all about.

This is a novel that is carnivalized to offset that "gory carnival" of "Middle Class Morality," the Great War itself. The true function of carnival is to affirm life, not death. It is also to do away with class distinctions that make one group of people better than another. Indeed, "Bakhtin . . . postulates the carnival spirit and carnival world as models for a superior world order that is organized horizontally rather than vertically" (Clark and Holquist 310). In carnival such basics as food, dance, song, and sexual love are reaffirmed as so essentially human as to be beyond class. The club claret is renounced permanently for sweetened coffee laced with rum that both Captain Tietjens and his subaltern, Aranjuez, can drink. The schoolgirls sing "Glory, Glory, Glory" and the "old pals" sing *"Ainsi font! font! font!"* and both groups long to dance: the girls with the crowds in the streets and the men with their women in Tietjens' flat. And monied ladies with class connections like Sylvia and Edith Ethel, who are perversely attracted to Tietjens as a sexual partner, have no better right to him than Valentine—as her name indicates—who has worked as a slavey and ash-cat. It is she who will bear his child in *The Last Post*. In short, Ford democratizes *A Man Could Stand Up* by carnivalizing it.

Valentine is very much in the carnival mood when she resigns her post at the Great Public Girls' School on Armistice Day. She walks out of the building "through gauntish corridors whose decorated Gothic windows positively had bits of pink glass here and there interspersed in their lattices" (529). She walks out of a Gothic world where the mistresses' good manners suggest a greater degree of madness than the girls' irrepressible high spirits: "The day before there had been a false alarm and the School—horribly—had sung: 'Hang Kaiser Bill from the hoar apple tree / And Glory, Glory, Glory till it's teatime'" (510). Valentine resigns not simply because she agrees with the girls and disagrees with the mistresses but principally because Miss Wanostrocht believes Lady Macmaster to be "a serious personality" (538). Edith Ethel telephones Valentine to tell her that Christopher has returned, but her underlying purpose in conveying this information is very much like the Head's in having Valentine on her staff at all. Lady Macmaster is trying to keep her own place in society, which she feels is threatened by Tietjens' return because Macmaster owes Christopher at least two thousand guineas. She offers to be a go-between for Valentine and Christopher if Valentine will get him to forgive Vincent his debt. Valentine responds to Lady Macmaster by pulling the telephone out of the wall. She literally severs her connections with the Edwardian society that Edith Ethel once upon a time so brilliantly entertained. Like Miss Wanostrocht, Lady Macmaster wants Valentine to help keep the old ways intact. But Valentine destroys the telephone and shakes the dust of the school from her feet. She goes to Christopher and crosses his threshold. They accommodate their passionate life to the reality of their changed circumstances.

At Tietjens' she gets a phone call from her mother who urges her not to become his mistress unless madness or death is the only alternative. Speaking to Christopher, Mrs. Wannop is unable to persuade him to delay his union with Valentine. When their conversation ends, he hangs up the telephone. Christopher breaks the connection with the Victorian society Mrs. Wannop represents:

> Early Victorian instinct! . . . The Mid-Victorian had to loosen the bonds. Her [Valentine's] mother, to be in the van of Mid-Victorian thought, had had to allow virtue to "irregular unions." As long as they were high-minded. But the high-minded do not consummate irregular unions. So all her books had showed you high-minded creatures contracting irregular unions of the mind or of sympathy; but never carrying them to the necessary conclusion. They would have been ethically at liberty to, but they didn't. They ran with the ethical hare, but hunted with the ecclesiastical hounds. . . . (661)

When he has Tietjens hang up the telephone, Ford himself breaks the connection between the realistic novel of James, Conrad, and Joyce and the moralistic fiction of the Victorians. He ends *A Man Could Stand Up* with a glance back at that volume of Victorian fiction he thought the best of its kind, *Vanity Fair* (*March* 811–14). Nevertheless, although he admired the novel, he regretted that it was more a record than a rendering of life and that Thackeray interfered too much with his characters. In the Dedicatory Letter to Isabel Paterson that serves as foreword to *The Last Post*, Ford says that he had not planned a sequel to *A Man Could Stand Up*: "I have always jeered at authors who sentimentalised over their characters and after finishing a book exclaim like, say, Thackeray: 'Roll up the curtains; put the puppets in their boxes: quench the tallow footlights' . . . something like that" (vi).[12] At the end of *A Man Could Stand Up* Valentine and Christopher are dancing to the cheers of the "old pals,"

Tietjens' comrades from the trenches. These men have taken the place of the likes of Lord Port Scatho and Sir John Robertson and the society set that Christopher and Valentine once mingled with at the Macmasters' Friday afternoons. The "old pals" are the nucleus of the new Republic of ground and soul. The song they sing for Christopher and Valentine to dance to—"*Les petites marionettes, font! font! font!*"—is the scrap of a street song popular among French children:

> *Ainsi font! font! font! les petites marionettes!*
> *Ainsi font! font! font!*
> *Trois petits tours et puis s'en vont!*

With a nod to Thackeray, Ford ends his novel with a reference to puppets. But his characters are not to be put away in the showman's box. With closure of the novel deferred, Christopher and his friends, full of their new life, sing and dance their way into the postwar world.

In *Some Do Not* Ford Madox Ford makes a case against the continuance of a society that is so bereft of the cardinal virtues that its hollow manners lead to the horrors of war. In *No More Parades* he shows that a man's confrontation with sexual existence can be so much of a riddle that judgment and hell follow logically on an inability to solve the problem. In *A Man Could Stand Up* he presents the solution to the riddle by casting off a superseded code and by presenting simultaneously the emergence of a new order built upon self-command. In *The Last Post* he allows the new man and woman in their new republic of ground and soul to be discussed from different points of view. The novel is a symposium on their love and the new order of things. *Parade's End* brings together case, riddle, republic, and symposium as ways of presenting the cardinal virtues as they confront the last things. Complementary lovers like Christopher and Valentine are played off against romantic lovers like Vincent and Edith Ethel as the myth of a new freedom is worked out in conflict with the myth of an old concern. *Parade's End* recapitulates the basic elements of the Gothic-manners tradition at the same time that it dramatizes the destruction of society as the inevitable outcome of a world in which manners are divorced from justice. After *Jude the Obscure* the only thing that seemed possible was to destroy a society that was killing its best people. In *Parade's End* that destruction takes place in the war. Ford does what Hardy saw needed doing. In *Parade's End* the novel of Gothic manners reaches its logical conclusion.

Conclusion

If Ford brought the tradition of Gothic manners to a logical conclusion, he did not necessarily bring it to an end. Some and in some cases all elements of the Gothic-manners tradition made their way into fiction that was written after Hardy. We even find those elements in contemporary novels.

Almost a score of years before *The Shadow-Line* absorbed the Gothic tale into a nautical novel of manners, Conrad explored Gothic manners in *Heart of Darkness* (1899), which in turn helped inspire Evelyn Waugh's naughty novel about gentlemen in the jungle, *A Handful of Dust* (1934). Both Conrad and Waugh elaborate as well as parody the conventions of Gothic manners to show how desire rooted in manners gone amock leads to "The horror! The horror!" Conrad does this in the mode of tragic quest; Waugh in the mode of black comedy that encapsulates a quest motif. In addition, Max Beerbohm reconceived *Jude the Obscure* in his mock-epical novel *Zuleika Dobson* (1911), which, on one side, gives us the ultimate English gentleman in John, Duke of Dorset, and, on the other side, gives us the ultimate femme fatale in Zuleika Dobson. The gentleman reveals the fatality of British decorum; the lady reveals the fatality of romantic convention. Beerbohm sends up the ideals both of ideal conduct and of love-death. He laughs these variations on love and honor, the deadly staples of heroic literature, out of the twentieth-century novel, which certainly has had little to do with either since modernism became a fact of twentieth-century fiction. John Fowles has been similarly irreverent in *The French Lieutenant's Woman* (1967), which presents Victorian conventions as intolerable realizations of a myth of concern. He argues that men and women must recognize such a restrictive social myth as outmoded if they are to achieve their own individual freedom. In concluding this book, then, I want briefly to look at the parodic elements of these four novels and examine the way they advance the critique of society associated with a Gothic-manners tradition.

"The horror! The horror!" at the end of *Heart of Darkness* anticipates the horror of World War I in *Parade's End*: both are bloody carnivals of a middle-class morality that has been taken to its logical extreme. Marlow admits he admires Kurtz: "He had something to say. He said it. . . . He had summed up—he had judged. 'The Horror!' He was a remarkable man. After all, this was the expression of some sort of belief; it had candour, it had conviction, it had a vibrating note of revolt in its whisper, it had the appalling face of a glimpsed truth—the strange commingling of desire and hate" (151). A civilized life has ended in savagery. That is the horror and the truth of both Kurtz's life and of World War I. Kurtz as overlord of the Inner Station—as god of his own little portion of the earth—is a remarkable man because he tells the truth about being a successful man. He sends out more ivory than any other agent of "the Company." As its best businessman, Kurtz has achieved the bourgeois dream: he has become very rich very quickly and has settled down to living like a great lord on his African estate.

From the outside Kurtz is seen as the hero of a Social Darwinism that promotes the superiority of Western civilization and values. From the inside he is seen as a man whose Western values have not survived his contact with the Congo. Not simply has Kurtz become savage, he has made himself over as a savage god. Thus he surrounds himself with images of death to make it evident that he determines who will live and who will die. This is a world of arbitrary justice where the myth of freedom has been taken to the extreme. Kurtz stands in contrast to the accountant at the Outer Station whose manners are those of King William Street and whose concern is that he dress the part. The chief accountant lives a life of Gothic manners in which his manners are a joke: "No hat. Hair parted, brushed, oiled, under a green-lined parasol held in a big white hand." Marlow finds him a "miracle" (67). Kurtz for his part sees the joke of pretending to be civilized in a savage situation and lives the life of Gothic manners in which the manners have become "The horror! The horror!"

Kurtz also stands in contrast to "his Intended," whose concern is that she remember him as her romantic lover. And Marlow, with the riddle of Kurtz behind him and the case of the Intended before him, finds it necessary to admire the truth of "The horror!" and equally necessary to lie about Kurtz: "Hadn't he said he wanted only justice? But I couldn't. I could not tell her. It would have been too dark—too dark altogether . . ." (162). Marlow sees this clearly. He can tell the truth only to a small group of select listeners. "The horror!" and justice are only for the few. There is the private Kurtz of "The horror!" and the public Kurtz of the Company and the Intended. Marlow therefore presents the Intended with the hero that her civilization expects her to worship: the man whose love and honor survive the savage world intact: "'The last word he pronounced was— your name'" (161). By presenting two versions of Kurtz's last words, Marlow presents two versions of Kurtz. The first is a realistic version, the Kurtz of the Inner Station; the second is a parodic version, the Kurtz that civilization demands. Conrad through Marlow's lying parody opens up the tradition of Gothic manners not only to the kind of logically realistic exploitation that we have already seen in *Parade's End* but also to a parodic exploration of the kind that we are about to see in Beerbohm, Waugh, and Fowles.

H. G. Wells tried his hand at a comic version of *Jude the Obscure* in *The Wheels of Chance*. That that novel is so little known today is an indication of the little success it enjoyed—in contrast, say, to the great success of *Kipps*, Wells's version of *Great Expectations*. Max Beerbohm, however, created his most memorable work as a parody of *Jude* and the Oxford novel tradition. It is not simply John, Duke of Dorset, who dies for love in *Zuleika Dobson* but all of the undergraduates at Oxford. Not satisfied with her good fortune in wiping out one great university, Zuleika hires a special train to take her to Cambridge, where she hopes to repeat her success and go down in history as the greatest femme fatale since Helen of Troy. In his story of Dorset the dandy and Zuleika the deadly lady, Beerbohm sends up the whole tradition of romantic love and *Liebestod*. For if John seems to die for Zuleika and Zuleika seems to love John, each really loves himself and herself the best. Their most satisfying scenes take place in front of mirrors where they admire themselves. And if all the undergraduates at Oxford do die with Zuleika's name on their lips, their motivation is not love so much as snobbery. Dorset as Oxford's greatest snob must be followed by all the lesser men lest they lose their title to being snobs too. And Dorset's death is his supreme act of snobbery and self-love. Having told Zuleika he would die for her, he keeps his honor unsullied by seeming so to die even though he has come to hate her. Even when he decides to renege on his promise—after Zuleika soaks him with a pitcher of water as he speaks her name beneath her window— he cannot because the gods have decreed that Dorset must die. The gods thereby become the guarantors of his honor.

Beerbohm confounds Dorset's freedom of choice with his concern for his fellows at Oxford who insist on following his example. Case and riddle therefore become one as death and honor, love and hate, fate and snobbery so interpenetrate each other that all logic leads the Duke to a love-death for the woman he hates. The example of his good manners has to be taken by all who would be gentlemen on the model of the Duke of Dorset. In a novel replete with mock-epical machinery, Max Beerbohm shows just how bizarre the Gothic manners of a great feudal lord can be and just how funny the tragic conflict between love and honor can become. Is Dorset required to keep his pledge to die for the woman he hates? Isn't Dorset obliged *not* to die for Zuleika once he knows his fellows will follow his example? Is it really a question of honor to abet the killing-off of a generation of undergraduates in order to seem to keep one's word? Indeed, hasn't one already drowned with Zuleika's name on one's lips when one is dowsed with a pitcher of washing water as one calls her name beneath her window? Having been so drowned and having in the process caught a cold too, need one drown again?

If this were simply a case, a decision could easily be rendered. But this case is a riddle. Zuleika is a witch: "I give you Zuleika Dobson, the fairest witch that ever was or will be!" the Duke tells the Junta (96). A modern-day Circe, Zuleika will have her victims. Moreover the moment that Dorset reasons himself back to life and sees himself as the savior of Oxford besides, his butler sends word that the owls that announce the death of the head of the Tankerton family have hooted the night through and that the Duke therefore must die. Well, if he must die, then he will die keeping his word, shouting Zuleika's name as he jumps into the river. And he does just that taking everyone with him except Noaks, who is eventually shamed by Zuleika into jumping out a window and bashing out his brains in her honor. Satisfied with this total destruction, Zuleika leaves for Cambridge to see whether romantic love and romantic death are as much a part of the curriculum there as they were at Oxford. After all, a femme fatale can always hope that chivalry is not dead.

This intense preoccupation of the dandy and the deadly lady with themselves is a comic rendering of the consequences of their attachment to mirror images of themselves. Nothing pleases Dorset more than seeing himself in his robes of Knight of the Garter: "with head erect, and measured tread, he returned to the mirror. . . . A dandy he lived. In the full pomp and radiance of his dandyism he would die. . . . In death they [he and his image of himself as a dandy] would not be divided" (196–97). Dorset's nickname is not "Peacock" for nothing (26). Likewise, when she is poor, nothing pleases Zuleika more than "the little square of glass, nailed above the washstand"; when she is rich, nothing pleases her more than her "cheval-glass": "always she seemed to herself lovelier than she had ever been" (16–17). This definition of the self by way of an image of the self is a perfect realization of Lacan's notion of the alienation of the individual from his and her real self. In these instances it leads to the extinction of all the undergraduates at Oxford, which is a socialization of Lacan's concept of *le corps morcelé*. Lacan's conception of the mirror image and of the dismembered body as its consequence is relentlessly tragic. And so it can be thought, as *Wuthering Heights* suggests and as one interpretation of the ending of *The Portrait of a Lady* indicates. But what we see in Max Beerbohm's parody of conventions that appear in these and other novels is a relentless movement toward laughter because what he does in *Zuleika Dobson* is laugh at the miseries of romantic love through which, as Aristophanes remarked in the *Symposium*, man and woman seek their original undivided self. That self, Lacan, who frequently cited Aristophanes' speech, saw as real. Consequently, in a novelist like Beerbohm, we laugh at the human condition as presented by Jacques Lacan, who, report has it, lacked a sense of humor.

Beerbohm, lightheartedly, takes Lacan's analysis of the human condition to a ludicrously logical conclusion:

> "The reason why there were no undergraduates in your Hall tonight is that they were all dead" [Zuleika tells her grandfather, the Warden of Judas College].
> "Dead?" he gasped. "Dead? It is disgraceful that I was not told. What did they die of?"
> "Of me."
> "Of you?"
> "Yes. I am an epidemic, grand-papa, a scourge, such as the world has not known. The young men drowned themselves for love of me." (240)

The Warden feels disgraced by the singularly foolish conduct of the men of Judas. Zuleika then tells him that they were not alone:

> "There were others? cried the Warden. "How many?"
> "All. All the boys from all the Colleges."
> The Warden heaved a deep sigh. "Of course," he said, "this changes the aspect of the whole matter. I wish you had made it clear at once. You gave me a very great shock," he said, sinking into his arm-chair, "and I have not yet recovered. You must study the art of exposition." (241)

"You must study the art of exposition": one can hardly imagine a more wonderfully ludicrous or totally characteristic statement from a schoolmaster at a moment like this. If all the undergraduates of all the colleges have committed the same act of folly, then he cannot be singled out for blame. The Warden of Judas, in short, keeps his mirror image of himself intact too.

Evelyn Waugh's *A Handful of Dust* announces its Gothic affinity in its chapter titles: "English Gothic—I" (chap. 2), "English Gothic—II" (chap. 4), "English Gothic—III" (chap. 7). These chapters make a sandwich with "Hard Cheese on Tony" (chap. 3), a chapter that indicates the novel's indebtedness to the manners tradition in British fiction. The two other chapters, "Du Côté de Chez Beaver" (chap. 1) and "Du Côté de Chez Todd" (chap. 6), show where the hard cheese is manufactured. They also announce the Gothic manners of the novel by transposing the morals of civilization into a key suited to the voice of Tony Last, who reads the novels of Charles Dickens aloud to Mr. Todd, Waugh's Amazonian version of Conrad's Kurtz of the Congo. But if Conrad suggests that civilized values cannot stand the test of the wild, Waugh suggests that civilization itself has gone wild. Tony Last is as much a victim of the Beavers of London as of Mr. Todd of the Amazon. Hetton as a silver-fox farm is no less savage than Mr. Todd's compound as a meeting place for the Dickens Society.

The English Gothic chapters of *A Handful of Dust* focus on Hetton, Tony Last's neo-Gothic estate built at the fag end of the Gothic revival in an "authentic Pecksniff" style (43). Almost an anachronism at its inception, Hetton is a total anachronism by the 1930s. Gothic style as Ruskin conceived of it was the expression of the religious and communal ethos of the Middle Ages, but Hetton as Waugh presents it has nothing to do with religion or community. In the Last world overrun by Beavers there is no community, only aberrant individuality; there is no religion, only its mockery. Thus the Sunday service is haphazardly attended, bizarrely celebrated, and morally inconsequent. The Reverend Tendril preaches sermons that he wrote while a garrison chaplain in India, and Tony goes to church to think quietly about renovating the bathrooms at Hetton. Consequently, the myth of concern in the novel focuses on Tony Last's attempt to live like a feudal landowner in a manor house where the bedrooms are named after Arthurian characters and the plumbing needs repairs. The competing myth of freedom focuses on London society where Brenda Last becomes a model of infidelity by her affair with John Beaver, who cares nothing for anyone but himself. The supposedly perfect couple, Tony and Brenda, give way to the imperfect couple, Brenda and Beaver, as the ideal romantic marriage gives way to the impossible affair in a mockery of both complementary married love and affined romantic love. Intemperance and imprudence are the guiding norms of society, and justice consists of an advantageous settlement in a divorce court. In such an atmosphere, case and riddle are one because there are no moral bearings to make a case make sense. Thus there is the farce of Tony's trying to act the part of a gentleman by pretending to have an adulterous weekend at Brighton. Brenda, pretending moral outrage, will use that against him so that he, not she, will be seen as the guilty party in the divorce proceedings. After all, a lady's honor must be protected. But only to a certain point. When Brenda demands an exorbitant settlement that will endanger Tony's keeping Hetton, he refuses to divorce her. Justice does not extend to Tony's buying Beaver for Brenda if Tony has to sell Hetton to do it.

The case for Brenda's marrying Beaver can be made only after Tony Last is pronounced dead. By that time, however, Beaver has lost interest, and Jock Grant-Menzies has taken his place. After Tony is pronounced dead, a monument is erected at Hetton to his memory as an "Explorer." But, of course, Tony Last is not dead. The monument to him at Hetton has no more meaning than his simple grave in the Amazon.

In all of this confounding of life and death, love and lust, profit and loss, Waugh is making a case against postwar England in the thirties, which he thinks more an animal farm than a human community. He gives us not only beavers but rabbits and pigs and foxes too. The law of the wild has somehow come to replace the law of society. In this context Tony's search for the Lost City as the partner of Dr. Messinger becomes Waugh's bitter indictment of his contemporaries. Everything about Tony Last is anachronistic, so Waugh has him play out his character in a romantic quest for the Lost City of the Amazon, which Tony envisions as a perfect Gothic creation: "He had a clear picture of it in his mind. It was Gothic in character, all vanes and pinnacles, gargoyles, battlements, groining and tracery, pavilions

and terraces, a transfigured Hetton, pennons and banners float-
ing on the sweet breeze, everything luminous and translucent; a
coral citadel crowning a green hill top sewn with daisies, among
groves and streams; a tapestry landscape filled with heraldic and
fabulous animals and symmetrical, disproportionate blossom"
(222). On his way to this city of his dreams, Tony meets the
beautiful Thérèse de Vitré of Trinidad, age eighteen, and they
fall romantically in love. But the moment she finds out he is married, she immediately drops him. Her social and moral code has
no place for a married man—even one soon to be divorced. The
island society of Trinidad proves more civilized than the island
society of England: concern and the moral virtues go hand in
hand in Trinidad but not in London. London is more like the
Amazon; thus the parallel titles of "Du Côté de Chez Beaver"
and "Du Côté de Chez Todd." Both city and jungle are governed
by *Tod*, Death; appropriately, Waugh cites T. S. Eliot's line from
The Waste Land—"I will show you fear in a handful of dust"—in
the epigraph of the novel.

Mr. Todd saves Tony's life so that he can have someone
read Dickens' novels to him for the rest of his life. And they
begin their reading with *Bleak House*, Dickens' scathing indictment of country-house life and the Court of Chancery in London.
Mr. Todd is deeply moved by the plight of Dickens' characters:
"at the description of the sufferings of the outcasts in 'Tom-
all-alones' tears ran down his cheeks into his beard" (293). But
Mr. Todd's feelings relate to no concept of justice that has any
application to Tony as his prisoner. Indeed, to keep Tony with
him, Mr. Todd pronounces Last dead to the search party that
comes to find him; he even shows them Tony's grave. Mr. Todd
gives the search party Tony's watch to prove that he has seen
Tony die—a gesture which nicely suggests that Tony has no time
of his own left to live. He is certainly legally dead by the time the
novel ends. Tony has fallen victim to a man to whom Dickens'
concept of justice means nothing.

Waugh recreates the ending of *Heart of Darkness* to dramatize that, after all, Mr. Kurtz is not dead but alive and well in
Mr. Todd. It is Mr. Last who is dead because he lives with *Tod(d)*
itself. But, of course, the last laugh is not on Tony; it is on English society. Tony's friends at Du Côté de Chez Beaver are no

more alive than poor Tony himself at Du Côté de Chez Todd. If Todd preys on Tony, the English prey on each other. There is no more justice in the world of the Beavers than in the world of the Todds. Waugh uses the quest format ·'to show that there is *no escape*, however far one journeys, from the power structures that rule society and dictate human behavior" (Boone 275). Todds and Beavers are the same breed.

The last chapter of the novel is "English Gothic—III" in which Hetton has been turned into a silver-fox farm. The last image of the novel is the feeding of fifty dead rabbits to the foxes in what Tony's cousins, the new owners of Hetton, call "the stinkeries." The genius of Evelyn Waugh in writing *A Handful of Dust* is to divert the tradition of Gothic manners into a totally satiric mode so as to render the traditional venues of English life and fiction, the country house and the city of London, convincingly as "the stinkeries." Waugh has rendered a last judgment on his dead countrymen by placing them in his version of an odoriferous hell—living with and cannibalizing each other. For Waugh, to live on and on without religious and social values for as many years as there are grains in a handful of dust is to live as dead men who just plain stink.

The French Lieutenant's Woman travesties Victorian fiction and morality. In doing so, John Fowles's novel revitalizes the fiction of Gothic manners while deconstructing it. Of the elements of Gothic manners that we have examined in this study, only two retain any importance as values in *The French Lieutenant's Woman*. They are the myth of freedom and the moral virtue of justice. In the final analysis the only concern in the novel is a concern for individual freedom, and the only justice is justice to oneself. The last things lose their power except as a way to abuse the horrible Mrs. Poulteney, whose soul, we are told is "well-grilled" (51) by the time Fowles writes his novel. The moral virtue of prudence gives way to the total imprudence of Charles Smithson, who tosses over a carefully arranged marriage and a tempting offer of financial security; and the moral virtue of temperance gives way to the fornication of Charles and Sarah, which moves the lives of both of them toward a greater, if more trying, moral good. Complementary love is discarded as useless in Smithson's repudiation of his betrothal to Ernestina Freeman, and affined love has only the briefest moment of satisfaction in the sexual encounter of Charles and Sarah. Indeed, Sarah goes on to become "la belle dame sans merci," who kills her lover's love so that he and she can find their own individual souls. And the whole novel is set up as a case that really is a riddle, as Sarah, the diagnosed melancholiac, becomes more herself and harder to understand. As the French lieutenant's woman she is neither the hysterical lady seduced by La Roncière in the story within a story told by Fowles nor the seduced and abandoned woman of the story of her own invention in which she is the victim of Varguennes. "Who is Sarah? Out of what shadows does she come?" the narrator asks. "I do not know," the narrator answers (80).

With those last four words the tradition of the omniscient narrator of Victorian fiction is ridiculed. Along with the omniscient narrator, the convention of realism is called into question too: "This story I am telling is all imagination. These characters I create never existed outside my own mind" (80). What Fowles does here is expose the contradictory nature of these two conventions of Victorian fiction, suggesting that nothing that someone knows all about can possibly imitate reality. Other conventions are travestied as well. The bourgeois dream, for instance, is mercilessly treated. Charles Smithson expects to inherit his uncle's estate, but loses it to Sir Robert's determination to end his bachelorhood in old age and marry the scheming Mrs. Bella Tompkins. Then his fiancée's father, a department-store mogul, offers to make Charles his heir and successor—"I have no son" (226)—and Fowles immediately presents Smithson as "Jesus of Nazareth tempted by Satan" (227). Having lost Sir Robert's estate, Charles refuses further to enter into the bourgeois dream by becoming rich and settling down on one of Mr. Freeman's making, just as he finally refuses to marry the boss's daughter and condemn himself to living the dream he repudiates.

The Victorian convention of naming characters to suit their roles is another that Fowles travesties in this novel. Mr. Freeman is the prisoner of commerce. Although a gentleman, Charles is merely a smith's son. Mrs. Poulteney's housekeeper, Mrs. Fairley is unfair; she is a sadist like her mistress (22). Smithson's unfaithful servant is named Sam after Pickwick's faithful Weller.

Dr. Grogan has embraced science as a way of salvation, but he is named after grog, an intoxicating drink. Sarah's name is Wood-ruff, but she changes it to Roughwood, and Charles is "crucified on *her*" (285). This religious imagery leads Fowles into a decon-structive play with language as he presents religion, the main-stay of Victorian morality, as a myth of concern that needs to be reanimated because, as Leslie Stephen indicates in the epi-graph to chapter 37, "Respectability has spread its leaden mantle over the whole country . . . and the man wins the race who can worship that great goddess with the utmost devotion" (222). "Respectability is what does not give me offense" (31), Mrs. Poul-teney says, which is enough to give it a bad name out of hand. Indeed, the Christian religion has become a religion of Respecta-bility, an idol supported by money, rank, and snobbery. But as Charles discovers in his "sin" with Sarah, "the right purpose of Christianity" is "to bring about a world in which the hanging man could be descended, could be seen not with the rictus of agony on his face, but the smiling peace of a victory brought about by, and in, living men and women" (285).

This is a reinterpretation of Christianity that is oriented to-ward the individual rather than toward the system. Thus it is that in Charles's love for Sarah "the moment overcame the age" (199). What is implicit in Fowles's questioning of Victorian ortho-doxy in a character like Mrs. Poulteney—her house "Stygian" (21), her manners those of the "Gestapo" (23)—or in a charac-ter like Mr. Freeman, an imitator of an "earlier generation of Puritan profiteers" (223), is an acceptance of Bakhtin's analysis of the vocabulary of Protestantism: "Calvin's language, the lan-guage of the middle classes ('of shop-keepers and tradesmen') was an intentional and conscious lowering of, almost a travesty on, the sacred language of the Bible" (*Dialogic* 71). Fowles tries to reanimate the "sacred language of the Bible" in relation to an existential reading of the meaning of "God" as "the freedom that allows other freedoms to exist" (82). To do this he has to call into question the conventions of Victorian morality and of Victorian fiction. As Bakhtin points out, "It is necessary to destroy and rebuild the entire false picture of the world, to sunder the false hierarchical links between objects and ideas, to abolish the divi-sive ideational strata. It is necessary to liberate all these objects and permit them to enter into the free unions that are organic to them, no matter how monstrous these unions might seem from the point of view of ordinary, traditional associations" (*Dialogic* 169). The contribution that John Fowles makes to the great tradition of a fiction of Gothic manners is to build it up and to knock it down by using its conventions for the purpose of construction and deconstruction simultaneously.

The fiction of Gothic manners is animated in its dying in *The French Lieutenant's Woman*. In this final fillip of parody only freedom and justice remain, and these must be redefined by each individual reader in the choosing of an ending for the novel.[1] The reader is not required to accept an interpretation of a hero such as Trollope's interpretation of Mr. Harding at the end of *Barchester Towers*; the reader is not required to submit to the author's picking one ending over another as Dickens did at the end of *Great Expectations*; the reader is not required to submit to a conclusion like that provided by George Eliot in the Finale of *Middlemarch*. The reader is not even required to submit to a character's sense of an ending like that given by Henrietta Stackpole in *The Portrait of a Lady* or like that given by Arabella in *Jude the Obscure*. The reader is left with a walk down a street in Fowles's novel, not unlike the way he is left with a song and a dance at the end of *A Man Could Stand Up*. The reader, like Charles Smithson, must go out upon life's "unplum'd, salt, estranging sea" (366) and find his or her own individuality, starting with the choice of an ending for this novel. In that way *The French Lieutenant's Woman* gives a final turn of the screw to the tradition of Gothic manners in which social vitality originates in individual freedom.

Notes

Works Cited

Index

Notes

Introduction

1   There is evidence of a resistance to associating these two novels too closely with Walpole's, just as there is evidence of a counterresistance to separating them from the old Gothic formulas. For example, George Levine argues that *Frankenstein* is "a psychomachia of the extremes of human consciousness aspiring to transcend the limits of thought and language by touching a new reality and to assert the compatability of that reality with poetic, moral, and religious ideals" (26). Viewed in this way, *Frankenstein* provides "both a pattern and a metaphor for the very different realist literature that followed" it (23). But writing at approximately the same time as Levine, Maximillian Novak places Mary Shelley's novel squarely in the old Gothic tradition: "The skeleton with its combination of deathly terror and horrible grin is the essence of the grotesque and the essence of the Gothic. . . . And . . . [its] involuntary grin plays over the 'straight black lips' of Frankenstein's monster" (51). Whereas Robert D. Hume argued that *Melmoth* was "the last and clearly the greatest of the Gothic novels of this period" [1764–1820], George Haggerty, while making a case for the novel's artistry, also demonstrated how that artistry fell short of Maturin's goals (389–90).

2   On *The Castle of Otranto* and its successors see the standard books of Sommers and Varma, the more recent books of MacAndrew and Day; also G. R. Thompson's collection of papers on the Gothic; in addition, see Hume's revaluatory essay as well as Novak's and Haggerty's reassessments of the Gothic tradition.

3   Jean Starobinski, arguing the case for Walpole, presents *Otranto* as "an intense dreamworld inhabited by the phantasms of violence, incest and catastrophe," which was Walpole's way of circumvent-

ing the dull, circumscribing rationalism of the Enlightenment: "It is as though this modest respectable gentleman, with his intellectual freedom, had wished to evade the dullness of an uneventful life by creating a universe overflowing with guilt and affliction" (188). But if dullness serves as an excuse for fantasy—manifested in violence, incest, catastrophe, guilt, and affliction—it does not make phantasmagoric characters, actions, and settings any more probable: it does not show that they have any logic of their own in *Otranto*. Thus Masao Miyoshi's insistence that "a more complete critical picture should take into account its mechanical plot, pasteboard characters, and the unashamed improbability of its supernatural events" (6).

4   MacAndrew (16–18) presents a different picture of *The Castle of Otranto*, arguing for its coherence as a symbolic allegory.

5   "Thus Cervantes allows the horizon of expectations of the favorite old tales of knighthood to arise out of the reading of *Don Quixote*, which the adventure of his last knight then seriously parodies" (Jauss, *Aesthetic* 24).

6   La Bruyère writes, "Il y en a une autre, et que j'ai intérêt que l'on veuille suivre, qui est de ne pas perdre mon titre de vue, et de penser toujours, et dans toute la lecture de cet ouvrage, que ce sont les caractères ou les moeurs de ce siècle que je décris . . ." (62). In short, when *Les caractères* appeared in 1688, manners were seen as directly related to character, which is formed by "habitual behaviour or conduct."

7   While pursuing a line of argumentation different from Heilman's, Judith Wilt explores ways that Gothicism survives the demise of the old Gothic novel in *Ghosts of the Gothic*.

8   Robert M. Polhemus echoes this tension between concern and freedom in his placing of tradition and dogma against comic vision, which enables one "to find or 'excite' mirth, to justify life, and to imagine the means of its benevolent regeneration in the future" (*Comic Faith* 20).

9   Jolles provides this example: Two experts were asked to judge the taste of a hundred-year-old cask of wine. One found that the wine tasted slightly of iron, the other that it tasted slightly of leather. When the cask was emptied, a leather lace holding a tiny iron key, which must have been dropped during the pressing of the grapes, was found at its bottom. Each expert was therefore correct in his judgment of the wine. This case clearly admits of more than one judgment as long as taste remains the norm for evaluation (152–53).

10 This is the end of a brief exchange in Hemingway's *Islands in the Stream*. The woman begins:

"Should I be you or you be me?"

"You have first choice."

"I'll be you."

"I can't be you. But I can try."

This is a more realistic version of a similar dialogue in *A Farewell to Arms*, where the woman again takes the lead:

"Oh darling, I want you so much I want to be you too."

"You are. We're the same one." (Crews 24)

11 Lacan presents at least three forms of alienation or "lack" in man. The first is sexual and occurs when the androgynous cell yields to the determination of one's sex in the womb. The second is personal and occurs at the "mirror-stage" when one determines one's identity through an agency outside oneself (rather than from within) by recognizing and idealizing an image of oneself. The third is cultural and occurs when in sacrificing one's desires in exchange for social accommodation one gives up the only real thing in oneself. These three phases of alienation create an insatiable desire to fulfill oneself in a real way, but one never can because one has been assimilated into a cultural code by language. That language as well as the cultural code it supports is "phallocentric" because it is the product of a masculine authority, which forms the social order. Everything that one does, then, is done not in the name of the real desires of one's being but in "the-Name-of-the-Father." One thereby sacrifices the penis, the organ of sexual desire, for the phallus, the symbol of male domination and a logocentric or rational system. Because in this culture men are not men and women not women—they act out the same social code, not individual desire— Lacan maintains that there is no such thing as heterosexual intercourse, the one thing that would help to heal the primal loss of one's androgynous entity in the womb. All intercourse, even that between the sexes, Lacan therefore calls "*hommosexuel*" (spelled in precisely that way) because the male and female victims of phallocentric society are one and the same. Insofar as the cultural system is self-perpetuating, thwarted "desire is affirmed as the absolute condition" of human existence. All men and women are therefore doomed to live fragmentary lives and to be unhappy. Whereas there is of course a great deal more to Lacan than this (see Silverman; MacCannell) this is enough to show in a nutshell why fragmentation (*le corps morcelé*) is the ordinary human condition.

12 Like Letwin's, Bakhtin's sense of the self as complementary rather than affined has a theological foundation: "Bakhtin's insistence on the necessity of 'understanding' the position not only of the other

but of all others, by adding communication theory to theology, extends the meaning of Christ's biblical injunction to treat others as we would be treated ourselves, to take on, in other words, the role of others with the same depth of sympathy and understanding that we bring to our own perception of ourselves. In Bakhtin's system this is not merely a moral imperative but an epistemological requirement" (Clark and Holquist 208).

13 See Bakhtin, "Forms of Time" (224–36), where he presents the idyll as helping to form the provincial novel, the *Bildungsroman*, the sentimental novel, and the family novel.

Chapter 1. *Pride and Prejudice*

1 The Austen novel that is most insistently a case is *Persuasion*. After her engagement to Wentworth, Anne Elliot reflects upon her case:

"I have been thinking over the past, and trying impartially to judge of the right and wrong, I mean with regard to myself; and I must believe that I was right, much as I suffered from it, that I was perfectly right in being guided by a friend whom you will love better than you do now. To me, she was in the place of a parent. Do not mistake me, however. I am not saying that she did not err in her advice. It was, perhaps, one of those cases in which advice is good or bad only as the event decides; and for myself, I certainly never should, in any circumstance of tolerable similarity, give such advice. But I mean, that I was right in submitting to her, and that if I had done otherwise, I should have suffered more in continuing the engagement than I did even in giving it up, because I should have suffered in my conscience. I have now, as far as such a sentiment is allowable in human nature, nothing to reproach myself with; and if I mistake not, a strong sense of duty is no bad part of a woman's portion." (248)

Robert Hopkins has made this statement the centerpiece of an article that begins by considering Anne Elliot's actions as "a hypothetical case" (143). He places the weighing of truth against morality—of "what is" against "what ought to be" (158)—in the context of ethical consequentialism, the norm for interpreting this case. Moreover, for Hopkins, the nicety of the moral problem generates aesthetic value too: "Precisely because *Persuasion* places a heavy burden on individual choice, on personal judgment by an agent when confronted with the complexities of consequentialism and the context of moral luck, it has become my favorite Jane Austen novel" (156).

Chapter 2. *Barchester Towers*

1   Asa Briggs writes that "the symbol of the Crystal Palace, built for
the Great Exhibition of 1851, dominates the whole period from 1851
to 1867. . . . Its destruction [by fire on an autumn night in 1936]
severed one of the most interesting visible links of continuity with
the mid-Victorian period: 'It was like watching the burning of a
Victorian Valhalla when the gods of our fathers sat in a solemn
circle awaiting the end'" (*Victorian People* 14).

2   In editions of *Barchester Towers* that number chapters consecutively,
vol. 2 comprises chaps. 20–34 and vol. 3 chaps. 35–53.

3   On other similarities between Arabin and Trollope, see Wiesenfarth, "Dialectics" 40.

4   "Then our guardians must not be fond of laughter. For when anyone gives himself up to violent laughter, his condition calls for a
strong reaction. So if any poet represents men of sense as overcome
by laughter, the verses must be deleted, and much more so if he
says it of the gods" (quoted in Gilbert 32).

5   "A novel in style should be easy, lucid, and of course grammatical.
The same may be said of any book; but that which is intended
to recreate should be easily understood,—for which purpose lucid
narration is an essential. In matter it should be moral and amusing.
In manner it may be realistic, or sublime, or ludicrous;—or it may
be all these if the author can combine them." (Trollope, *Thackeray*
184).

6   *Spectator* (16 May 1857) quoted in Smalley 42. For alternative views
of Madeline, see Daniel 533; Knoepflmacher, *Laughter and Despair*
37–39; Krieger 251; Polhemus, *Anthony Trollope* 48.

7   See Polhemus, *Anthony Trollope* 45; also Daniel 533; Edwards 26;
Kincaid, *Novels* 107–8.

8   On the condition of English universities, see Wiesenfarth, "Dialectics" 44–46.

9   "I had already made up my mind that *Pride and Prejudice* was the
best novel in the English Language,—a palm which I only partially
withdrew after a second reading of *Ivanhoe*, and did not completely
bestow elsewhere till *Esmond* was written" (*Autobiography* 35).

10 Trollope goes on to say that "the novelist creeps in closer than the
schoolmaster, closer than the father, closer almost than the mother"
(*Thackeray* 203). Trollope recommended Thackeray as wholesome
reading: "The girl will never become bold under his preaching, or
taught to throw herself at men's heads. Nor will the lad receive a
false flashy idea of what becomes a youth, when he is first about to
take his place among men" (206).

11 "Without the lesson the amusement will not be there. There are

novels which certainly can teach nothing; but then neither can they amuse any one" (*Thackeray* 207).

12   Trollope's politics are treated in Kincaid's "*Barchester Towers* and the Nature of Conservative Comedy" and at book length in Halperin's *Trollope and Politics*. Subsequently, Halperin published an article entitled "Trollope's Conservatism," which traces the novelist's conservative views in the face of his profession of "advanced conservative liberal" principles and his membership in the liberal party.

Chapter 3. *Wuthering Heights*

1   Walter L. Reed, *Meditations*, also notes the similarities between Brontë's novel and Scott's.

2   Other instances of violence are catalogued by Wade Thompson, "Infanticide."

3   On Heathcliff's predisposition to sadism, see Homans 16–19.

4   "The act of observing another person, often, though not always, secretly, is a paradigmatic Gothic motif; it is the act of watching one's self" (Day 64).

5   Robert Kiely discusses "heaven" and "hell" at length in *The Romantic Novel in England* (233–49).

6   T. E. Apter writes, "The novel insists that passion is a force with its own laws, a cosmic, inhuman thing that cannot be denied or treated lightly" (206).

7   Mr. Linton's violent and arbitrary way of solving a problem seems to be a reflection of the West Riding magistrates of the day, according to their contemporary, Sir Charles Napier: "The Tory magistrates are bold, violent, irritating, uncompromising" (David Wilson 98).

8   For a psychoanalytical reading of Cathy's illness, see Homans 16–19.

9   On the riddle as a literary form see Jolles 103–20.

10 J. Hillis Miller (*Fiction* 55–57) assigns significance to the Catherine Earnshaw–Catherine Heathcliff–Catherine Linton passage but is anxious about its "imperialistic will to power" over other significant passages; this leads him to read it differently from the way I do. Miller's deconstructive reading of *Wuthering Heights* has been formidably met by Clayton: "For Emily Brontë, the 'undecidability' of a work of literature relates neither to the presence or absence of a 'transcendent cause' nor to the meaning or lack of meaning of ghostly traces; it relates to the otherness of the power that she and countless readers have felt her texts to possess" (86).

11   Homans writes that "the whole form of the novel is a diary." The
     implications of diary form have been worked out in detail by Ber-
     nard Duyfhuizen in *Narratives of Transmission: Communicating Fic-
     tional Texts*, a forthcoming book, which contains a chapter on *Wuth-
     ering Heights*.
12   Leo Bersani discusses other effects of repetition in the novel (197–
     203).
13   C. P. Sanger's chronology of events shows that Edgar Linton dies in
     August or September 1801, that Lockwood arrives in late Novem-
     ber 1801, and that Heathcliff dies in May 1802; see Sanger 17–18.
14   Winifred Gérin uses these lines from Wordsworth's *Prelude* as the
     epigraph of her biography of Emily Brontë.

Chapter 4. *Great Expectations*

 1   "Nüchtern, amüsiert, zynisch, mit Hilfe von Ironie und grotesker
     Darstellung, aber unter Vermeidung übertriebener Rhetorik deckt
     er seine früheren Irrtümer und Fehler auf" (163); the translation in
     the text is my own.
 2   David Craig sees the two selves of Pip as giving the whole novel
     its structure and even as explaining the revised ending. He argues
     that Pip's self of fantasy (Pip the gentleman) and Pip's real self (the
     bundle of shivers) represent a progressive self and a self of origins.
     They are played off against each other and symbolized in various
     ways (the marsh land; the ruined garden); these selves create a
     dialectic of action that lasts to the novel's end where Estella, the
     object of Pip's fantasy, turns up a time-worn beauty, but a beauty
     nonetheless: she satisfies both his real and fantasized need. This is
     one example of a sustained reading of Dickens' personalization of
     Great Expectations.
 3   Ruth M. VandeKieft shows that a similar pattern is worked out
     completely in the life of Mrs. Joe (176). G. Robert Stange argues
     that the novel is "a parable which illustrates several religious para-
     doxes: he [Pip] can gain only by losing all he has; only by being
     defiled can he be cleansed" (77). John H. Hagan, Jr., sees Pip as
     a "scapegoat," taking upon himself "society's vices, its selfishness,
     ingratitude, extravagance, and pride." Pip represents more than "a
     study of personal development. In his lonely struggle to work out
     his salvation, he is atoning for the guilt of society at large" ("Poor"
     91, 93).
 4   Julian Moynahan offers a further psychological analysis of the "fan-
     tasy element" in "the drive for power and the drive for more
     mother-love" in the novel (156).

5   Humphry House makes a similar observation when he asserts that "it is a remarkable achievement to have kept the reader's sympathy throughout a snob's progress. The book is the clearest triumph of the Victorian bourgeoisie on its own special ground. The expectations lose their greatness, and Pip is saved from the grosser dangers of wealth; but by the end he has gained a wider and deeper knowledge of life; he is less rough, better spoken, better read, better mannered; he has friends as various as Herbert Pocket, Jaggers, and Wemmick; he has earned in his business abroad enough to pay his debts; he has become third partner in a firm that 'had a good name, and worked for its profits and did very well.' Who is to say that these are not advantages? Certainly not Dickens" (44).

6   On Orlick as giving a definition to one side of Pip's character, see Moynahan 106–63; Wintersdorf 219–21; and Axton 285–87, who writes, "Pip must come to an understanding of Orlick as an alter ego representing what evil really is as practiced by himself and by the society envisaged in this novel" (285).

7   "Miss Havisham has a function only comparable to that of the justice of the peace or clergyman in a marriage ceremony," writes VandeKieft: "the lovers must make their vows to each other . . . not the presiding official. Joe turns this potentially disagreeable business interview into a ceremony of love; he makes vows of duty and affection" (174).

8   There is a provocative discussion of all these types of gentleman in David Castronovo's *The English Gentleman* 5–61.

9   I cannot agree with Brooks's argument that "the pages that follow [Pip's recognition and acceptance of Magwitch] may simply be *obiter dicta*" (137). To do so would be to scrap chapter 57, which stands in vital relation to chapter 1, where Pip's world is turned upside down by Magwitch; and to chapter 39, where Magwitch's return makes Pip dizzy ("the room began to surge and turn" [337]). In chapter 57, after Magwitch dies, Pip experiences like sensations in his fever and delirium. But chapter 57 is significant not only to this incremental repetition in the novel but also to chapter 56, where Pip's actions with Magwitch anticipate Joe's with Pip in chapter 57. By their very placement in a climactic series, Dickens is suggesting that chapter 57 is more important than chapter 56; indeed, he suggests that chapter 57 builds on chapter 56 (as well as on chapters 1 and 39). Dickens has Joe do for Pip exactly what Pip did for Magwitch: attend him in a grave illness. In acting toward Magwitch as Joe will act toward him, Pip achieves the status of gentleman, not socially but existentially, the way Joe has. Because it takes one to

know one, Pip the gentleman can now recognize Joe as the greater gentleman. Beside Magwitch's deathbed Pip earns the right to decipher the riddle of "a J and a O" (" 'Is it Joe?' . . . 'Which it air, old chap' ") and affirm the blacksmith as "gentle Christian man" (472).

10   Sir Edward Coke writes: "For a man's house is his castle, & *domus sua cuique tutissimum refugium*; for where shall a man be safe, if it be not in his house."

11   Lawrence Jay Dessner asserts that Wemmick is "the novel's most deeply imagined victim" (66). Anthony Winner, quoting Graham Smith, remarks that "Wemmick can maintain his Walworth self 'only at the expense of spiritual fragmentation' " (109).

12   Stanley Tick rates the law higher than Mr. Bumble does. "Like literature itself," Tick writes, "the law is an expression of morality abstracted and formalized: it offers an essential text for any man who seeks truth in phrases" (146).

13   Almost every critic of the novel has something to say about its ending. For a variety of ways of preferring one ending to another, see David Craig, Greenberg, Meisel, and Millhauser. Kestner argues that it is "completely acceptable to consider both of them [the endings] as part of the architecture of the novel" (*Spatiality* 121). "Both conclusions intend a physical parting, but with a spiritual unity, between Pip and Estella. Commentators ignore the fact that in the revised conclusion, presumably including all data Pip wished one to know, the final phrase is 'friends apart.' Had Dickens's intention been otherwise, that expression would not have been the final statement from Estella, who never lied. There will be no 'shadow of another parting' for the reason that there will not be another meeting" (186 n. 66). Brooks argues that one need not trouble oneself to choose among endings (Millhauser identifies three endings) because "the real ending may take place with Pip's recognition and acceptance of Magwitch after his recapture" (136). Raina is equally uninterested in choosing among endings, arguing that Pip's growth is made manifest in his self-imposed exile in Cairo and in his realization that "what he owes Joe can never be repaid in money" (128–29). In other words, Pip's coming to maturity is much more important than his deciding how he is going to spend his mature years: with or without Estella.

Chapter 5. *Middlemarch*

1   Taking aim in *Little Dorrit* at gentility and propriety, the first cousins of respectability, Dickens creates the character of Mrs. General with as devastating an accuracy as he does that of Mr. Vholes in *Bleak*

House. For a trenchant discussion of Mrs. General, see Castronovo 65–69.

2   The essence of carnival is that it "is not a spectacle seen by the people; they live in it, and everyone participates because its very idea embraces all the people" (Bakhtin, *Rabelais* 7). Carnival also involves a free intermingling of people of all ranks and professions in society. During carnival authority conferred by age, law, church, and society counts for nothing. All men and women are equal (Bakhtin, *Problems of Dostoevsky's Poetics* 122–23). To carnivalize an institution, a character, or an event is to bring it into the mainstream of life and to deflate its pretensions to superiority through laughter, ridicule, and even through outright scorn.

3   Bakhtin points out the "connection between digestion and dialogue" (Clark and Holquist 302). A kind of "prandial libertinism" in which all sorts of people eat with each other is characteristic of carnival (*Rabelais* 297). Respectability, however, tends to place one group of people apart from another. Usually such people are fastidious about the way they eat or, like Vholes and Casaubon and Bulstrode, have poor constitutions and are poor eaters. Dickens and Eliot carnivalize Vholes, Casaubon, and Rosamond, not by having them *eat with* people but by having them *eat* people. Eliot further parodies Bulstrode's respectability with Raffles' deviltry, which is also essential to carnival.

4   For a different reading of Rosamond from a feminist point of view, see Gilbert and Gubar 514–21; there she is valorized by the similarities between her characterization and Dorothea's. Her similarities with Casaubon are consequently overlooked while Lydgate's are emphasized.

5   George Eliot added this passage—from the word "found" to the word "summons"—to her manuscript to emphasize Casaubon's transformation; see Brit. Mus. Add. MS. 34,035, fol. 296; see Wiesenfarth, *George Eliot's Mythmaking* 207.

6   On the "perfectly complementary nature" of Raffles and Bulstrode, see Carroll 82.

7   See Wiesenfarth, "*Middlemarch*: The Language of Art."

8   See U. C. Knoepflmacher's elucidation of George Eliot's punning on "will" in his *Religious Humanism* 110.

9   See George Eliot, *A Writer's Notebook* 135, 221 n. 8. Ford Madox Ford explains succinctly just how and why the artist must hate: "I do not mean to say that a writer of novels should hate governments, or institutions, or organised cruelties. Such a man is a Social Reformer. But a certain hatred for certain types, a certain cynical dislike for the imbecile, gross, and stupid nature of things, for the meannesses of

the human heart, for want of imagination, and for the measure of hypocrisy that is necessary to keep us poor human things all going on—that sort of hatred is an almost necessary motive power for the artist" (Hueffer, "Miss May Sinclair" 599).

Chapter 6. *The Portrait of a Lady*

1 James reworks some very specific new Gothic elements of *Middlemarch* in *The Portrait*. Casaubon haunts his library, drawing imaginery lines of connection between antique myths; Osmond sits in his study "drawing . . . an antique coin." James called Casaubon an "arid pedant" in his review of *Middlemarch*; Ralph calls Osmond a "sterile dilettante." These unproductive husbands despise their young wives' ideas and demand obedience to their own judgments. They darken their wives' worlds and make them miserable. "Dorothea, shrouded in darkness," finds her life a "nightmare" in which "every energy" is "arrested by dread"; Isabel, sleepless in a darkened world, is "assailed by visions." Their husbands' ever-narrowing minds imprison the women in suffering. Casaubon's dark mind is projected in Lowick and Osmond's in Roccanera, each house suitably named for its darkness. These houses contain dungeons in which Dorothea and Isabel suffer: Dorothea longs for a "lunette [to be] opened in the wall of her prison, giving a glimpse of the sunny air"; Isabel sees Osmond's beautiful mind "peep[ing] down from a small high window [to] mock at her." Dorothea is a "virgin sacrifice[d]" to Casaubon, who grows "grey crunching bones in a cavern"; Osmond grinds Isabel "in the very mill of the conventional." The irony of the horror is that Casaubon and Osmond are monstrous and devilish because they are, impeccably, gentlemen. The one is "a man of honour according to the code"; the other is "convention itself." Nonetheless, Casaubon is "a dragon"; Osmond is worse, "the deadliest of fiends." If Dorothea, "shut . . . in prison," has a purgatorial life, Isabel's has a "hellish" life, "her soul . . . haunted with terrors."
2 Birute Ciplijauskaite discusses James and Ibsen as well as the convention of marriage in *La mujer insatisfecha* 123–44.
3 Ann B. Tracy notes that the "obsession with putrefaction, though not exclusive to the Gothic novel, does suggest an interest in death as something more than a lurid plot device." She continues: "The point of all this wormy circumstance is that death is a peculiar, even distinguishing, characteristic of the fallen world" (5).
4 Martha Banta gives a detailed account of James's indebtedness to the Gothic tradition in *Henry James and the Occult* 169–78.

5 Robert Emmet Long works out this imagery in detail in *The Great Succession* 110–16.
6 The sexual aspect of the Goodwood scene has been reemphasized by Dennis L. O'Connor. Whereas I do not wish to deny the sexual significance of the Goodwood scene—Isabel does feel "she has never been loved before" (589)—I want to suggest that Isabel's last moments with Ralph are more subtly erotic than anything else in the novel; whereas she does not love Goodwood, she does love Ralph. To experience a man's passion and to give her own love are clearly distinct events for Isabel.
7 Donne writes, for example, "Women are like the Arts, / . . . unpriz'd if unknowne" ("Change," lines 5–6). "Then since I may knowe, / As liberally as to a midwife showe / Thy selfe; cast all, yea this white linen hence" ("To his Mistress Going to Bed," lines 43–45). "Call us what you will, wee'are made such by love; / Call her one, mee another flye, / We'are Tapers too, and at out owne cost die" ("The Canonization," lines 19–21).
8 MacAndrew points to the sentimental tradition to discover the pattern and value of such a love-death: "Mackenzie's Harley goes into a 'decline' and dies. His Julia de Rubigné is poisoned. Virginia is drowned. Werther shoots himself. Such chronic failure, however, does not detract from the ideal itself [of "complete spiritual union with one like themselves"]. These novels affirm the Sentimental concept of virtue by showing that to know oneself virtuous, to develop one's sensibilities to the full, is more important than worldly 'success' and even than life" (67–68). Boone also discusses *Liebestod* lucidly and succinctly (38–39).
9 By what "seems right" Isabel does not mean what "looks right"; she means, as far as she can determine, what is the best thing to do. Irene Santos catches this substantive sense of "seems right" when she writes of Isabel: "As she confides to Ralph right before he dies, her final decision will be dictated by what 'seems right' (577). To ratify retroactively [by her decision to return to Rome] her initial choice of fate [to marry Osmond] had meant to choose her destiny again, to redefine her marriage as freedom fulfilled, to assume her identity as Mrs. Osmond, without which she would now be lost" (514). For Isabel "to redefine her marriage" is what "seems right" to Santos.
10 James complains about George Eliot's endings in novel after novel: "Her conclusions have been signally weak, as the reader will admit who recalls Hetty's reprieve in 'Adam Bede,' the inundation of the Floss, and, worse than either, the comfortable reconciliation of Romola and Tessa. The plot of 'Felix Holt' is essentially made up,

and its development is forced. . . . . The termination is hasty, inconsiderate, and unsatisfactory—is, in fact, almost an anti-climax" (*Literary Criticism: Essays* 907). James also finds the treatment of Dorothea's movement toward Ladislaw in the last two books of *Middlemarch* "almost ludicrously excessive" (961).

11 Patricia McKee reaches the same conclusion in her reading of James's *The Golden Bowl* (270–346).

12 *The Cimabue Madonna*, an 1855 painting by Frederic Leighton, was famous in its time and known to James, who used Leighton as a model for Lord Mellefont in "The Private Life" (1892). As an art critic, James noted in Leighton's depiction of women a lack of animation: "his texture is too often that of the glaze on the lid of a prune-box; his drawing too often that of the figures that smile at us from the covers of these receptacles" (*Painter's Eye* 214–15). Leighton's canvases were well known for the waxy completions and masculine features of his female figures. As president of the Royal Academy, he refused to allow women to be voting members. Joseph A. Kestner has pointed to the misogynistic character of Leighton's political attitudes and of his paintings in *Mythology and Misogyny*. If James is thinking of Leighton when he mentions the *Cimabue Madonna* in *The Portrait*, given all the implications of Leighton's misogyny, it is certainly an unhappy and forbidding analogue for Isabel Archer.

Chapter 7. *Jude the Obscure*

1 Lennart A. Bjork gives an overview of Hardy's appreciation and lack of appreciation of James as an individual and novelist in *Literary Notebooks* 1:357.

2 Hardy composed the epitaph for Antell's tombstone, which reads: "He was a man of considerable local reputation as a self-made scholar, having acquired a varied knowledge of languages, literature and science by unaided study & in the face of many untoward circumstances" (Gittings, *Young Thomas Hardy*, fig. 14b).

3 Hardy never acknowledged the influence of Dickens or Eliot. In "Charles Dickens: Some Personal Recollections and Opinions," he said "his literary efforts did not owe much to [Dickens'] influence. 'No doubt they owed something unconsciously, since everybody's did in those days' " (Orel 246; also see Collins). Bjork notes, "Hardy was not willing to acknowledge any aesthetic influence" of George Eliot's and was annoyed that *Far from the Madding Crowd* was attributed to her. Hardy characterized her as a "great thinker" but not "a born storyteller" (F. E. Hardy 98).

4 Hardy laments natural conditions to the extent that he portrays God

in the image and likeness of Jude: "the world resembled a stanza or melody composed in a dream; it was wonderfully excellent to the half-aroused intelligence, but hopelessly absurd at full waking; . . . The first Cause worked automatically like a somnambulist, not reflectively like a sage; . . . at the framing of the terrestrial conditions there seemed never to have been contemplated such a development of emotional perceptiveness among the creatures subject to those conditions as that reached by thinking and educated humanity" (417). God is a dreamer who creates his world from heaven very much as Jude created his from the roof of the Brown House: "It is a city of light," he said to himself" of Christminster. "It would just suit me" (66). God's world like Jude's is an illusion. The small world projected from Jude's personality proves so discordant and horrible that he chooses to die. The large world projected from God's personality is equally deadly. Nature's laws prove unsuited to human survival.

5   Sue asks Jude to quote "Epipsychidion" (309). C. H. Sisson, in his notes to the Penguin text, thinks that Sue's request is "an occasion for an exhibition of her silly vanity" (508). Such a comment misses Hardy's point in alluding to the poem; Miyoshi provides a much better explanation of Sue's quoting Shelley (so too does Clayton [20]) in recognizing the "Shelleyan theme" in the novel and in indicating that Sue "thinks of herself as Jude's epipsyche" (307): his "self-duplicate" (72), his " 'soul within a soul' " (67).

6   Peter Cominos argues that "married love was an immature association of dominance and submissiveness" in the Victorian period, "corresponding to the structure of the Respectable family and congruent with the entirety of family associations" (243).

7   "To the Romantic poets, the imagination is a mode of transcending raw reality, a means of overcoming the world as given" (Miyoshi 47). "The world as given is continually being transformed into a Higher Reality of the poet's own making" (ibid.).

Chapter 8. *Parade's End*

1   Ford expressed his admiration for *Jude the Obscure* in *Portraits from Life*: "*Jude* is at any rate so far and away his best book . . . is to such an extent inspired by the passionate mind of a great nature . . . that one can be pretty certain that in its working out he did employ some sort of conscious artistic knowledge. And it is interesting to speculate as to what he would have done in the way of novels if he had not abandoned the trade just at the moment when he seemed to have awakened to the fact that that avocation was really an art" (101).

2 Marlene Griffith writes that "Sylvia likens Christopher to Christ, with particular reference to her desires and his abstentions. Actually it is only when Christopher is in the army, when he suffers for and with his men, shares the suffering and puts it onto his own shoulders, when, in other words, he identifies with his men and ceases to be the detached observer, that this simile works. Christ, by embracing our sin and guilt, atones for them" (144–45). Melvin Seiden offers another explanation of the Christ analogy: "Christopher Tietjens is an enigma inside an anomaly, and this is why he invites the crucifixion that the world willingly bestows on him" ("Persecution and Paranoia" in Cassell 159).

3 Sondra J. Stang writes that "By 'no more parades' he [Ford] meant, in addition to the more obvious sense of the phrase, no more hollow rhetoric, no more heroic abstractions like hope and glory and honor—an end of traditional moral language, those words that, compared to the concrete names of villages, indeed seemed obscene to Hemingway in *A Farewell to Arms*" (97).

4 Barbara Tuchman indicates that the Germans had so carefully scheduled their railway transportation that the generals refused the opportunity to halt mobilization on the premise that once started "it can not be altered" (79). On transportation and the war, see Tuchman 74–79.

5 "Guggums" was a pet name that Dante Gabriel Rossetti gave to Elizabeth Siddall. Ford writes that Ford Madox Brown recalled that "Gabriel commenced telling me how he intended to get married at once to Guggums . . ." (Hueffer, *Memories and Impressions* 22). Ford also reports that when Rossetti used his grandfather's studio he would stand "before his easel in the silence of the studio . . . uttering over and over again the words, 'Guggum, Guggum'—a pet name for Miss Siddall" (Hueffer, *Ford Madox Brown* 113).

6 Robie Macauley writes that Tietjens is terrifying to his enemies because "they are fragmentary people, uncertain, confused, without values. They sense that Tietjens belongs to a moral frame of reference that both makes the world intelligible and wards off its shocks. To their jumbled and neurotic lives he stands as a reproach, and they must destroy him if possible" (xii).

7 "For him [Ford], as for James, ultimate reality is not some event in time and space; it is the conception of that event in a consciousness" (Mizener 496).

8 For an extended discussion of the hourglass form of *Some Do Not*, see Meixner 235–39.

9 Writing of *The Last Post*, Robert Green says that "Ford's commitment there to values now called 'ecological,' the need for man to

locate his life within natural rhythms which he had attempted to
destroy between 1914 and 1918, was his attempt, one among many,
to introduce some meaning into a demented world." He continues:
"The epilogue to *Parade's End* has customarily been seen as suffering from a lack of direction, from Ford's flight into 'romance.'
On the contrary, its weakness is rather that, unlike the rest of the
series, it is too nakedly perceptive in its desire to eulogise a way
of life that in spirit is closer to Social Credit than to either of the
period's extremisms, Fascism or communism" (166, 167).

10   Although he clearly pays tribute to *The Shadow-Line* in *A Man Could
Stand Up*, Ford also seems to model Vincent Macmaster on Conrad.
Macmaster is a small man with a black pointed beard who wears a
monocle; that is, he has Conrad's most salient physical traits. Macmaster also draws on Tietjens' imagination—the statistics arguing
against a single command that Christopher fabricated for his own
amusement are stolen by Vincent—to gain notoriety. That event
may be Ford's backward glance and partial evaluation of his col-
laboration with Conrad, who eventually gained money and critical
acclaim, which came to Ford, and then rather briefly, really only
with the publication of *Parade's End*.

11   Ohmann writes: "Again and again in *Parade's End*, Tietjens and his
fellows record, with exclamation, stress, and repetition, the aston-
ishing emergence of the subconscious into the conscious" (150).

12   Ford praised Thackeray because he saw that *Vanity Fair* was not
"founded on any conventional scheme of ethics" and "pro-
pound[ed] no conventional solutions of evils" (*March* 811). Whether
he was as acute about the significance of Thackeray's puppet metaphor is not as clear. It seems that he did not read it the way
Polhemus does in *Comic Faith*. See above, Introduction, p. 20.

Conclusion

1   Julian Barnes has recently complained that such a choice is not
choice enough: "After all, if novelists truly wanted to simulate the
delta of life's possibilities, this is what they'd do. At the back of the
book would be a set of sealed envelopes in various colours. Each
would be clearly marked on the outside: Traditional Happy Ending;
Traditional Unhappy Ending; Traditional Half-and-Half Ending;
Deus ex Machina; Modernist Arbitrary Ending; End of the World
Ending; Cliffhanger Ending; Dream Ending; Opaque Ending; Sur-
realist Ending; and so on. You would be allowed only one, and
would have to destroy the envelopes you didn't select. *That's* what
I call offering the reader a choice of endings; but you may find me
quite unreasonably literalminded" (92).

Works Cited

Abrams, M. H. *Natural Supernaturalism.* New York: Norton, 1971.

Adam, Ian, ed. *This Particular Web: Essays on "Middlemarch."* Toronto: University of Toronto Press, 1975.

Alvarez, A. "Afterword." In *Jude the Obscure.* Signet Classics. New York: New American Library, 1961.

Annan, Noel. "How Should a Gentleman Behave?" *New York Review of Books,* 3 February 1983, 11–13.

Apter, T. E. "Romanticism and Romantic Love in *Wuthering Heights.*" In Smith, 205–22.

Arnold, Matthew. *The Portable Matthew Arnold.* Ed. Lionel Trilling. New York: Viking, 1956.

Auerbach, Nina. *Communities of Women: An Idea in Fiction.* Cambridge: Harvard University Press, 1978.

Austen, Jane. *Northanger Abbey.* Ed. Anne Henry Ehrenpreis. Harmondsworth: Penguin, 1974.

Austen, Jane. *Persuasion, with A Memoir of Jane Austen by J. E. Austen-Leigh.* Ed. D. W. Harding. Harmondsworth: Penguin, 1975.

Austen, Jane. *Pride and Prejudice.* Ed. Tony Tanner. Harmondsworth: Penguin, 1972.

Axton, William F. "*Great Expectations* Yet Again." *Dickens Studies Annual* 2 (1972): 278–93.

Bakhtin, M. M. *The Dialogic Imagination: Four Essays.* Ed. Michael Holquist. Trans. Caryl Emerson and Michael Holquist. Austin: University of Texas Press, 1981.

Bakhtin, M. M. "Discourse in the Novel." *Dialogic* 259–422.

Bakhtin, M. M. "Forms of Time and the Chronotope in the Novel." *Dialogic* 84–258.

Bakhtin, M. M. *Problems of Dostoevsky's Poetics.* Ed. and trans. Caryl Emerson. Introd. Wayne C. Booth. Minneapolis: University of Minnesota Press, 1984.

Bakhtin, M. M. *Rabelais and His World*. Trans. Hélène Iswolsky. Bloomington: Indiana University Press, 1984.

Banta, Martha. *Henry James and the Occult*. Bloomington: Indiana University Press, 1972.

Bareham, Tony, ed. *Anthony Trollope. A Vision Critical Study*. London: Vision, 1980.

Barnes, Julian. *Flaubert's Parrot*. New York: McGraw-Hill, 1985.

Baudelaire, Charles. *Les Fleurs du Mal*. Ed. Wallace Fowlie. New York: Bantam, 1964.

Beerbohm, Max. *Zuleika Dobson; or, An Oxford Love Story*. Harmondsworth: Penguin, 1983.

Bersani, Leo. *A Future for Astyanax: Character and Desire in Literature*. Boston: Little, Brown, 1976.

Bjork, Lennart A., ed. *The Literary Notebooks of Thomas Hardy. See* Hardy.

Boone, Joseph A. *Tradition Counter Tradition: Love and the Form of Fiction*. Chicago: University of Chicago Press, 1987.

Bosanquet, Theodora. *Henry James at Work*. N.p.: Folcroft Library Editions, 1976.

Bowie, Malcolm. "Jacques Lacan." In *Structuralism and Since: From Lévi-Strauss to Derrida*, ed. John Sturrock, 116–53. Oxford: Oxford University Press, 1979.

Briggs, Asa. *A Social History of England*. New York: Viking, 1983.

Briggs, Asa. *Victorian People: A Reassessment of Persons and Themes, 1851–1867*. Colophon Books. New York: Harper and Row, 1955.

Brontë, Emily. *Wuthering Heights*. Ed. David Daiches. Harmondsworth: Penguin, 1971.

Brooks, Peter. *Reading for the Plot*. New York: Vintage Books, 1984.

Carlyle, Thomas. "Memoir of the Life of Sir Walter Scott, Baronet." *Westminster Review* (American ed.) 28 (January 1838): 154–82.

Carroll, David. "*Middlemarch* and the Externality of Fact." In Adam 73–90.

Cassell, Richard A. *Ford Madox Ford: Modern Judgments*. London: Macmillan, 1972.

Castronovo, David. *The English Gentleman: Images and Ideals in Literature and Society*. New York: Ungar, 1987.

Chapman, Raymond. "'Arguing about the Eastward Position': Thomas Hardy and Puseyism." *Nineteenth-Century Literature* 42 (1987): 275–94.

Cicero. *De Finibus Bonorum et Malorum*. Trans. H. Rackham. Loeb Classical Library. London: Heinemann, 1951.

Cicero. *De Officiis*. Trans. Walter Miller. Loeb Classical Library. London: Heineman, 1928.

Ciplijauskaite, Birute. *La mujer insatisfecha: El adulterio en la novela realista*. Barcelona: Edhasa, 1984.

Clark, Katerina, and Michael Holquist. *Mikhail Bakhtin*. Cambridge: Belknap Press of Harvard University Press, 1984.

Clayton, Jay. *Romantic Vision and the Novel*. Cambridge: Cambridge University Press, 1987.

Coffin, Charles M., ed. *The Complete Poetry and Selected Prose of John Donne*. New York: Modern Library, 1952.

Coke, Sir Edward. *The Third Part of the Institutes of the Laws of England*. London: W. Lee and D. Packman, 1648.

Collins, Philip. "Pip the Obscure: *Great Expectations* and Hardy's *Jude*." *Critical Quarterly* 19 (1977): 23–35.

Cominos, Peter T. "Late Victorian Sexual Respectability and the Social System." *International Review of Social History* 8 (1962): 18–48, 216–50.

Conger, Syndy M. "Nature in *Wuthering Heights*." *PMLA* 93 (1978): 1003–4.

Conrad, Joseph. *Heart of Darkness*. In *Youth* 45–162.

Conrad, Joseph. *The Shadow-Line, Typhoon, The Secret Sharer*. Ed. Morton Dauwen Zabel. Garden City: Doubleday-Anchor, 1959.

Conrad, Joseph. *Youth and Two Other Stories*. Canterbury Edition. 26 vols. Vol. 16. New York: Doubleday for Wise, 1924.

Craig, David M. "Origins, Ends, and Pip's Two Selves." *Research Studies* 47 (1979): 17–26.

Craig, Randall. "Plato's *Symposium* and the Tragicomic Novel." *Studies in the Novel* 17 (1985): 158–73.

Crews, Frederick. "Pressure under Grace." *New York Review of Books* 34 (13 August 1987): 30–37.

Daniel, Robert W. "Afterword." In Anthony Trollope, *Barchester Towers*. Signet Classics. New York: New American Library, 1963.

Day, William Patrick. *In Circles of Fear and Desire: A Study of Gothic Fantasy*. Chicago: University of Chicago Press, 1985.

Dessner, Lawrence Jay. "The Tragic Comedy of John Wemmick." *Ariel* 6 (1975): 65–80.

Dickens, Charles. *Bleak House*. Ed. George H. Ford and Sylvère Monod. Norton Critical Edition. New York: Norton, 1977.

Dickens, Charles. *Dombey and Son*. Ed. Peter Fairclough. Introd. Raymond Williams. Harmondsworth: Penguin, 1970.

Dickens, Charles. *Great Expectations*. Ed. Angus Calder. Harmondsworth: Penguin, 1965.

Dickens, Charles. *Oliver Twist*. Ed. Peter Fairclough. Introd. Angus Wilson. Harmondsworth: Penguin, 1972.

Dickens, Charles. *Our Mutual Friend*. Ed. Stephen Gill. Harmondsworth: Penguin, 1971.

Donadio, Stephen. *Nietzsche, Henry James, and the Artistic Will.* New York: Oxford University Press, 1978.

Dry, Florence Swinton. *Bronte Sources.* Vol. 1, *The Sources of "Wuthering Heights."* Vol. 2, *The Sources of "Jane Eyre."* Cambridge: W. Heffer and Sons, 1937.

Duyfhuizen, Bernard. *Narratives of Transmission: Communicating Fictional Texts.* Forthcoming.

Edwards, P. D. *Anthony Trollope: His Art and Scope.* St. Lucia: University of Queensland Press, 1977.

Eisenstein, Victor M., ed. *Neurotic Interaction in Marriage.* New York: Basic Books, 1956.

Eliot, George. *Middlemarch.* Ed. Gordon S. Haight. Riverside Editions. Boston: Houghton Mifflin, 1968.

Eliot, George. "Middlemarch." Brit. Mus. Add. MS. 34, 035.

Eliot, George. *A Writer's Notebook, 1854–1879, and Uncollected Writings.* Ed. Joseph Wiesenfarth. Charlottesville: University Press of Virginia, 1981.

Engels, Frederick. *The Origin of the Family, Private Property, and the State.* Ed. Eleanor Burke Leacock. London: Lawrence and Wishart, 1972.

Everitt, Alastair, ed. *"Wuthering Heights": An Anthology of Criticism.* New York: Barnes and Noble, 1967.

Ford, Ford Madox. *The Good Soldier: A Tale of Passion.* New York: Vintage Books, 1955.

Ford, Ford Madox. *The Last Post.* New York: A.&C. Boni, 1968.

Ford, Ford Madox. *The March of Literature.* New York: Dial, 1938.

Ford, Ford Madox. *Parade's End.* Ed. Robie Macauley. New York: Vintage, 1979.

Ford, Ford Madox. *Portraits from Life.* Boston: Houghton Mifflin, 1937.

Ford, Ford Madox. *Your Mirror to My Times.* Ed. Michael Killegrew. New York: Holt, Rinehart, and Winston, 1971.

Fowles, John. *The French Lieutenant's Woman.* Signet Book. New York: New American Library, 1970.

Freeman, Lucy, and Harold Greenwald. *Emotional Maturity in Love and Marriage.* New York: Harper, 1961.

Frye, Northrop. *Anatomy of Criticism.* New York: Norton, 1967.

Frye, Northrop. *The Critical Path: An Essay on the Social Context of Literary Criticism.* Bloomington: Indiana University Press, 1973.

Frye, Northrop. *The Educated Imagination.* Bloomington: Indiana University Press, 1964.

Frye, Northrop. *The Secular Scripture: A Study of the Structure of Romance.* The Charles Eliot Norton Lectures, 1974–1975. Cambridge: Harvard University Press, 1976.

Gallop, Jane. *Reading Lacan.* Ithaca: Cornell University Press, 1985.

Gérin, Winifred. *Emily Brontë: A Biography*. New York: Putnam, 1971.

Gibson, Jennifer. "Behind the Black Veil: Gothic Epistemology in the Fiction of Borges, Beckett, Nabokov, and Pynchon." Diss. University of Wisconsin–Madison, in progress.

Gilbert, Allan H., ed. *Literary Criticism: Plato to Dryden*. New York: American Book Co., 1940.

Gilbert, Sandra M., and Susan Gubar. *The Madwoman in the Attic: The Woman Writer and the Nineteenth-Century Literary Imagination*. New Haven: Yale University Press, 1979.

Gilmour, Robin. *The Idea of the Gentleman in the Victorian Novel*. London: George Allen and Unwin, 1981.

Girouard, Marc. *The Return to Camelot: Chivalry and the English Gentleman*. New Haven: Yale University Press, 1981.

Gittings, Robert. *Thomas Hardy's Later Years*. Boston: Little, Brown, 1978.

Gittings, Robert. *The Young Thomas Hardy*. Boston: Little, Brown, 1975.

Goetsch, Paul. *Dickens: Eine Einführung*. Munich: Artemis Verlag, 1986.

Goodridge, J. F. "A New Heaven and a New Earth." In Smith 160–81.

Gordon, Sheila. "*Parade's End*: A Reading." *Antaeus*, 56 (1986): 86–92.

Graves, Robert. *Collected Poems, 1914–1947*. London: Cassell, 1948.

Green, Robert. *Ford Madox Ford: Prose and Politics*. Cambridge: Cambridge University Press, 1981.

Greenberg, Robert A. "On Ending *Great Expectations*." *Papers on Language and Literature* 2 (1970): 152–62.

Greene, Donald J. "Jane Austen and the Peerage." In *Jane Austen: A Collection of Critical Essays*, ed. Ian Watt. Englewood Cliffs, N.J.: Prentice-Hall, 1963.

Gregor, Ian, ed. *The Brontës: A Collection*. Englewood Cliffs, N.J.: Prentice-Hall, 1970.

Griffith, Marlene. "A Double Reading of *Parade's End*." In Cassell 137–51.

Hafley, James. "The Villain in *Wuthering Heights*." In Lettis and Morris, *Handbook* 182–97.

Hagan, John H., Jr. "Control and Sympathy in *Wuthering Heights*." In Gregor 59–75.

Hagan, John H., Jr. "The Poor Labyrinth: The Theme of Social Injustice in Dickens's 'Great Expectations.'" In Lettis and Morris, *Assessing* 88–98.

Haggerty, George E. "Fact and Fancy in the Gothic Novel." *Nineteenth-Century Fiction* 39 (1985): 379–92. ✓

Haight, Gordon S. *The Portable Victorian Reader*. New York: Viking, 1972.

Halperin, John. *Trollope and Politics*. London: Macmillan, 1977.

Halperin, John. "Trollope's Conservatism." *South Atlantic Quarterly* 81 (1982): 56–78.

Hardy, Florence Emily. *The Early Life of Thomas Hardy, 1840–1891*. New York: Macmillan, 1928.

Hardy, Thomas. *The Collected Letters of Thomas Hardy*. Ed. Richard Little Purdy and Michael Millgate. Vols. 2, 5. Oxford: Clarendon, 1980, 1985.

Hardy, Thomas. *Jude the Obscure*. Ed. C. H. Sisson. Harmondsworth: Penguin, 1978.

Hardy, Thomas. *The Literary Notebooks of Thomas Hardy*. Ed. Lennart A. Bjork. 2 vols. New York: New York University Press, 1985.

Hardy, Thomas. *Personal Writings*. Ed. Harold Orel. London: Macmillan, 1967.

Heilman, Robert B. "Charlotte Brontë's 'New Gothic.'" In Gregor 96–109.

Homans, Margaret. "Repression and Sublimation of Nature in *Wuthering Heights*." *PMLA* 93 (1978): 9–19.

Hopkins, Robert. "Moral Luck and Judgment in Jane Austen's *Persuasion*." *Nineteenth-Century Fiction* 42 (1987): 143–58.

Houghton, Walter E. *The Victorian Frame of Mind*. New Haven: Yale University Press, 1967.

House, Humphry. "[Pip's Acquired 'Culture.']" In Lettis and Morris, *Assessing* 44–48.

Hueffer, Ford Madox. *Ford Madox Brown: A Record of His Life and Works*. London: Longmans, Green, 1896.

Hueffer, Ford Madox. *Henry James: A Critical Study*. New York: A. C. Boni, 1915.

Hueffer, Ford Madox. *Memories and Impressions: A Study in Atmospheres*. New York: Harper, 1911.

Hueffer, Ford Madox. "Miss May Sinclair and 'The Judgment of Eve.'" *Outlook* (2 May 1914): 599–600.

Hume, Robert D. "Gothic versus Romantic: A Revaluation of the Gothic Novel." *PMLA* 84 (1969): 282–90.

James, Henry. "Far from the Madding Crowd." *Nation*, no. 495 (24 December 1874): 423–24.

James, Henry. *Literary Criticism: Essays on Literature, American Writers, English Writers*. New York: Library of America, 1984.

James, Henry. *Literary Criticism: French Writers, Other European Writers, The Prefaces to the New York Edition*. New York: Library of America, 1984.

James, Henry. *The Painter's Eye: Notes and Essays on the Pictorial Arts*. Ed. John L. Sweeney. London: Rupert Hart-Davis, 1956.

James, Henry. *The Portrait of a Lady*. Harmondsworth: Penguin, 1978.

James, Henry. *The Scenic Art*. Ed. Alan Wade. New Brunswick: Rutgers University Press, 1948.

Jameson, Fredric. *The Political Unconscious: Narrative as a Socially Symbolic Act*. Ithaca, N.Y.: Cornell University Press, 1981.

Jauss, Hans Robert. *Aesthetic Experience and Literary Hermeneutics*. Ed. and introd. Wlad Godzich. Trans. Michael Shaw. Minneapolis: University of Minnesota Press, 1982.

Jauss, Hans Robert. "Theses on the Transition from the Aesthetics of Literary Works to a Theory of Aesthetic Experience." In *Interpretation of Narrative*, ed. Mario J. Valdes and Owen J. Miller, 137–46. Toronto: University of Toronto Press, 1978.

Jauss, Hans Robert. *Toward an Aesthetic of Reception*. Introd. Paul de Man. Trans. Timothy Bathi. Minneapolis: University of Minnesota Press, 1982.

Johnson, Samuel. *A Dictionary of the English Language*. 7th ed. London: W. Strahan et al., 1783.

Johnson, Samuel. *The Rambler*. Ed. W. J. Bate and Albrecht B. Strauss. The Yale Edition of the Works of Samuel Johnson. Vols. 3–5. New Haven: Yale University Press, 1969.

Jolles, André. *Einfache Formen*. Trans. as *Formes simples* by André Marie Buguet. Paris: Seuil, 1972.

Kestner, Joseph A. *Mythology and Misogyny: The Social Discourse of Nineteenth-Century British Classical Subject Painting*. Madison: University of Wisconsin Press, 1988.

Kestner, Joseph A. *The Spatiality of the Novel*. Detroit: Wayne State University Press, 1978.

Kettle, Arnold. *An Introduction to the English Novel: Defoe to the Present*. Rev. ed. Perennial Library. New York: Harper and Row, 1968.

Kiely, Robert. *The Romantic Novel in England*. Cambridge: Harvard University Press, 1972.

Kincaid, James R. "*Barchester Towers* and the Nature of Conservative Comedy." *ELH* 37 (1970): 595–612.

Kincaid, James R. *The Novels of Anthony Trollope*. Oxford: Clarendon, 1977.

Kinkead-Weekes, Mark. "The Place of Love in *Jane Eyre* and *Wuthering Heights*." In Gregor, 76–95.

Knoepflmacher, U. C. *Laughter and Despair*. Berkeley: University of California Press, 1971.

Knoepflmacher, U. C. *Religious Humanism in the Victorian Novel: George Eliot, Walter Pater, and Samuel Butler*. Princeton: Princeton University Press, 1965.

Krieger, Murray. *The Classic Vision*. Baltimore: Johns Hopkins University Press, 1971.

Kubie, Lawrence S. "Psychoanalysis and Marriage: Practical and Theoretical Issues." In Eisenstein, 10–43.

La Bruyère, Jean de. *Les caractères de Théophraste traduits du grec. Avec les caractères ou les moeurs de ce siècle.* Paris: Garnier Frères, 1962.

Lacan, Jacques. *Ecrits: A Selection.* Trans. Alan Sheridan. New York: Norton, 1977.

Lacan, Jacques. *The Four Fundamental Concepts of Psycho-Analysis.* Ed. Jacques-Alain Miller. Trans. Alan Sheridan. New York: Norton, 1978.

Lang, Andrew, ed. *The Blue Fairy Book.* New York: Dover, 1955.

Lehan, Richard. "Urban Signs and Urban Literature: Literary Form and Historical Process." *New Literary History* 18 (1986–87): 99–113.

Lemon, Lee T., and Marion J. Reis, ed. and trans. *Russian Formalist Criticism: Four Essays.* Bison Books. Lincoln: University of Nebraska Press, 1965.

Lettis, Richard, and William E. Morris, eds. *Assessing "Great Expectations."* San Francisco: Chandler, 1960.

Lettis, Richard, and William E. Morris, eds. *A "Wuthering Heights" Handbook.* New York: Odyssey, 1961.

Letwin, Shirley Robin. *The Gentleman in Trollope: Individuality and Moral Conduct.* London: Macmillan, 1982.

Levine, George L. *The Realistic Imagination: English Fiction from Frankenstein to Lady Chatterley.* Chicago: University of Chicago Press, 1981.

Lewis, C. S. "A Note on Jane Austen." In *Discussions of Jane Austen*, ed. William Heath, 58–64. Boston: D. C. Heath, 1961.

Lindsay, Jack. *Charles Dickens.* New York: Philosophical Library, 1950.

Litz, A. Walton. "'A Development of Self': Character and Personality in Jane Austen's Fiction." In *Jane Austen's Achievement*, ed. Juliet McMaster. New York: Barnes and Noble, 1976.

Liu, Alan. "Wordsworth: The History in 'Imagination.'" *ELH* 51 (1984): 505–48.

Long, Robert Emmet. *The Great Succession: Henry James and the Legacy of Hawthorne.* Pittsburgh: University of Pittsburgh Press, 1979.

MacAndrew, Elizabeth. *The Gothic Tradition in Fiction.* New York: Columbia University Press, 1979.

Macauley, Robie. "Introduction." In Ford Madox Ford, *Parade's End*.

MacCannell, Juliet Flower. *Figuring Lacan: Criticism and the Cultural Unconscious.* Lincoln: University of Nebraska Press, 1986.

Mann, Thomas. *The Magic Mountain.* Trans. H. T. Lowe-Porter. Harmondsworth: Penguin, 1980.

Mathison, John K. "Nelly Dean and the Power of *Wuthering Heights*." In Lettis and Morris, *Handbook* 143–63.

Matthiessen, F. O. *Henry James: The Major Phase.* Galaxy Books. New York: Oxford University Press, 1963.

Maturin, Charles Robert. *Melmoth the Wanderer*. Ed. William F. Axton. Lincoln: University of Nebraska Press, 1961.

McKee, Patricia. *Heroic Commitment in Richardson, Eliot, and James*. Princeton: Princeton University Press, 1986.

Meisel, Martin. "The Ending of *Great Expectations.*" *Essays in Criticism* 15 (1965): 326–31.

Meixner, John A. *Ford Madox Ford's Novels*. Minneapolis: University of Minnesota Press, 1962.

Miller, J. Hillis. *The Disappearance of God*. Cambridge: Harvard University Press, 1963.

Miller, J. Hillis. *Fiction and Repetition: Seven English Novels*. Cambridge: Harvard University Press, 1982.

Millgate, Michael. *Thomas Hardy: A Biography*. New York: Random House, 1982.

Millhauser, Milton. "*Great Expectations*: The Three Endings." *Dickens Studies Annual* 2 (1972): 167–78.

Miyoshi, Masao. *The Divided Self: A Perspective on the Literature of the Victorians*. New York: New York University Press, 1967.

Mizener, Arthur. *The Saddest Story: A Biography of Ford Madox Ford*. New York: World, 1971.

Morgan, Charlotte E. *The Rise of the Novel of Manners: A Study of English Prose Fiction between 1600 and 1740*. New York: Russell and Russell, 1963.

Moynahan, Julian. "The Hero's Guilt: The Case of *Great Expectations.*" In Lettis and Morris, *Assessing*, 149–69.

Nettels, Elsa. "*The Portrait of a Lady* and the Gothic Romance." *South Atlantic Bulletin* 39 (1974): 73–82.

Newman, John Henry. *The Idea of a University*. Ed. I. T. Ker. Oxford: Clarendon, 1976.

Novak, Maximillian E. "Gothic Fiction and the Grotesque." *Novel: A Forum on Fiction* 13 (1979): 50–67.

O'Connor, Dennis L. "Intimacy and Spectatorship in *The Portrait of a Lady.*" *Henry James Review* 2 (1980): 25–26.

Ohmann, Carol. *Ford Madox Ford: From Apprentice to Craftsman*. Middleton, Conn.: Wesleyan University Press, 1964.

Orel, Harold, ed. Thomas Hardy, *Personal Writings*. London: Macmillan, 1967.

Paulson, Ronald. *Satire and the Novel in Eighteenth-Century England*. New Haven: Yale University Press, 1967.

Plato. *Laws*. Trans. R. G. Bury, 2 vols. Loeb Classical Library. London: Heinemann, 1952.

Plato. *Lysis. Symposium. Gorgias*. Trans. W. R. M. Lamb. Loeb Classical Library. London: Heinemann, 1925.

Plato. *The Republic*. Trans. Paul Shorey. 2 vols. Loeb Classical Library. London: Heinemann, 1946.

Polhemus, Robert. *The Changing World of Anthony Trollope*. Berkeley: University of California Press, 1968.

Polhemus, Robert. *Comic Faith: The Great Tradition from Austen to Joyce*. Chicago: University of Chicago Press, 1980.

Price, Martin. "Manners, Morals, and Jane Austen," *Nineteenth-Century Fiction* 30 (1975): 261–80.

Radcliffe, Ann. *The Mysteries of Udolpho*. Ed. Bonamy Dobrée. The World's Classics. New York: Oxford University Press, 1983.

Raina, Badri. *Dickens and the Dialectic of Growth*. Madison: University of Wisconsin Press, 1986.

Rajan, Tilottama. *Dark Interpreter: The Discourse of Romanticism*. Ithaca: Cornell University Press, 1980.

Reed, Walter. *Meditations on the Hero: A Study of the Romantic Hero*. New Haven: Yale University Press, 1974.

Rickaby, John. "Cardinal Virtues." *Catholic Encyclopedia*. New York: Appleton, 1908.

Robinson, F. N., ed. *The Works of Geoffrey Chaucer*. 2d ed. Boston: Houghton Mifflin, 1957.

Rosenberg, John D. *The Darkening Glass: A Portrait of Ruskin's Genius*. New York: Columbia University Press, 1961.

Routh, Michael. "Isabel Archer's Double Exposure: A Repeated Scene in *The Portrait of a Lady*." *Henry James Review* 1 (1980): 262–63.

Ruskin, John. *The Crown of Wild Olive*. *The Works of John Ruskin*, ed. E. T. Cook and Alexander Wedderburn. London: George Allen, 1905.

Ruskin, John. *The Genius of John Ruskin: Selections from His Writings*. Ed. John D. Rosenberg. Riverside Editions. Boston: Houghton Mifflin, 1963.

Sadleir, Michael. *Trollope: A Commentary*. New York: Farrar, Straus, 1947.

Said, Edward. *Beginnings: Intention and Method*. New York: Basic Books, 1975.

Sanger, C. P. "The Structure of *Wuthering Heights*." In Gregor 7–18.

Santos, Irene Ramalho de Sousa. "Isabel's Freedom: Henry James's *The Portrait of a Lady*." *Biblos* 56 (1980): 503–19.

Secor, Robert. "Henry James and Violet Hunt." *Journal of Modern Literature* 13 (1986): 1–36.

Seiden, Melvin. "Persecution and Paranoia in *Parade's End*." In Cassell, *Ford Madox Ford: Modern Judgments* 152–68.

Shelley, Mary. *Frankenstein*. In *Three Gothic Novels*, ed. Peter Fairclough, introd. Mario Praz. Harmondsworth: Penguin, 1968.

Shelley, Percy Bysshe. *Shelley's Poetry and Prose*. Ed. Donald H. Reiman and Sharon B. Powers. Norton Critical Edition. New York: Norton, 1977.

Shklovsky, Victor. "Art as Technique." In Lemon and Reis 3–24.

Silverman, Kaja. *The Subject of Semiotics*. New York: Oxford University Press, 1983.

Sittler, Joseph. *The Structure of Christian Ethics*. Baton Rouge: Louisiana State University Press, 1958.

Smalley, Donald. *Anthony Trollope: The Critical Heritage*. London: Routledge and Kegan Paul, 1969.

Smiles, Samuel. *The Life of George Stephenson, Railway Engineer*. London: John Murray, 1857.

Smiles, Samuel. *Self-Help*. London: John Murray, 1859.

Smith, Anne, ed. *The Art of Emily Brontë*. New York: Barnes and Noble, 1976.

Sommers, Montague. *The Gothic Quest*. London: Fortune Press, 1938.

Stang, Sondra J. *Ford Madox Ford*. Modern Literature Monographs. New York: Ungar, 1977.

Stange, G. Robert. "Expectations Well Lost: Dickens' Fable for His Times." In Lettis and Morris, *Assessing* 74–87.

Starobinski, Jean. *The Invention of Liberty, 1700–1789*. Trans. Bernard C. Swift. Geneva: Skira, 1964.

Tamm, Merika. "Inter-Art Relations in the Novels of Jane Austen." Diss., University of Wisconsin–Madison, 1976.

Tanner, Tony. *Adultery in the Novel: Contract and Transgression*. Baltimore: Johns Hopkins University Press, 1979.

Tanner, Tony. "The Fearful Self: Henry James's *The Portrait of a Lady*." In *Henry James: Modern Judgments*, ed. Tony Tanner. London: Macmillan, 1968.

Thompson, G. R., ed. *The Gothic Imagination*. Pullman: Washington State University Press, 1974.

Thompson, Wade. "Infanticide and Sadism in *Wuthering Heights*." In Everitt, 139–51.

Tick, Stanley. "Towards Jaggers." *Dickens Studies Annual* 5 (1976): 133–49.

Todorov, Tzvetan. *Mikhail Bakhtin: The Dialogical Principle*. Trans. Wlad Godzich. Minneapolis: University of Minnesota Press, 1984.

Tracy, Ann B. *The Gothic Novel, 1790–1830: Plot Summaries and Index to Motifs*. Lexington: University of Kentucky Press, 1981.

Trilling, Lionel. "Manners, Morals, and the Novel." *The Liberal Imagination: Essays on Literature and Society*. Garden City: Doubleday Anchor, 1954.

Tristram, Phillipa. "Divided Sources." In Smith 182–204.

Trollope, Anthony. *An Autobiography.* Introd. Michael Sadleir. World's Classics. London: Oxford University Press, 1968.

Trollope, Anthony. *Barchester Towers.* Ed. Robin Gilmour. Harmondsworth: Penguin, 1983.

Trollope, Anthony. *Clergymen and the Church of England.* Victorian Library. Leicester: University of Leicester Press, 1974.

Trollope, Anthony. *Thackeray.* English Men of Letters. London: Macmillan, 1912.

Tuchman, Barbara. *The Guns of August.* New York: Macmillan, 1962.

VandeKieft, Ruth M. "Patterns of Communication in *Great Expectations.*" In Lettis and Morris, *Assessing* 170–81.

Varma, Devendra. *The Gothic Flame.* London: Barker, 1957.

Walpole, Horace. *The Castle of Otranto.* In *Three Gothic Novels,* ed. Peter Fairclough, introd. Mario Praz. Harmondsworth: Penguin, 1968.

Waugh, Evelyn. *A Handful of Dust.* Boston: Little, Brown, 1977.

White, Hayden. "The Value of Narrativity in the Representation of Reality." *Critical Inquiry* 7 (1980): 5–27.

Wiesenfarth, Joseph. "Dialectics in *Barchester Towers.*" In Bareham 36–53.

Wiesenfarth, Joseph. *George Eliot's Mythmaking.* Heidelberg: Carl Winter, 1977.

Wiesenfarth, Joseph. "*Middlemarch*: The Language of Art." *PMLA* 97 (1982): 363–77.

Wiley, Paul. *Novelist of Three Worlds: Ford Madox Ford.* Syracuse: Syracuse University Press, 1962.

Wilson, David. "Emily Brontë: First of the Moderns." *Modern Quarterly Miscellany* 1 (1947): 94–115.

Wilson, R. B. J. *Henry James's Ultimate Narrative: The Golden Bowl.* St. Lucia: University of Queensland Press, 1981.

Wilt, Judith. *Ghosts of the Gothic: Austen, Eliot, and Lawrence.* Princeton: Princeton University Press, 1979.

Winner, Anthony. "Character and Knowledge in Dickens: The Enigma of Jaggers." *Dickens Studies Annual* 3 (1974): 100–121.

Wintersdorf, Karl P. "Mirror-Images in *Great Expectations.*" *Nineteenth-Century Fiction* 21 (1966–67): 203–24.

Wright, Andrew. *Anthony Trollope: Dream and Art.* Chicago: University of Chicago Press, 1983.

Index